The Snare of the Fowler Series

Whom The Son Sets Free
Book 2

Carol S. Lacey

What People Are Saying About "Whom The Son Sets Free"

Right from page one, I was swept up into Daphne's tragic life and times. Carol's descriptive penning of this young woman's story is so detailed, I could easily picture each scene. I found myself holding my breath one moment and rejoicing at the small kindnesses shown her in the next. Her deep grappling in reconciling what she hears the apostle Paul preach, with what she has been taught as truth all her life will resonate with many.

Pamela Wellington
Bible Study Leader

"Whom the Son Sets Free," continues Daphne's story with her riveting struggle to obey her master or her conscience. I was swept along by her fascinating journey of the necessity of obedience to the evil spirit that indwelt her, while continually searching to find a way to be free of the demon. The details conveyed in all the characters make it easy to imagine yourself right there experiencing the events taking place. It was such a good read, I didn't want to put it down. Looking forward to the next book.   **Larry Mueller**
Heartland Church
Fort Wayne, IN

In "Whom the Son Sets Free," Carol Lacey brings biblical stories to life and puts the reader in the middle of them with context and background. Her character development and historical references will transport you to the year 51 A.D. Read this page turner. I loved it, and so will you!

William R. Wieringa
Attorney & Counselor at Law

An exciting sequel to the first book! Daphne continues to fight her demons. Paul arrives in Philippi, Nicanor returns from Rome. There is so much going on, lost sleep--couldn't put it down.

Barbara Johnson
Bible Study Teacher

Following the pattern established in "Ensnared by Evil," Lacey's follow-up novel picks up with full-bodied characters and engaging plots. Once again, Lacey's meticulous research doesn't go unnoticed - whether it's riding upon the slave ship that transports Daphne to her new life, or setting eyes on her new home for the first time: as a slave. Readers will engage with the girl's inner turmoil and despair as unwanted circumstances are thrust upon her at an innocent age, and ponder what choices – good and bad – will be made along the way.

Lisa Mackinder
Writer for magazines &
Chicken Soup for the Soul books

If you love historical fiction, a story filled with suspense, and dialogue that grabs your attention from the get-go and keeps you turning page after page, this book is a great read for you! My husband and I both loved Lacey's book, and you will too!

Mary Jane Mapes
Founder and President
The Aligned Leader Institute, LLC

Carol Lacey has done it again...in her newest novel! It's a page-turner with a wonderful and transformational message woven throughout. I highly recommend Carol's new book!

Beth Jones
Author& Co-Founding Pastor
Valley Family Church

DEDICATION

*I am dedicating this book to all those whom
I have studied God's Word with through the many
years. You have greatly enhanced my life.*

ACKNOWLEDGEMENTS

I am so grateful for my faithful Lord, Jesus, who's precious Word, inspires me daily. His promises to…strengthen me, help me, and uphold me with the righthand of His righteousness. (Isaiah 41:10) and, just as He spoke through the apostle Paul to the Philippians, that through Him I could do all things, (Philippians 4:13) and if I would bring my anxieties to Him in prayer, He would give me peace. (Philippians 4:6-7)

I am thankful to those who helped me with this project through prayer or counsel. And those who encouraged with praise for book one and frequently asked, *"when is book two coming?"* I am especially thankful for Joshua Lacey, who cheerfully bailed his tech-challenged grandma out of printer mishaps or computer trials. And for my family who believed in and encouraged me in my venture to write and publish a book. Also, I appreciate the help of my publisher, Liz Lawless and her editor, Janice Robinson, who will help me get the last book in this series, *Free Indeed*, out in late fall.

INTRODUCTION

I hope you enjoy *Whom the Son Sets Free*, the second in my *Snare of the Fowler* series. Book one, *Ensnared by Evil*, left Daphne (who becomes the demon-possessed slave girl who harasses the Apostle Paul, in Acts 16) invaded by a demon of divination at the temple of Apollo in Delphi, Greece. After which she and her family are sold into slavery to pay her deceased father's debts. Her journey into a life she's never known brings lots of challenges she struggles to overcome.

"Daphne's ineptus to be shielded from abuse secured the entrance of her snare, keeping her helplessly trapped in the ruse. Thoughts of her on-going dilemma rose like a child's kite. She let them unwind, persuaded the winds of her circumstances would never change course."

I found it to be a faith-adventure to write about Bible persons, and an awesome responsibility to put words in their mouths. I hope you find this fictional effort in my could-have-been scenes, true to their characters and acceptable.

I have been writing for thirty years, mostly for Christian magazines, Bible studies, or blogging, but this series is my first attempt at novels. It has been a lot of work, but something I delight in doing.

There was a point in my life where I wasn't sure I had anything to offer others. On a prayer walk, feeling useless, I came across a patch of acorns, broken and cleaned out by squirrels. As I shuffled through the debris, I heard the Lord say, *"It is easier to glean from broken people than from those surrounded by a hard shell."* He went on to assure me He had a plan and a purpose for me, and I was to rejoice and follow His lead. I hope the honest struggle of Daphne's life will influence you to keep on keeping on in tough times and embrace the journey.

I would love to hear from you at my website, CarolLacey.com, where you can sign up or read my blog, Nuggets from God's Word.

Blessings, Carol

PROLOGUE

Our soul has escaped as a bird from the snare of the fowlers; The snare is broken, and we have escaped, our help is in the name of the Lord, who made heaven and earth.

– Psalm 124: 7-8

Chapter One

There was none to help.
– Psalm 107:12

The captain tipped his hat to Daphne's new owner, but his eyes remained on Daphne. "Welcome aboard, I see you acquired some…ah, merchandise." He lowered his voice and stuck out his lower lip. "And you said you were only here to buy supplies and set up a new venture." He poked Patharus with his elbow, unmindful he laughed alone. "Looks like a pretty good investment. Want me to take her to the slave quarters?"

Her chest heaved. The man's face sported the same leer as the ship's captain who abused her mother.

Patharus looked away. "No, I will see to it. When do we sail? I need to get back as soon as possible."

The captain's gaze swung back to his passenger. "We leave at high tide. There's only two or three weeks of good weather left, and we don't want to run into a *euroclydon*. It can be worse than a northeaster. Your boy loaded your supplies, so you are all set."

"Good. I will be back shortly to settle our passage. I need to instruct my girl in some matters."

The captain gave a knowing smirk. "Leave your trunks, I will see to them." His gaze drifted back to her. "And whatever else you want delivered to your quarters."

She followed Patharus down the deck relieved to leave the captain's presence, but bile flushed her mouth at the reality she was decreed property of this stranger, subject to whatever pleased him.

He headed to a quiet spot between the ship's few upper cabins and the side rail with instructions to wait there for his return.

Alone for the first time in months, she relished the quiet and let her thoughts drift, grateful he did not return right away. What kind of a man held her life, her future, in his hands? His countenance revealed little.

The captain's call for his crew to take their positions brought the sound of rhythmic splashes. The ship cleared the harbor and loud snaps replaced the creaking of oars, as unleashed sails flapped like newly released birds.

The sun hung almost to the horizon as the port grew smaller, its waning light reflected its dying hold on the Parthenon's marble pillars. She sighed. It is so beautiful. I wish I could have seen it up close.

Her gaze drifted to the hill across from it, the one Cassandra said displayed monuments to all the gods. Tears filled her eyes at the memory of her friend reluctantly succumbing to her mother's demand she ignore the plight of Daphne's family.

Athens faded and it struck her that she did not know the ship's destination. Was she being taken back to Corinth, or Delphi? Hope surged at the thought. The Port of Piracus disappeared and left her to wonder about the fate of her family. Would she ever see her mother or brothers again? She wiped her cheeks and took a deep breath. At least I was not given over to Talsta. She shuddered, grateful to have escaped an arranged marriage to the temple's high priest.

Weariness lowered her body to the deck. To soften the ship's vibrations, she pillowed her head with her arm, curled up and fell asleep. Something grazed her back. Her mind drifted to the filthy shed where she had waited to be sold. Had Nectari rolled over and bumped her again? She struggled against the pull of slumber and strained into the shadows. Where am I? Oh…the ship. I am back on a ship.

She lay perfectly still, desperate to know what nudged her but afraid of what she might find. A sandaled foot swept past her face and jostled her knee. With panic, she recalled Bentalla's warning of the likelihood of rape by her new owner.

With her heart in her throat, she jumped to her feet, ready to resist even if it meant death. Her arm bumped her attacker and she backed up several steps.

The young slave who traveled with her owner stared open-mouthed. Her hand flew to her lips, too late to cover a moan. "I...I am sorry, I thought...."

His tall, athletic physique towered over her, and she was sure laughter twitched his lips. He raised the remains of a bowl that had sloshed over his hand and onto his tunic. "They have put out the evening meal." He searched for something with which to wipe off the container. With a shrug, he handed her a spoon and the bowl. "Better eat up. It is nearly time to go below."

She took the food and sat as far from him as she could. When she did not begin to eat immediately, he raised an eyebrow. "It could be a long time before your next meal. This ship is not generous with food for slaves, so you need to eat all they offer…sometimes we only get one meal a day."

She brought some of the gruel to her lips. *Syssitia.* How she hated it. He leaned against the railing and followed the progression of her spoon. She forced down the contents, conscious of his stare.

"There you are, Nicanor. Everything finished here?" At the young man's nod, their owner dismissed him and turned his attention on her.

She avoided his eyes and ignored the curiosity that lurked behind them. He did not move. The syssitia began to swirl. Now what…could he plan to…?

When he spoke, she jumped. "Have you been transported by boat before?"

She nodded but did not raise her head.

"Then you are familiar with the area under the hold. This ship is not designed to carry slaves, but it is one of Rome's finest. Captives are few and women are housed separate from men." When she did not respond, he continued. "The quarters are small, but you will be safe…from everyone."

She chanced a glance at his face. His stern expression belied the kindness in his voice and unnerved her. Had he noticed how the captain leered at her. Why would he care?

She wished he would leave, but he leaned against the outer rail and appeared to be in no hurry. "Tell me about this gift of yours."

She jerked in his direction, her face blank.

"Come girl, I know you can see into the future. Tell me how you came to receive this ability. Was it granted by Jupiter?"

She grimaced. Hurle! Hurle must have told him about my idol. That is why he and the others bought me. They believe I am a sorceress.

And why would he assume it came from a Roman god? The idea disgusted her.

Chapter Two

Do not walk in the ways of darkness.
– Proverbs 2:13

Daphne swallowed the lump in her throat. "How did you…know about…."

"Did you expect to hide it from me? Your former overseer told my fellow investors of your gift…that you possess a *teraphim* used by Apollo worshipers to divine the future. Was he wrong?" Patharus sounded impatient.

She chewed her lower lip. Should she admit the Voice had counseled her in the past? What did it mean to him? What did he expect? It was not as if she could control the Voice's presence. If she said she had the ability to see into the future, what if it never spoke again?

Grooves crossed his broad forehead and lined his face.

She breathed a prayer, "Help me."

Tell him you have the gift. He knows its value and will protect you as it proves true. Have I not told you you have been given to know things others cannot know? I have much more to show you and I will! Tell him…it will assure you of a better life.

A vague caution festered, and she hesitated. Perhaps an-ill-defined omen hovered to warn her about the risk of dependence and trust on this mysterious being.

Patharus cocked his head. "Well, do you have the gift or not?"

She opened her mouth, but confusion hobbled her senses. Why the gift increased her value and would make life as a slave more tolerable, escaped her. Still, his tone confirmed its importance. Despite her doubts, fear of being vulnerable to men like the captain made her decision. "Yes…my overseer said rightly. I have been granted the ability to see into the future." She hoped she sounded confident.

"And have you used it to profit your previous owners?"

Her breath caught. Profit? How? Maybe I should not have said that.

"Never mind, it is enough that you have it. We will discuss our plans later. It is time to go below. Follow me."

She found herself confined with others also being transferred to places over which they too held no control. The room was small and stuffy, filled with the smell of unwashed bodies, not unlike her own. She searched each face, but none had been detained with her in Athens.

Days fell into a monotonous pattern: breakfast, a short time on deck, the evening meal and sleep. Only at night, in the obscurity of darkness, would she set aside her humiliation and use the pot set rudely before all. It made her skin crawl. She longed for her lovely marble tub filled with scented water and oils. I wonder who is using it now?

She crept to her pad each night as darkness unfolded like an unwelcome presence. Snores of her companions highlighted her loneliness. Sleep became an escape even though the sparse pile of straw made her back ache. As dawn filtered through the locked grate on the second morning, she breathed a sigh of relief to leave the cramped quarters. Waves on the Aegean were much larger than those on the gulf and her stomach had been slow to adjust to the ship's roll. For the first time it growled from hunger, not nausea.

While they waited for their food, a sailor called the women captives to attention. "Your daily confinement has been relaxed. You are free to remain on deck until after the evening meal...if you stay away from the crew and caused no trouble." The male slaves grumbled. Their restrictions had not been altered.

She ate all her gruel. It was bland and tasteless, but it strengthened her. The sailors left the area after they swamped the deck and checked the sails. No sound competed with waves that broke under the bow or the groan of ropes that stretched to accommodate the sails. She found a spot near the stern where she seemed out of the way and could watch the water.

Thoughts of the gulf and the trip to Corinth her father had promised brought a whimper to her lips. "Father...." The memory rekindled concern for the rest of her family. "What a far cry this voyage is from what you planned."

You will never see your family again.

Cruel in its simplicity, she was not sure if it was her thoughts or that of the Voice. Her heart plummeted with the probability of its prophecy and released tears stored with her longing for them. She turned from the water.

Ropes threaded through poles on either side of the huge, gopher-wood mast drew her attention to its highest point. Directly above the owner's flag, Rome's proud emblem topped the pole. The lines of the largest sails swept nearly the entire length of the ship and intertwined in every direction, ready to defy unruly winds.

The mast creaked as the wind changed directions and refilled the slackened sails. They swayed and flapped as if they danced to the music of an unseen harpist. The highly polished deck glared in the sunlight.

A thick, multicolored rope startled her. It stretched down the deck where it wound around a bright copper ball. She shuddered at the memory of a close call with a coiled snake on her walk to the temple. A permanent fear of the reptiles remained and never lessened.

She inhaled deeply of the salty air and exhaled the hold's putrid smells. An occasional spray vaulted the rail. She welcomed the only water to refresh her body or clothing. Lacy white bubbles topped each glassy swell as they crested and broke under the weight of the powerful surge. Like the froth that topped Belte's milk pail, they did not last. She could almost hear her servant as she scolded a rambunctious nanny goat. Would thoughts of home never release their torture?

A sailor walked up behind her. "Well, what have we here?"

"Looks like a chance for some fun," another said.

"How about it girly…want to have some fun?"

She froze as she remembered the order to stay clear of the crew. The closest sailor took hold of the hem of her tunic and pulled it up when she tried to leave. "Stop that. Get away from me." She broke free and started to run but his mate blocked her escape.

"Come on, pretty girl, how about a kiss?" With that he grabbed her and thrust his mouth on hers. She bit his lip and pushed him away.

He wiped the blood from his chin. "Well, you little… I have a notion to…."

An angry voice chimed from behind. "Maybe you better rethink that notion."

The sailor spun and faced the angry scowl of Patharus. A young man with clenched fists stood beside him.

The sailors backed away. "We were just, just…."

He glared at him. "See that it never happens again, or I will report you to the captain."

In a panic, they stumbled in their haste to leave. "Yes sir! Yes sir."

Her owner turned to her. "Are you alright?"

She wished she could sink through the deck.

He motioned to Nicanor. "Walk her down to the other end of the ship and get her some water."

She hung back so Nicanor would not see her crimson cheeks. He led her to the skiff she often rested by. "This is where you like to spend your days, right?"

She folded her arms across her chest and wished he would just leave.

"I will bring you some water. And do not worry. Patharus often travels on this ship and those sailors will not dare come near you again."

Nicanor turned and left. How did he know she liked this spot?

Chapter Three

Now is high time to awake.
– Romans 13:11

The next day Daphne decided to stay near the skiff, but soon grew restless. She decided to walk and get some exercise.

She assured herself no sailors were around and wandered nearer the bow. Deserted except for the man at the helm, she studied the prow. The expertly finished wood extended upward out over the water, well above buffeting waves. Like crudely knitted doilies, knotted ropes hung on each side and enhanced its artistry.

The figurehead of a seductive woman had been sculptured into its peak. With flowing red hair that swept down her shoulders and curled around a milky-white bosom, she appeared to lead the ship. Her serene expression designed to beguile, promised peace and safety to all who traveled with her.

The unspoken pledge mocked Daphne. She scoffed at its presumption. "All is not well." The words hardly left her lips before contempt faded to a whimper. "It may never be well again. I ought to slip over the side and disappear…who would care?"

Waves dashed against the bow and disintegrated. Who would care, echoed across the sea and into her heart. Swells beckoned, their hypnotic pull heightened her desire. Daphne despaired, "Why not? I cannot help my family and I have nothing to live for."

"I care. I love you with an everlasting love."

She gasped at the voice of Belte's God, but, as he had when she first heard him after they were sold into slavery, he seemed a distant reality.

She gripped the rail several times, arms tensed, ready to spring, but at the last moment her nerves melted like snow on Mt. Parnassus. Determined, she swallowed her fear, wiped the sweat from her hands, took a shaky breath, and grabbed the rail.

Loud voices foiled her plans. She panicked but before they could reach the area, she crossed to the opposite side. The first mate and Patharus passed, deep in a disagreement. Her owner eyed her with suspicion but looked away. Had he guessed her intentions? To her relief, both men kept their pace.

She grimaced, dismissed the despair that tugged, and marched toward the stern. "No…I will not surrender!" she thought. "If I give in, I will never find my family." Instantly, the heaviness lifted, replaced with something close to peace. Each step became a commitment to rebuke the tentacles of self-pity that threatened to erode her hope.

She sat in the shade of the little dinghy, the small skiff hung on iron hinges just above the deck, ready to rescue or carry men into coves. Like a giant cradle, it rocked with each motherly breeze. Its patient demeanor lured her thoughts to Belte, her sorely missed servant and friend. She wondered where Belte and her family were and what happened to that precious granddaughter she loved so much.

Tears stung at the recall of Belte's patient explanation of Jesus, her newly found God. She was so sure of His love and care. "I wonder if he is still her God?"

Her stomach growled. There would be no food until just before dark. Days of nausea and restricted water rations had taken their toll. Sharp hipbones were all that rippled the dirty tunic that hung from her skeleton-like shoulders, and the daily climb out of the hold took all the energy she could muster.

She crossed her arms and tried to calm her thoughts. The effort fell flat. "Only a few more days, I can do it. Then what?" she thought. Despite her resolve, negative thoughts drained like a nursing child. What would life as a slave amount to? Would she be like those who had worked under Belte? Where would she live…in a hovel like she had in Athens? And how did they plan to profit by her gift?

The full force of the afternoon sun bore down. She closed her eyes, stretched, and soaked up the late-summer heat against the dampness of the hull.

"Be careful, Daphne. Remember, the midday sun can sear your skin." Her mother's wisdom brought a catch to her throat. Before she could heed her advice, a shadow enveloped her. She expected a cloud but found herself centered in a man-shaped shade. She jerked to her feet, ready to flee, but was arrested by Patharus' stare.

Her heart pounded. She lowered her eyes and waited. Why did he seek her out? She had not read anything in his expression. Like a wary hummingbird she searched around her feet, as if the answer might be written on the deck.

He handed her some bread and water. "Do not forget the restrictions about the deck… understand?" She nodded and without another word, he walked away.

So taken back by his kindness, she forgot to thank him. She clutched the precious gifts to her chest and pressed the jug to her parched lips. She drank the water and ate the bread.

Too much water too fast caused her stomach to cramp but the spasm soon passed. She sat the jug between her thighs, eased her back against the bracket that supported the rowboat and sipped the rest. Hunger abated, she fell asleep, roused too soon by the clang of the dinner bell.

Strengthened by the bread, she took advantage of the empty hold and climbed below to relieve herself before she joined the food line. The fare, cabbage, and potatoes with less than a hint of mutton, a poor excuse for stew. She ate her portion, using her allotted crust to soak up the watery soup.

The signal that announced time to go to the hold, came much too soon. Despite the circumstances, she discovered she loved sailing and how the sky looked as it darkened. She tried to remember her father's explanation of the star placements and wished she could sleep on deck. Do the stars looked different out on the open sea?

Reluctantly, she followed the other women and drew in great gulps of fresh air to offset what waited in the hold. Like a heavy cloak, oppression closed in. She tried to recall the wind on her face and the warm afternoon sun. Images played of the swells rising to heights too great to sustain. Each glassy exterior soon folded, its foam a picture of lace curtains against a dark window.

Finally, she drifted off and dreamt that a relentless god mounted on high waves chased their ship. He waved an overseer's whip and gained on the vessel. Terrorized, she tried to hide, but her feet would not move. The evil being neared and bore the face of Talsta. She sat up and clutched her chest, unable to dismiss the memory of her last moments in the *adytum*. Would she never stop replaying the moment he stabbed the high priest to eliminate the only obstacle able to thwart becoming his successor? Was he still after her? What unlikely methods might he use to follow the ship and seek her out? Sleep did not come for hours.

At the first glimpse of light, she rubbed her eyes and climbed from the hold. Beneath purple-gray clouds, the horizon glowed as if fire burned at the end of the water. A tiny red sliver broke through, grew to a half-circle, and then to a huge ball that rose above the surface of the water and cast a choppy red path across it.

She frowned, "Do not go…Do not disappear." Her hopes dangled like the sun. But inch by inch it was gobbled into the dark abyss until nothing remained but a silver halo etched into the edges of the clouds. She sighed. The majestic light submitted to its fate, and so must she.

The sun's inability to change its destiny still on her mind, she leaned her back against the rail and pondered the turn her life had taken. Apollo's Spring Festival just months ago had truly changed her life, but not in ways she expected. She attained the adult status she coveted, but not the freedom she hoped for. In the bowels of the temple something had invaded her, something that wanted to control her life. And the loss of their home to the Romans had rendered her a life of slavery.

Daphne mused, "Why was I so anxious to leave childhood and embrace the grownup world? Is this what life is about? You get one brilliant moment after you break free, only to be drawn into an ominous thunderhead that douses your light forever."

Chapter Four

...compassion on those who are ignorant and going astray...
– Hebrews 5:2

The bustle of sailors as they readied the ship for the day disrupted Daphne's reverie. At the signal she lined up with the others to receive breakfast. While she waited for her food, they approached a distant island. A sailor pointed it out to his mate who manned a huge pot of gruel. "It means we are halfway to Neapolis."

She lingered to hear more, but others jostled her from the spot. Neapolis? Where was that? Maybe it was near Thessalonica where mother's cousin lived.

They drew nearer the island close to a small fleet of anchored sponge boats, close enough to witness men preparing for the dangerous dive. With bulging cheeks, one was girded with a long rope just above his waist. He attached a massive lead weight and clutched a sharp bill before he climbed out on the prow.

Calls of comrades incited him to jump. Without fanfare, he leapt into the sea. She tried to picture him spewing the clear white oil at the bottom, its bright gleam a beacon in the murky darkness.

For several minutes she scanned the area where his head would likely clear the water. He did not surface. She leaned further into the rail. Where was he? His fate became hers and that of her mother and brothers. Had he found a bumper crop and overstayed the capacity of his lungs? She whispered into the depths that concealed him, "Oh please, do not run out of air…survive."

By the time his fellow workers manned his lifeline, her mouth was as dry as the creeks in summer. In unison, they pulled with great heaves. Seconds later his body flew out of water, gasping for air. He sank again before he reached the ship. With one hand he flung the sharp bill onto the deck, and with the other raised his waterlogged treasure at his cheering comrades.

She resisted the temptation to cheer along with them and released her breath in a whoosh.

The vessels became tiny dots as her ship sailed further north and passed island after island to the east. On some, they passed close enough to see families going about their daily business. She turned her gaze toward the open water.

For the next two days the ship languished, captive to an eerie calm. She spent her time tucked close to the skiff, grateful for its shade. Up on the windless deck, the sun beat without mercy, while at night stillness rendered the lower quarters unbearable. She slept fitfully and awoke to a soaked tunic and clammy skin. On deck, the garment dried, but became stiff and uncomfortable until the temperature rose and the cycle repeated.

She longed to scrub her tunic but at first hint of a calm, fresh water was monitored and cautiously doled out. To bathe or wash one's clothes was not a priority to the dirty-looking men who manned the ship.

Her hair hung in rigid clumps. She tried to tidy it but found she could hardly run her fingers through the matted jumble. The odor it left on her hands made her wince. Escape from her offensive stench would have to come after they landed. She gazed at the glass-like sea. Gone were the swells. "If I could only jump in and cool off, I would not care if it was salt water…if it would remove some of this filth."

"Your clothes would still be stiff when they dried," said Nicanor.

She pivoted and found herself face to face with her owner's other slave. "I, ah, I was...."

Nicanor swiped at the sweat that poured from under his hair. His tunic stuck to his frame and his chest heaved. "I was commandeered to row on the lower oars with the other slaves and we all long for cool baths and clean clothes. Have they passed out any water?"

She shook her head and fingered a loose clump of hair that hung over her eyes. Why was she so tongue tied? They were both slaves.

He smiled. "That is better, now I can see your pretty brown eyes."

A flush crept up her neck and into her face. She had never been spoken to like that by a young man. She should probably leave but nothing about him felt threatening. Should she say something? What? And why did he make her feel.... what was it she felt?

"There you are, Nicanor. I need you to attend...." Patharus spotted Daphne, frowned, and waved Nicanor off. "Find the man in charge and see to it that our cargo is first off when we land."

She shrank at the impatience in his command. Had she violated another rule? She had seen him pace while they waited out the calm. The ship's owner approached and Patharus motioned him over. "Captain, surely something can be done. I have an important meeting with the city fathers in Philippi just days from now. Could you not assign fresh oarsmen? Perhaps if you directed the prow to one side it would pick up a bit of breeze."

She cocked her ear. Philippi? Daphne thought they were going to Neapolis. That must mean they would travel inland from the port.

As the two drifted from earshot, the captain's effort to explain his inability to modify their plight faded.

At dawn the third day, a wind rustled the sails. In the stifling hold, whispers of gratitude rose. The sound lasted only a few moments, but every ear strained as lips beseeched their gods for relief. They were not disappointed. Zeus or Jupiter as some called him, had relented, and loosed his hold on the wind.

She climbed out to the cheers of bondsmen and personal servants as they let go their oars, came out and stretched their aching backs. Sailors ordered to the higher tier of the oared biremes felt the sway. Their roars merged with those of the captives.

Passengers and staff alike revived, eager to complete the journey. Cargo shippers congratulated one another as sailors dashed to adjust the tension on the sails. She stretched her arms to the breeze. Her *chiton* was drenched, and her stomach growled. Water and their meager rations had been cut further the first day of the wind stopped. By mid-afternoon, a sailor with a spyglass spotted a large landmass. "Thasos," he said to his less experienced shipmates, then expounded on its proximity to Neapolis.

Her heart leapt, only to sink at the unknown. By the time they finished the evening meal, they neared the island of Thasos. Its marble cliffs gleamed a golden orange in the sun's lower rays. Their heights hosted streams that plunged thousands of feet to the Aegean. Despite the painful reminders of families, she searched the island for signs of life.

The cliffs gave way to a valley and a narrow inlet with fishing boats lined to unload their catch. Nearby, children gathered to watch a young man beat a squid against the rocks. They squealed with delight as the blows released its protective, inky stream, and rendered the creature tender and edible.

She could not take her eyes off a small boy with a pudgy body. He could have been Theo. Just as her little brother would, the child crept ever nearer to the scene. More than once the older boy gestured him out of the way. She could almost smell Theo's damp hair after a day in the warm sunshine. She choked back tears.

Patharus' footsteps startled her. His expression curious. "I saw you at the rail. Is there a problem?"

The rail...he had seen her there before. Did he think she planned to jump. She shook her head. "No. No, I...." How could she explain her anguish to him, to anyone? She swerved from his stare and wiped her cheeks. "I came to walk awhile before. ..."

"I will see you to the hold." His tone left no option as he fell in step beside her. "Be ready to depart at dawn. My people will have wagons ready to load once we are off."

She nodded and quickened her steps. The dark outline of the harbor rose in the near distance. His frequent glances made her squirm. For the first time, she welcomed going below.

Chapter Five

To give them beauty for ashes…
– Isaiah 61:3

Daphne sensed dawn was near. She tried not to speculate on what the day would bring. At the click of the hold's gate, she tiptoed around the other women and climbed to the solitude of the deck. The misty air revived her body and nourished her soul.

Pink-tinged clouds promised a clear sunrise. She whispered to the god of the dawn. "Come, Eos, allow the sun to clear the water and begin its journey across the sky."

A husky voice responded. "The Romans call him Aurora."

She whirled and found herself but a few feet from the bronzed face of Nicanor. His smile reached his eyes. She nodded and forced herself to turn from his gaze.

He pointed toward the port. "That's Neapolis, and to the west is Mount Pangaion. We will soon be on our way home."

She studied the mountain, grateful for a reason to avoid his eyes. "Is Philippi your home?"

"Yes, this was my first trip to Athens. I was born in Philippi of Greek parents. Where was your home?"

Where was her home? She wanted to scream, "Delphi is still my home," but she explained it was a small city on the northern Gulf of Corinth.

He did not comment. "Patharus has arranged for our immediate departure. Our cargo will be first off so you must be ready…with or without the morning fare." He left but his presence lingered.

"Nicanor," She said it aloud. She liked the way it rolled off her tongue.

Even in the diffused light the city gleamed. Lush green hills covered with tiny white houses that bore terra cotta roofs, rose on both sides of the port. Like orange daylilies, they peeked out of the abundant foliage.

She ate the figs and dry bread the crew hastily offered. Others tethered the ships anchors, ready for the drop. With nothing to fetch from the hold, she fingered her only possession, safely hidden under a fold in her tunic. Gorgeous beaches on both sides of the harbor reminded her of Delphi. She sighed and focused on the port.

Mountains towered in the distant north and west. According to her grandmother, Mount Pangaion was sacred to the god, Dionysus and filled with gold. The matriarch's disdain for the outlandish god of revelry resurfaced. Daphne snorted, "Is that where you hide your evil ways each spring after Apollo returns from the land of Hyperborean?"

She dodged the crews who readied the cargo for transfer, and the captain who shouted orders from the middle of the deck. The ship had nearly reached a standstill by the time the rowers propelled it the last few yards.

Patharus appeared at her elbow. "This is it. The anchors are secured. Stay close behind me."

She followed him through the maze of cargo. As promised, his goods were stacked, ready to be first off. As they passed, the captain stretched forth his hand for the expected drachmas, but his eyes remained on her. "Farewell for now, and may your, ah, new goods, serve you well."

She turned from his leering grin as her owner helped her into the dinghy that would take them to shore.

Patharus led the way after they left the dinghy and headed for his wagons. With a nod, the servant in charge acknowledged her and welcomed his master.

Nicanor supervised the dock hands hired to load the wagons. With well-practiced precision, they stacked vats marked exotic wines, leather goods, pottery, and oil. He motioned to her and helped her squeeze into a small area cleared in the owner's wagon.

She half-expected to be tied as before, but Nicanor simply pointed at the wooden floor and shrugged. "I apologized for the lack of comfort. Our owner did not plan to buy slaves this trip, so no space was allotted to transport them."

He backed up, climbed onto the driver's bench, and sat beside Patharus. With a low whistle, the driver signaled the wagons behind them, flicked the reins, and led the way to Philippi.

Though surrounded by cargo, a gap on each side allowed her a view of the countryside, and a bigger slot between two barrels opened the view of where they had been. To her relief, the wagon had no cover. To the front, a slit between boxes gave view of the men and horses. She could hear them talk but paid little attention until Patharus peppered the driver with questions.

"The harvest…how does it fare? Have the fruit trees held their bounty, not dropped early? What about the grapes, any blight shown up?"

"All are well, my lord. The figs are right on schedule and the barley crop should be the best in years."

"And the slaves…any problems surface? Has Stello…."

The driver shot him a knowing glance. "There has been no ah, incidents with the overseer, my lord. All has been peaceful."

Patharus nodded and dropped the inquiry. Occasionally he checked to make sure his load had not shifted but took no notice of his passenger.

The port grew smaller and disappeared. With folded arms she pressed her stomach and hardly moved. Nothing, other than what awaited her, on her mind.

The ride proved dusty and uncomfortable. Her bones ached from rattling around on the hard floor and her limbs stiffened in the cramped quarters. Finally, they stopped to refresh themselves. Nicanor handed her some fruit and a pouch with vegetables and dried lamb wrapped in grape leaves. His hand lingered on hers as he handed her a skein of water. "Here, you will need this." He smiled. "You can keep it with you."

She nodded and he climbed back onto the driver's bench.

She stared at her hand. Surely, she had imagined that kind gesture. She ate the first decent food given her in months. How long would the journey take? Days? Weeks? With each turn, the distance from home pierced her heart. She gazed at the road behind, jostled as the wagon lurched and tossed her against its side. How far had they come? Philippi sounded as distant as the far peaks of her beloved Mt. Parnassus.

Once they left Neapolis, there were no signs of civilization. The rut-filled road encompassed the east side of a lengthy marsh.

Her grandfather once told of a famous Roman battle around the swamp between Neapolis and Philippi. For her brother, Alexander's eager ears, her grandfather dramatized the scene: "It happened nearly a hundred years ago, right after Brutus and Cassius assassinated Julius Caesar. They fled to Macedonia with their large army and camped beside the swamp not far from Philippi.

But Mark Anthony and Octavius tracked the renegades and settled on the opposite side of the marsh."

Alexander crouched close, eyes wide. "How did they cross the marshland, Papose?"

"Well, with their supplies nearly gone, by night Mark Anthony's men dug trenches through the swamp and by day pretended to await their fatal end. The reeds hid the trenches, so when they reached their enemy's camp, their surprise attack brought a decisive victory. Confusion and defeat led both Cassius and Brutus to commit suicide."

Long after she had lost interest, Alexander pestered their grandfather for more gruesome details.

She welcomed the distraction of little ringed plovers and smiled at their antics. Black marks circled their throats like a necklace of misshapen, onyx beads. They darted about the cattails that bowed under the weight of their uninvited guests.

Patches of bluish-purple and pink hydrangeas edged the swamp grasses, intertwined with marsh myrtle and flowers she did not recognize. The scene delighted her senses and cushioned her discomfort. "Oh mother, you would have loved to see this."

On the windswept plains, fields of red poppies defied the rocky terrain. Nearer the port, their bright splotches squeezed into every unattended nook, whether a roadside dump or parks with statues of city's gods. Silently, she cheered the tenacity of the joyous blossoms and returned their gentle, welcoming nods. She sat a little straighter. They survive and bloom in a hostile climate and somehow, she would too.

In the distance she spotted a flock of the largest birds she had ever seen. Long scrawny necks connected to pink and white-feathered bodies, with equally gangly legs. Black, hook-like beaks curved out of heads that looked too small to hold their bills. Her head swiveled as they passed, fascinated by gigantic wings that arched in rhythmic slow motion. Delphi had no such birds.

The marsh faded from view long before they entered the foothills that surrounded Philippi.

Chapter Six

...gone like a shadow when it lengthens...
– Psalm 109:23

At the crest of a bluff Patharus called a halt. He climbed up on the bench and surveyed both sides of the road. It led to the front gate of a manor that sprawled in three directions. Fruit and olive orchards, vineyards and fields of barley or wheat stretched as far as one could see. The cherry trees were bare, but apricot and apple trees bowed under the weight of promise. Stables, and structures built to store crops surrounded the main house.

Daphne gulped. She had never seen such opulence, her father's lands would not have filled half of it. Along one side of the property well away from the main house, roughly constructed small shanties lined the area nearest the barley crop. She wagged her head. He must be very powerful. How can I...how will I....

At his signal, the wagons lurched forward. A ram's horn sounded and a pudgy man with a turban coiled around his head stepped from the gatehouse and opened the iron barrier. Dozens of men clad in scant garments that wound around their waists and between their legs rushed to attend the wagons.

She pictured her father's joyful returns. Would this man's wife or children rush to greet him?

None but workers milled about. Her curiosity dwindled to a stark reality: her former life was forever gone. A bitter bile climbed her throat as she thought, A slave! I am a slave, like Belte or one of her helpers…or worse yet, a field hand.

Nicanor seemed taken care of, but how would she be treated? Her father's kindness and fair management kindled loyalty among his slaves, but her friend, Semiele's father, was cruel and violent. Daphne startled when the driver came to help her down from the wagon. He pointed to a nearby mulberry tree. "Wait over there."

As the cargo unloaded under Nicanor's trained eye, Patharus withdrew into his house. To her relief, he did not glance her way or appear to instruct anyone concerning her. Still Bentalla's prediction made her stomach flipflop. She focused on the workers and forced back the persistent dread.

For over an hour she stood in the shade. Nicanor removed his tunic and helped lift the heavier cartons, his muscles rippled with the weight. She lowered her eyes each time he glanced her way. No one spoke to her or offered anything to eat or drink, and the dropped berries discouraged sitting on the grass.

Thirsty and weak from hunger, she pictured the heron-like bitterns back at the marsh. They had lifted their thorn-shaped beaks to protest the intrusion, then dove deep into the reed-beds. She wanted to protest too and nestle where no one would find her. Instead, she leaned into the tree, grateful she had shade.

"Would you like something to hold you over until dinner?"

The voice came from a girl not much older than herself. She bore a tray of figs, olives, and a cup of watered wine. Daphne picked up the wine. "Oh yes, Thank you." She swallowed it in one gulp, reached for a fig but stopped midway. "Is it all right, I mean...."

"Of course. The master did not set out to buy slaves, so you were forgotten until I happened to notice you. I am glad you speak Greek...so many do not."

She finished the fruit while the girl fetched more water. "Oh, thank you, I have not had much to drink for days."

The girl's smile revealed gleaming white teeth behind a tiny mouth. "I am Kawit, I am a house girl."

She returned the smile. "I am Daphne." She liked the girl's easy manner. Her heart-shaped face and dark skin fascinated her. Small round eyes peered under arched brows that nearly met her hairline. Her tiny, upturned nose created a bit of a shelf, and the combination forged a look of perpetual surprise. Daphne stared. She must be from somewhere far from Greece.

The short, practical tunic worn by household slaves barely covered Kawit's curvy frame. Void of frills, it had no extra drapes or folds that might interfere with her tasks. Her light brown hair swept to one side at the nape of her neck and circled her head in a braided coil.

Her brows twitched. "You do not look very strong. Why did the master purchase you? Are you a weaver or have a special skill?"

Daphne shrugged.

"Were you bought at the slave auction in Athens?"

She nodded but added nothing.

Undeterred, Kawit chirped a stream of questions. Not sure how she should answer, she faltered, but the girl's sincere demeanor convinced Daphne, she could trust her. "I...I really do not know. He seems to think I have special powers to discern the future and tell people's fortunes."

"And do you?"

"I have known of some things before they happened, but I cannot explain how I know."

She waited. Daphne searched the girl's face. It held only compassion. "Ummm, can you tell me what, ah...."

It was no use. She did not have the courage to ask what was foremost on her mind. She tried again, her cheeks red at the thought. "I mean, do you know how the master might use me...or what to expect?"

"Well, I...."

A surly voice cut into their conversation. "That will do, Kawit. Get back to your duties."

She stiffened and lowered her head, but not before Daphne saw something akin to dread or fear flash across the girl's face. She left without another word.

The man stepped close to Daphne. He made it no secret as he checked her form. "I am Stello, the master's overseer. I am over all slaves." He watched her face for a reaction.

She swallowed hard and nodded. His steely eyes never left her face. His muscular body towered over her, arms crossed, his face a portrait of intimidation. She dropped her eyes and waited, her heart beating wildly.

"You will be under my command and do as I say at all times. Is that understood?"

Again, she could but nod.

"The master wishes to speak with you. Follow me."

With leaded steps, she trailed into the large foyer inside the front entrance. On each side elegant staircases led to the upper quarters. Polished wood railings topped with vine draped marble pillars highlighted the gentle curve of every stair.

Busts she assumed were Roman emperors graced the bottom columns, with frescos of animals, birds and dolphins that ascended one outer wall. A larger fresco depicting a Roman regiment engaged in a victorious battle covered much of the other side. Light shone from windows near the ceiling, giving the vestibule a bright, airy aura.

Stello headed down the hall and knocked on a door carved with the figure of Jupiter, Rome's dominant god. At Patharus' response, the overseer gestured for her to enter the room. The door clicked and sent her hand to her throat. Did her owner see himself like that god...powerful and at liberty to do whatever suited his mood or desire?

Chapter Seven

The thing I greatly feared has come upon me.
– Job 3:25

Patharus glanced up briefly from work on a huge, table-like desk. "Well, let us see, Daphne, right? This is now your home. You will be given a place to sleep, food and clothes. If you do the work assigned and do not shirk, you will find it an acceptable place." He paged through the papers laid out before him as he spoke. "Do you have any questions?"

She shook her head, not sure how she was expected to address him. His speech sounded like one he had given a hundred times. An uncomfortable silence followed until he looked up. She cowered and looked at her feet. He had caught her staring. She clenched her hands and pressed them to her stomach to quell a rising nausea. He would not see them shake.

He stood and she jumped back a step. Her response startled him. His brows twitched. "What is it girl?" He waited. When she did not respond, he came around his desk.

She gasped and thrust her arms up in front of her. Vivid images of the long-anticipated defilement flowed. She shook her head and backed toward the door, whimpering. "Please… please!"

He took a step in her direction.

Tears streamed down her face and her cries grew louder "Please, please do not…" She shielded her chest with her arms.

He frowned and jammed his chin into his neck. "Do not do what?"

She fell to her knees, covered her face with her hands, and sobbed hysterically. He stood over her, fists on his hips, his face a snarl.

"D…do not. Please do not…"

Alarmed by the commotion, Patharus' personal servant stepped through the door with his hands on his sheath. "Master?"

He looked at him and back at the quaking figure at his feet. "No…leave us."

The servant disappeared as quickly as he had come.

Patharus lowered his voice. "Daphne, tell me, where did you come from…were you beaten by a former owner?"

She shook her head. "My family, my family is…" Shudders stifled her efforts.

"You do not speak like a slave. How did you come to be in the Athens auction?"

She tried to speak but could not catch her breath.

He allowed her time. "Tell me."

Exhausted by the fear and despair of the past months, she gave way to emotions that ballooned within. The need to unleash her pain overwhelmed every semblance of reason. She told him how her father's unwise business decisions had caused his estate to falter after his death. She told him of the unscrupulous magistrates who controlled Delphi, who despite guaranteed payment, auctioned off her father's estate to pay his debts. She told him how those in authority sold her mother, herself, and her two brothers into slavery to satisfy his creditors.

Tears dripped as she spoke of her family. She wiped her eyes with a corner of her *peplos* and shared the despair of her inability to prevent the uncertainties her loved ones likely faced.

He listened until she quieted. "And when did this take place?"

His gentle demeanor melted her vow to hide her past. Despite hiccups she could not stop, she whispered, "Shortly after the *Pythian* festival of the games."

Disarmed by his kindness, all resolve fled. He now knew how recently she had led the life of a protected girl in a respectable family. To deduce that she had not yet lost her innocence would easily follow.

He put his hand on her elbow and pulled her up. She searched his face, aware he held full sway over what might yet happen. His expression did not threaten.

He ignored her final shudder. "Here, sit on this couch and tell me about life in the Peloponnese. I have been to Athens countless times but have not traveled beyond Corinth."

She did as he directed, grateful he sat opposite her. She explained Delphi was in the lower part of northern Greece and answered his questions as best she could. He listened with nods and inquired further into their community and customs.

"Now," he said, as if anxious to get to what he really wanted to find out. "Tell me how you acquired this ability to tell fortunes?"

She sighed and leaned into one hand. Where to begin? He looked expectant. "Apollo's most important temple is in Delphi…."

"Yes, yes. Even in Rome we know of the great divination initiated there. Are women allowed to seek guidance? Did they give you the ability?"

She covered her lips with her knuckles. How could she explain what happened? "I officially became a part of Apollo's followers last spring with other girls my age. Women are not allowed in the *adytum* where the *pythia* receives word from Apollo. We can sacrifice and attend festivals, but not games."

She decided to keep the part about sneaking into the *adytum* to herself. "I had an accident and fell while there, and soon after I began to hear a Voice within that would tell me things, I could not know on my own." She tried to further explain the presence of the Voice, but stumbled, not fully understanding it herself.

He asked for examples, and she told him about the murder of Semiele's mother, and how she knew Neptari would be sold to a brothel. He leaned in, eager to absorb every word. "Have people sought you out…asked for your insight or paid you to tell them their future?"

She shook her head. "I have mostly kept it to myself, but some people discovered it works within me."

He stood to his feet. "Daphne, life has been cruel and it cannot be altered. You must accept your circumstances and go on. But I promise you this…you will be safe here. I will not allow you to be abused."

Chapter Eight

Where then is my hope?
– Job 17:15

Patharus did not allude to the assault Daphne anticipated, but her cheeks reddened knowing he knew, and it made her squirm.

He folded his arms across his chest and locked his eyes on hers. "You will go each day into the city and use your ability to tell men's future for a price. Your profits will be reported directly to me at day's end. If you obey and do your task you will have nothing to fear."

She listened intently. His eyes conveyed compassion, but his tone spoke expectations of compliance. At his pledge of protection, gratitude and relief flooded her heart and filled her eyes. But how was she to tell fortunes? The Voice said she would know things others could not know, but she had no control over what or when it spoke. What if it refused to tell her what to say? And who would teach her how to become a sorcerer?

"Your Apollo will look after you." Melench's prediction rang in her head. It confirmed her belief that somehow Apollo had arranged things, she could trust this man who controlled her very life.

She wiped her cheeks and took a deep breath. Fear of what might develop from the life he laid out dissolved as hope rose like a thunderhead in her heart. "Thank you. I will do as you say."

He rang and his servant instantly appeared. "Take her to Jahtel and tell him to set her up in one of the inside slave quarters."

The servant reached for the door but stopped when Patharus spoke. "And tell Stello to report immediately. I have special instructions for him."

The servant bowed and led Daphne down the white-washed halls. They entered a stark, but clean area well away from the owner's section of the villa.

He found the manager of the master's inner household and pointed at her. "Here is a new slave, Jahtel." He conveyed the special instructions and left.

Jahtel leaned his wiry body and squinted into her face as if he expected to see something unusual, then fussed with some papers. She could hear him mutter something about specific orders and an individual's housing.

He ushered her into a small, narrow room. "This will be yours, I am told you will answer directly to the master as to your assignment, but I am in charge of all those who work inside, so you will come to me with questions or needs… understood?"

She lowered her head to hide a frown and avoid his unpleasant demeanor. What should she do if his orders conflicted with those of Stello or the master?

"Yes…thank you." She wanted desperately to ask for water to bathe but could not bring herself to verbalize such an intimate need to a stranger, especially a man. The thought sent a flush up her neck and dampened her skin. She started to speak, but hesitated.

He arched a brow, cocked his head, and waited. "Well, what is it you wish?"

Restrictions of a world far removed from the life forced upon her faded, overruled by a strong desire to rid her body of weeks of filth. She looked him in the eyes. "Ah, may I please have some water…to bathe?"

His eyes widened. Daphne's blush deepened. Had she breached a procedure? He rolled his eyes and scowled.

Her courage shrank.

Finally, he spoke. "I will send a girl.to show you where things are." He cleared his throat. "….and bring you some clean clothes. One change is allowed each slave. You are responsible to keep them clean."

She flinched at his tone and waited to peek down the hall until he passed through the curtain that served as her door. To her relief, she was alone. She leaned against the wall and blew the tension from her lungs. In the farthest corner, covered with pale muslin, lay a rolled bed mat filled with straw. She lifted it and a woven blanket folded across one end.

No vermin or smelly mold rose from the bedding. Grateful, she replaced it. Nearby, a crudely carved table held a water pitcher and a towel. A rough wicker bench completed the furnishings. As she caught sight of the room's tiny window, a light breeze grazed her bare arms.

She had a window! She brightened at the meager concession. It had been chiseled from the upper wall, well above eye level. She stretched up on her toes to see the view, but an opposite roof and the tops of a few trees were all she could see. She huffed. Well, at least she would know when it was morning.

• • • • •

The wicked watches….and seeks to slay him.

– Psalm 37:32

The spirit of divination sneered at her spunk. Yes, and I will see that it is a profitable morning for both of us. The sooner I finish with you, the sooner I will be returned to my true calling.

Are you inferring our Master has made a mistake?

The voice of Delphi's head demon. How he dreaded it. He ruled without mercy over Apollo's temple, posing as their beloved god. Divination knew the order. Delphi's head demon was accountable to his superior, the guardian principality over all of Greece who held a commission of power and authority invested by the Father of Lies, himself. He scoffed. Ignorant humans believed the guardian principality to be their all-mighty Zeus, but those under him knew him to be a powerful demonic stronghold with no patience for failure.

He shrank at the question. Ever since he vacated the lifeless body of the pythia in Apollo's temple and inhabited Daphne, his superior had been on his case. N...no, Mighty One. No, I was just....

Just what? Do you really think you have a better plan than the ruler of darkness? Or maybe your assignment is too hard for you...shall I find someone else.

The divining spirit cowered. Why was his superior always spying on him? His beginning went back more than six hundred years to the onset of the Apollonian myth. He certainly did not need to be monitored. No! No, I can do it. I will....

The head demon stepped close. See that you do. And make sure she does not come to "an accidental" end.

His superior sneered, See that you do not! Your talent was aptly appointed eons ago to complement the great hoax. The Prince of Darkness devised his plan to bring millions into his domain through deceit instilled in displaced spirits with your expertise. Remember, these superstitious, gullible people have bought the enslaving myths of Greek gods for generations That includes your present vessel. She pledged herself to one other than the creator of the universe...the god they call Apollo. That makes her eligible for our master's use.

Now, let me hear you repeat your assignment.

I am to use my expertise to develop a fortune teller who will lead people astray as they put their trust in her insight. That will separate the creatures to the god of this world and keep them from the knowledge of our master's ancient foe.

At his monotonous spiel, his superior leaned closer. And?

Through their ignorance and greed our ruler will gain an irresistible foothold and cause them to worship our Father of Lies as the provider of all they want or need. The despicable creatures will believe they can get knowledge of the future and receive supernatural guidance from a source other than our powerful Adversary.

Right, and just as you deceived Apollo's priestess to believe she served a god rather than the ruler of darkness, you will teach this girl how to deceive men. She has been exposed to the truth and has not fully swallowed the fallacy, so take care to keep her from knowledge of our great ruler's advocate.

He glared with contempt at the underling who sniveled with his chin on his chest. Over eighteen years have passed since our great Adversary implemented a plan that resulted in salvation for any who would receive it. No one knows how much time is left. I have my eyes on you and expect quick results.

With that, Delphi's head demon disappeared in a whiff of smoke. His heinous laughter echoed in the ears of the Apollonian spirit of divination. He sighed, relieved his superior had accepted his commitment, but determined to make it work in his favor. Careful not to speak it aloud, he vowed again to mold Daphne into the most sought-after diviner Lucifer has ever seen.

Chapter Nine

A time to gain and a time to lose.
– Ecclesiastes 3:6

Daphne tried not to compare her coarse surroundings and the days ahead of her with what she left behind. They shriveled in contrast to the pampered life and beautiful home she took for granted in Delphi. No lovely tapestries would adorn her walls, nor would soft carpets cozy her bare feet.

The Romans had not let them rescue even the most personal things before the auction. Greedy for everything Greek, the wives of the Romans had gobbled her jewelry and even her clothes at the auction. She fumed at the memory of how they gleefully pounced on her mother's treasures, then fled like thieves with all they could carry.

She looked at the only dress she owned. How would she ever get it clean and fix the tears? And her sandals. The strings had been knotted many times, soon they would be too worn to hold to her feet.

A cheerful voice charged through her makeshift door. "Hello again."

Daphne's face lit up at Kawit's welcome smile, her gloom dispelled by the sight of one she sensed would be a friend. She resisted an impulse to hug her but reached out and took her hands. "Hello! I am so glad to see you again. Did they send you to show me where things are?"

Kawit grinned. "They said you wanted to bathe." She looked at the ceiling and huffed. "I do not think Jahtel ever had such a request."

Daphne groaned. "Oh, did I ask too much? It is just that I cannot remember the last time I…."

She shook her head. "No…no. It is that only the master's household bathes before the evening meal. Slaves must wait until before bed." She studied her more closely. "Have you been a slave for long?"

Her family' routine had been the same. Had a rule been enforced on their slaves? How could she not know? "About two months. How about you?"

"Oh, I was born into it." Her comment lacked emotion or self-pity. "I know nothing of my father. My mother was Egyptian and very beautiful. She named me after an ancient queen. Mother was badly used by her owners…forced many a night to leave me alone and lie with whomsoever her master desired to please. I had just passed eight summers when he sold me off. I never saw her again."

"Oh, Kawit, I am so —"

"It is alright. A lot of time has passed since then."

The trauma of being torn from your family at such a young age, struck Daphne's heart. Would that happen to Theo? Could he survive such a shock? She had barely managed herself.

That Kawit could view the tragedy she endured as a likely progression of being owned without bitterness, amazed her. She openly revealed the ups and downs of times she had been sold and where she had lived. "But this is not a bad place. I have been here three years, and believe me, have known much worse. The master is a kind man, fair and reasonable...but watch out for the overseer. He has a mean streak and an eye for young girls, besides a love to flaunt his authority."

Her assessment of Stello confirmed the uneasiness Daphne felt during her brief time in his presence.

"Come on, I will show you where the tubs are. Jahtel said he would allow an early bath this time and you can tell me how you came to be here." She took Daphne's arm then pinched her nose. "Whew, now I know why."

They laughed at Daphne's dire need to bathe. Kawit helped her carry pitchers of water and a copper tub back to her room. "You go ahead, and soak and I will fetch you a clean garment."

Daphne pointed out her sandals. "These are nearly worn through. Do you think you could find me some others?"

Kawit nodded and handed her a rough cake of soap. "This won't be what you are used to, but it is all we get. I will see what I can find. And after you finish, you should wash your *peplos* in the water. It will save having to refill the tub."

Daphne watched the flimsy curtain sway into place. She looked at the tub. The desire to submerge overrode her concern. In seconds she undressed and sank all but her face beneath the tepid surface. She groaned, closed her eyes and leaned against the metal back.

The pleasure brought thoughts of her alabaster tub with Belte in close attendance. It was a gift from her father from the island of Crete. His love of history led him to explore the ruins of an ancient palace in Phaistos where he saw a quaint tub in the queen's quarters and had a replica made just for her.

How she missed him. Out of habit, she sniffed the soap. One whiff brought reality. It contained none of the fragrant oils she had long taken for granted. She sat up. "It does not matter." It took several washes to clean her hair and her skin tingled from its first scrubbing since she bathed in the sea the day before they entered Athens.

Kawit brushed through the door. "Let me wash your back for you."

Daphne hugged her knees to her chest. "Oh, I am so relieved it is you."

She scoured Daphne's back and poured several pitchers of warm water over her. "Feeling better?"

Daphne rubbed her wet hair with the rough towel left on her table and snickered at her pruned fingers and toes. "Nothing has ever felt so good. How can I thank you?"

A mischievous smile curled from Kawit's lips up into her eyes. "Oh, I will find a way one day." She laughed and tossed Daphne's filthy *peplos* into the water. Here is a clean tunic. You are awfully thin but I think it will fit. That will change, we are well fed here…that is not always the case. And here is an old tunic you can sleep in. It is worn, but better than sleeping in your clothes."

Daphne finished drying and wrapped the towel just under her arms. Both tunics lay across her bed.

Kawit chattered as she worked the snarls from Daphne's long locks. "Shall I fix your hair like mine? I will never forget a time I failed to secure my braid. When I bent to serve a guest, my hair worked loose and fell into the man's food. The beating that followed is a forever reminder."

Daphne's eyes widened. Would she make a mistake and be beaten for it? Her tension unraveled under the familiar sense of being cared for. "You are so kind, do you think I could just put on the older tunic and go to bed? I know it's early, but I am so worn, and that bath relaxed every part of me."

Kawit cocked her head. "I do not know. The master has ordered a feast to celebrate his successful trip. We eat after he retires, and then do the cleanup. It usually runs quite late and Stello expects all of us to be there."

She put her forefinger against her upper lip. With a flick of her hand, she gestured toward the bed. "Go ahead and lie down. I will try to get you excused for tonight, and if he insists you be there, I will come for you after the guests are served." They washed her *peplos* and emptied the tub. Daphne unrolled the straw mattress and laid down. Her sleepy thanks followed her new friend through the curtain.

She closed her eyes. How many menial tasks did Belte do for me that I never even noticed or thought to thank her for? How she wished for one last opportunity to speak to her former servant. Twilight had yet to fade as she drifted into a deep sleep with thoughts of what she would say if given the chance.

She awoke and sat up with a start. In the near darkness it took a moment to remember where she was. The villa. She was in her new owner's villa.

A cool breeze played across her shoulders, carrying a familiar sound. She pulled up the blanket and cocked her ear toward the window. That is the cry of a warbler.

The sky began to lighten, and a cardinal's whistle joined the chorus. Her stomach growled. Kawit had not fetched her for the evening meal and cleanup. She must have slept since early evening.

She listened for signs of movement but heard none. She slipped out with her water pitcher. In the dim quiet she filled the vessel and returned to wash her face and dress before anyone came for her.

She held up the tunic Kawit had given her. It stopped above her knees like the garments she wore less than half a year before. She scoffed. The thrill she felt when she reached the age where she could dress in longer *chitons* seemed eons ago. She reached for the dress she had worn since she left Delphi, but it was still damp. She clutched her *teraphim* for strength. Better get used to wearing a slave garment.

She finished tying her sandals before she heard, "Good morning…I am so glad you are up and dressed. Did you sleep well? You sure look better…good that Jahtel said you did not have to come out last night."

Daphne grinned at her friend's chatter. Together they went to the cookhouse where the slaves ate breakfast. The sun had not yet risen before the area cleared. Those assigned to the house gathered what they needed to serve the household and guests, while the others headed for the orchards and fields.

Jahtel approached with a young boy as Kawit bid her goodbye for the day. "This is Dendril. He will accompany you and show you the way into the city. It's not a far walk." He lifted his chin and looked at her through half-closed eyes. "Should you have thoughts to leave us, remember Philippi is a very isolated city surrounded by mountains and the sea. Penalties for those who decide to run away are extreme and unforgiving."

She listened, amazed. Escape had never entered her head…where would she go?

His face bore no hint of mercy. "The cooks have prepared food and a flask of water for you. Be back well before sundown."

He left before she could think to ask for further instructions. The boy looked much too young to answer her questions. He said something and handed her the cook's provisions. She took the packet, unsure of what he said. He paused to be sure she followed, then started toward the gate with gestures flung over his shoulder.

Daphne hurried to keep him in sight, fearful he would disappear around the next bend. Despite his unfamiliar tongue, he left no doubt he expected her to hurry.

Chapter Ten

So he shall open and no one shall shut.
– Isaiah 22:22

The path led continually west as it rose into foothills like a symphonic prelude to the majestic mountains above them. To keep Dendril in sight, left Daphne little time to admire the view. She tried to imagine the city. Would it resemble Delphi or sprawl like the metropolis of Athens?

They passed a Roman cemetery. Lush flowers and ivy native to Macedonia graced marble vaults or tombs. The lids of the largest had artfully sculpted gardens with either nude bathers and dancers, or scenes of fierce soldiers on horses in battle.

She admired the ornate carvings but felt they compared poorly to the crypts that surrounded the temple at Delphi.

The bright morning sun made the inscriptions difficult to see. She chuckled. Most Romans living in Greece had been born there and spoke fluent Greek, Even in Delphi no one she knew spoke the language of those who ruled over them. To exalt the virtues of the deceased, she affirmed, certainly required their native language.

In a weedy, less desirable section, the poor lay in burial pits, covered with roof tiles. She thought of her father's bier and shook her head. Why would they want to bury their dead, anyway?

Surely burning is a more honorable way to dispose of remains.

The thought spurred a premonition: many of the ways of these people would be strange to her.

At last, the route looked down upon the city. To her relief, it looked more like Delphi than Athens, though considerably larger. Official buildings and the *agora*, as well as the theater and an area set aside for homes were located within a high wall of thick, multi-shaped bricks. Towers protected the western and northern gates as well as the one through which she would enter, the eastern passage that led back to Neapolis.

Dendril, pointed to the entrance below and turned to leave. Daphne called to him, "Wait, I do not know what I am supposed to do. How do I...."

The boy pointed to his ears, lifted his palms, shrugged his shoulders, and ran off. She had never felt so alone. She looked down at the city and back at Dendril but he was gone.

"Will you give me your pledge?" Only her promise to Patharus kept her from trying to find her way back to the estate.

For a while she took in the scene stretched below. The half-moon shaped theater chiseled out of the rocky terrain looked much like the one back home except for the flat center for its orchestra. There were thick retaining walls where spectators entered before they climbed the twenty-five rows of the eight sections to find seats. Later Daphne learned, these walls and rows remained untouched from the time King Phillip II had it built in 400 BC. Near the city's middle, lay the forum where a busy *agora* surrounded it with a courtyard in its center.

She decided it would not hurt to go look around. She started down the path that led to the Neapolis gate but stopped. Wait, I do not know how they feel about women in the marketplace. What if they stop me...or worse? Her courage disappeared. She twisted back toward the foothills and chewed her lower lip. No...Patharus would not have instructed her to go if she could not serve him by doing so. She shook off the concern and tromped toward the opening in the dingy gray wall.

Below the rectangular tower a guard stood over a group of men who were deep in conversation. He barely glanced as she passed under the stone arches, but the men's eyes followed her. She lowered hers and scooted onto the well-known *Egnatia* that led from Rome to the far east. She had learned of it as a child, but it surprised her that the well-touted road split Philippi in two.

Her father's tales returned of deep grooves that were formed in the marble blocks by legions of ancient chariots that traveled to and from Rome. Now ruts around each grime-filled segment threatened a twisted ankle. At its eastern end, the road wound onto a path that led to the commercial section.

The market bustled with shoppers and noise of merchants who hawked their wares. To her relief women in slave garments moved about the *agora* as they inspected the goods and bartered with the merchants.

She wandered through displays awed at the abundant produce. Her mother had spoken with envy of the great variety of vegetables and fruits grown on the Macedonian plains; a benefit the mountainous terrain in Delphi could never sustain.

"A fine melon, *Kopela*, you buy?" Her jaw dropped. No merchant back home would have dared speak to her, much less address her as 'young girl'. She shook her head, but he followed for several steps. "Picked this morning...a fine addition to your master's table."

He had hardly given up when another man pushed glossy red tomatoes in her face. "For your master's salad, *Kopela*, fresh this morning. You buy?"

She shook her head, painfully aware they saw her as a slave. She hurried out of earshot and away from their aggressive behavior.

Many of the newer, marble buildings had more than one story. Ancient limestone ones like the library had been built before the Romans conquered Macedoni. She admired its sculptured facade, grateful "Library" was chiseled in Greek, not Latin. "How wonderful," she whispered, surprised to hear herself compare something favorably over Delphi which had no library.

Shops on the longer, south side of the *agora* backed up to the forum. Like the market in Athens, vessels for every use, garments and household items competed with poultry, meat, and seafood. Aside from the merchants, no one noticed her. She walked the full length and peeked into the buildings alongside the shops, but could not see inside.

She rounded the corner and discovered a few more shops that ended at an entrance into the courtyard. Across from the public fountain, the rounded platform of an *exedra* was not occupied by anyone who lectured or held a meeting, so she sat in the small recess in the wall and pulled out the dried goat meat and bread, given her at the start of the day.

The sun was high in the sky. She grimaced. What should she do? She had no idea where to begin or how to find people who would need their fortune told. She studied the shoppers that milled around the fountain. Most left before she walked over to replenish her jug. Behind a monument on the other side of the fountain, voices came from the next *exedra*.

A man sounded worried "But how will I know what to do?"

A woman's raspy voice replied. "The gods have revealed the outcome. Follow my instructions and it will come to pass."

Daphne drew closer and peered around the monument to see the man walk rapidly past the fountain and exit the courtyard. The woman still knelt before an idol. She picked up the *teraphim* along with several coins before she labored to raise herself. Like Bentalla, she was shrouded in dark clothing. Wisps of gray hair sprouted like unruly cowlicks from under her head piece, becoming one with the deep wrinkles on her face.

Daphne ducked behind the monument before the woman straightened enough to see her. Her heart raced. She had found her answer...the woman was a sorceress.

Chapter Eleven

Consider your ways.
– Haggai 1:5

Daphne remained hidden until the old seer tottered across the courtyard and back into the marketplace. She followed, careful not to draw attention to herself.

The sorceress wended her way among the crowds. From time to time, she paused and turned her ear to arguments or discussions. She stopped and observed when she heard loud voices or an argument. The seer pushed her way to the front of a small crowd that gathered around two men.

Daphne pretended to examine some fabrics in a booth but stayed close enough to hear the conversation.

A heavyset, older man shouted, his face contorted. "This is not the price we agreed on!"

The other man countered, "Nor is this the merchandise you promised. These skins are poorly tanned…not fit for fine leather work!"

The argument went on until the buyer threw down the goods and walked off. With that the sorceress approached the merchant. "I see you have been badly swindled, good sir. Would you like the help of the gods to bring justice to your situation?"

The merchant eyed her coldly until she brought out her idol and assured him of her ability to see into the future. He looked at his rejected skins, back at her, and grunted. "Meet me behind the *palestra* in a couple of minutes."

The woman nodded. The *palestra* was a gymnasium type building that sat directly across from his booth. The sorceress moved slowly between it and the small building beside it to reach the back.

Daphne frowned as the old seer left. What should she do? The seer would see her if she followed. Should she ask permission to observe how to contact and receive direction from one's gods? She knew she lacked the courage. Disheartened, she veered toward the courtyard.

Go around the smaller building. There are no athletes training at this hour and you can cut through and get close enough to hear and not be seen.

Unsure, she repeated, "around the smaller building." The counsel of the Voice had never failed to prove right...surely, she could trust it. She eased toward the smaller building and ducked around its eastern end. To her relief, the area proved empty. She forced herself to move unhurriedly around the back and into the courtyard of the *palestra*. As the voice predicted, it was empty. She moved quickly across the back of the practice area close to the wall.

Hidden behind the corner of the building, she turned her ear to listen. Her face fell. She could hear nothing. Had she confused the directions? Everything within her wanted to peer around the opening, and make sure she had the right place. If she sees me, I will lose my chance. Soon shuffled footsteps made her heart race.

The slow patter stopped not ten feet from where she waited. The seer's hoarse chant grew louder. Moments later, heavy vibrations announced the merchant's arrival.

The sorceress spoke with confidence. "Sit there, across from me; the gods have much to tell you."

*****

The walk back to the estate seemed much shorter than it had in the morning. Daphne studied the mountains that surrounded Philippi. She wondered if they created flash floods and mudslides like on Mt. Parnassus? Her concern did not linger with perils but returned to the old seer. From the moment the woman maneuvered herself into the situation, till how she collected her fee, Daphne paid close attention. She rehearsed the skill with which the woman had plied her craft and implanted the pattern in her mind.

As she passed the cemetery, she was surprised at how far she had come. In awe, she recounted how the sorceress had manipulated the man's anger and cultivated his greed for her own purposes. Between clenched teeth she vowed she could do that. Even as she spoke, she winced. To dispel the doubts that lodged like barnacles to the bottom of her heart would require more than a hearty confession.

How could she become confident enough to boldly step up to a prospective seeker and convince him she could ascertain the counsel of a god? And what of her scruples? The woman had not concerned herself with the second man's claim of fraud. Could she encourage deceitful practices? What would her father think? Everything she observed conflicted with her nature and what she had been taught.

She glanced at the barren terrain. Abandoned and silent now, it mirrored the desolation of her soul. Solace lay in the wind that rustled the trees and the chatter of *sousliks*. The beady eyes of the squirrel-like creatures stared as she approached. They stood on their haunches, tiny ears raised, forehands pressed against their breasts, ready to scold her for the intrusion.

Despite qualms that weighed her heart, she smiled at their antics and likened their stance to Apollo's priests as they chanted prayers or chastened errant contributors. She sniffed as the animals dove for their sanctuaries.

Patharus' charge echoed from the desolate landscape. "Can you agree? Will you give me your pledge?"

No defensible reason for existence surfaced in the forsaken foothills that surrounded her, nor could she fathom any within the mandate forced upon her. She cried out at the deserted path that stretched before her. "No, it is impossible." How could she prey on men's troubles or convince a stranger she could tell his future? She could not even convince herself.

Have I ever failed to give you needed counsel or help? Have I not told you I will tell you what to say?

The message rang, almost audible in its intensity. Instinctively, Daphne jerked, expecting to see someone. The Voice no longer frightened, but the permanence of its presence frustrated her.

Apollo knows the future and he has chosen you to show men he is the one who has all knowledge and can help them. You are simply the vessel he works through.

She shivered. Did she want to be a part of the kind of help she just witnessed? "I cannot. It is not —"

The Voice cut into her nagging conscience. *Trust me, Daphne, and I will lead you. I will always be with you. Together, we will do great things and men will honor you for it.*

With mixed emotions, she approached Patharus' gate, the promises foremost in her mind.

Uneasiness quickened her steps, but the assurance sparked a glimmer of hope. She sighed, reconciled to her lack of choice. If she was to remain under Patharus' protection, she must accept the Voice's guidance...where else would she get wisdom to pass to men?

She ran her hand over the *teraphim,* snug in the fold of her tunic. Maybe she could be of help to some. A contrary thought followed. Beltre would say this piece of wood is useless except for the confidence men put in it. She cocked her head. A part of her knew that to be true.

Rybic, the gate keeper shut the barrier behind her and waved. She returned the gesture. What contentment did he find in belonging to another? Would Patharus be waiting for her? Would he be angry she had not made a profit or excuse her lack of experience?

She fretted over the possibility. In the end, she decided she would simply tell him what she learned and how it would help her earn her keep in the days to come. She slipped through the servants' entrance and into the courtyard. "Go before me, Apollo."

Chapter Twelve

House slaves scurried as they prepared the evening meal. The smell of roasting foul made Daphne's stomach cramp. When would she stop feeling empty much of the time? Kawit waved from behind a table laden with fresh fruit, dried figs and raisin cakes. "Are you hungry?"

She flushed. "Am I that obvious? I cannot seem to stay filled."

"It is no wonder, you have been half-starved for months. Here, no one will mind if you eat a little. Our meal won't be for hours…but you will get used to that." She handed Daphne a tangerine and a bit of bread. "Here, eat. See you at dinner."

Daphne entered her room and wished she could bathe. The tempo of a leisurely bath to relax before the evening meal, now a forbidden luxury.

Exhaustion accompanied her regrets over privileges taken for granted, buoyed by the emotion of the day. Too tired to deal with past failures, she lay down aware Patharus would soon demand she report. Dusk had not yet fallen when Jahtel's deep voice invaded her room. "The master awaits you in his study. My assistant will accompany you."

"Yes…may I have a moment?"

He harrumphed a sharp answer. "We do not make the master wait."

She splashed some water to remove the dust that powdered her face and crusted her eyes, then smoothed her hair. Her sandal caught on the curtain, and she stumbled into the arms of the surprised assistant.

He caught her against his chest. "Whoa, the call is not that urgent."

Nicanor's face was inches from hers "Oh... forgive me, I did not...."

He smiled. "No harm done."

His clean, manly scent unnerved her. She jerked herself upright and lowered her eyes, mortified at her clumsy entrance.

"I did not see you at the celebration dinner. Are you all right...your quarters comfortable?"

"Yes, yes, it is fine."

"I am glad they gave you an inside room. You look ah.... more rested. I hope you like it here. That was a long voyage...we were all glad to get home."

She squirmed but forced a calm expression. Why did he not move? Finally, she glanced up. He still stared. A flush climbed her neck and colored her face. What did he want? Her heart sank. Could he plan to...no, Patharus said she would be protected. She must trust his control or be in a constant state of anxiety.

"I am Nicanor. What is your name? I never heard anyone use it...on the ship, I mean."

To her dismay, her voice wavered. She knew his name, but simply said "Daphne."

"Daphne," he repeated, as if pleased with the sound of it. He gestured toward the master's end of the house. "Follow me then, Daphne," already several steps ahead.

She hurried to pace her stride to his. She studied him from behind, relieved to be free of his gaze. Who was he…and why had he made her feel so uneasy? Now and on the ship. Jahtel referred to him as an assistant, but Patharus relied heavily on the young man on the ship and after they arrived at the estate. Was he part of Patharus' household? No, he wore the plain tunic of a slave. Still, he did not carry himself like a slave…much too confident.

The way his hair curled around his neck and ears brought a catch to her throat. Alexander's had been as unruly. He stopped outside Patharus' receiving room, pointed at the door, smiled, and left. A smile tugged at the corners of her own lips.

Patharus' personal servant saw her, but he did not bid her enter. She crossed her arms and waited. At his nod she hastened past him and wished she had honed her response to Patharus' inquiry.

The room was entirely in order. Patharus demanded order, according to Kawit who knew everything about everybody, plus all the inner dynamics beneath the surface.

With caution born of uncertainty she followed the plush wool rug that led to his desk. The pile nuzzled her feet like a lamb's coat as it brushed through her sandals. She pushed thoughts of home it resurrected into the furthest recesses of her mind. A confident, clear head was necessary if she were to explain her failure to make a profit.

Patharus was engrossed in the work before him. She waited and took in the wonder of the room she had hardly noticed the day before. It boasted more windows than Delphi's most elite homes. Exquisite designs painted in gold leaf outlined each one. Across the tops a pale-yellow, silk fabric cascaded down the sides and nestled in billows on the floor.

The stucco walls and ceiling were white with additional gold leaf scrolled around the ceiling and down the corners. Oil lamps cast subtle shadows and gave a luminous glow to the frieze-covered walls.

He sat on a cushioned chair behind his massive, wooden desk. A frown accompanied the hand that flew over an open ledger. She could not see his face but recalled when she first saw him in Athens. About the age of her father, dark hair circled a bald spot, brows framed intense eyes, and strong features that gave no clue to his nature.

An ivory statue of an incensed bull sat on one corner of his desk. The ferocious beast seemed a poor representative of the man whose character according to Kawit, and the kindness shown to her, concealed a sensitive heart.

At last, he looked up. Warned by Kawit, she quickly bowed her head, careful not to raise it or look any authority in the eye unless they insisted. Out of the corner of her eye she could see him squint, as if he did not recognize her. He leaned forward, apparently pleased with the change in her appearance, he spoke. "Ah yes, I see you have been well ah, taken care of."

She nodded, not sure if she should reply.

He folded his arms and leaned upon his desk. Gold and silver rings adorned both hands, regalia he had not worn on their voyage. One had emerald eyes that glared from a lion's head. Daphne squelched a grimace. More intimidation… like the bull?

Patharus somehow looked even taller sitting than when he stood. He wore a fine, wool chiton dyed a dark indigo. Her mother had told her the dye came from the grapes of Attica. A gold fibula forged into the likeness of a gazelle with diamond horns, pinned it in place.

"And how did you do in the city today? Were you successful?"

She gulped back her nerves. "Sir, I mean master, I have never told a fortune to earn money before, but today I learned how it is done. I observed a seer at her craft…an older woman who has practiced the art for many years. Please be patient with me and I will bring you a profit tomorrow and in the days that follow." She did not dare to look and try to judge how he took her explanation.

Chapter Thirteen

I would fly away and be at rest.
– Psalm54:6

Patharus closed his ledger. "All right, tell me exactly what you observed, and look at me while you do."

Daphne breathed a sigh of relief and raised her head. She left nothing out as she filled him in on the events of her day. He listened, his chin supported on one hand and did not interrupt. "You have learned quickly." He rubbed his chin thoughtfully. "Undoubtedly the gods will honor the power of your *teraphim* and move at your bidding, but you must stay on track. My fellow investors are anxious to hear of your conquests. I will hear of your progress tomorrow. You may leave." His attention already on his ledger.

She wanted to say wait. What if nothing happens? What if no one who needed her trade? What if I cannot…? In silent surrender, she backed through the door. Doubt and fear waved like the frost-nipped dahlias by the gate. She leaned against the wall, her head resting in icy hands. Tomorrow…I will hear of your progress tomorrow, bounced around her head.

The command faded along with the pulsing in her throat. Who knew what tomorrow would bring. She lifted her eyes and declared her confidence. She had a plan and she would make it work.

Light shone from an open door across the hall. She tiptoed over and peered into the room. It opened to a suite decorated as lavishly as the one she had just left. Silk fabrics in various shades of blue and cream draped across the top of a bed and down each corner. A large window overlooked an area she had yet to discover. It extended into a garden, but she could see little beyond the entrance.

A woman lay billowed amidst a stack of pillows. Shiny blond hair, popular with fashionable women of the day, curled around her head and down her shoulders. Beneath her exquisite makeup her face was as pale as the sheets she lay upon.

Daphne's jaw dropped at the woman's beauty. She forgot her manners and stared. Who was she?

The woman saw her and gave a weak smile. At the same moment a hefty servant noticed her. She sat the tray she carried on a stand and with a scowl slammed the door. Daphne flinched at the woman's rudeness, but let it go. After all, it was she who had snooped. Back in her room she made a mental note to ask about the woman; Kawit would know.

She tidied her room and looked around. What would she do until dinnertime? She sat on her wobbly bench and stared at the small window where a thrush nightingale flitted in and out of sight. Its trill haunted. "You can go wherever you wish, little bird…I wish I could join you."

If you are faithful to Apollo, one day you will be free to do as you please.

She jumped to her feet and repeated the Voice's promise. She would be free! She would find her family and return home. Her spirits lifted, she left and entered the area around the villa.

The promise of a full moon urged her to explore the grounds. An opening on the side of the main building appeared, well hidden from the front of the manor. She gasped. Maybe it is that lady's garden.

She approached the shrubs that disguised the entrance with caution. Did she dare enter? None but statues looked over the greenery, so she stepped through the gate. Words failed her. Before her lay a carefully attended oasis flush with late blooming roses, wild orchids, giant marigolds, and flowers not familiar to her. The similarity to her family's garden made her eyes tear. She ambled over and touched a mosaic-topped table with matching benches. Its presence flashed a painful picture of Theo ready to eat his breakfast.

A well-manicured path led to a pond with a fountain and statues entwined with ivy. She ran her fingers along the back of a wrought-iron bench. "So like at home…" She grimaced, knowing the Roman who forced the auction, now enjoyed their garden.

Around the next curve a familiar object brought a squeal. "A sundial!" She clapped her hand over her mouth, relieved nothing stirred.

She sat on a bench tucked behind a hedge of witches'-broom. The delicate yellow flowers quivered in the evening breeze and assured she was hidden. Gratitude filled her heart. In the midst of all things foreign, surely the god had led her to this place of solace. "Thank you, Apollo."

She whispered to a tiny frog about to leap into the pond. "This will be my refuge too." She closed her eyes and drew in the earthy smell and fragrances of flowers. Enthralled with her find, she stayed until chill forced her to leave the garden and return indoors.

Back in her room, she feared she might fall asleep before the call to dinner. She sat on her mat with her arms around her ankles. Anxiety about tomorrow's jaunt into the city returned but she dismissed its threat. Exhausted and hungry, she concentrated on the images she had seen in the garden.

Kawit finally ducked her head through the curtain. "We have nearly finished the meal. See you there."

Time in the garden had revived her, minimized Patharus' expectations, and waylaid her own. She hesitated, but hunger and Stello's blanket-attendance policy drove her to assemble with the rest. To mingle with a group of strangers confirmed this new station in life was not going away. Not now…maybe never.

Kawit motioned to join her at a long table filled with house slaves. She recognized a few from breakfast. Field hands and cooks, house girls and groomsmen, all lined up to receive their generous portion. Kawit led her to the end of the line and back to the table.

She smiled and nodded at the introductions. Guilt twinged. How many servants back home could she have called by name? She vowed to remember these.

To her surprise, the mutton stew was flavorful, full of green beans, onions, carrots, and tomatoes, and well-proportioned with meat. Cider from the master's orchards flowed from large wooden urns.

The hot food energized her and to her surprise she enjoyed the company of those around her. She marveled at the light-hearted bantering, teasing about slackness and preferred assignments. Abruptly, all conversation stopped. Everyone feigned great concentration on their plates.

Kawit instantly joined those who averted their eyes. She shook off Daphne's questions with a jerk of her head in the direction of the food pots. Everyone seemed fearful. What did it mean? Daphne lowered her head. What did they expect…was this unusual?

Stello walked among the tables he carried a stick with leather thongs on one end and slapped them against his palm. A smug smile stretched his lips but did not reach his eyes. Occasionally he stopped to ask a slave how their day went. None answered with more than a few words.

He approached on the opposite side of their table. Kawit stiffened as he stopped across from them. "And how was your day, ah…Daphne, is it not?"

Chapter Fourteen

He changes the times and the seasons
– Daniel 2;21

Daphne froze, her voice but a squeak. "It was... good."

Stello barely nodded before he turned his attention to Kawit. "And tell me about your day. Did you render your services in an, ah...pleasing manner?"

Kawit's color deepened, her words barely audible, "Yes, my lord."

He studied her face, sneered, and grunted a "Humph." When she refused to rise to his taunt, he moved on.

Kawit pressed her elbows to her waist and stifled a shudder. Daphne squeezed her friend's forearm and thrust her jaw to one side. She would not let him intimidate her.

After Stello sauntered out of the area the untroubled atmosphere returned with tangible relief. Kawit nudged Daphne. "Come, we can fill our tubs before the crowd gathers...some will linger another hour or so."

Daphne followed Kawit as they made their way through slaves that milled about. She tried to dodge around some young men who stopped unexpectedly but tripped. Nicanor caught her arm and steadied her.

"Oh," she gasped, "I am so sorry, I...."

His eyes danced, as if he relished her embarrassment. "Seems we are destined to meet like this." He swept his hand across his body in an exaggerated bow. "Perhaps you need a guide. At your service, madam."

"I am fine. I mean…I can find my way. Please excuse me." She tried to walk around him, but he moved in the same direction, anticipated her shift, and blocked her again. His dimple divulged a repressed smile.

She put her fists on her hips "Please, someone is waiting for me, I…."

He moved to one side and gestured toward a group of his peers who all sported grins. "Of course, and welcome to our family."

She barreled past him and did not look back. To her relief, Kawit had not waited. Who was he and why was he so bold? An image of his warm smile and eyes so blue eyes they could reflect the gulf on a sunny day, accompanied her every step.

Kawit met her at the well. "I thought I had lost you. Let's fill both in your room. I want to hear of your day."

Daphne made several trips with her pitcher, her mind back in the courtyard.

Kawit removed her sandals and sighed. "The likelihood of more misery from Stello is all that squelches my response when he taunts me like tonight. He makes life miserable for anyone he singles out…and sadly I am one of his 'favorites.'"

She filled Daphne in on the overseer's ugly tactics and the background of the beautiful lady in the bed. Her face reflected the sadness of the woman's story when she told Daphne she was the master's wife. "They grieve the loss of their son. She will never have another. It has been eight years and she is no better. The master visits her often."

"Does he not have concubines to bear him an heir?" Daphne asked.

"Plenty are willing, but house servants say he truly loves his wife and while she lives, he will not give his seed to another."

Daphne said, "He is not old, but time could run out…then what?"

Kawit shrugged and moved to more current gossip. She warned Daphne about the garden. "Be careful not to get caught there, my friend, it is strictly off limits."

Daphne explained how she learned from the seer and of her relief at Patharus' patience with her effort to learn.

With carefully cloaked words, Daphne inquired about Nicanor and his status in the household. She had no history with young men. Did they all act like him? Kawit confirmed he was a slave, but with it dropped unwelcome news: Jahtel was his father. The thought made Daphne wince.

Kawit went on, "Nicanor is Patharus' favorite. The master calls upon him for special tasks and sometimes takes him on business trips."

"Is that all that is required of him?"

"Well…no, I think he helps Jahtel manage the household slaves, not sure what else."

"Yes, he accompanied me to Patharus' office yesterday."

They talked far into the night. Daphne's mind still spun as she climbed into bed to the rattle of a thunderstorm. Heavy rain pelted the roof, the sound a comfort until drops began to bounce off bricks at the bottom of her windowsill and spray her bed. She jumped up and moved her mat then rescued her sandals and tunics.

Lightning highlighted its presence across the wall opposite her window. She counted, "One… two…three…four," and listened for thunder to follow. Images of forked flashes were forever etched in her memory and were not deterred by the blanket she pulled over her eyes. Panicked horses and a picture of her father thrown to his death merged with the persistent horror of she and her mother as they dangled over the edge of a cliff in their storm-washed vehicle.

The reflections faded with the thunder. The storm had long passed before she stopped pondering all Kawit tried to make clear.

******

Light poured through her window when she opened her eyes. She grabbed her old *peplos*, splashed water on her face, and tied her sandals while balancing on one foot. Minutes later Kawit peeked through her curtain.

"Coming, Sleepy?"

"I will be right there," Daphne smoothed her hair before she dashed to catch up.

The courtyard had partially emptied by the time she arrived. Kawit waved from the food table. Daphne gathered a bit of bread, goat cheese and figs as she went.

Kawit yawned. "Are you as tired as I am? I know it is late but sit with me a moment."

Daphne tore off a bit off the bread she intended to eat on the way to the city. Kawit's eyes sparkled. "The master has planned a huge party sometime next week. Rumor has it he will make some big announcement. No one knows what it is."

She listened, not sure why the news was important. Surely the master's business would not affect their lives. A few field workers clustered, each vocal about what to expect.

A food tender asked, "Do you think he has decided to become a city magistrate?"

A house servant spoke up. "Not likely, I have heard him with his friends…he disdains politics, has little to say about it that is good."

"Well…maybe he is going to buy that adjoining land to the north of us." The muscular field hand filled his plate as he spoke. "You know, the one that Greek landowner has tried to keep from his creditors? I hear the man is but one step out of the courts."

The man who dished out the morning fare cocked his head. "That does not seem worthy of a big announcement."

"Maybe. But could be the master's tired of paying the *obels* it cost him to rent additional slaves he needs. He might want to expand and buy the man's slaves as well as the land. Anyway, we had best get at it. There is much to harvest if Zeus is bent on an early fall."

The speculation continued until the workers left. Daphne touched her friend's arm. "Please beseech your god on my behalf. I am so nervous about how to find someone in need of the counsel of the gods...let alone convince him I can help."

Kawit squeezed her hand and pointed a finger up on each side of her head. "I will call upon Hathor."

Daphne frowned. "Who...what does that mean?

Kawit lowered her eyes.

Her heart sank. "I am so sorry, please forgive me.

A grimace twitched before Kawit's lips relaxed. "She is the powerful Egyptian goddess my mother taught me to depend upon. On each side of the sun disk on top of her head, she has a curved horn...like this." Once again, she modeled the goddess for her. "Seconds before they dragged me from my mother, she reenacted our signal on each side of her head. Hathor is the protector of women…it is my mother's legacy to me." Her head drooped. "A promise of protection she could not provide."

Daphne's eyes stung as she hugged Kawit to her chest. "Thank you, I…."

Kawit, placed her finger to her lips, and chirped a jovial tata. "Hathor is also the goddess of joy, music and dancing, so why should we worry, my god will look out for both of us." Her words silenced Daphne's attempt to apologize more.

Kawit's bravado belied the pain behind her eyes, but before she raced off, she hunched her shoulders, smiled, and flicked her signal of protection again.

Daphne flicked it back and picked up a lunch bag, filled her jug and headed for the gate. Dendril was nowhere to be seen and no other stepped up. She guessed they knew it would be futile for her to try to leave.

"Wait…Come back!"

She turned, not sure the call was meant for her. Jahtel stood at the top of the path that led to the gate. He motioned vigorously for her to return. She zipped back, alarmed by his irate tone. "Yes, my lord? Do you have further instructions for me?"

Chapter Fifteen

A door was opened to me.
– 2 Corinthians 2:12

Jatel's voice blared as she approached. "That *peplos*…you are never to wear a long dress. Slaves wear short tunics." He jerked his head toward the slave entrance. "Go change and you will be given a replacement."

Daphne staggered at his harsh rebuke. He did not bother to wait for a response. Head down, she raced for her room, sure everyone heard him chasten her. His rant burned like fire in her heart. Would she never get used to being humiliated? She snuffed deep breaths, changed quickly, and left for the city. His callous berating churned and quickened her pace. Did he have to embarrass her? Could he not have told her ahead of time…or at least privately?

A brisk climb on the newly dampened path helped put the incident behind. Her thoughts reverted to the things she learned last night. She slowed, passed landmarks but saw only faces, Jahtel's, the lovely woman's, Stello's, Patharus', Nicanor's. Jagged rocks, a menace to her sandals, jarred her back to the task she felt ill prepared for.

She rehearsed her plan. She would find someone in trouble or upset…a person who faced a great difficulty. She would show them her idol, that will bring credence to her claim, then she would convince them she could hear from the gods. Then she, she....

It was no use. Her mind refused to remain where her head needed to be. Images of Nicanor blurred her thoughts. Last night's light-hearted teasing played like a drama on the stage of her mind. She smiled at the memory of his elaborate bow and courteous words. "Perhaps you need a guide...at your service madam."

The bleating of sheep interrupted her thoughts. Around the next bend her path was hemmed in by a ravine at the base of the foothills. Parched and dry yesterday, it now held a deep runoff from the night's torrential rains. Grass around its shallow banks already showed signs of green, a shepherd's treasure.

Her hopes of getting through vanished. Like a living carpet, the large flock pushed toward her. Their woolly bodies bobbled against each other on the narrow path. She did not fear the sheep but climbed a few feet up onto a ledge to avoid having her feet trampled.

The shepherd saw her but made no apology. He led his flock toward the fresh supply of foliage with only a nod and a whistle at his busy dog.

Resigned to no recourse but to wait, she held her shawl to her nose and hoped the odor did not permeate her hair and clothing. How much time had she lost? She glanced at the sun and refocused on the task ahead. As the path cleared, she clutched the shawl Kawit found among spare clothing and was quick to dodge mud puddles the storm created.

On the rise that overlooked the city, she paused and admired the mountains on either side. She clutched her chest as the "what ifs" retuned. If the voice was silent could she make something up?

She shook off her fears, I am here Apollo…go with me, and please alert your Voice to guide and give me the insight I will need.

Vendors crowded the gate, eager to set up in choice spots before shoppers arrived. The gatekeeper inspected each one, tally in hand. A man near the end of the line, his wagon heaped with cabbage, eggplant, and carrots, shouted. "What is the holdup?"

The man ahead of him spit an answer. "Some have not reported their profits, so the Romans have decided to keep track of who comes in and with what."

She followed those on foot who worked their way around the wagons and walked unhindered through the gate.

A scraggy dressed merchant with a load of apples called out as she passed. "What is your hurry, pretty girl?"

The lane led to both sides of the *agora*. She hesitated, which way? How would she ever….

Do not be anxious. I will lead you.

Yes, she would follow where the Voice led.

She ambled through the market's three sides, eyes on the merchandise and determined to avoid worry. At midday she ate her lunch and hoped she had not missed a prospect. The old seer passed, a man close on her heels. She sighed. *I wish I found him first.* Her conscious countered. *It is wrong to covet the woman's livelihood.*

A search of the courtyard proved futile. People met, shared food, laughs, or complaints. Life was simple, seemingly without concern.

She put aside negative thoughts and gathered her shawl and water jug. *You need to get back into the* agora. *Opportunity will not search for you.*

Go out the second entrance and turn to the left.

She shivered. *Finally, some instructions!* She made a hasty exit and soon heard a commotion. Across the walkway, a booth had collapsed, its merchandise scattered in the mud.

A man waved his arms and cried out. "My silks...my silks! They are ruined."

Nearby merchants stared at the mess. Several left servants in charge and went to help. Poles that gave way in the soft ground were shored with hefty boulders. Some tried in vain to brush the residue from the man's tent and off the mud-soaked fabrics. Helpless, they left but compassion filled her heart. *The poor man.*

You can help him. Go tell him so...and show him your teraphim.

She had no idea what to say that would help. *Silk is so new to our country, and no one was sure how to clean it...and that mud.*

I will give you what to say.

She took a deep breath, fingered the idol, and pulled her shawl over her head. A few steps brought her to the man who paced and wrung his hands.

She tried to sound confident, "Sir, I can help you. Apollo, the god of light and good has seen your plight." She drew the *teraphim* from her pocket and held it up for him to see. "He has sent me to give you counsel, if you will receive it."

Chapter Sixteen

And plan deception all the day long
– Psalm 38:12

Struck dumb, the man stared. He looked at the idol and back at Daphne. Skepticism chased disbelief across his face. He glanced again at the idol and for a second his expression reflected hope.

Her expectations lifted, but just as quickly the man scoffed. Anger and frustration darkened his eyes. "You are too young…what do you know of the wisdom of the gods?"

She ignored his surly tone. "Apollo's spirit of divination has graced me with the ability to see into the future. He will give me wisdom to rescue you from ruin." She held her breath, amazed at her boldness. Would he believe her?

Several times he glanced from her *teraphim* to the muddy bolts of fabric at his feet. At last, his face relaxed and he hung his head. "Yes, I want to hear from your god. I have visited many of Apollo's temples, with offerings…perhaps he will remember me in my time of need."

She wanted to weep at the defeated slump of his shoulders. She did a quick search for a place to meet and pointed at an area behind a Roman temple. "I will meet you there in a few moments."

She trembled as she made haste to the place they agreed upon and began the seer's pattern.

With the *teraphim* on the ground before her, she closed her eyes and circled it with her hands "Oh, great Apollo, you who hold all wisdom and light, draw near for the sake of this one who needs your counsel."

Hesitant footsteps approached. She did not look up, but boldly instructed the man to sit opposite her. "Bow before the glorious Apollo, the god of mercy and wisdom. Pay him the homage due his name."

The silk merchant fell to his knees and lowered his head to the ground. The hot, fall day had grown humid and the smell of sweat seeped from his body. Through squinted lids she peeked, grateful he could not see her face. "Keep your mind free of your trouble. Let your thoughts remain on the one who can get you through this misfortune with knowledge too high for mere men."

She waited, not sure of what to do next. Nothing came. She swallowed the panic that threatened to climb her throat. Do not fail me now, Voice.

She lowered her eyes and continued with the only things she remembered the old seer did, to chant and circle her hands over the *teraphim*. What were the characteristics of Apollo her grandmother instilled in her years ago? Her mind was blank. It crossed her mind to get up and run. Something popped into her head. Crops. Apollo was the god who granted abundant harvests.

Zealously, she began again. "Oh, great Apollo, you who cause the trees to leaf in the spring, who sends the tiny worms in a country far from here to feed upon them and make beautiful strands of silk, visit us with your great knowledge, grant us a portion of your wisdom."

She peered at the man. Was he convinced Apollo led her? He remained bowed at waist level.

You shall receive my counsel. Obey every detail and your merchandise will be renewed.

Her hand sprang to her throat. The grating words had come from her, but she had no part in their content.

The next words were hers, mysteriously inspired. "Make haste and take your soiled fabrics outside the city to the river Gagitus. Gather large urns of water and allow it to warm to the day. Dip your silks briefly in the cold stream to remove the mud, then gently ease them into the tepid water and let them soak for a time. Discard that water and soak them again. Add a bit of the mild cleanser from Israel's Dead Sea mixed with olive oil. From time to time, swirl it gently with your hands. Now, rinse it in cooled water, with a small amount of vinegar. Be sure to use a fresh, active mother of vinegar, squeezed from white grapes, not red. Rinse it a final time in clear water. The fabric is weak when it is wet, so be careful not to twist or pull on it or you will damage it. Roll it in clean cotton blankets and lay it on cloths in a well-shaded place to dry. You will lose a bit of its sheen and a small amount to shrinkage but assure your customers it will retain its size after they fashion it into garments they can clean in the same manner."

Stillness moved like fog into the silence that followed. She clamped her teeth on her lower lip to keep them from chattering. The man's eyes zinged from left to right and back to her as he lifted his chest. Wide-eyed and expectant, his stare pinned her in place.

What did the old seer do at this point?

Give him ample assurance the word came from our god and charged him to pledge his life to Apollo.

She clutched her hands in front of her so he would not see them shake. Like a starving hawk, she seized the soundless counsel but chose her words with care. "Apollo has spoken. Follow his counsel without fail and give him credit for your triumph. He deserves great praise. See that you pay homage due him alone…forever."

The merchant rose to his feet and nodded vigorously, his face wreathed in relief. "I will, I will. Here," he handed her some coins, backed a few steps, and ran toward the market.

Her breath released with a woosh. "Whew!" A snicker bubbled as the merchant nearly danced down the path. She swooped up the *teraphim*, held it at arm's length and spun around with a laugh. That was not so bad, was it?

Amazed and delighted, she clasped the idol to her chest. She had helped someone find a way out of his trouble! Like ants on a mission, goose bumps crept up her arms. She hugged herself and rubbed at the chill. She could do it! She could actually do it.

She brushed the dirt from the back of her tunic, sobered by the uneasiness she felt as the Voice first spoke through her. But the counsel was amazing, and if the man followed it his goods would be restored. Maybe that was all that mattered. She almost skipped toward the market, one of her grandmother's odes to Apollo on her lips.

Her joy faded as she stopped to drink from her water bottle. That same crusty sound that instructed the merchant growled a threat within her.

No, what matters is if he heeds your charge and dedicates his life to the god who gave you the power to divine his future... and yours depends on it.

She tightened her shawl against the icy spasm that passed between her shoulders. Her entrance into the busy *agora* carried a reluctance to find another prospect.

Your future depends on it.

What did it mean her future depended on it? She covered one side of the market, gave up and headed back to the estate. She thought Apollo wanted to help people through her. Is complete allegiance to him his true priority? If he is the god of love and light who desires justice and good, is that not enough, and why would he need to use her? Is he not happy the man found help? Had she misunderstood?

The further she walked the deeper her brows creased. People back in Delphi worshiped Apollo by offerings brought to the temple to honor him. What more did he desire? Why did he want to go through her, if not to help people? What else might he require?

Chapter Seventeen

The heart knows its own bitterness.
– Proverbs 14:10

Daphne reached for her jug mindless she forgot to refill it. She grimaced. How far had she walked? The area where the sheep slowed her lay ahead. She groaned. Would they be on their return too? To her relief, they were nowhere to be seen. For the first time she searched out the coins she had tucked into her tunic. Two *obels*. At least Patharus would be pleased.

When she reached the estate she drank deeply of the spring's fresh cool water and fought an impulse to soak in a tub despite the restrictions. The notion persisted while she wiped the grime of the day off her face and arms. I am just tired. Someday I will return to Delphi and bathe when I please. At least I can change.

But the peg that bore her tunics held only a replica of the one she had on. Where was the *peplos* she wore from Delphi? She hopped over and jerked the tunic from its hook. The fastener was empty. Someone had removed the only thing she owned.

She sank onto her bench. No…they cannot It was hers! How could they come and take it…it was all I had left. She covered her face with her hands. To protest would get her nowhere. No possession was hers…she was the possession of another.

You have a right to be angry, but do not despair. I will see that you get another.

The dour tone the voice had used earlier was gone, its pledge of help a comfort. What would she do without its encouragement and guidance?

*****

The reining spirit of divination motioned. Over here, Anger, and bring Resentment with you. She is discouraged and has given in to the damning emotion twice today. She is ripe for your entry.

Anger whined his response. "What about Bitterness? We always work together…can it come too?

Alright, but hurry, I will not be able to keep the door open if she starts repenting of her feelings and forgives her offenders.

*****

Daphne sat on her bench, arms folded across her waist and rocked herself until her anger subsided. No fanfare alerted her to the three uninvited guests that joined those she already harbored.

The serenity and peace she found in the garden called to her. Did she dare? Kawit had already warned her. Would she have time to make a visit?

She checked the sun's position and tried to remember what time she had been summoned yesterday. Better not chance it...Patharus might call while I am gone. Maybe she should ask him for a garment more suited to a seer. She snickered. Jahtel would love that.

Would Nicanor be called upon to summon her again today? She brightened at the prospect. Time dragged. Her thoughts took her back to the cliff above the Gulf of Corinth, where she waited for her father's ship to appear on the horizon. She indulged herself in joyful memories of his homecomings, until footsteps sounded outside her door.

An unfamiliar voice came from outside her curtain. "You are to report to the master, immediately."

She bounced up and peered through the opening. The lone form of a servant moved down the hallway. She made sure she had the *obels* and followed him.

The doorway where she had seen the lovely woman was tightly closed. Her heart went out to her. How sad, to lose your only child and your health at the same time. Not surprisingly, Patharus had never mentioned his wife...or even spoken of a family. She wished she could express her sympathy, but it would be unseemly.

Upon reaching Patharus' door, his servant quickly ushered her in. She walked quietly to his desk and waited. His brisk manner in Athens and aboard the ship, the glaring ring and ferocious bull all faded in contrast to the compassion she felt as she studied him. Father would have died for Alexander...or Theo. How he must suffer.

He shut his ledger. "Ah, Daphne. Tell me, how did your second day go? Were you successful?"

Her mind snapped back. "Yes, my lord. I believe I was." She held out the *obels* for him to see.

He nodded his approval. "Well, tell me about it. Whom did you advise?"

She related the whole incident. His interest in the details surprised her. She did not speak of her confusion over the Voice's questionable purposes.

He came around the desk to collect her profits. "Very good...very good. Your other owners will pay a visit before long. They too want to hear of your progress. You are dismissed."

She turned to leave. "Wait. There is one more thing. I am giving a large banquet soon. I plan to call upon you to demonstrate your talents for any guest who desires to know his future."

At the thought, doubts stole her breath. But she must trust the Voice would guide her. "I will call upon my god for your guests, if that is your desire, sir, but would it be possible for me to have a garment more suited to a seer?"

"And what would that look like?"

"Well, a woman I knew and the seer in the market wore long dark shawls that went over their tunics and hung from their head to their knees."

Patharus' face scrunched. "Hmmm-wonder where I would find that? All right. I will look into it. You are excused."

Out in the hall, she considered his request. No, she could do it, and to look the part would help.

You do not control Apollo's willingness to perform. He grants wisdom through me...you are merely the vessel through which he operates.

She shrank at the Voice's rebuke and longed for the serenity of the garden. Dusk had yet to fall so despite Kawit's warning she decided to go. It would be risky, but she needed its calm and wanted to see the flowers while daylight lingered. She eased herself around the hedges and checked continually for movement. No sound could be heard so she let herself through the gate, mindful to ease the latch and avoid a loud clunk.

The lustrous foliage delighted her. Like protective green arms the leaves shimmered, highlighted by the setting sun. Nestled in clusters at her feet, fall crocuses poked their blossoms for all to admire. A rare, reddish-purple variety drew her attention. Of course, Patharus would have the rarest and best. Shame quickly dismissed the sarcasm, her mother's garden boasted of the same. Chrysanthemums golden blooms glowed in the sun they modeled. Each section beckoned but to tarry near the gate was risky.

She strolled the length of the garden, oohing over each flower before she returned to the cover of the hedge of witches'-broom. In the pond near her bench, fragile clusters of lily-of-the-sea grew inside the shallow edges. She bent over and picked a few of the dainty white blossoms and pressed them to her nose. The fragrance transported her back to her mother's dressing table.

Memories flood her mind at the smell. "May I hold the bottle, mother? I promise to be very careful." Hebee smiled at the growing moppet that clamored to be her exact replica. "Alright… but just for a moment, Kalon." Up on her toes Daphne had pressed close and reached for the delicate vessel. Hebee steadied her impish cherub between her knees and cupped the crystal container in her daughter's chubby hands. Her eyes shone as Hebee withdrew her hands and allowed her little girl to raise the vessel on her own. With each sniff her tiny nose wrinkled until her mother retrieved it and sent her off to play.

Anger wilted the blossoms she deliberately crumpled. The scent had been her mother's favorite. Bitterness enveloped her as she threw them to the ground. Still, the fragrance lingered, a reminder of all that had been torn from her. Mother, oh Mother. She covered her eyes. Where are you now?

Her mood reflected the promise of darkness. As the last bit of twilight waned, she rose, wiped her tears, and pushed the agony of her family's whereabouts into the deepest recesses of her heart.

The rumble of men's voices startled her. In seconds the heated discussion was nearly upon her. Panic paralyzed her feet. What could she do. Where could she hide?

Chapter Eighteen

Therefore, I turned my heart and despaired.
– Ecclesiastes 2:20

The Voice wasted no time. *Back into the hollow space between the bushes behind you.*

Daphne followed the advice. The quarrel grew more heated as the men drew near her makeshift shelter. Her heart thudded, would they discover her? Would she be punished...beaten? They stopped not ten feet from where she hid. She could hardly breathe.

"My son, you have much to learn...."

"Father, please...can we sit on that bench and talk this out?"

Daphne pressed her fist to her lips. Please, do not come over here.

"No...you need to hear me. You are young and do not understand what Roman schooling would do for you."

Relief gushed from her lips as she leaned into the sound. Was that Jahtel?

"Father, how can you be so sure of what is best for me? What about what I want? I may not be cut out for life as a Roman. You could very well be mistaken."

She squelched a gasp. That was Nicanor! Why would his father want him to seek a Roman education?

Jahtel's voice rose in anger. "Nicanor, do not be foolish. Patharus has favored you since you were young. He has no heir and is not likely to get one. I am sure he is about to announce his desire to adopt you and make you his successor. You would be insane to rebuff the future he offers."

"But I am not an orphan. Why would he even consider me for adoption?"

"Because he knows I would be thrilled to publicly announce your eligibility…for your own good. That is the only requirement. You already belong to Patharus, so it would be a natural transition. Once you are officially adopted you will be his heir, even if another child were born to him later. Roman adoption is stronger than the birth of a natural born child. Their laws are very strict. An adoption cannot be dismissed once it is official."

Nicanor's voice softened. "But you…and the memory of my mother. I cannot turn my back on who I am."

His tender profession spurred his father's zeal. "We would still be of the same household. Your mother, were she still with us, would rejoice at your chance to become a free man. Imagine her joy in your status as the master of Patharus' estate…think of how you could provide for your children, her grandchildren, born free, because you are free. Your mother would be ecstatic."

Daphne moved a few branches so she could see their faces. Both looked strained.

Jahtel put his hands on his son's shoulders. "I am not mistaken, Nicanor. This has been in the heart of our master for a long time. All I ask is that you keep an open mind and remain in Patharus's favor."

Neither spoke for a moment. Nicanor's head drooped. The discussion faded as they drifted back toward the manor.

She had not meant to eavesdrop, but how could she not have heard? Nicanor, Patharus' heir? What a great opportunity. Why would he hesitate? He has no idea what it would mean to be free.

She slumped on the bench, her heart torn. Joy in Nicanor's good fortune wrestled with regret he might soon leave for Rome. She envied him. His god had surely favored him. Could Apollo have such a miracle in store for her?

The hard, blank eyes of the statues near the gate seemed to stalk with their eyes, to scorn her intrusion. Wispy clouds that obscured much of the moon deepened the shadowy condemnation on their faces. She turned her back. Marble and stone, that is all they are. Nevertheless, she hurried to her room.

Full of her usual chatter, Kawit lingered in Daphne's room after dinner. She listened, half-hearted and nodded from time to time.

Kawit pushed up from the mat where they had flopped "You have not heard a word I said." She put her fists against her hips and cocked her head.

"Are you alright? Did something bad happen in town today?"

Daphne assured her she was fine and talked about the man and his ruined silk. "And when I reported it all to the master, he asked me to entertain his guests by telling fortunes at the big party he has planned."

Kawit sat slowly back on the mat. "Really? That is a great opportunity. The master must really be impressed with your ability. Let me see, what I can glean out of the storage room for you to wear."

"I asked him for a gown more suited for a seer." Daphne responded.

Kawit exclaimed, "You did? Good for you...did he agree to it?"

"I think so, said he would look into it."

Kawit hurried off to the storage room and returned with every possible thing she thought Daphne might need, including new sandals. From there, she started on how they should arrange her hair.

Daphne stifled a yawn as Kawit jabbered. "It's late, Kalon, how about we work on it tomorrow."

"Kalon? What is Kalon?"

Daphne smiled and pulled Kawit up with her. "Oh, it's a Greek term of endearment...we use it for people we love."

Kawit's eyes filled with tears. She grabbed Daphne, held tight and smiled into her face. "I love you too." They hugged again, and Kawit scurried through the curtain.

*****

Daphne left for the city the next morning, resigned to find someone she could help. She needed to practice before that party. She wondered if any guests would respond to Patharus' offer.

Her success with the man and his silk encouraged her, but the outcome could have been a disaster. Surprised to be at the gate already, she lifted her head and entered.

Fewer people waited to get past the inspectors, so she weaved her way through the wagons with little trouble and stepped toward the *agora's* busiest section.

A loud voice called out "There she is! See, over there, she is nearly here."

She stopped and searched the crowd for the source of the outcry. It was the silk merchant... and his finger pointed at her.

What is wrong? Is he angry...was the counsel of no help? Her insides wrenched. Should she run? It was too late. In seconds, the merchant had reached her side with another man not far behind.

"You, Sorceress, wait, I need to talk to you." He grabbed her arm, his breath in gasps. "Please, please, my friend needs to talk to you." He released his grip and gestured toward the man who had yet to catch up.

"She can help you!" he called to his friend. "She sought her god for me yesterday and saved my business. Ask her…she will tell you."

Relieved, she nodded at the man, determined to appear calm. "Do you have need of help from the gods?"

Worry pinched his brows. "I am in danger of losing my land." He searched her face. "Can your god tell me what is ahead? How to avoid the loss of all I own?"

She waited in silence. No council stirred from the Voice. "I will seek the gods for the wisdom you need." Surely Apollo would not fail her. "The gods will choose whether they can help you. Is that acceptable?"

He nodded vigorously. "Yes, I must have help. What should I do?"

Chapter Nineteen

A time to tear and a time to sew.
– Ecclesiastes 3:7

No secluded nook caught Daphne's eye. The place the old seer used rushed to mind. "Go behind the *palestra*. It will be deserted at this hour. I will meet you there shortly."

He took off for the gymnasium at a near run. He paced as she arrived, but flew to her side, eager to explain his misfortune. "It has been in my family for generations…almost to the time of Alexander. You must help me. I have done all I can, even rented my slaves to my wealthy Roman neighbor. He has no trouble paying the heavy taxes his government demands."

Her heart leapt. Was this Patharus' neighbor? The one the field hand referred to. What should she do? Her loyalty lay with her master and yet this man needed her help. "Let us seek the god of wisdom and light and gain his counsel." She hoped she sounded surer than she felt. *Do not fret. Apollo holds the answer to his future. Trust him.*

She pulled her shawl over her shoulder and sat on the ground, placing the *teraphim* between them. "Sit there."

The man was quick to follow her lead. He bowed low while she chanted. Again, she circled her hands over the *teraphim*. "You who are a god of the crops, who bids Eos to rise each morning and directs the sun to shine its warmth so plants will prosper and grow, hear our plea for help. You who beseech your father, Zeus, and he sends timely rains, speak to this one who reveres you and looks to you to take up your cherished bow and to target your arrow of wisdom in his direction."

She instantly heeded the impression to stop speaking. As soon as she obeyed the deep Voice from within began to chastise the man.

You have brought no offerings to my temple for many years. Your household replica of me, designed to bring me honor, gathers dust on an obscure shelf and receives no attention. Your neglect has brought about failure to manage your resources. Apollo is not pleased. and his blessings have been withheld.

She chanced a quick glance at the man. He squirmed but did not lift his head. She waited for the Voice to continue. Would he condemn the poor man to poverty, to lose all as her father had?

Your estate will be sold to pay your creditors. Do not fight this action but go to those who hold authority in these matters and ask that your house and surrounding acres be excluded. That will leave you enough to feed your family and not lose their home. See that you do not fail to honor the great Apollo in the future, or you will lose it all.

Her voice returned. "Apollo has spoken. Submit to his charge, and do not fail him again. He is worthy of all your homage and will reward all who honor him."

The man heaved a loud sigh. He made no attempt to defend himself, rose and laid a coin before her, and left without a word.

Her heart was heavy. She hated being the bearer of such ruinous news. Did Patharus' neighbor really deserve to lose his land? Her father had not failed to honor Apollo, and yet everything he had built was lost...even his family. Was Apollo not known as the god of love? Was there no mercy? Why was he sometimes so harsh?

With little enthusiasm, she picked up her idol and the coin, surprised to see the man had given her a drachma. She shot a quick glance in the direction he took but he was gone. She stared at the coin. He needed this more than Patharus ever would.

The sun had not reached its peak, so she slipped the coin into her tunic with the idol and walked among the shops until her stomach growled. No one that needed help appeared, so she turned into the courtyard, guilty of closing her ears to any skirmish.

Sitting in the courtyard refreshed her. Large bushes of oleander graced all of one side and filled the air with their sweet fragrance. She refilled her jug at the well and contemplated the long, thirsty walk home.

Home? Would she ever have a proper home again? The breeze rippling the Oleander swept the thought from her mind, along with her hope.

You belong to Apollo...he is your resting place.

She scoffed at the thought and dismissed the despair that threatened to engulf her. Much of the day lay before her, but already she longed to return to her room and the solitude of the garden.

The garden. She recalled Jahtel and Nicanor's argument as she sipped her fresh water. What would Nicanor do…surely, he would not reject this generous offer. Guilt chastised a brief hope that he would. She would miss his lively manner and engaging smile.

Go through the far gate. There is one in need of help.

She obeyed but her heart lingered on Nicanor's life-changing decision. Nothing in the market drew her attention, so she continued to walk. After she turned the corner, she crossed behind the portico's first pillar. Its roof brought instant relief from the sun. She had nearly reached the end of the sheltered portion when something caught her eye. A young woman stood hunched over, nearly hidden behind the last pillar.

She slowed. The girl looked distraught. A generous shawl covered much of her but not the extended curve beneath her breasts. Daphne gasped. She is pregnant and no older than me… should she go to her?

The girl's sobs pierced Daphne's heart. She held out her jug. "Please, here is some water. Can I be of help to you?"

The girl looked up and swiped her hands across her face. "No…I will be alright." She snuffed tears that did not let up. "I have to wait, the East temple is not open yet and, I, I....” Sobs choked her words. She bent over and clasped her abdomen with both hands.

Daphne grabbed the girl's waist and eased her to the stone floor of the portico. “The baby, is the baby on its way?” She shot a desperate look for help but saw no one.

The girl gave her a weak smile and shook her head. “No…no, it is not yet time.” She winced. “The little one’s kick is strong.” Pride shone in her eyes as she tenderly caressed her stomach. “I think my precious baby may have moved into the birth position to make its grand entrance.”

“Can I help you home? Maybe you should….”

The reply was curt. “I cannot go home. I must find out if, if….” She closed her eyes and covered her mouth.

Tell her who you are, that your god can help her.

Daphne drew out her *teraphim*. “I am…I mean, the gods have given me the ability to discern the future. Perhaps I can help you.”

The girl stared at the idol and then at her, a frown ringed her face. “But you are so young….” She eyed the idol again. “Can you really tell the future? I mean, the baby, could you tell me if I carry my husband’s heir, or if, if….” Terror tremored from her lips.

She hugged the girl’s shoulders and held her until she relaxed and leaned awkwardly into Daphne’s slight frame. She sniffled. “I could not bear it if the child is a girl.” Watery eyes searched hers. "How could I live with the horror that might befall my baby if my husband demands my child be, be...."

The thought brought fresh hysterics. She clutched Daphne's arm. "How? How? Oh, my baby....my poor baby."

She let her cry as the kindred sorrow that tortured her grandmother returned. The haunting wails that echoed for a lifetime after her husband demanded their infant daughter be cast into the deserted wastelands.

Call upon me.

She patted the girl's hand. "Come, let us listen to the counsel of the gods." She placed her idol and knelt beside the girl. Silently she beseeched Apollo for mercy and wisdom.

The young mother complied, hardly able to still the quiver of her chin. She shifted her cumbersome body until she sat opposite her and strove to stifle the deep shudders that convulsed her chest.

Daphne set the *teraphim* close to the girl and began to chant. With all her heart, she praised Apollo for his reason and light as she wholeheartedly beseeched his wisdom for this girl and her baby. She did not pause or change her routine. Janaeze's face flashed behind her closed lids. Would her childhood friend have to face this same dilemma? What would Apollo say to the girl? No words would comfort if she did not carry a male child. She could hardly bear the suspense

as the voice began to speak, relieved its tone had
gentled.

Chapter Twenty

How can you being evil, speak good things?
– Matthew 12":34

Daphne spoke the words that the Voice gave her.

Artemis, the goddess of fertility, has smiled upon you. The voice paused to let the words impact the young mother. *She has granted you the desire of your heart. You will bear your husband an heir. Raise your son to honor her twin brother, Apollo. It is he who grants you this good news. He alone is worthy of all your honor and sacrifice. Make no more visits to the foreign god of this temple…honor Apollo and listen to none other.*

As if targeted by a sunbeam, the girl's child-like face lit up "A boy! An heir! Oh, thank you, thank you." She grabbed Daphne's hands. "How can I thank you? Oh, thank you…a boy! Thank Artemis, I mean Apollo."

The Voice was silent, but a familiar mocking resounded deep within her. She had heard that evil snicker before, a vague hint that things might not be what they seemed.

The girl noticed her expression. "What is it? You look worried. Is there more…is something wrong?"

She forced a smile. "No…no, everything is fine. You heard what Apollo said, now I think you should go home. You cannot take a chance this close to...."

The girl struggled to her feet. "I will...I will." She reached into her tunic and thrust some coins into her hand. "Please, take this. I brought it for the temple gods, but the one who gives you what to say, deserves the sacrifice. It is he I will honor, I promise." She brought her face close, her voice choked with gratitude. "Goodbye and thank you...thank you."

She watched the girl waddle toward the gate and disappear, disturbed by the jeering inside. Slowly, she picked up her *teraphim*. Daphne struggled to remember...the god who gives you what to say....

Where had she heard that before? Semiele. The evil god who tells you things. Words she screamed at her after her friend's father killed her mother, convinced Daphne's revelation of a drastic change was at fault.

The evil god? Surely Apollo was not evil. All Greece revered him. Most of the educated class had renounced the ancient practice of serving many gods, but still honored Apollo and held his temple in high esteem. True, he had not prevented the Roman government from reducing their country to one of its colonies, but many welcomed the stability its occupation brought. No, none would call Apollo evil.

She brushed the dust from her tunic and polished the idol with her hem before she hid it in the folds of her tunic. She stared at the coins the girl gave her. Three *drachmas*. That made four. Indeed, Patharus would be pleased. She left the portico and headed for the gate. A smile tugged as she reflected on the face of the young woman. She dismissed her uneasiness. Would she herself ever know the joy of motherhood?

She climbed the first hill mindful the warm sun she welcomed that morning now called for protection. She draped her shawl over her head and down her back, weighted by the cares of the day. The pain of the man's lost land and the young girl's terror became hers, quick to sink or spike if joy returned. Her shoulders drooped. How was she to detach herself from troubled people...and could she? She welcomed the sight of her master's gate and avoided chats with a quick nod to those she passed.

The cool water of Patharus' well revived her. Back in her room she lay on her mat with a wet cloth on her forehead while she speculated on the delay of fall's cool weather.

Too soon a servant announced that the master awaited her. She jumped up. She should have used the time to wash the dust from her body. "I will be right there," she called out. How she wished she could skip the obligation, but gave her face a quick swipe and dashed down the hall

Patharus' servant nodded permission to enter before she reached the door.

She entered the room but stopped short. He was not alone. She lowered her eyes, but the faces of his partners, remained. She remembered {how they had urged Patharus to buy her at the slave market in Athens. What did they want? She swallowed her nerves and clutched her hands at her sides.

"Well, Daphne, your other owners have come to hear of your progress. Did you have a profitable day?"

She nodded. Maybe he would dismiss her quickly. "Yes, my lord. Here is your profit." She laid the coins on his desk.

Like puppets yanked by dual strings, Sergius and Amplias bent toward the money. Amplias gestured at the coins. "Not much for a full day's work,"

Sergius agreed. "You said she made much more in only half a day yesterday."

Before the two of them went off on a tangent, Patharus interrupted. "Yes, but you cannot put the spirit world on a timetable, and it will not be that way each day. You must understand these things take time. She must not only convince people she can see into the future but call upon the power within to tell her what to say. It is not a command performance."

Daphne was amazed at his perception.

Amplias cleared his throat and eyed Daphne closely. "Tell me about your, ah…customers?"

She hesitated. "I…."

Patharus interrupted. "It is alright, tell them about your day and look up while you do."

She focused on him and hoped they would be satisfied with the telling of the man about to lose his land. To explain the horror the young woman faced would be much harder. She swallowed the lump in her throat and began.

Patharus leaned in her direction "That must be my neighbor! Tell me, what did the man look like?"

She had hardly noticed. "Well, he was about your height, but much thinner. I believe he had a mustache. Yes, it was dark, and bushy."

Patharus turned to his partners. "That sounds like him. I will send my servants to investigate this sale first thing tomorrow. I have need of more land and am far short on workers."

She lowered her head, disappointed in his reaction. Where was compassion? In Delphi, neighbors pulled together and helped each other in hard times.

Sergius slapped Patharus' shoulder. "A stroke of good fate, friend…and on us, with our little sorceress." He spoke to Patharus, but his eyes swept her form.

She squirmed and hoped to be dismissed.

Sergius' eyes narrowed. "Perhaps she should spend some time in my villa. I am within the city walls and travel time would not cut into her profits."

Her knees grew weak.

Patharus shook his head. "No Sergius, the agreement stands. She will remain housed on my estate."

She covered her sigh, grateful Sergius' poorly veiled intentions were upended.

Impatient with Sergius' all-too-familiar desire to exploit those he owned, Amplias broke the silence that followed. "What of your other encounter, girl?"

Patharus gestured at Amplias and took Sergius's arm. "Let us go out on my veranda and save that for another time. Appetizers and wine await us and we have much bigger concerns to deal with. Come and let her enjoy the evening. You may leave, Daphne."

Relieved, she backed toward the door.

A shiver swept her body as she contemplated the fate that would be hers without Patharus' protection, especially after Sergius undressed her with his eyes. Gratitude flowed to Apollo who had surely arranged for her to live in this villa rather than with either of her other owners. Her nook was safe, stark, but decent. Even her master's overseer was not allowed to harass or abuse her.

Patharus' voice carried to the door. "Please stay for the evening meal. The girl will use her skill to entertain at the banquet I am planning. You can talk to her then."

She scurried down the hall, thankful his plans did not include her, but wary of what the banquet might bring.

Chapter Twenty-One

Guilt has grown up to the heavens.
– Ezra 9:6

Near the end of the first month of going into the city, Daphne sat across from the courtyard fountain eating a late lunch. The day had been productive. One after another, as if prearranged by some phantom overseer, rendezvous with customers materialized. She slipped off her shawl and laid it beside her. Perhaps her new garb authenticated her position. The densely woven fabric was too warm on hot days, and almost spurred regrets she asked for it. She wished she could save it only for special events like the banquet Patharus planned.

She leaned back on the bench and relished time to relax. The initial satisfaction she found in helping people had eroded, tarnished by the motives of the majority of those who sought her counsel.

A burly man had sought her out. "I need a way to drive my competitor out of business…can your god show me how?" Another approached when he thought he could not be seen. "My neighbor reneged on his promise to sell me some sheep. Sold it to my former partner! I want vengeance."

The last was the worst. "I want you to put a curse on a man I thought was my friend. He knew I hoped to marry our well-to-do neighbors newly eligible daughter and I just found out he swayed her father to betroth her to him!"

Few came to gain wisdom or spiritual guidance, nor did they seem eager to delight in the one who initiated their launch into her hands.

Disappointed but unable to alter the outcomes, she gave Voice to Apollo's underhanded instructions. To fret over her inability or whether she was clever or knowledgeable enough to perform her tasks faded like the last of the roses in the garden. It did not really matter.

A sparrow gleaned crumbs around her feet. She sat still and quietly vented her frustrations at her newly found companion. "Your source of supply does not matter to you either, does it?"

The bird's head jerked nervously but returned to its search.

"And Apollo doesn't want my opinion or care how I feel about anything. He works solely through his messenger who tells me exactly what to say or do unless he decides to verbalize his will aloud. I merely house the mediator between myself and the god who has chosen me to speak his plans."

She followed the tiny bird's flight toward the lone cloud that blocked the sun. Why does Apollo help those bent on taking advantage of another? Surely the god of light and good sees the blackness of their hearts. Why would he support deception that enables them to steal from or destroy a fellow citizen? And why does he value the homage of such wicked men anyway?

The cloud drifted. It brought light to her face but not to her questions.

Despite a concerted effort, she could not distance herself from her daily reality. Pity for those ravaged by circumstances not of their own doing wound its way around her heart. Likewise, seeking guidance for the vicious and the greedy tweaked her sense of right and wrong, and heaped layers of guilt upon her badgered conscience. Surely father had not done business this way. She wondered who she had become, and if she truly cared about the downtrodden. Why did she continue to help men with no scruples?

The fountain's plume reached for some unseen target, scattered, and hung midair before it plummeted back into the pond. As the highest drops finished their journey, she closed her eyes. She was like that, about to burst into the wonderful future she thought was hers, but her dreams shattered like that spray. Now she is a nameless face, submerged in a pool of dehumanized souls with no hope of escape and no chance to live out her dreams.

Her thoughts reverted to those she dealt with. Were they any better off? Blind to their inability to protect their possessions from thieves or loss they all grasped for more...more wealth, greater prominence, never satisfied. Were those heady with wealth and power entitled to a life free of want, absent of sorrow or pain?

She sneered. No matter, before long, they too will fade from memory, forgotten and unfulfilled.

She stood and stretched. As always, what she pondered led to the reality she could not deny: without the gift that set her apart, she would likely be owned by someone less benevolent than Patharus and lead a much more difficult life. Backbreaking work or subjected to the whims of a master like Sergius could be her lot. Even worse, she might have shared Nectari's horrible fate and landed in a brothel. She hated the life thrust upon her but could see no way out. There was no choice. She had to protect herself.

Her thoughts ran to Nicanor. He does have a choice. What great fortune has befallen him. She hoped he…. The thought hung, undefined.

The courtyard began to fill with shoppers in need of respite from the heat. She counted the coins she acquired. One gold and three denarii, more than enough to satisfy her owners. She picked up her shawl and removed the pins from her hair so it would fall around her shoulders in the manner of free women.

If she arrived back at the estate too early, it might give a wrong impression. She needed something to do. To dawdled through the market seemed her only option. She laughed and thought she would pretend to be Patharus' daughter.

She stepped into the *agora* and gasped. Not far from where she stood her master rounded a corner. Nicanor kept pace, tuned to his every word.

She ducked back into the courtyard and cowered behind an arch. Within seconds they passed, their attention on each another. She released her breath, relieved they had not seen her.

What were they doing in town…together? Had they come to spy on her, to check her diligence? It did not seem likely. Patharus had never failed to respond positively to her daily reports. She decided to follow at a distance, close to the stalls, but vigilant should they turn around.

They moved into the South *stoa* and turned into the building that housed the office of the Roman magistrates. With a painful whisper, Daphne realized, Patharus has arranged a meeting for Nicanor's adoption!

She backed up and leaned against the *stoa* wall, unprepared for the surge of abandonment that swept like a plague of locust across her heart. Disappointment welled in her chest and spilled from her lids with facts that created sorrow and ignored reason.

She wiped her tears on her shawl. How could she be so selfish? Did she not want him to be free?

His long absence and the position he would hold after he returned, was hard to envision. Like the first blast of winter, its chill heralded the unwelcome change.

There was no place to hide along the *stoa*, so she left the walkway and returned to the market. Baffled by her unmerited speculation, she sat somewhat hidden behind a well-stocked stall they would pass as they left. It is not as if they were friends. It is…is what?

She could not bring herself to admit how drawn she had become to those dancing blue eyes and ready smile.

Chapter Twenty-Two

As for my hope, who can see it?
– Job 17:15

An hour passed with no sign of Patharus or Nicanor. Could she have missed their return? Should she wait? Daphne's eyes rolled with indecision. The ground she sat on was hard. She could not head back. She might catch up with them along the path.

She stood and stretched. At the same moment they burst through the exit nearest her and into the *agora*. Patharus had one hand on Nicanor's back, headed for the Eastern *stoa*. She panicked, in seconds they would pass the shop where she tried to hide. Where was her head?

She pulled her shawl over her head, turned her back, and withdrew into the thickest part of the crowd. Patharus wove purposefully through the throngs of people. In no time they moved so close she could hear him speak.

"The school in Rome will open your eyes to a whole new world, Nicanor. You are very bright. You will do well."

"But the language, Master. I do not speak or understand your tongue. How will I—"

Patharus beamed and cut him off. "I know, I know. It has been well over two hundred years since the Battle of Philippi. It was easier for the soldiers and their descendants who settled here after the skirmish to adopt your language, than to teach the whole city their own. It is rare to hear our mother tongue anymore. I will hire a tutor to work with you until you leave in the spring. The straits of the Mare Hadriaticum would be too dangerous now, always the chance of an *euroclydon* this far into the fall."

His enthusiasm grew, "And since we are situated on the Via Egnatia, we have a direct link to the port. The road is well traveled and safe from marauders. We will time our overland travel to make the first ship that sails next spring. There will be time. Meanwhile...."

She strained to hear what else Patharus planned but they turned the corner that led to the gate. The long portico of the Eastern *stoa* left no place for her to hide. She glanced at the sun. Darkness fell noticeably earlier this time of year but there was still time.

The market held no interest now. She waited until Patharus and Nicanor would be halfway home before she started out, grateful for the cooler part of the day. Her thoughts remained with Nicanor.

Rome. What would such a place be like? How long would he be away? Her thoughts wandered as she began the walk home and ended with a picture of Nicanor sitting at Patharus' desk. The image brought a gasp. Nicanor would be her owner one day! How will he feel about the work Patharus has assigned me?

Deep in thought, she nearly fainted when Nicanor jumped from behind a thick stand of aloe. "Hello. Mind if I accompany you the rest of the way home?"

She pressed her hand to her throat. "Oh, you frightened me. Did not your mother ever tell you it is cruel to scare people?"

Nicanor pressed his palms together "Look, you are right. I am truly sorry, please forgive me... please?" Beneath the shock of black hair, his eyes twinkled.

"What are you doing here anyway? I saw you leave...." She put her hand to her lips, but it was too late.

Nicanor grinned. "I know, I saw you too. Why did you hide from us?"

Heat rose to her face. What could she say? "I, I...." no excuse came to mind. She dropped her voice. "The master...did he see me too?"

Nicanor fell in step beside her. "No, his mind was fully occupied...he saw nothing but the future."

She marveled at the ease she felt as they walked and talked. "You have been given a wonderful opportunity. Are you excited about going to school in Rome?"

His jaw dropped. He stopped and stared at her, his face a platter of questions. "How did you know about Rome...and school? No one is to know."

She fidgeted with the hem of her shawl. "I did not mean to listen, I was in the garden one evening last week and I overheard…."

"You heard my father urge me to allow Patharus to adopt me."

"Please forgive me, I did not mean to eavesdrop, but I could not expose myself. I have never asked for permission to be allowed in there and it probably would not be given."

They walked in silence for a while. From time-to-time she stole a glance at him. A scowl darkened his face. They were not far from the estate when he gripped her arm. "Have you told anyone else what you heard?"

His tone frightened her. She pulled away and shook her head.

The muscles in his jaw twitched. "I ask you to keep this solely to yourself. Can you do that…can I count on you to keep it a secret?"

Impaled by his stare, she nodded, fascinated by the way his dimple deepened when he spoke. "I promise…I will never speak of it to anyone."

"Besides the master and his wife, only my father knows. The news must not be leaked before he announces it at his banquet. It is very important."

"Then you have agreed to his plan? You will become his legal heir…his son?"

"Patharus has been good to me, but I will always be my father's son. This is somewhat of a…a business arrangement."

She searched his face. "Do you care about Patharus?"

He pulled his chin to his chest. "What kind of a question is that? Patharus is, well, he is a good man."

She looked away. "I see."

He grabbed her arm again. "No...you do not see. I am not, I mean I have not taken advantage of his good nature. My father, my whole family have served him faithfully all my lifetime. Patharus initiated this plan, not me nor my father."

She glanced at the hand that clutched her arm. He released her as if her arm were a hot coal.

At the crest of the foothill that led to the estate, she paused. Nicanor stopped and faced her. Her words were soft. "Nicanor, I hope it all works out wonderfully for you. And you have my word, I will not breathe a word of this to anyone."

For a moment he did not speak. His eyes narrowed as if he searched for any reason to not trust her. At last, a sheepish smile crossed across his face and his eyes held hers, "Thank you." He reached out and touched her shoulder. The brush of his hand was gentle. She still felt the touch of his warm grip on her arm.

She backed away and started out, aware her face had flushed again. She could not let him see how his smile affected her...how everything about him caused her head to spin.

He called after her. "By the way, why did you try to hide from us in the *agora*?"

His question caught her off guard. She could hear the amusement in his voice. What if she said she feared Patharus had come to check on her? She could not say she followed because she cared whether he left for Rome. "I am not sure, but thank you for not pointing me out to the master."

He caught up with her. "We are even then." The twinkle had returned to his eyes.

Before the passage turned sharply toward the estate, he paused and gestured toward the trail. "Umm, I guess, I mean, well, you had best go on from here. I will wait a bit and follow."

Daphne covered the affront with a quick smile, too hurt to ask why. She nodded and continued. So, he did not want to be seen with her.

From what she observed slaves were not prohibited from mingling. Perhaps it is his coming status, or maybe Patharus or his father instructed him to distance himself from fellow slaves.

She could feel his eyes upon her as she jogged down the path. What did it matter? He would soon be the master's newly adopted heir and off to Rome.

It mattered.

Chapter Twenty-Three

By pride comes nothing but strife.
– Proverbs 13:10

Patharus summoned her shortly after she entered her room, so Daphne had no time to brood. She approached his door just as Stello pushed his way past the master's servant and walked unannounced into the room. The overseer's gait warned something had not gone his way. Silently, she thanked Apollo their paths seldom crossed.

Patharus glance darted from her to his overseer. He cocked his head and frowned. She lowered her eyes, waited and realized she had forgotten to refasten her hair. Had he noticed?

He finally spoke. "You may bring your earnings, Daphne."

Stello's eyes followed as she laid the coins on Patharus' desk. She ignored the overseer's glare. Something must have happened, his jaw seemed tighter than a jackal's. Could he have learned of the master's decision about Nicanor...but why would he care?

Kawit's enlightenment returned. *Despite his lofty position, Stello cannot accept less than total charge over all of Patharus' household. I have heard him and Jahtel argue over things that are not his concern. He thinks he should be consulted over every decision and men like the one he picked on tonight bear the brunt of his rage…or I do.*

Daphne shifted her weight and hoped for a quick dismissal. Patharus poked at the coins, nodded, and flicked his hand in her direction. "I look forward to your performance at the banquet. You are dismissed."

The banquet. She searched for courage to say something to temper his expectations, but his attention had turned to Stello. Thoughts of a room full of leering men who wanted to be entertained or seek knowledge of who knew what, sent dread to the pit of her stomach.

Out in the hall she sighed, "What if I cannot…"

Remember my promise to give you what you are to say.

She left for her room. "Yes." The Voice had never failed to give her what to say. When would she stop questioning it? She sipped some fresh water and lay on her mat. Patharus' expectations competed for her attention with Nicanor's snub until she dozed.

"Daphne? Daphne, are you in there? I need to talk to you. Will you please meet me in the garden by the pool in a few minutes?"

She rose on one elbow and blinked several times. Shadows darkened her room. Had she dreamed Nicanor called her? She strained into the twilight and listened. Nothing. She cleared her throat, her voice tentative. "Who is there? Did someone call?"

"Yes, it is me, Nicanor. Please come, Daphne, I need to talk to you."

She bolted upright. What did he want of her? The way he acted before they reached the estate spiked a caution. Should she go? She could not deny her heart leapt at the thought of time with him.

"Daphne, did you hear me? Will you come?"

"Yes, I will come. But give me a little time."

"I will wait. Do not be long, it is important."

She scurried to her washstand and filled the bowl. She wished she could bathe but this would have to do. She discarded the wilted tunic she had worn all day and washed her face. Her hair! For the hundredth time she wished for a looking glass.

With her comb clutched in her teeth, she groaned. "I cannot take time to wash it." She dampened her hands and smoothed her locks into a fresh coil and secured it with the comb at the nape of her neck. She frowned at the only other tunic allowed her. At least it was clean. She donned the garment and left the dirty one in a heap.

Darkness enveloped the statues by the gate as Daphne searched the area for any late visitors. She did not stop by the oleander bush but plucked a few of its blossoms to tuck into her hair. How she missed her scented oils. Dark clouds that rolled across the sky, played hide and seek with the moon and made it hard to see the path.

Nicanor called in a loud whisper. "Over here, Daphne."

"I can hardly see…it is so dark."

He extended his hand. "Here, let us sit on the bench."

She let him lead her the last few steps. His fingers curled around hers, their warmth a balm of comfort. They sat close but she withdrew her hand. He noticed but did not comment.

Dampness from early dew on the stone seat penetrated her tunic. How could she have forgotten her shawl? She shivered and hoped he did not notice.

"Here, sit on my waist wrap, these seats get cold after sunset."

Daphne took his wrap and dismissed her outlandish desire that he would pull her close and hold her.

He shifted sideways on the bench. "I want to explain why I could not walk up to the manor with you earlier today."

Her heart raced. Her fingers caressed the back of the hand he had held and drew from his touch that lingered there. She did not look at him. "There is no need, I…."

He held up his hand. "Yes, yes there is." His voice demanded she face him. "I did not stay back because I did not want to be with you or anything like that."

She shook her head. "Really, I was not—"

"Please, let me finish."

She lowered her eyes and nodded. Why did he seem so nervous?

"My father, umm, well, my father, he watches my every move these days. You know what the master has proposed, and well...." He paused and took a deep breath..

"My father is very concerned that I might do something that will ruin my chance to become Patharus' heir before he makes the official announcement." His words rushed on pent-up emotion. "He has asked me to pull back from my friends and...well, from anyone he considers...." His voice dropped. "To be of a...a lower station."

Her head snapped in his direction. A lower station? Is that how he would view her once he became Patharus' heir...part of a people with less value than his own? Incensed, she fumed. I was not born a slave. I was raised in a beautiful home that....

As quick as the recent storm, truth struck with a desolate finality. It devoured all pretense of the past she longed for. She was a slave and Nicanor would soon be free, a world apart.

No longer could she deceive herself to believe her old life would return. What a fool she had been. She jerked her face from his gaze and forced a serene expression.

She hoped darkness hid the heat that colored her face. With her emotions marshaled, she jumped to her feet and faced him. Her voice oozed feigned comfort. "Please do not concern yourself, Nicanor. I certainly will not, I would never cause...."

Her voice began to waver. How could he believe she would presume upon their brief friendship? Were they friends? More than friends? How could she bear to live in the same estate and have him treat her as one of a "lower station?" Unsanctioned betrayal poured throughout her being like fine sand through an hourglass.

You have a right to be angry. He sees himself as better than you are now. Do not let him pass the blame to his father...he feels the same or he would not avoid being seen with you. A friend would not treat you this way. Do not accept his excuses.

The Voice continued to harp on Nicanor's offenses. It confirmed the truth she grasped and added fuel to the pain that gnawed a hole in her heart. Anger quickly filled the opening with bitterness. She was nothing to him, and so he must be nothing to her.

It was a lie, and she knew it, but her bruised pride screamed to lash out and hurt him back. He saw her as a threat to his future. Well, so be it. How could she have allowed her imagination to lead where it had no right to go? Disgusted with her weakness, she squelched the upbraiding perched on the edge of her tongue and covered it with a half-truth. "I must get back. Kawit waits for me." With that, she turned and ran toward the gate. He would not see her tears.

"Daphne, no…wait. Daphne, wait! Let me explain." He started after her but tripped over a small statue of a nymph half hidden by vines. As he tried to untangle himself, she slipped out of his sight.

Chapter Twenty-Four

Do not be overcome by evil.
– Romans 12:21

Daphne made sure she was up early and on her way before many gathered around the food tables, especially Nicanor. At the city's gate, she found herself well ahead of the crowds. She moved slowly through the inner passage, relieved to avoid rude remarks by vendors or pompous merchants.

She passed the self-appointed city fathers gathered inside the gate and scoffed. The elite. What would *they* do if they lost their wealth and positions in society?

She overheard a man much older than Patharus ask his companion, "Say, what is this I hear about your plan to buy my neighbor out? Sounds like you have captured the head magistrates' ear."

Another jumped on the news, "Maybe you could put in a word for me, I...."

Their politicks disgusted her but she moved on and kept an eye out for an early prospect.

She caught a glimpse of Sergius. He did not acknowledge her but followed her every step with his eyes. He was typically too dignified for crude remarks, she knew what was on his mind and he made her skin crawl. She wished Patharus would buy out his share in her.

She tried to picture Patharus among those who gathered there.

.... he disdains politics, has little to say about it that is good....

She smiled at the ardent defense of his loyal house slaves. A flush of pride in her owner's stand swelled like wet grain and lifted her chin as she maneuvered through the passage. Her lack of experience with politicians aside, she admired Patharus' disdain of them.

She refused to meet anyone's gaze. Should a candidate for her counsel desire to meet he would signal. She slowed to a leisurely pace and enjoyed the solitude of deserted streets. Buyers would not arrive for an hour or so.

The early quiet gave way to the market's usual din and by mid-morning the scarcity of solicitors frustrated her. She wandered over to the *palaestra*, sat on the shaded stone ledge that surrounded the building.

The north side faced a brook that ran under the gymnasium. She relaxed, soothed by the sound of water that bubbled gently down the slopes of the landscape. It disappeared into a rock-lined chasm and plunged well beyond the nine steps that led to the room below ground.

She marveled at the Roman engineers who rebuilt the city and placed their public toilets beneath the building on a circular ledge directly over the stream's flow. Water that rushed from the peaks of Mt Orvilos' extended range, coursed beneath the latrine's forty-two communal stone seats before it disappeared under the exterior wall and out of the city.

Early on she had observed that the men congregated at the *palaestra* or around the public baths after they left the city gates. Opportunities had surfaced before, perhaps they would today. Men came and went but none glanced her way. In the lull her thoughts returned to the garden and Nicanor. Why had she reacted with such anger? Where did it come from? Perhaps he did despise his father's precautions but could not bring himself to disobey…any more than I would have.

She leaned her chin on her fist. "He did seem distressed at what he had to tell me."

Do not be a fool! He is about to become a member of Patharus' family…there will be no place for a slave in his life.

She frowned. Was the Voice right? Did she believe that? One thing is sure, I must be on my guard and distance myself…I cannot let him see or take advantage of how my feelings for him have grown.

A merchant dressed in finery passed. His heavily loaded slave shuffled at his heels. The slave's head was bowed, and his eyes did not lift. She stared at the welts on his back and shuddered. Slaves seldom ran away twice, the price was too high. Punishment for a failed escape would be as horrible as a rape.

The sun shrank the shadow of the *palaestra* as she sat and mulled thoughts of her future. She kept a sharp eye, but no noticeable need surfaced. Heat on her bare arms prompted a glance at the sun. Nearly midday, maybe she would do better in the market.

She slid off the ledge and gathered the heavy shawl, along with her lunch as two stragglers absorbed in conversation emerged from the latrines. Neither glanced her way nor roused any hope, but she decided to wait. They paused close so she listened, drawn by the anguish in one's voice.

The taller of the two lamented a business disaster he had suffered the day before, his discourse laced with self-pity. "I never saw it coming." Bitterness spewed with the complaint. "How was I to know he would take his contract to that pig…after all these years?" He shook his head at the injustice.

The shorter man reached up and patted his friend's shoulder. "Come now, it will right itself. Men like that eventually get their comeuppance."

The first man raised his arms and shook his fists. "An honest man has no chance." Did he half-expect some deity to see his plight and intervene on the spot? "My prices are fair. He will be cheated along the way. Mark my words."

The discussion continued for a considerable time. After failed attempts to console his friend, the second man gave a weak excuse and left.

With her shawl over her head, she stepped over and seized her chance. With a boldness that surprised her, she took a deep breath and addressed him.

"Good Master. I could not help to overhear of your misfortune. The gods have brought me here to serve you." She held up her *teraphim*. "I can see into the future through the power of our great god, Apollo, and cause you to triumph over that rival. My god will tell you what will come to pass so you can take advantage and bring back your disloyal customer, begging for your goods."

She held her idol close to his face, amazed at how quickly she had learned to exploit a man's desire for vengeance. A familiar haunt of regret filtered through her conscience. She rued the day Bentalla had recognized the divining spirit of python within her and insisted she keep the idol. Its powers to conjure up visions and entreat the spirit world had proven true…but at what cost? And where would she be without it?

Minus an advocate, she had been helpless to stay the power behind the Roman seal that authorized the auction of her family and home. No leeway had been granted…no time to arrange to pay the debt. Just as the authorities in Delphi had failed her, no authority in Philippi would free her to live a decent life either.

Patharus' orders were stamped indelibly on her mind. *….. if you use your ability and obey… nothing to fear….*

If. She scowled. As if she had a choice.

Her inner struggle continued…her future or those she dealt with? She pushed aside the conflict, barely aware she had decided. The same conclusion evolved: she could not risk the consequences of the rule of her conscience.

She spoke with contrived confidence. "This *teraphim* has all the answers." Each day, the familiar words spewed more easily, but they still made her cringe.

The man jerked back as if he expected the god to appear. He studied the idol several seconds then searched her face. Doubt embraced his countenance. Many believed to collaborate with a diviner was a risk. Maybe he agreed.

She lifted the *teraphim* again. That the tiny image could bring such fear to a man, surprised and amused her. She tried to ease his apprehension. "It has special powers to conjure visions of what is to come and to counsel you with an oracle directly from Apollo."

Would her words appeal to his greed or his drive for vengeance? Both, she discovered, had power to blind men to the consequences of dabbling in the spirit world. Few grasped what she had only begun to understand: an inroad to their very soul.

Chapter Twenty-Five

In the multitude of anxieties within me…
– Psalm 94:19

The man was weakening. Daphne had seen him at the marketplace many times and knew he was a reputable merchant, but anger and misfortune might result in bad judgment. While he vacillated, she pressed her case, determined to profit from his dilemma.

Her words dripped with honey. "A wise merchant such as yourself can easily grasp the wisdom of seeking help from the gods. The justification you seek is well deserved. A recompense for your years of loyal service to this ungrateful customer."

She moved the *teraphim* slowly in front of her and flattered his intelligence as she coaxed him to a quiet place back near the *palaestra*. He hesitated but followed several steps behind. She rehearsed what she would say should he suddenly change his mind.

She found a spot shaded from direct sunlight, sat cross-legged, and motioned for him to sit across from her. He fingered his tunic, glanced behind and back at the idol propped in front of her. The moment he lowered himself she began to ply her trade.

"Oh, great Apollo, god of all knowledge who holds power to intervene in the lives of mere mortals. I beseech thee to grace us with your presence. You who grant justice and circumvent the plans of the wicked, hear your maidservant."

Over and over, she extolled the virtues of her god and pleaded for him to speak forth his wisdom. Wide-eyed, the man still peered from side to side. He kneeled on his haunches with his hands pressed the ground, ready to run. Her voice droned on. Its hypnotic effect induced a calm and his body slumped, glazed eyes fixed on the idol. Concern she might yet lose him lifted.

A twinge of pity twisted her heart…she had heard of bad things that happened after some patrons opened themselves to a god.

The man stirred. She could not turn back, already she sensed the familiar churning within. She chided herself. Concentrate, perhaps they ignored Apollo's warnings.

With tireless repetition, she resumed her chant and reaffirmed her dependence on the supernatural manifestations of the god to whom she had submitted her future. Her hands moved in a circular motion over the idol. Hidden behind a glassy stare, nothing revealed her repulsion of the motives or intentions behind her voice.

The submission of the man's heart to the false god would release power to rise in Apollo's messenger and reveal itself through her.

Hear the plans I have for you, man of faith. The tone rang with authority. *I am a messenger of the great Apollo, who has seen your injustice and wills to help you. Bow your face to the ground and give Apollo, the beautiful god of all vengeance and justice, your homage.*

The man's head jerked at the unexpected tenor of the Voice. Wide eyed, he froze, a gasp his weak response.

Bow before the great Apollo, the Voice demanded, louder now and raspy.

Obediently, the man fell forward until his head touched the earth. Hunched on all fours, he cowered, as if he expected a lash to break across his back. Seconds later he pushed his legs out behind and lay prone, his face in the dirt. When the Voice began to wail, he did not venture a glance.

Great and mighty is the wisdom of Apollo. Awesome and terrible are his powers. Pay heed to the god who has all understanding. He alone can instruct you.

On and on the Voice harassed the quaking man. Daphne waited, conscious she had no inkling of what might happen next. No session was like any other…each unpredictable. With shallow breaths, she struggled to mask her dread, desperate to not flinch each time a new command erupted.

A frigid wind blew over them. The man shivered under the ominous chill. As quickly as it came it dissipated and left oppressive heat. Sweat poured from under the man's hair and dripped onto the ground. Her heart went out to him. Why must the god torture him so?

From out of nowhere a scene appeared before her eyes.

Speak what you see. The prompt was insistent.

Daphne gulped and obeyed the Voice. "I see a landowner just past the great bridge over the river Gagitis. He is distressed because he has fallen on hard times."

Ask the man if he is familiar with the place.

"Are you familiar with the place, good man?"

The man croaked a response. "Yes, I know of the place."

Tell him what else you see.

"The man is rounding up his herd of swine to ready them to sell at the market".

"But…this is not the time to sell," the merchant protested. "The man will not get a good price unless he fattens them over the winter."

Go, the Voice charged after a brief silence. Its gritty whisper grated like rough coral on her throat. *Buy them yourself, but do not accept the man's first price. He will agree to whatever you will pay. Fatten the herd yourself. Your competitor will not be able to match your prices. The man who took his business elsewhere will be forced to buy from you. You can make a great profit and retrieve your lost business.*

The man's forehead rubbed the ground with each nod, hardly able to contain his rapture. He began to push himself up but dove for the ground as the Voice hissed again.

Remember to give glory to the great Apollo, and honor him before men. Forever pay him the homage due him alone. Revere him, or continued disaster will fall upon you and all you own.

The Voice faded but neither Daphne nor her patron moved. The eerie silence held several minutes before the man inched his head off the ground. His eyes darted in every direction then settled on hers. He stared, drawn and expectant, his face as gray as one laid out on a bier. She nodded and he slowly pushed himself upright. He dug some coins from his girdle and jabbed them into her outstretched hand, backed carefully then bounded for the street.

She sighed and waited for her uneasiness to leave. Would it ever get any easier? She thought about the man who owned the swine...was she responsible for his losses? Would he too lose his land and livelihood? "Oh father," she groaned. "What am I doing? How will I ever...."

Be concerned for your own welfare. No one else will...or care.

The words held no comfort. As she rose, she swore the *teraphim* sneered. She glared at it and used her foot to bury the idol under a pile of loose dirt and pebbles. "Stay out of my life! I hate you. I wish I had never set eyes on you."

Chapter Twenty-Six

Men who suppress the truth in unrighteousness
– Romans 1:18

Daphne pulled her shawl to her face and sobbed. She walked a short distance and sat on a ledge until her shudders quieted. After a few deep breaths she picked up her lunch and headed for the courtyard, grateful no one was around.

Apart from me you can do nothing.

She shook off the message. "You are finished pervading my life...I hate what you do."

What will you tell Patharus when you are not able to please his guests or earn wages?

She sputtered and sped up. "I will think of something."

He purchased you for one reason. You have no other use unless it is the fields...subject to Stello's whims.

She could not dismiss the awful truth. Her drive evaporated. Her heart raced at an image of herself at Stello's feet, stripped, brutally raped, and beaten, with a cruel brand burned into her forehead.

Within, the Voice coaxed. *You are a help to people, Daphne. You are not responsible for the farmer's poor management. If this man did not take advantage of his situation someone else would. Come now, go retrieve your teraphim. Apollo has great plans for you...he is well pleased with your service and wants only to protect you.*

The plea faded, but fear and dread volleyed with an upper hand. Even in her struggle she knew what she would do. The consequences of deserting her gift were more than she could face. She thought of her father's high moral standards. Tears dripped on her feet as she retraced her steps. "Father, I am sorry, I cannot…I do not have your strength." She retrieved the dusty idol and stuffed it into her tunic, convinced it smirked as she did.

The market had resumed its post-noon business as she joined the crowds. To her relief, the courtyard was nearly deserted. Her appetite gone, she tossed her lunch into a receptacle and refilled her water jug.

She looked at the sun and inspected the coins she had collected. Fewer than on most days, but she decided to risk Patharus' ire. With a shuffle not unlike the cowed slave she witnessed, she made her way back to the estate. At the crest of the hill, she checked the grounds. Satisfied she would not be noticed, she slipped through the gate and into her room.

She stripped the dirty *chiton* from her body and washed the dust off her skin. She longed to go to the garden but could not chance it this early in the day. With no place to go, she donned her tunic and lay on her mat, convinced she had failed everyone.

Her thoughts traveled to the beginning of her relationship with the Voice, to the path that led her to this day. Mercifully, sleep brought escape. Someone screamed and called for help. She tried to get up but something heavy on her chest weighed her down. As in the *adytum*, a *pythia* with a haggard face whirled and pointed a finger at her. Talsta withdrew his dagger from the high priest's bloody body and glanced at her. At last, she stood, but her feet would not move. Talsta was almost upon her. Frantic, she screamed and searched her room. Where was he?

A young slave burst through her curtain. "What is it…what is it? I heard you scream, what is it?"

She thrust her hands over her face, relieved and embarrassed. "Oh…oh, I am so sorry. I must have fallen asleep. I dreamt that…." How could she explain what she saw? The dream had not reoccurred in months. Would it never go away?

The youth stared, reluctant to leave.

"Please, did anyone else…I mean were their others that heard me?"

He shook his head. "No, I was on my way to the master's room when I heard you. All are occupied with the ever-growing plans for his banquet."

She sighed. "Thank you, I am alright now… thank you for checking." He nodded but paused when she spoke. "Do you think…I mean do you have to say anything about this to Jahtel?"

The young man smiled. "Nah, it was a bad dream. It will remain between you and me."

She blushed and thanked him again. Deep breaths released her gratitude…an arm of the great sea lay between her and Talsta. She wished she could change her clammy tunic, but the other was dirty from the day's travels.

She freshened as much as she could and soon the same young man alerted her to Patharus' call.

He beckoned her from the hall. "Daphne… come in. How did your day go?"

She forced a smile and held her breath. "It was not one of my better days, my lord. I have only these coins, but I am sure it will be better tomorrow."

He poked at the coins she laid on his desk. "Fine, fine, I am sure it will be. We have more important things to discuss. I have set the day of my banquet for the fourth day. Will you be ready to entertain my guests?"

She pressed her elbows into her waist and steadied her voice. "I will do my best, my lord."

Tell him you need some time to seek wisdom from the gods.

A frown flicked her brows. Why did the Voice want her to say that?

Say it. He will not object.

"My lord, to seek the gods for such an undertaking requires time. A commitment to assure they will be comfortable and can easily respond. I will need a respite from my work in the city and some undisturbed time to seek their guidance."

He cocked his head. Seconds later he nodded, as if he had been given special insight. "Of course, of course. I should have thought of that. You are relieved from your duties and can seek as you see fit. I will hear of your progress the night before my guests arrive. You are dismissed."

She made her exit relieved but anxious. What did the Voice have in mind?

Did she want to know?

Back in her room anticipation built. Four days. Only her dread of how the Voice planned to use the respite tempered her joy.

Kawit arrived and insisted she hear it all. "Tell me again, exactly what did the master say? I cannot believe he will expect no profit for three days." She lifted her arm to her forehead, closed her eyes and sighed. "Would that I might be granted such a reprieve from Stello." A trace of envy seeped as she clowned.

Word for word, Daphne related the conversation again. "I do not have any idea what Apollo has planned, and I do not know what I am supposed to do. What if I embarrass Patharus in front of his guests?"

Kawit frowned, "No...do not worry, it will not happen. Look how well you have handled your tasks in town. I will ask Jahtel if I can help you get ready that day, do your hair and help you dress."

Daphne chuckled. "That should be easy, shall I wear this tunic and cover it with the black shawl or the other one? That reminds me, I have not yet washed them out, and it is late. We should fetch our bath water…you coming?"

Kawit yawned. "I am tired. I plan to do a quick sink wash and get to bed. Jahtel has us busy from dawn to dusk with his preparations. See you in the morning."

Daphne hugged her friend and set out for the well. It was late, but to not have to hurry into the city in the morning would be a luxury. She stepped into the courtyard and her breath caught. She backed into the hallway and breathed his name. "Nicanor."

Chapter Twenty-Seven

...as the serpent deceived Eve by his craftiness...
– 2 Corinthians 11:3

Daphne peeked around the wall for a few moments. Nicanor stood near the well caught up in conversation with friends. One jostled his shoulder in response to a jibe and the rest joined with laughter and mocked accusations.

Quietly, she retraced her steps. Hurt lumped in her chest as she made her way into the villa. Humph, she guessed he had decided he could mingle with some of his friends.

Back in her room she paced trying to sort anger from pain. After a good while she returned to the courtyard, sure it would be deserted. The moon cast an eerie glow across the vacant tables and cold ovens. The shade trees where the help lingered in the evenings to play with their children or talk, were empty. Barren and quiet at the late hour, its emptiness struck her. Everything lacks purpose and is useless without someone to bring life into it, even people.

She approached the well, aware Nicanor had stood earlier in the same spot. Did he ever think of her? The yawning pit captured her gaze, its murky gloom a perfect match for her mood. She drew her water and returned to her room.

Although she slept fitfully, she woke at her usual time. She determined to stay in bed, but sleep eluded her. She frowned, what good was the opportunity to rise late if you cannot sleep? She swung her feet around and sat up.

Enduring rest will come in good time.

She huffed. What did the Voice mean by that? She took her time to dress, relieved that both tunics had dried overnight. She chose the lighter one. Most of the house servants and field slaves had left the courtyard by the time she arrived.

A lone girl looked up from the table she scrubbed. "About time you showed up Miss Daphne."

Daphne cocked her head and returned the grin. "Anything left, Femi? I know I am awfully late."

Femi stopped scrubbing and put her hands on hips. "Hear you have some days off...some assignment you got."

Daphne pretended to wilt at the mocking chide.

"There is some bread and maybe a bit of goat cheese. You real hungry?"

"No, this will do," She scooped some cheese onto a large chunk of bread. "I think I will take this with me. Bye Femi."

"Bye Daphne and do think of me hard at work in the hot sun while you enjoy your leisure."

Daphne chuckled and waved a goodbye. She started for her room, but midway stopped and looked up into the trees. To her delight, little wind troubled them, and the sky held no threat of fall's frequent rains. It is too beautiful a day to eat inside, where should she go?

The garden. Of course! It would be perfect. Had not Patharus told her to seek as she saw fit? She turned and boldly made her way toward the entrance.

The sun's warmth radiated from the bench. She ate her breakfast and enjoyed the pleasant chirping of corn buntings. From time to time, a brazen wagtail strutted his yellow breast and eyed her with a wary cock of its head. She knelt by the pond and scooped water to satisfy her thirst.

The time has come for you to drink fully of Apollo's divine calling.

Was this the great plan the Voice spoke of, the reason she needed time apart? She returned to the bench and listened.

You have been granted much, but you are not wholeheartedly wedded to our god. Apollo. He is not pleased with your doubts and frequent tendency to vacillate with concern over his methods and purposes.

She writhed in the silence that followed. What more did he want from her?

He desires that you voice your praise and pay homage to his name…that you speak of his greatness to those you meet. He saved you from a life of horror or drudgery and has the ability and power to grant you all you desire, power and riches…even the freedom you long for, but you must worship him alone and fully adhere to his will.

The accusations were true. She had not voiced her trust in Apollo to those who befriended her. Even what she shared with Kawit centered on the problems people brought for counsel. Slaves had their own gods. She could not impose hers upon them, could she? Had she been so caught up in hating Apollo's harshness had she forgotten he alone had rescued her? Freedom. Did he have the power to grant her the freedom she so earnestly desired? The kind Nicanor would soon enjoy?

Would he?

Fall on your face before your god.

She jumped at the forceful command. It vibrated like a never-ending echo throughout her being. Her heart pounded as she slid off the bench and crumpled to the ground.

Worship me; I am god.

A chilling breeze swept over her. She shivered and her voice wavered. "Oh, great Apollo, you who—"

Louder! Apollo deserves great glory and honor, not whispers.

Frightened and uncertain, she recalled how the *pythia* extolled Apollo in the *adytum*. She took a deep breath and mimicked the priestess. Rhythmic chants pealed from her lips and clamored like the gong in front of her mentor's temple.

"Oh, great Apollo, you deserve all my praise. You who delivered and saved me, I revere you great son of Zeus. I declare you to be god over all gods...."

The last phrase brought a gasp that left her mouth ajar. She shrank at a conviction that the declaration was other than truth. The certainty brought her accolades to a halt. Was that not what her servant said years ago about Jesus, her God? That He alone was God over all gods? But Belte's God did not keep the Romans from tearing apart her very own family and selling them to the highest bidders.

Daphne shook off the conflicting thoughts. Apollo was here and now...all she could count on. She repeated his promises again and clung to the first bit of hope she received since she left Delphi. Freedom! Apollo promised to grant her freedom. He was her hope, her help. He deserved her allegiance and worship.

She filled her lungs and began again. Each time she faltered, the Voice urged a deeper commitment. A light rain had moved into the area by the time a release welled inside her. Her mind swam with Apollo's demands and his assurance of freedom, if she held fast and obeyed his commands. She would do what he demanded.

Chapter Twenty-Eight

...give the more earnest heed to the things we have heard.
– Hebrews 2:1

The next day the Voice commanded Daphne repeat her homage and prodded that she speak of the supremacy of Apollo to her fellow slaves. Only by the promise of freedom could she bury her resentment at the persistent goading.

Her first effort brought an uncomfortable encounter with a male slave. "How is it you believe your god is more powerful than Amun, the revered king of the Egyptian gods, or Jupiter, the powerful ruler over Rome? And if Zeus is the most powerful deity, how is it that Rome conquered all of Greece? Is he not Apollo his son?"

Tell him you have been given a special insight into the world of the gods. Tell him if he believes the overseer will soon give him a higher position.

She repeated the message. The man's eyes narrowed. She waited until a glimmer of hope challenged his doubts. He slunk off, his brows pinched.

She sighed and wished she were more effective. Secretly, she avoided the busiest mealtimes to avoid further conversations, or a chance run in with Nicanor. She need not have worried...he was nowhere to be seen.

That night after the house had eaten, Kawit lined up to fill her plate. "One of Jahtel's assistants told me Nicanor is busy with the arrangements for the banquet." She turned and gave her a guarded look. "You favor him, do you not?"

Daphne turned to hide the denial that reddened her cheeks. "No, no! I happened to notice he has not been with the young men that usually eat together."

Kawit snickered and returned her attention to the food.

Daphne gave her friend's shoulder a playful push. "Go on with you,"

The morning of the third day, after breakfast, she decided to take advantage of her brief freedom and explore the area that surrounded Patharus' estate. Where should she go? She wished the colorful coast of Neapolis and the beautiful marsh she admired were closer. To the east lay the Pindus Mountains. Where could she go…anywhere but the city.

She packed her parcel then passed through the house gate and cast a glance at the distant mountain crest. "I guess the foothills will have to do." A wave of homesickness for Delphi and Mt. Parnassus blurred the unfamiliar skyline. She lifted her chin. "No, today is to be a time of joy, not sadness."

The minute the manor passed from sight, she set her things on a stump and loosened her hair. It bounced around her shoulders as if it too cherished their freedom. She laughed and shook the curls from her face and began her adventure.

To have no destination or time constraints perked her senses. She started down the path with bits of her grandmother's songs on her lips and danced as she once did on a pilgrimage to the temple. Tiny brown squirrels scurried up trees in protest. Lush green ferns that grew beyond a gorge on one side of the path, resembled lacy tablecloths that beckoned she pause and enjoy their beauty.

She slowed to catch her breath. "Freedom, this is how it felt!" The fresh mountain air coaxed deep breaths that left in grateful sighs. "Somehow, someday, I will have it again...I know I will." Her voice fell to a whisper. "I have to...I will die without it."

With each crest of a foothill the lack of agenda urged her on. She finally stopped at the base of a mound that sloped to the bank of a creek. A sizable shelf of solid rock hewn by the stream projected out over the water.

She refilled her jug and climbed onto the ledge, surprised how the heights revealed how far she had traveled. The warm fall sun and the wind that rustled a stand of poplar trees, soothed her soul. She moved closer to the edge to eat her lunch and listen to the current as it surged over the rocks.

Zeus formed this valley and mountain…he holds it and all life in his hands. His son, Apollo holds your future too. If you obey him and —

"No, I do not want to hear anymore. This is my day and I want to be left alone."

And so shall you be.

She sniffed at the ominous message but hoped she had not thwarted Apollo's promise of freedom. A stillness encompassed her whole being as she leaned backwards and enjoyed the solitude. The sight of clouds blown by the wind brought a scoff at her grandmother's stories of Apollo's travel beyond them. She fantasized how she would regain her freedom and travel back to Athens and search for her family.

Nicanor's warm smile invaded her thoughts. For a moment she allowed herself to imagine being betrothed to him, but quickly forced herself back to reality.

The sun's mild rays and the water that babbled created an aura of lazy contentment. The sound rekindled the memory of the river in Delphi where she once pretended to be the nymph that became her namesake. The warm surface lulled her into a dreamlike state where time stood still. How far she had walked that morning and how long it would take to return, did not enter her mind.

The cackle of a pair of Eurasian jays broke her reverie as their rusty heads and blue wings darted from tree to tree. She stretched and hopped down from her perch, surprised at how close the sun was to the mountain top. She upbraided herself for forgetting how quickly dusk fell at this time of year. But she could surely make it back before dark.

She refilled her jug. A second look at the sun challenged her calculations. Again, she assured herself there was time, but set off at a brisk pace.

The wind shifted and blew clouds over the mountains. It pushed her along, grateful it was at her back and no thunderheads had formed. Her thoughts tumbled like the leaves that swirled across her path, piled with concern for tomorrow's banquet.

Her mind sped to how she would keep her promise to satisfy Patharus if a guest's future was sad or horrible. There you go again. Can you not remember it is not you that sees into the future or knows what to say? She ducked a low-hanging branch. Apollo promised to give me what I need...I must trust him.

At a fork in the path, she bent to adjust her sandal and studied both directions. Which way led to the estate? Each resembled the other and nothing looked familiar. Hills on both sides blended into one mass of rock and trees that prevented a view into the distance. She stammered. "Apollo, which way should I go?"

Silence.

She waited. Where was he? "I do not know which way to go, Apollo, please..." Her voice caught. "Please, help me."

Again, she heard nothing. She looked at the horizon, the sun hung just above the farthest foothills. Once it set, darkness would quickly follow. Resigned to being on her own, she shrugged. "Alright, I will find my own way." Both probably lead past the estate. She straightened her shoulders and started out but kept a sharp eye for anything she might have seen earlier. In less than an hour, she came upon another fork. Her hand flew to her lips. She did not remember the path splitting like this...she must have taken the wrong one.

She looked back and her heart sank. There would not be enough daylight to retrace her steps.

Chapter Twenty-Nine

Do not be overcome by evil.
– Romans 12:21

The sun had yet to set but the hills diffused much of its light. Dark shadows cast by the heightened terrain swept deep into the gorge that followed the path.

Fear raked like a predator's talons into Daphne's chest and riveted her to the spot. To be lost overnight in the hills terrified her. Shivers swept her spine as the wind heightened. A desperate plea quivered on her lips. "Please, please Apollo, send your messenger to help me."

Silence devoured all sound but that familiar, evil snicker. She ran until her sides ached. Finally, she stopped and stooped over, hands on her thighs as she struggled to catch her breath. Where were the landmarks she hardly noted hours before? "What shall I do…what shall I do?"

Something crashed through the stand of Cypress trees she had just passed, rousing a flock of crows. She jerked as the birds took flight, their objections as zealous as the offensive crow who desecrated her grandmother's funeral bier. Her hand flew to her lips. "A wild boar! What if it's a wild boar?"

Stories of aggressive boar attacks and their vicious tempers spawned an adrenalin rush that propelled her feet in a rush down the path.

Branches avoided earlier now whipped her upper body while humped tree roots snagged her sandals. Blinded by tears, she tripped, sprawled to the ground, cut her knee, and sobbed.

Apart from me you can do nothing…do you still wish to be left alone?

Relieved to hear anything, she pushed up onto her knees. Regrets over her caustic response hours earlier taunted. Her head fell into her hands. "I am sorry…truly sorry. Please, please help me."

You are helpless apart from Apollo, as lost as you are now. He is your guide in everything. You must always listen to my counsel and honor him.

"Yes…please, I am sorry! I will, I promise."

Bow and speak to him of your undying devotion. Perhaps he will forgive you and lead you to safety.

Smugness buried beneath the fake concern, mocked, but she did not hesitate to prostrate herself on the ground. Pain seared as her injured knee hit the rocky surface. She shifted her weight to the other knee but could not keep her balance. Each time she wobbled it throbbed afresh.

She babbled whatever came to mind. "Oh, great Apollo, please forgive me. You are the great and mighty warrior, the god of the bow. In your light blessings fall upon our people and on their crops. You are the god of music, benevolent and faithful to judge fairly. I give you my life and loyalty. Please help me. I pledge complete devotion to your cause."

Darkness fell and except for an occasional break in the clouds, the moon shed no light. By the time the Voice bid her rise, the temperature had dropped, and she wished she had brought her shawl.

Take the path to the left and keep left at every turn.

She hobbled as fast as she could. A near miss down the gully stressed she keep an awareness of the of the pebbles beneath her sandals to know she held to the path. No turns had yet to present themselves. Had she missed any in the dark? Every sound caused her heart to plummet. She stumbled again but avoided more injury to her knee. Each time the moon broke through she ran as fast as she could, but the pain increased and forced her to walk. She wiped at the dark streak that ran down her leg with the hem of her tunic and winced at the sting.

Something large crossed several yards in front of her. She jerked to a stop and stifled a scream. Every nerve tensed as she stared into the darkness. Nothing moved. Was it hidden behind the thicket, ready to attack?

Despite her pain she raced past the spot. Her eyes remained on the place where the creature crossed, relieved darkness covered whatever might yet decide to follow. Her chest heaved. She could not see her feet let alone the path. "Oh please, where am I? Am I going in the right direction?"

Trust me. Have I ever failed you? Just keep going.

She swallowed her reluctance, comforted to not be alone…even with a presence she could not see. Still, she jumped at every sound and pictured danger behind every object. A final fork rounded a mound at the bottom of a foothill and torches lit up the distant skyline.

A sob caught in her throat. Home…it must be. She whispered her thanks to Apollo, grateful for his forgiveness. She staggered on, thankful her knees did not buckle.

Apollo is your hope and protection. There is great danger in scorning him. Beware, least he leaves you to your own resources again.

She nodded at the gruff rebuke, ran, and stumbled through the entrance and onto the path where Nicanor paced.

He grabbed her shoulders. "Daphne, where have you been? You should have been in hours ago." He glanced over her head. "Has someone chased you?"

She shook her head.

"Patharus asked about your return shortly before dark. I had to tell him you had not yet returned. Stello was ready to send out a search party an hour ago, but no one knew where you had gone or if you intended to come back. You are lucky. The master made him wait, said he had given you special time away from your duties."

Her heart sank, she was in trouble. She looked up at Nicanor and burst into tears.

"What, what is it?"   He checked behind her again.

Her knees buckled but he caught her against his chest.

"I am so sorry…so frightened. Lost in the hills, darkness fell, and I heard strange animal sounds, so I ran and ran." Reasons gushed between sobs she could not control. She knew she should back away, but she could not find willpower to forgo the comfort of his arms.

"Let us sit in the courtyard a moment." He lifted her into his arms and carried her to a nearby bench. Her head rested against his shoulder, too worn to object.

He gently sat her down. She tried to sit erect but wove to one side. He pulled her to his shoulder and steadied her with his arm.

She struggled to catch her breath, "I am so embarrassed, please forgive me, I…."

"Nonsense, you have had quite a fright. What in the world were you doing out in the hills alone? Do you not know how dangerous that can be? Besides wild boars and mountain lions, there are marauders, groups of men who would think nothing of robbing you or…well a woman is far from safe around them."

She nodded. "Patharus said I could seek, I mean go wherever I wished. I wanted to be alone, to be free of — "

"That kind of freedom could get you killed! I am amazed you found your way home in the dark." The concern behind his reprimand swept like a gentle wave that tugged and soothed at the same time. "Would you give your life for one day of freedom?"

She shook her head and continued to lean against his shoulder. He ran a protective hand over her upper arm from time to time, but neither spoke nor moved. Her shudders finally ceased, but it took all her willpower to push herself upright. "I had no intention of being out there after dark. Thank you for your help. I will be alright now."

Light from the torches highlighted his chiseled features. He pushed a disheveled lock of hair from her face and held her captive with his gaze. His fingers lingered as he gently wiped a tear-stained smudge from beneath her eye. Both spoke at once.

"I am so sorry about...." At the same instant, they stopped and grinned at their mutual desire to set things straight.

He took her hand and spoke first. "I do not know what changes my life will take Daphne, but I want us to remain close friends."

She did not dare speak. A friend, he called her a friend. Maybe he did see her as more than a slave. She grew desperate to escape the pull of those piercing blue eyes. She jumped to her feet, "I must go."

"Oh," she gasped and grabbed her knee.

"What is it? What is wrong with your leg?" He sat her down again and looked at her knee. "You have a nasty gash, did you fall?"

"I tried to run…it was dark…I fell."

"That needs attention. Here, lean on me, our physician needs to look at it." Nicanor put his arm around her waist and helped her walk. "Patharus brought the man here years ago, He is well schooled in the art of medicine. I know he has a salve that will help it heal."

Not far into the courtyard they came upon a scowling Jahtel, hands clenched on his hips.

Chapter Thirty

And we will take our revenge on him.
– Jeremiah 20:10

Jahtel's eyes darted from Nicanor to Daphne then settled on his son. "What have we here?"

Nicanor ignored his irate tone. He eased Daphne onto a nearby bench and turned back to his father. "Daphne fell and cut her knee. It is not good. Dirt and bits of gravel are deeply embedded. It needs to be cleansed and swathed with that ointment Halaten makes. Without it, I am afraid it will fester and not heal properly. Will you stay with her while I fetch him?" He did not wait for a reply, nor see Jahtel's reluctant sneer, but left for the healer.

Daphne brushed at the dirt-crusted scratches on her arms and legs. To smooth her torn tunic proved as futile as her wish rain would douse the torches and shield her from the scrutiny of this man who held power to decide her fate.

He had not moved. With even less success, she tugged at the hair that hung in tangles across her face. The pain in her knee paled in comparison to the silence that hung like an impenetrable wall. It took every ounce of her will to ignore waves of anxiety that rose as she imagined the punishments he probably had in mind.

He stared hard at her with one elbow perched on an arm that pressed firmly to his waist, and tapped his knuckles against his teeth.

She lowered her eyes What was he thinking?

He cleared his throat as if about to make an announcement. "I am aware the master gave you time away from your duties, but I do not believe it granted you permission to leave the estate."

She squirmed at his disapproval. Did he expect an answer?

Nicanor's admission stabbed at the forefront of her mind…*my father has asked me to avoid people of a lower station.* Was that behind Jahtel's annoyance?

He continued to stare. "Well?"

She swallowed the urge to justify her actions and kept her voice to a near whisper. "The master said I could seek the gods as needed. He did not set any limits on where I might go."

She hated that her voice shook.

He shifted his stance and cocked his head. "I believe you were told to always be in before dark. Perhaps you are unaware of the dangers of time alone in the hills after nightfall." He scowled at her silence.

His pretense of concern did not mask his intent. She shivered, his accusations matched the chilly air that seeped through her tunic. She swiped at the goose bumps that climbed her upper arms. If it were not for Nicanor, how might his father deal with her?

Instinct told her not to cower but to answer with calm respect. She raised her head but did not look directly at him. "I am truly sorry. "I did not mean to…" He huffed his doubt. Sheer determination kept her voice serene. Perhaps a reminder of Patharus' permission would help. "I wanted to be where I could be alone to seek the gods, as I was instructed. The day was so beautiful, I stopped by a rock by a stream to meditate and lost track of time." She did not know where to stop. "I started back but could not remember which way I came. It was too late to turn back and I, I…."

She finally looked up at him. His sneer made her flinch. Did he plan to beat her?

Nicanor called to the physician who hustled but a few steps behind and gestured at her knee. "Here she is, Halaten. It is a nasty cut."

The physician knelt in front of her and plopped a tapestry bag near her feet. A quick scan of the wound sent a glance at Nicanor. "Fetch me some clean water and cloths. And grab a shawl, she is cold." He turned to Jahtel. "Good evening, Master Jahtel. Would you be so kind as to bring one of the torches a little closer?"

Jahtel balked briefly, but complied.

A nearly inaudible chant rose from Halaten's lips as he waved his hands over her knee and extolled the god he regarded as healer. A sincere request followed on a whisper. "Grant me wisdom and power to follow your lead."

His smile eased her anxiety. "So young lady, how did this happen?"

Tell him your god is Apollo and it is he who will heal to your knee.

"I panicked and ran. It was dark and I fell, but my god will—"

"At a good clip, I would guess. But do not be concerned, the skin that covers one's kneecap is unusually tough, enough to protect what lies behind. Did you twist it when you fell?"

"I do not think so. I only remember that I got back up and ran as fast as I could, but Apollo will—"

"Good. You would not have been able to run if you had wrenched it."

Just as Jahtel secured the torch to a nearby pole Nicanor arrived, his breath in heaves. "Here are the cloths and water." He draped the shawl around her shoulders. "I will be right back. Patharus insisted I inform him as soon as you returned." She nodded and gave up on the Voice's command.

The physician carefully swung Daphne's leg closer to the light. Using a flattened stick, he probed the wound as gently as possible. "It does not appear to have chipped the bone, but I am afraid there is a good bit of dirt and gravel ground beneath the surface." He looked straight at her. "It is going to sting, but it must be cleansed."

Daphne clamped her teeth on her lower lip, determined not to cry out.

Halaten flushed the dirt and dried blood with the water before he wiped the wound with a wet cloth. She bit her lip and clutched the shawl, grateful for something to hang on to. Would he never finish?

Nicanor returned and stood behind her, his hands on her shoulders. Jahtel craned his neck as Halaten pushed deep into the gash. Blood flowed and Daphne turned pale. The physician squeezed her hand. "Do not be alarmed. Bleeding is a good thing. It helps wash the wound from places I am not be able to reach."

Jahtel's jaw twitched with impatience. "Are we about finished?"

Halaten covered his exasperation with his superior. "We are nearly done."

Nicanor glared at his father whose face grew more purple by the minute. He turned his attention back to Daphne and winced at her every cringe.

Nicanor signaled Halaten. "How bad is it?"

He shook his head. "Do not worry. It will heal. She will be good as new in a week or two."

Jahtel gripped his son's shoulder and gestured for him to follow. They moved a short distance from the bench. "Nicanor, it is time to make the nightly rounds. You get started, and I will join you shortly." His expression left no room for debate.

Nicanor scowled at his father's ill covered intentions. "I will as soon as Halaten is finished."

The physician applied salve to her wound, placed a splint and bound a bandage around her knee. "That should do it." He fished in his bag and handed her a tiny cloth sack. "Take some of this powder with water for the pain, it will also help you sleep." He gathered his things and stood. "Try not to bend that knee, and do not let water get to it for several days, that gash needs time to mend. You can change the binding day after tomorrow, come see me and I will help you."

Her eyes teared at his gracious manner. "Thank you for your help, it was very kind of you." Nicanor touched the physician's shoulder. "Thanks, Halaten."

Nicanor stepped close to Daphne and took her hand. "You do what he says and take care of that leg, promise? I must go attend to things."

After Nicanor left, she hobbled stiff-legged toward her room.

Jahtel's tenor did not softened, "I will send Kawit to help you."

Daphne turned to face him. "Thank you. I am so sorry to have been such trouble."

He waved her off with a smirk.

She winced. Had plans to punish her began to hatch.

Chapter Thirty-One

A friend loves at all times.
– Proverbs 17:17

Kawit arrived moments after Daphne eased herself onto her mat. "Daphne...where in the world were you? Jahtel ordered me to get up and help you...even allowed me to bring a lamp."

She fastened it on a wall hanger. "What is going on...hey what is wrong with your leg? And those scratches...and your hair? It is a mess. What happened?" She dropped beside her and inspected her arms and legs. "Look at you!"

Moved by her friend's concern, Daphne burst into tears. Kawit pulled her to her chest and rocked her in her arms. "Are you alright, did someone attack you? Are you hurt, besides your knee?"

Daphne snuffed her tears and shook her head. "No, I am alright. It was so, so awful."

As her misadventure poured out in nonsensical bursts, Kawit stroked her hair and whispered her sympathy. At last, she quieted and Kawit pulled at a thorn-covered twig wound firmly into Daphne's curls. "And was this the fashion of the day for your outing?" The piece of a bramble bush brought a mutual chuckle. "Thank the gods you are alright. Come, let us get you cleaned up."

"The physician said I could not get my knee wet for several days or the wound would not close properly."

Kawit scratched her head. "Hmmm, how are we going to wash your hair without getting you into the tub? The wash bowl is too small."

"Maybe I can lean over the tub, with your help."

"But your knee, you cannot lean on it or bend it."

"Right, but my hair is awful. I cannot wash it and oh…oh, Kawit! She smacked her forehead. Tomorrow is the master's banquet! What am I going to do? He expects me to entertain his guests."

Kawit shut her eyes and leaned into her hand. "Daphne, your timing is terrible." Neither spoke for a moment. "Alright, this is not the end of the world, we will think of something. Jahtel already promised I could help you get ready tomorrow. What you need now is a good night's sleep. I will fetch enough water for a sink bath, and we will worry about your hair tomorrow."

Daphne grimaced. How could she possibly face Patharus after today? Kawit was right, she needed to sleep. With her help, she bathed, surprised at the sting of angry red welts on her arms and legs. In her terror she had felt none of them.

"Do not worry, things always work out. I will be by as soon as you wake, and we will figure it out…alright?"

Daphne forced a smile. "Thank you, dear friend. What would I do without you?"

Kawit's eyes shone as she lifted the lamp from its stand. "Just remember, I am going to collect one day."

Gratitude filled Daphne's eyes. As promised, the powder the physician provided reduced the pain. Exhausted, she fell asleep.

She awoke with a start, surprised her room was as bright as midday. She pushed herself up on her elbows and rolled to sit up. Pain surged up her leg and brought a loud groan.

Kawit brushed through the door. "You are awake. I have peeked in for the last two hours. It is midmorning already. I will be right back."

Daphne rubbed her eyes. She could not believe she slept so long…it must have been that powder Halaten gave her. She put her weight on her good leg and tried to push herself into a stand but lost her balance.

Kawit arrived in time to catch her. "Here, hang onto me. To get up and down will be tricky until you can bend your knee." She helped her over to her bench. "I saved you some breakfast." She unfolded the cloth on Daphne's lap and sat beside her while she ate.

"Thank you, I am hungry," her words muffled by a large chunk of bread.

"I am not surprised, when did you eat last?"

"Must have been lunch yesterday. I found the prettiest spot. It was near a ledge that overlooked a stream. We should go there someday."

Kawit huffed. "After what you went through you would go back?"

"But the fault was not in the place. It was my careless loss of time."

"Well, it may be a while before another opportunity comes. Jahtel is not happy with you."

Sparks popped like live embers from Daphne's eyes. She grasped her friend's arm. "Do you think he will have Stello beat me?"

She covered Daphne's hand with her own. "No, no, I am sure he will not. Before he waved me off, I overheard Nicanor tell him he had smoothed things over with Patharus…that you had no intention of disobeying the rules but got lost. But if I were you, I would be careful. You do not want Stello or Jahtel for an enemy."

"Oh, how could I have been so irresponsible? I could be in such trouble. Where was my mind?"

Kawit cocked her head. "Well, I would guess you were distracted by the joy of a whole day to yourself…or maybe you unleashed your pledge to forget and mooned over a young man whose name I know."

She rolled her eyes. "Oh you. I am not…."

Kawit grinned. "I know, I know, but let us get you out of your nightdress and figure out how we can wash your hair. Patharus may want to see you before the banquet, and you sure cannot go like you are."

Memories of Delphi's servants returned as she watched Kawit fetch the water and fill her tub. Most of them had served her because they had to. Kawit followed orders, but she did it out of love. Daphne's eyes welled, humbled by her friend's unselfishness. "You are such a good friend."

"Hey, this is much more interesting than my usual duties. Let me see, first we need to wash your hair, somehow." Her mouth twisted to one side as she leaned her chin into her fist.

"Maybe I could bend on one knee and still keep the other one straight...."

"Oh no. We will not take a chance you might slip and open that wound." She stared at the floor. "I have it! I will pile some pillows at the end of your mat, and you can hang your head over them. I will put the tub under your head to catch the runoff and pour water from the pitcher to wet and rinse it."

She grinned. "You are so resourceful."

"Tell it to Patharus next time you go to his office. *I* never get called there." She ran off to fetch more pillows.

Daphne called after her. "I may just do that."

It took some doing to arrange the pillows to the right height and get Daphne into position without bending her knee, but they managed. Soon her dark hair shone.

She beamed as Kawit helped her sit up "Oh, thank you. I feel like a new woman."

A woman. *...a woman is far from safe....*

Nicanor's words brought a smile and sent her thoughts adrift.

Kawit finished towel-drying her hair. "What made you smile?" When she did not respond she nudged her. "Daphne? Are you still in there? "

"What? What did you say?"

Kawit laughed and tapped the top of Daphne's head. "What is going on in there, anyway?"

Chapter Thirty-Two

...do I seek to please men?
– Galatians 1:10

Daphne wiped the grin from her face. "Oh, nothing. Tell me Kawit, did you ever ask Jahtel about something for me to wear tonight? All I have is that heavy dark shawl that covers my tunic. Patharus did not insist I wear it."

"No...he has had us so busy, I forgot." She gestured at Daphne's torn, blood-stained tunic. "Maybe it is just as well...you will never wear that one again. Let me get you started on your sink-bath, and I will dump the tub and see what I can find."

"Do you think there is any chance Jahtel would let me have a longer one...just for tonight? I would love to hide this bandage."

Kawit shrugged and sprinted for the door. "I will ask."

By the time she returned Daphne had finished her bath. Her knee throbbed so she hobbled over to her bench, careful to keep her leg straight. Kawit held up a garment and dangled a newer pair of sandals when she returned.

Daphne arched her neck to see what she had gleaned from the storage room. "You found something... did you get a longer *peplos*?"

Kawit shrugged. "I am sorry. I found Jahtel knee-deep in arrangements for tonight's seating.

Something was amiss and he was in a foul mood. He glared and said, 'She will wear what every other slave wears.' I knew better than to try to change his mind."

"Thanks, I know you tried. No one will care what I wear anyway. Let me see what you found."

Kawit showed her the tunic. It was light blue, constructed exactly like every tunic they were allotted. Both girls looked it over and sighed. Kawit held up a matching shawl. "I almost forgot this…could not believe I found one in the same color. It will hide some of those scratches"

Daphne winced. "I had not thought of that."

Kawit laid the tunic across the mat. "Let me get started on your hair," Neither spoke as she worked the tangles from Daphne's hair. While it was still damp, she plaited it into sleek braids and skillfully wound them in an arrangement around Daphne's head. At each temple, she left a ringlet that hung just above her shoulder. She stepped back to admire her work. "That should do it."

Daphne patted it with care. "I wish I had a mirror. It must look great." She pushed herself up until she stood. "Thank you, dear friend…again."

Kawit brushed off the thanks and picked up the tunic. "Here, I will help you put this on." She smiled. "You look wonderful…but I am not sure that is good, since you will be in a room full of lecherous old men."

Daphne sighed. "I have no choice."

"I know…none of us do. Here, sit down and relax. I am going to fetch us something to eat. Patharus probably will not call for you until the men have had plenty to eat and drink. You may be in for a long night."

She returned and sat cross-legged on the mat while they ate a late lunch.

Someone called from the hall. "Kawit, master Jahtel has need of you. He said you should be finished in there by now."

Daphne's brows twitched.

Kawit squeezed her arm. "Do not worry. You will do fine. I had better help with your sandals. I do not know if I will get back and doubt you will be able to put the right one on without bending your knee."

The curtain swung to a shut behind Kawit. Now what should she do? She hobbled over to her stand and mixed a small amount of the physician's powder. She could not show up half drugged.

Before she could lower herself to her mat, a voice sounded outside her door. "The master requests that you come to his receiving room."

She recognized the voice of the young slave who had been kind to her. "Thank you, I will come right away." She wished she remembered his name.

"Jahtel said you might need some help. I will accompany you."

"Oh, I can walk by myself, but it may take me a bit longer." She draped the shawl over her shoulders and stepped into the hall. "See." She smiled. "I must simply swing my leg to the side. It is fine if I do not bend it."

He followed her down the corridor, ready should she wobble. She thanked him and was ushered into the room.

Patharus noticed her struggle to work her way to his desk. "Ah, Daphne, I was told of your misfortune. How is the knee?"

She kept her eyes lowered. "I am sure it will heal, my lord. I am so sorry to have inconvenienced the household."

"I will expect you to remember the rules in the future. Failure to arrive back to the estate before dark might lead to…ah, an unfortunate misunderstanding. You have the freedom to come and go but you are not above discipline, so I am glad you arrived without…." He cleared his throat.

She froze. Without what? Had they really wondered if she tried to run away?

His voice softened. "We were all relieved you found your way back and were safe." Oblivious to her uneasiness, he continued. "My guests will be arriving in a few hours, and I trust your time away from the city prepared you to entertain them." It was more than a question.

Entertainment? Is that what he really thinks to speak for the gods amounts to? What if she said no? She did not know what might happen. She did not know what she should say or do if someone's future was full of pain or even death. She was terrified because she had no control over what the Voice might say or do. No! No! No!

She brought herself up short. Enough. She was just grateful he did not plan to punish her. "I believe I am ready, my lord. I have spent many hours seeking the gods and I am sure you will be pleased."

He rose from his chair. "Good, good. I knew I could count on you." He glanced at her bandaged leg. "I see you cannot bend your knee." He rubbed his chin. "I think I will set you up on some cushions in that far corner where my guests can confer with you at will. And it would be better if you wore a longer *chiton* to cover your bandages. It would be less of a distraction. I will see that one is sent to your room."

She nodded and expected to be dismissed.

"One more thing, I want you here near the start of the evening. The guests will arrive long before dinner. It is possible some may want to seek your skills before the meal is served. You may eat along with us. I will send word at the proper time."

She backed awkwardly from the room. To her surprise, the young slave waited to accompany her. She took his offer and leaned on his arm. At her door she waved him off with another heartfelt thanks.

She sat on her bench and wished the night were over. With little more than a whisper, "Great Apollo, I give you praise for your faithful answers each time I have asked you to speak into the life of those who seek your wisdom. Please be with me tonight and give me words that will not cause distress or…"

You will speak the words Apollo gives you. It is not your concern over whether they cause distress. You are not in control, I am, and I will speak what is required. Be sure you point each one to our god and give him the homage he deserves.

"But…" She stopped, reminded afresh of her vow never to cross Apollo again.

Kawit charged into the room. "Who you talking to?"

"Oh, you startled me. No one…what is it you have?"

She grinned and held out her arm. "A long *chiton*! You are not going to believe this, but Jahtel shoved this at me just minutes ago and told me to take it to you. I can tell you the man looked agitated. Do you know what changed his mind? Did you get Patharus to agree you should wear a longer dress?" Her eyes danced with expectation.

"It was not my idea…honest." She related how the decision came about.

Kawit choked back a giggle. "Oh, this is good… but I am afraid you lost points with Jahtel again." Her expression sobered. "He is sure to assume you went to Patharus with the request he denied and will see it as undermining his authority."

Daphnes eyes widened. "I cannot win! How can I make him see it was not my doing?"

"I do not think you can. Let us hope the truth comes out somehow. He would not believe it was not your idea from either of us. Come, let us get you changed."

Chapter Thirty-Three

He does not abhor evil.
– Psalm 36:4

Kawit unfolded the dress. "I would wager this *peplos* belonged to the master's wife. It is of that lightweight wool we are not allowed to wear… how lovely."

Daphne fingered the dress and smoothed it with her hands. Her voice shook. "I had a dress like this once, out of this fabric. I wore it to the temple the day I became a full-fledged member. My mother she…." Her eyes filled.

Kawit hugged her shoulders. "Wear it for her. You will look beautiful."

"It is alright…it was a long time ago."

Careful not to undo Daphne's hair, Kawit helped her slip the cream-colored garment over her head. It fell in graceful folds that ended inches above her feet.

Kawit backed a few steps. "Perfect. It hides the bandage and could not be a better fit. He did not offer a shawl." She picked up the pale blue one. "This will complement it well enough if you want it."

Daphne reached for the shawl and ran her hands down the skirt "It is so beautiful."

"I cannot stay, or you know who will be after me, but I will see you get something to eat." She grabbed Daphne and looked her in the eye. "You will do just fine. I will call upon Hathor to bless you. Do not let anyone intimidate you. This is your *destiny*." She smiled, flashed the sign of her god, and dashed from the room.

Rather than deal with unknowns at the banquet, Daphne ate the food sent to her room. The sun was still bright. It could be hours before she was called. She longed for the peace and distractions of the garden but did not dare miss her call. She eyed her mat and decided resting her knee would be best. She backed to her mat, swung out her stiff knee and eased herself down.

Lying so as to not disturb her coiffure, she closed her eyes and tried to think of anything but what the evening might bring. Despite a small dose of the powder, sleep eluded her. Her thoughts ran to Nicanor. His big night. She wondered how he felt about it.

She tried to imagine him as Patharus' son. Would his newly acquired status separate him from longtime friends he grew up with? Would he miss their easy relationships, lively banter, and camaraderie? A future she struggled to deny, pricked her conscience. What did she hope he felt?

Her desire that she and Nicanor remain on equal ground spawned guilt. How could she want less for him?

She closed her mind to the 'what ifs' and let her thoughts drift to the task ahead. What kind of counsel might a guest desire? Surely, in front of one another, they would not request anything underhanded like to cheat or take advantage of less fortunate people…would they?

Patharus called it entertainment. She sniffed. Did he really see seeking the wisdom of Apollo as something to enjoy? How naïve and uninformed he and those who surrounded him are, blind to the intentions of the gods. Like I was, ignorant of the unseen dangers in opening oneself to the spirit world. A recurring wish she could relive the last years of her life, passed, unspoken. They are Romans. They do not understand Apollo's ability to control the destiny of nations or influence a man's fate. How could they, none of their gods have such power.

She listened but received no more instructions from the Voice. Her mind journeyed through dozens of possibilities. Each distracted her to another. No. She thought. She can only do what she is told. All Patharus probably has in mind is to indulge those interested, no matter how foolish.

The call to report startled her. Had she dozed?

She scooted as best as she could down the hall. Patharus' personal servant pointed to the out-of-the-way corner. "You are to seat yourself there, where the cushions are piled."

She moved slowly to minimize her limp, surprised a crowd already gathered. The first time she entered this room was like yesterday and yet forever. She had not noticed the plush couches with tasseled cushions that lined the walls, or how the settees swooped in the center to enable a servant to serve the occupant from behind. Patharus' exquisite taste never ceased to impress her, but none more than the presence of the man himself.

She found her way to the assigned place, grateful he appeared too busy to notice her. She squeezed behind a boisterous group and eased herself down upon the cushions. Several eyed her with lustful glances and a few made crude remarks. She ignored them, lowered her head, and folded her hands in her lap.

Rakish laughter from those near the wine *krat'er* soon waylaid their sinister interest. A shiver convulsed her. A man staggered and stepped on the hem of her *peplos*, his sloshed wine left a stain on a pillow near her feet. She inched as far as possible into the corner.

She avoided every guest's gaze. To her relief, only an occasional glance swept her corner. Had Patharus forgotten she was there, or at best forgot to inform his guests of her presence?

She took in the activities when no one was nearby. Where was Nicanor? This was probably as unfamiliar to him as it is to her.

She peeked at Jahtel. Engrossed in a flurry of refills at the *krat'er*, he evidenced no sign of regret or sadness over the transfer of his son's identity. Could her father have released Alexander or Theo to the care and upbringing of another? Sons were a man's heritage.

The room was half full before she spotted Nicanor slipping into the room. She followed him with her eyes. I wonder if he has had second thoughts about this arrangement.

He looked as uncomfortable as she felt.

Chapter Thirty-Four

My sorrow is continually before me.
– Psalm 38:17

Nicanor stood close to a wall. He took in the crowd, grateful Patharus was busy with his guests.

Two Romans in dress uniforms were ushered into the host's presence. Patharus reached out a hand, "Welcome, welcome." Behind the Romans, a wealthy Greek merchant waited to be greeted. Alert to their master's plan, the servants subtly steered every arrival toward the *krat'er*, freeing Partharus to personally welcome each guest. The room soon filled with business associates, magistrates, and friends eager to delight in his generous hospitality.

At his nod servants scurried to set tables beside each couch. Wary of spilling on a guest, they were mindful as they filled the individual basins with citrus water in preparation of the need to cleanse fingers between courses. Wide-spouted ewers to hold the wine were placed on each table, but the *promoma*, the herbed wine would not be poured until just before the main meal.

Jahtel stood at the *krat'er*, where he lavished a gracious welcome along with the wine. Nicanor noticed his father's theatrics. Had he seen him?

Guests were in constant motion. Each moved from group to group, always with a cup in hand.

Voices escalated in proportion to the number of emptied vessels. Flute girls arrived and their music added to the challenge of hearing any announcements.

At a lull in Jahtel's animated interaction with guests, Nicanor wandered over to him. "Well, Father, the time has come, I hope that you have —"

Jahtel scowled. "Do not be seen here. Remember you are no longer part of the help. Think about who you are about to become." He jerked his head toward Patharus. "You need to be there beside him." With that he recast a smile and swung his attention to a newly arrived guest.

Nicanor's face fell. He backed like a scolded child and waited until Patharus beckoned his staff to pour the herbed wine. He walked over and stood at his right, hands clasped behind his back. Everyone held up their cup in anticipation of the opening toast. The room grew quiet as their host worked his way into the center of the crowd.

Patharus' gaze encompassed the entire room "Gentlemen, good friends, and constituents, tonight as you have honored me with your presence, I invite you to celebrate with me this very important occasion. The wait-period has passed, and I am pleased to announce the official sanction of my newly adopted son." He reached for Nicanor's hand and held it up. "I present to you Nicanor, from this day forth my son and legitimate heir."

Nicanor glanced at his new father. He knew this moment would come but could hardly believe it arrived. Patharus' eyes welled as he put his hand on Nicanor's shoulder. A lump rose in his own throat. He returned the smile and nodded at the man he had admired for years, awed that yesterday he was a slave and today he was the man's son and heir. The reality he would one day manage this enormous estate sent chills down his spine.

Cheers broke across the room. Amplias raised his glass as they waned. "Friends, raise your cups with me. I propose a toast to our friend Patharus and Nicanor, his beloved son."

Guests noisily complied. Someone slipped a silver cup into Nicanor's hand. Amplias continued, enjoying the limelight. "May your union be one of great enjoyment and fulfillment. May the gods bless you with many years of prosperity and abundance. May you enjoy the blessings of numerous descendants and great peace in your household."

Shouts of "hear, hear," concurred and led to one toast after another. Nicanor received the good wishes with gracious bows. As the night wore on, his frozen smile left his eyes.

He studied his birth father. Jahtel beamed. He made no effort to make eye contact with his son. Nicanor's jaw flinched, and he shifted his gaze. Patharus maneuvered him around the room. Joyfully he introduced him as his son and heir.

At last, the congratulations died, and the hubbub ebbed. Guests gravitated to the couches as servants set out the required bread and platters of meats and vegetables. Nicanor sat at Patharus' right, surrounded by Roman officials.

He ate very little and refused much of the never-ending wine. Awed at the magnitude of all Patharus arranged, he surveyed the room. His gaze passed the corner where Daphne sat, backed, and held fast. His jaw dropped. What was she doing here?

Patharus' nudge forced his attention back to a guest. "Tell the general about our plans for next spring."

Nicanor made a sincere effort to share his new father's enthusiasm for a Roman education. Throughout the many courses he peered at Daphne. Their eyes affirmed a mutual desire: I wish I could get out of here. The main courses had been cleared by the time the flute girls returned. Once again, music blared. Guests circulated and much of the time his view of Daphne was blocked.

Chapter Thirty-Five

There is nothing covered that will not be revealed.
– Matthew 10:26

Daphne tried to follow Nicanor's trip around the room. She hoped he would come near, and at the same time that he would not.

Sergius spotted her, moved close and smirked. "Well, what have we here?"

In a loud voice, he addressed those closest to him. "Gentlemen, this is the sorceress Patharus, Amplias and I bought in Athens. She has been summoned for your entertainment...if you like, she can tell your fortune. I hear she is *very* good."

She dismissed his innuendo and forced a smile.

He pulled a nearby guest toward her. "Here, Malatus. "Would you like to know what your future holds?"

Too much wine slurred his response. "Certainly, tell me *Kopela*, what is ahead for me?

She took a deep breath. Would her insides never cease to quake? With as steady a voice as she could muster, she told him to sit down. She pulled her *teraphim* from her tunic and sat it in front of her.

The man hesitated, shot a glance at the idol and then at Sergius. "Looks like she means business."

Someone taunted, "Go on Malatus...you are not afraid of an idol, are you?"

Matalus brushed off the jeer with a wave of his hand, bent in her direction but lost his balance and fell. She pulled back and raised her arms to keep him from landing in her lap or on her injured knee. He righted himself and cursed those who hooted and declared him a hopeless drunk. Through glazed eyes he reached back for the goblet an onlooker held for him.

"Well?" His fouled breath blasted like the smell of a decomposed animal.

She shuddered and stared at the *teraphim*. Could she even hear the Voice in such noise and turmoil?

Do not let them intimidate you, it is your destiny.

She circled her hands over the *teraphim*. "Great and mighty Apollo, god above all gods...."

A man in a Roman uniform heckled. "That is not true. He is not greater than Jupiter. Murmurs of agreement swept the room. She tried not to react, but what to do?

Tell the man to look at the coin in his left pocket.

She drew herself up as straight as she could. "Good sir, please look at the coin in your left pocket."

Eyes shifted to the man. Embarrassed, yet defiant, he held the coin beneath his fingers.

Tell him it is not an ordinary coin. Ask him if it is not a rare, silver-plated fourree, a denarius of one hundred years past that honored Pompey the Great, whose portrait on the coins' back is shown as Neptune, with a ship of his fleet.

She repeated the instructions.

The men closest to the heckler confronted him. "Let us see if she is right."

The man reluctantly held out the coin. Another examined it. "She is right! That is exactly what it is."

By now Patharus and Nicanor had joined those gathered around her. Patharus nodded his approval, but Nicanor's jaw dropped. Confusion, disappointment? She hoped it reflected his desire to rescue her from the situation and swallowed her misgivings.

Patharus signaled and a servant hushed the flute girls. He caught her eye and urged her to go on. The man in front of her squirmed, suddenly sober.

As many as could, crowded around the increasingly quiet room. Daphne held her forearms against her churning stomach. Every eye had shifted to her. She had grown accustomed to the scrutiny of customers who sought Apollo's counsel, but a room filled with skeptical onlookers caused beads of perspiration to trickle from beneath her hair and down her back. She shivered but proceeded with her homage. Her hands shook, would her voice betray her? Perhaps they would not think it strange if it wavered.

She finished the attributes and addressed the man. "You are one of many brothers who dwell on and work your father's land."

Malatus' eyes grew wide.

"You are not the first born, but your contributions have not gone unnoticed. Your father will reward your devotion."

Obviously relieved, Malatus smirked and glanced with pride at his peers, but his smug demeanor soon faded.

"But be warned, Apollo will not be taken lightly. He is god of the crops and blight will fall upon all you have built unless you honor him with your life and a yearly pilgrimage to sacrifice at his temple."

As he rose, Malatus jerked his head and sneered. Some encouraged him to heed the advice, but others slapped him on the back and scoffed along with him.

She hoped with all her might that it would end there. It was not to be. A man with gray hair and of slight build knelt before her. "I would like to talk to my dead son. Can you bring him back to speak to me?"

Daphne hid a gulp. No one had ever asked that of her.

Tell him you can, but he must be in complete submission to your bidding.

She repeated the message. The man slowly nodded his consent.

"Prostrate yourself before the mighty Apollo. Repeat after me as I extol our mighty god."

"Great and Mighty Apollo, god of all gods." She waited for the man to repeat her words and tried to dismiss the conviction the phrase instantly resurrected. Her heart quickened. Did Apollo know how her loyalty vacillated? She shook off the distraction. This was no time to wrestle her conscience.

"You who hold all men in your hands, you who causes the rain to fall and the sun to bless our crops...."

On and on she chanted, waiting each time for the man to respond and for the Voice to whisper. A picture flashed before her eyes.

Tell him what you see.

"I see a rock quarry. Men are hewing large stones from the pit. One has fallen and crushed a man."

The man's head shot up. "My son! It is my son...how did you know?"

I was there, a raspy voice spewed from Daphne. *I am the great Apollo. I watch over and see the works of mere men.*

The man stared, open mouthed. He struggled to compose himself, bowed his head to the floor once more and whispered, "please, please...may I speak to him?"

"He can hear but I will have to report his response."

The man gave a quick nod, his words muffled. "Dulacus, Dulacus, this is your father."

He hears you.

"Dulacus, I....Dulacus, please forgive me. I did you a terrible disservice. Can you forgive me, son?"

Questions darted among the onlookers and whispers filled the awkward silence.

Your son says he will forgive you for dishonoring his wife if you take her into your protection from this day forth and make her an honored part of your household. The child she carries is yours, not his. It is to have your name and is to be considered an heir, equal to all the rest of your sons."

An audible gasp rose in unison from those gathered around the scene. Adultery was readily tolerated, but incest or an incestuous relationship within one's own family or in-laws was an abomination to Greeks and most Romans.

Daphne wished she could sink through the floor but ventured a glance at the crowd. To her relief all eyes were on the man. Her Voice returned to normal as she admonished him. "See that you honor Apollo with your life and your sacrifices."

"I will. Yes. I will do all you say." He worked his way up from the floor, shaken and sapped of all dignity. The crowd parted, aghast at their colleague's exposure. Condemnation bulged from every eye as head down, he cowered and shuffled toward the entryway.

Patharus motioned for the flute girls to resume their music. Amplias waved his glass, "What say we have another toast?" His effort fell flat. Men clustered in small groups as a solemn buzz replaced the boisterous din of the early evening.

Patharus signaled his servants and soon fresh wine filled every glass.

It did not take long for the celebration to resume. Servants set out honeyed raisin cakes along with fruit and goat cheeses for the guests to enjoy. As if nothing had happened, each drank his fill and expounded unheeded monologues at each other. She remained seated, sure none would willingly approach her now.

Most avoided her corner. A few paused and discreetly let her know they intended to seek her counsel in the city. None lingered long enough to be noticed. At last, Patharus made his way over to where she waited. Her heart sank. Was he angry?

"Well Daphne, you gave us quite a show." His tone revealed nothing. She kept her eyes lowered. "It was not what I had in mind, but it certainly will be a night to remember."

"Master, I am so sorry, I…."

"Nonsense. You did what you were asked. However, I do not think there will be any more requests. You may leave."

To her surprise, he held out his hand and helped her up from the cushions. She returned a shy smile and thanked him, then wound her way through guests that scrambled to get out of her way.

Nicanor followed her every move. His eyes filled with questions, but he was trapped by men too drunk to know that he was not listening to their prattle.

Chapter Thirty-Six

No lie is of the truth.
– 1 John 2:21

Daphne had nearly reached her room when quick footsteps caught her attention. She turned as Nicanor rushed toward her.

"Daphne, Daphne, wait up."

Negative impressions of what he witnessed bombarded her imagination. She twisted the fringe of her shawl tighter with his every step,

He caught up and stopped abruptly. "Are you…alright?"

Her cheeks burned. She nodded and lowered her head.

He lifted her chin with his forefinger and searched her face before he found courage to pour out his confusion. "I, I guess I did not understand exactly what you did, ah, do, when you go into the city each day, and…"

She tried to lower her head, but he forced her to look at him. Tears born of a desperate longing for his acceptance, welled and wetted her cheeks.

"That strange Voice…the things you said, where does it come from? How did you know all those things?"

She studied the face that lit up her dreams. What lay beneath the surface? Curiosity? Disgust? Embarrassment? Did he despise what he saw? She longed to fall against his chest and feel the comfort of his strong arms as when she collapsed in the garden.

"I, I...." How could she explain? Surely, he had seen diviners ply their trade in the city.

The Voice boomed within. *He realizes what you are, and he is appalled. You are far below his newly acquired station, better protect yourself. Remember, he owns you now.*

A familiar fountain towered in her mind. She pulled from his reach. Why had he come? What did he want from her?

Her thoughts scrambled as despair rose from within. Concern etched on his Nicanor's face evolved to something more sinister. Eyes that searched hers became an inferno of lust; the touch of his hand the first step toward using her for his pleasure.

She lifted her chin and spoke in as confident a voice as she could muster. "I am the handmaiden of the great Apollo! I am an instrument for his Voice to those who seek his wisdom."

She spat all the Voice prompted. "His spirit dwells within me, speaks to me and through me, that men might gain his wisdom for their lives. I am of a different world, under the special protection of Apollo. Beware, least you anger him by offending me. He is all powerful, the defender of those who revere and serve him." With that, she hastened through her curtain.

Shock and pain wracked his voice as he called after her. "Daphne? Daphne, please come back. I did not mean to upset you. I, I.... Daphne? Can you hear me?"

Her heart thumped in her chest. Did she dare refuse him? Would he charge through the flimsy curtain that separated them?

"Daphne, I must get back to the banquet. Please, can we talk?"

She did not answer. In time, his footsteps faded. She flung herself on her mat and sobbed till she had no more tears. Surely, he was lost to her forever. He would leave for Rome as soon as it was safe to sail. Patharus had probably already decided on a great match for his newly acquired son, a girl of his own station who could give him legitimate grandchildren.

A thought wove through her pain and brought her to her feet. She had sought Apollo for others, why not for herself? She began to pace and quietly paid Apollo the homage demanded of seekers, then made her request.

"Oh, great Apollo, answer your servant; show me my future. Unveil the path my life will take."

She closed her eyes and concentrated as never before.

You are well pleasing to me. Your continual obedience has not gone without notice. Do not fear, I am your protection. Follow me without question and I will lead you into the service of great and powerful men. Your reputation will swell and bring you much respect and eventually your freedom. I will not fail you. My kingdom is greater than any other, and in it you will gain an honored position to which all will look up.

Despite the warm night, she hugged her arms to ward off a sudden shiver. She lay back on her mat and pondered what Apollo laid out. The promise of protection bathed her with a warm flush of relief. Service to powerful people, respect, and a place of honor. That had to mean she would not suffer the humiliation of being a fortune teller forever. And freedom! Best of all, Apollo promised freedom. Nicanor's troubled face returned. He must not occupy her thoughts, but if she were free? Her heart returned to hope they might one day…. She scolded herself. "One day what? She must let go of her fantasy. The Voice was her only friend."

Still, the prospect of being on equal ground with Nicanor lingered. Patharus was a great and powerful man. He could decide to give her an honored position and grant the freedom she craved. Excitement brewed at the possibility. She would work hard to impress him. Spring was months away, maybe her freedom would come before Nicanor left. Had not Apollo promised?

She closed her eyes to shut out the image of a laughing hyena the moon etched upon her wall. To close the longing that seeped through the crack in her heart was not as easy.

To avoid Nicanor, she left early each morning. From time to time, they passed but she eluded prolonged contact and willed her feet to scurry, though her heart longed to linger.

While in the city, affluent guests who attended Nicanor's adoption celebration sought her out. "I saw what you did at Patharus' party, will you seek your god for me? I need supernatural insights and wisdom from Apollo." Their patronage greatly enhanced her profits and spurred her to greater boldness.

One who had sided with Malatus found her and grabbed her by the wrist. "I want you to meet me behind the public baths. We could spend some time together and I would pay you well." An icy stare and a reminder of who her master was, wilted his sinister scheme. Shamed, he ran off.

…. I will protect you, important men will seek you out. You will be respected….

Many of the Voices' predictions had already come to pass and proven true.

She mused. "But it is the freedom I long for, freedom and…." She stopped, reluctant to give name to her desire. An uninterrupted lunch in the courtyard invigorated her to face the chaos of the *agora.*

She held out her idol and brazenly approached a man who wrung his hands and paced near an *exedra.* "Good sir, the mighty god Apollo has great power and will give you insight to solve your problems. Shall I seek his wisdom for you?" The man was taken aback by her boldness, but soon agreed. He left and after she scouted out several others, she counted her profits. Good. Patharus would be pleased and that is all that mattered.

Chapter Thirty-Seven

If you serve their gods, it will surely be a snare to you.
– Exodus 23:33

Daphne decided to head home but stopped when a man's voice soared above the din. "*Kopela,* tarry a moment. I have need of your services."

Daphne turned. She recognized a Greek merchant who had attended the banquet by his heavy mop of hair. He pointed and gestured toward a place to talk.

She waited. "Yes, my lord? Do you want me to seek the wisdom of Apollo for you?"

He caught his breath. "Yes, I most certainly do! Shortly, I have a very important meeting. Would you be willing to come to my shop and meet with me and my colleagues?"

Wary of a session in closed quarters, she cocked her head and studied the man. Lust did not appear to be his motive. She nodded. "Yes, I will come."

The man's head bobbed as he beckoned for her to follow. "Good, good."

She quickened her pace to his and wondered how she might seek her god for several men at a time. He led her to one of the rooms that faced the inner courtyard. She raised her brows. He had to be very wealthy to house his business there.

He motioned to an inner room with a stool that sat apart from the couches. "Wait here. The others are due soon."

He left and shut the door behind him. The space was larger than she expected. A table laden with ledgers and scrolls dominated one end. At the other, skins of wine, olives, cheese, and other delicacies were laid out close to the couches. Flames appeared to dance on the walls from lamps that gave light to the windowless room.

Voices drew her attention. She clutched the sides of the stool as she recognized one of them. Sergius! How could she have known? She lowered her eyes.

Pulmer, the man who had solicited her grinned, his introduction brimmed with expectation. "I have enlisted the help of the best diviner around, right, Sergius?" His comment merged with that of the other guest. She ignored their remarks and did not encourage their expectations.

The host directed his guests to the couches and served them wine. "Now, let us put our heads together." He droned on about his ideas for securing the property they considered. The others offered suggestions as they debated the merit of such a large investment.

Sergius' gaze drifted in her direction. She shuddered. The power he held over her brought reminders of his lustful glances and ugly remarks. Silently, she begged Apollo to keep him far from her.

She tried not to fidget. The stool was hard, and she longed to stand and stretch. An hour of unfruitful discussion passed before Pulmer stood. "All right, let us see what the gods have to tell us."

He motioned and she made her way over to their couches, aware every eye followed. She sat her idol in front of her. "Please join me here on the floor."

Sergius groused but joined the circle. As if she had not heard, they briefly explained their desire to know if the purchase they considered would be lucrative. To quiet her nerves, she began to chant her pattern of extolling Apollo. Faithful to his promise, the Voice manifested.

Apollo encourages you to make an offer for the property, but do not try to steal it. He will agree to a reasonable price. The investment will be large, but so will be your profit. Make haste to seal the agreement as there are others who have heard of the opportunity. Do not fail to sacrifice generously at Apollo's temple and see that you worship him and give him credit for your success, or you will court failure."

After the Voice became silent, the owner stood and clapped his hands. "Wonderful! Wonderful!"

He placed a generous offering in her palm and beamed at his guests. "I will go and find Abacus and try to solidify an agreement. Please, help yourself to the wine and refreshments." With that, he scurried out into the courtyard.

The other colleague followed the owner to the door. "I cannot stay. My helper needs to attend his wife and I need to cover my shop."

She rose to leave, but Sergius stepped between her and the door. Her heart began to pound.

He stepped closer. "Do not be in such a hurry, Daphne. I need to speak to you."

A futile glance confirmed there was no other exit. His intentions made her gasp and left her dizzy.

His tongue stroked his upper lip as a lustful gaze swept her body. Her stomach churned. Would this chance meeting fulfill his long-denied opportunity to use her for his pleasure? He waited until he was sure they were alone, then purred with a smug grin. "Patharus is not here, now, is he?"

"You do understand that I too am your master, do you not? And a wise slave submits to her master's wishes. A girl could be beaten or even killed if she does not obey, and we certainly would not want that now, would we?" He wagged his head with trumped up sympathy and moved slowly toward her.

His eyes fixed on her, prepared to intercept should she try to leave. He motioned toward a couch. "Come over here with me girl."

Daphne froze. The cold marble floor seeped through her thin sandals, as icy as his evil intentions. Every part of her wanted to scream, to run, but she was unable to do either.

In an instant, he covered the few steps between them.

She backed and tried to appeal to his greed. "I, I cannot stay. I promised a wealthy customer I would meet with him, and I am late."

He pursed his lips and smirked. "I have so admired you, Daphne."

Would Patharus' wrath discourage him? She tried not to sound desperate. "You know Patharus would not want me to disappoint such a man."

Sergius slipped off his outer robe and ignored her ploy. Her distress appeared to amuse, even please him. "I will take care of Patharus. You know I would never hurt you… you are so lovely."

He ran his hand up her arm, across her shoulders and pulled her close. She shrank at his touch. His hot breath reeked, and she struggled to free herself. He grabbed her in a vice-like grip and pushed one arm behind her back. With his free hand he pulled the front of her tunic down one side.

His mouth covered hers, stifling her scream as he pushed her toward a couch with a force she was helpless to fight.

She pushed his face from hers. "No, please, no!"

He tightened his grip. "You will…."

"Sergius?" Pulmer's voice came through the outer entrance and startled them both. "Sergius, I did not know if you had already left, but…."

He released her and grabbed his outer tunic. She straightened hers as the owner stepped into the room, his attention on the opened scroll he carried.

Sergius had hardly donned his wrap before the shop owner looked up. "Sergius, I am so glad I caught you. I was thinking, Abacus said he would come over here in just a short while. This would be a great time for you to meet him and help me negotiate the deal, even seal the bargain right here and now."

Pulmer's glance shifted, and he realized Daphne had not left. He looked curiously at Sergius and back at her, cleared his throat and continued. "Abacus has only a short time before he leaves for Thessalonica. Could you spare a few more minutes or do you have urgent business with your girl?"

He continued to elaborate on the opportunity but did not allude to what he had seen.

Sergius glanced between her and Pulmer. Disappointment and indecision pursed his lips. She held her breath. Which of his lusts would triumph…her or certain profit?

It seemed forever before he finally cleared his throat. "Of course Pulmer, a great opportunity." He nodded at her as if they had dealt with a matter of importance. "We will attend to this business later, Daphne,"

His eyes pierced hers with an intent she knew would never fade.

Chapter Thirty-Eight

Daphne rushed into the sunshine, shaken, but grateful to have escaped Sergius' clutches. She ran back into the *agora* and did not stop until she reached the courtyard. The money she earned before Pulmer approached, and his generous addition, was more than enough for today.

She refilled her jug at the fountain and found a deserted place near the city baths to relax until time to head home. The close call with Sergius continued to shake every part of her until fears melted to anger. She would tell Patharus and have him demand Sergius leave her alone. Even as she fumed, she knew she could not bring it up. To disclose Sergius' lecherous intentions would be useless.

The warm fall sun calmed her quaking but did not dispel her frustrations or the resentment that threatened tears. She would never, never again go into a room or an enclosed area with anyone. She despised that man…but how was she going to avoid him?" She would have to be smarter, more alert and find ways to protect herself.

With clenched teeth, she muttered useless possibilities. No recourse over the slave demands of one's owners, along with the helplessness of every female slave, brought pity for herself and all those she knew. Is it not enough that they own our lives and our time, must they invade our bodies too?

Do not fear, I protected you there and will continue to keep you from harm.

She scoffed. "Humph. If Pulmer had not come back, I would still be at Sergius' mercy."

Who do you think arranged for him to find Abacus and return so quickly?

She stumbled and nearly fell. Her hand flew to her mouth and her stomach felt like it had taken a blow.

Did I not promise to protect you? Trust wholly in me and give thanks to our benevolent god who rescued you.

She did not feel like it, but dutifully extolled Apollo's goodness the rest of the way home. Near the estate, she paused. She wished she could be alone until morning, but Kawit said tomorrow was some kind of a Roman festival they needed to plan for. She headed for her room, slightly buoyed by the prospect of a less traumatic day.

Her accounting with Patharus was brief. She watched him record her coins, eager for his approval. To her disappointment, he merely nodded and dismissed her. Disheartened, she rounded the corner, less than elated to see Kawit outside her door. With trumped up enthusiasm, she waved.

They met part way up the corridor. "I could not wait to find you Daphne. Tomorrow is the Roman festival of Feronia. Remember?"

A blank stare betrayed Daphne's disinterest.

"Oh, right. You were not here this time last year. Well, it means we are excused from most of our duties." She linked her arm in Daphne's. "We need to do something special. What should we do?"

"Oh Kawit, what I really need is to relax and catch up on some rest. It would be good not to have to go into the city…are you sure?"

"Yes. And I understand, I am tired too. But to get away will be so good for us. As long as we are back before dark, no one will much care what we do."

Chapter Thirty-Nine

...favor is like dew on the grass.
– Proverbs 19:12

Daphne could hardly believe Patharus sanctioned a day off for everyone. A different environment sounded nice, but the day's trauma had sapped her energy. "Kawit, I had a horrible day." She choked at the memory. "Let me unwind and I will likely be eager to join you in the morning."

Kawit touched her arm. "Get some rest. I will call you when the meal is ready, and we can figure out something. Maybe even go to that place you loved by the stream."

A weak grin tweaked her lips. "Oh, sure and get lost again."

She lay on her mat and fought scenes of the encounter with Sergius. Despair weighted her thoughts, but she drifted into a fitful sleep. At Kawit's call, she awoke with a start, grateful to escape a dream in which she fled but did not know from what.

Her heart still pulsed. "Do you think I dare skip dinner?"

"Frankly, I do not think it would be wise. Stello has been in a terrible mood since the master's party. Rumor has it he had set his hopes on becoming Patharus' heir."

She groaned and held her head. "Alright. I will be along, do not wait for me."

Mindful of Stello's unpredictable vengeance, she tidied herself and joined the others. Mealtime passed swiftly, but the overseer dragged out his instructions. She did not pay much attention to what he said, her mind stuck on Sergius' plans to set up another opportunity.

"....*so, be sure you do not violate the conditions,*" cut into her thoughts. "There will be no exceptions." Stello's threats seemed directed at her. At his final dismissal, she turned to Kawit. "What was he saying? I am sure he glared right at me."

"Tomorrow, you know, what is allowed in our time to ourselves. Did you not listen?"

She shook her head. "I am sorry. I cannot seem to concentrate. Did I miss something important?"

"It is alright, nothing new. Stello just wants to make sure we all bow to his authority. He is so, so...." She grimaced and rolled her eyes. "Come on, you need to tell me what so upset you today."

They passed the group of young men Nicanor usually chummed with. He had not joined them.

"Kawit, what is this festival about? Why is everyone so excited...because they have the day off?"

"Oh, lots of reasons. Feronia is a fertility goddess revered to secure a good harvest, besides being a goddess of travel, fire, and water. She is the mother of Hercules. You know who he is, right?"

"Yes, but I still do not see—"

"Listen, if the goddess blesses the crops and brings a good harvest before the rains, it goes better for all of us. None of us are Romans but we honor her too. And the Master...." She cast her glance at her feet and shook her head. "Ever since his young son died, the poor man has strictly commanded the goddess of fertility be revered by everyone. Year after year he petitions for another child."

"That is so sad! Does he go to her temple to pray?"

"No temple near here. There is one at the base of Mt. Soracte in Copena and a few others besides the one in Rome." She paused, "Perhaps he goes there on his voyages. I wish one were close. I would run to it."

She wheeled and caught Kawit's arm. "Why? Why would you go?"

"Because she is also the goddess of freedom. Every slave knows that if you sit on a holy stone in one of Feronia's sanctuaries, it guarantees you will be set free. You never heard of her?"

"No, but if that is true, I would go with you." They stopped at Daphne's room. "Right now, I cannot talk about what happened today. Could we meet as soon as you finish in the morning and plan to leave right after?"

Kawit hugged her and left. Daphne did not fetch water to bathe or even light her lamp. She flopped on her mat in the clothes she wore, curled into a fetal position, and fell asleep. When she awoke it was still dark. The night air had hardly cooled, leaving her clothes damp and clammy. She should have bathed.

How long before sunrise? She stretched up on her toes before her window. To the east only a glimmer of light broke the darkness. She picked up her pitcher and started for the well. It would not be long before the courtyard would bustle and expose her intentions. By the time she had enough water, it was light out. She relaxed in the cool water and quelled thoughts of yesterday. Today is mine and Kawit's to enjoy.

After dressing and arranging her hair, she began to empty her tub of water. On her last trip, she ran straight into Jahtel.

"And what is it you are doing?"

She cringed and quickly lowered her eyes "My tub needed to be emptied, my lord."

"And why would you need to do that in the morning?"

The accusation behind his question frightened her. Kawit's warning flashed. *Do not make him or Stello an enemy.*

"I, I, well, ummm, I…."

"What is the problem, Father?"

Nicanor approached him from behind. Her heart sank.

Jahtel lifted his chin. "A simple matter, Nicanor, er, my lord. This *slave* has disregarded a rule about bathing."

Nicanor looked aside and gave his head a slight shake. "Alright. Let us not allow a small incident to mar the day of festival." He looked his father in the eye. "I will take care of it."

Jahtel grimaced, unable to hide the twitch of his jaw. He glared at her, spun on his heel, and left.

Daphne swallowed the lump in her throat. "Thank you. I did not mean to break another rule or cause trouble."

He did not dismiss her, only stared. It had been weeks since she had seen him. Were his eyes always that blue? She bowed her head, aware heat crept up her neck.

"Why did you wait for morning to bathe?"

The question caught her off guard. What could she say? "I, I had an especially difficult day yesterday. I was very weary and fell asleep in my clothes."

"You know the rules about bathing?"

She nodded. "It will not happen again, I promise."

"Well, in that case I will not turn you in for a beating or...."

She gasped and looked up.

His eyes twinkled. "That is if you will agree to meet me in the garden after the morning meal." His brows rose. "Promise?" He went on his way, and she stood there, mouth agape.

Chapter Forty

Back in her room Daphne's heart raced. Was it fear of Jahtel's reprisal or the joy of a chance to be with Nicanor again? She dismissed their unpleasant exchange after the banquet and wondered what was on his mind. When Kawit arrived for breakfast, Daphne told her that they would have to start later as Nicanor requested to meet her.

Kawit covered her disappointment with a nod. "I will wait, do you have any idea—"

"No, we met by accident. It is not like he came to find me. Oh, what if he…."

"Put abuse out of your head. He has never treated you with disrespect. He probably missed you." The sparkle had returned to her eyes. "You would not object to that, would you?"

Daphne wrinkled her nose and smiled at her friend. "I promise not to be long." With a quick hug she left for the garden.

Nicanor was not near the gate. She walked farther down the path. Maybe he changed his mind.

She approached the pond where they had met before.

The hedge of witches'-broom had lost its yellow flowers, but its foliage clung and created a hidden cove beside the water. He called out before she saw him. "Daphne, over here."

Her heart jumped to her throat. How should she greet him? Nicanor? My lord? Master? "Hello," was all she managed.

He rose and walked toward her. "I am so glad you came. Come sit on our bench with me."

Our bench? Her knees felt weak. He called it "our bench."

His eyes held hers. "You look lovely,"

She blushed and lowered her head. "My lord, I...."

"Come and sit. It has been so long since we have talked." He cocked his head. "You have avoided me." He led her to the bench. "I am so sorry, I did not understand the assignment Patharus gave you. I do not know anything about...special powers." He paused and cleared his throat. "How is your, your work going? Are you alright with it?"

She sensed his uneasiness and hesitated, not sure how to answer. "It goes well my lord." Had her voice wavered?

"No, do not call me lord, here." He was emphatic. "We are friends, you can use my name."

Despite herself, her lips softly caressed his name. "Nicanor."

His expression softened and he reached for her hand. For a moment their eyes locked. She withdrew her hand and concentrated on the water lilies. She needed to protect herself. He must never suspect how his presence affected her. "Did you need to speak to me about something, my… er, I mean, Nicanor?"

He did not speak for several minutes. Her anxiety increased until she noticed he chewed his lower lip, his face a blank. A breeze stirred the trees that surrounded them and sent a parade of red and yellow leaves to the water' surface.

"Our lives are like that. A man gets an idea and before long a breeze of change sends us on a course we never anticipated."

He appeared deep in thought, his expression sad, or was it confusion? Did he refer to his new status? Surely his life had not changed that much, had it?

"I am very hesitant about going to Rome. I cannot tell Patharus, and my father will speak of nothing except my great fortune and opportunity." He winged a few pebbles into the pond. "I feel like my life is totally out of control, as if something important is being swept to the side. Patharus has untold plans for my future. He wants me to learn all about his business and to help him run it when I return."

A squirrel chattered in the boughs above them. "….and after I return, he is going to seek a suitable wife, someone I do not even know."

She did not grasp a word he said after that. A suitable wife! Patharus is seeking a wife for him. Her heart sank like the stones he tossed into the pond. Of course, he would want a suitable wife for his heir. A free woman to bear him grandsons and continue his name. She listened but did not hear, only added a nod from time to time as she forced back tears that edged the corner of her eyes.

He twisted to face her. "You are attuned to the spirit world, what does it all mean? Will the spirits that talk to you tell me what is in store for me?"

Her throat clamped. Never would she expose him to the wiles of the spirit world. Never. She vigorously shook her head. "No, Nicanor, no…no!

"Why? What is it? You look like I asked you to stab me. Do you not help people with guidance from the spirits every day?"

She swallowed the lump that closed her throat and clutched her hands to her chest. How could she explain the danger without risking loss of his respect? She took a deep breath. "Nicanor, I cannot explain the work of the spirits, but I want you to know that if you dabble in the spirit world it can open doors of tragedy into your life."

Tears spilled down her cheeks. "Please, please do not seek that kind of direction for your life. You are a strong person. You will find what is right through your own wisdom."

He wiped a tear from her cheek, his face a wreath of concern. "It will be alright. Do not worry. I trust that you know of these things. I do not understand, but I promise I will not seek that kind of help if it means so much to you."

She sniffed. "I must go, I promised Kawit I would spend the day with her, and she is waiting for me."

Nicanor stood with her. "Promise you will not avoid me anymore?"

She nodded and forced her feet toward the gate.

You should have sought my counsel for your friend. I could have advised him about his future.

She ran down the path, desperate to put plenty of distance between Nicanor and the Voice. She nearly tripped as she rushed through the gate.

*****

Upon leaving the estate, Kawit would not let up until Daphne shared about her run in with Sergius. "You poor thing, no wonder that fear haunts you. That man is trouble. You need to be on your guard. Whoever owns you can do whatever they want, and nobody will interfere, except maybe Patharus…if he were present. Now, I want to hear every word Nicanor uttered."

Daphne was quiet. Her friend was right, but how could she protect herself against unforeseen circumstances? As they neared the foothills, she opened about her time with Nicanor.

Kawit sighed. "It is so obvious that he cares for you. It would be wonderful if he—"

"Hold on, friend. Did you hear me say he knows Patharus intends to find him a suitable wife?"

They arrived at a deserted valley between two hills with a stream nearby. She walked over to refill their jugs while Kawit laid out their lunch.

Stello stepped from behind some bushes. "Well, this is a cozy setup."

She clutched the jugs and shot a glance at Kawit.

Stello drew close, his eyes on Kawit. "Looks like lunch is ready, maybe I will join you."

Kawit pointed at the food. "We are ah...about to leave, but you are welcome to...." She backed, ready to run.

Daphne took a few quick steps and grabbed Kawit's arm. "Yes, I need to prepare for tomorrow. Come, we have a lengthy hike before us."

Stello's words were syrupy. "It is a shame to waste all this food, Kawit. I would be happy to see you back if you can stay awhile."

Kawit's face paled.

Daphne pouted, "But remember Kawit, you promised to help me mend my tunic when we returned."

As if rescued from quicksand, Kawit brightened. "Yes, I almost forgot...I promised."

Stello smirked at their discomfort. "Do be careful. Things can....ummm, happen out here so far from help."

The girls whisked past him, their ears tuned for footsteps but too fearful to look back.

Chapter Forty-One

Every intent of the thoughts of his heart was only evil.
– Genesis 6:5

On her return the next day, Daphne shivered, grateful for the warmth of her heavy shawl. Winter's chill had settled upon the Philippian countryside. She huffed. Delphi's temperature never fell this low. Would she ever again feel those warm winds off the gulf?

She quickened her pace. The day had been productive, except for a prospective client who accused her of having an evil eye, and to her relief, ran off.

The mountain range drew her attention. The peaks of Dionysus' dwelling place lay beneath piles of fresh snow. Back home his feast would be well under way. I wonder if anyone there ever thinks of my family or wonders what became of us? She kicked a stone and watched it bounce until it fell to one side of the path.

Helene and Semiele are probably married, Cyrene too. Her chest heaved at the memory of Cyrene's helpless tears while she witnessed Daphne's family sold into slavery. Cyrene was my true friend, the only one who really cared.

Thoughts of her brothers and her mother followed. It was warm when I last saw them, seems a lifetime ago.

Mother. She found it hard to picture her face. Tears squeezed from beneath closed lids until Hebee's image materialized. She forced her anguish into the vault in her heart and relocked the chamber. Scenery. Concentrate on the mountains.

She passed the bend where she and Nicanor had met a few days before he became Patharus' official heir. The place on her cheek where he wiped her tears in the garden seemed to radiate warmth.

The memories soothed her. He cared, she knew he did. Oh, Nicanor.... Despite the promise he extracted, their meetings were brief and unplanned. Maybe he is avoiding me now.

The smile that lit his face when their paths crossed told her that was not true. But why had he not sought her out? Had Jahtel mentioned their friendship to Patharus? Had the master instructed Nicanor to cut off all relationships with slaves?

She was surprised to see Kawit waiting outside the gate. She pointed at a clearing beside the path. They sat on a rock that overlooked the valley, eating raisin cakes she wheedled from of one of the cooks.

Kawit picked crumbs from her lap and tossed them at a white-throated warbler. The bird pecked nervously at the offering, his light gray breast puffed against the chilly air. "So, how did your day go?"

"Mostly good. It is such a relief when Apollo is not so harsh with people. He always demands their undivided homage, but I guess that is not too much to ask, granted he usually gives them a way to solve their problems or secure their future." She kept the incident of the man who ran off to herself. "How about you?"

Kawit's eyelids drooped. "Not so good."

She spun to face her friend. "What? Stello again?"

Kawit breathed a heavy sigh. "He has it in for me." Anger welled with her tears. "I try to avoid him as much as I can, do exactly as he says, but it is never enough."

Daphne put her arm around Kawit's shoulders.

Kawit's voice shook. "Jahtel assigned me to serve the master's wife. I had her lunch tray ready, when Stello breezed by and demanded I do it over. I guess I did not respond quickly enough. He grabbed the tray from my hand and threw it to the ground."

Daphne gasped. "That makes no sense. What displeased him so?"

"I have no idea. When I bent to retrieve it, he shoved me to the ground and shouted, 'Start over, and see that it is fit for the master's wife.'" She covered her face with her hands. "He is looking for an excuse to beat me again. Ever since, since I did not..."

Daphne bristled "Did not what? You have never failed to do anything but what you are told."

Kawit hesitated. "He found me alone in the wash house last week. He pretended to inspect my work, then forced me into a corner. I tried to leave without making a scene, but he grabbed my arm and, well you can imagine. When I refused him, he laughed, shoved me into the laundry tubs and declared me too ugly for his tastes anyway. He treats me with such contempt, and I am so afraid."

Daphne drew her friend into her arms and rocked her against her chest. "I am so sorry, I wish I could do something, help somehow."

"I know, I have never told anyone. How can I complain to the one in charge when he is the problem? I have asked Jahtel for assignments that are likely to keep me out of his reach, but Stello's the overseer and he is everywhere." Fear glistened in her eyes. "I must get away before he kills me." She turned and looked out over the valley. "Please pray to your god to keep Stello from me."

They lingered until the sun disappeared behind the peaks. Each wracked their brain and speculated on what more she could do to avoid him.

Kawit stood. "Come on, Patharus will call for your report and I need to be about the evening meal." She gave a weak smile. "Hathor has promised to protect me, why should I panic?"

Daphne put her arm around Kawit's waist and ignored the fake bravado that weighted her friend's usually bouncy steps. The mischievous expression Daphne loved crept back into Kawit's eyes. "By the way, you never did tell me everything Nicanor said before Stello ruined our day in the foothills. Did he propose marriage?"

Daphne gave her a playful push. "Why would you say such a thing?"

"Well then what was it?"

"He merely wanted some counsel about seeking advice from the gods about his future. I told him to forget it and we agreed to be friends. That was it."

"Uhuh. And I am about to be promoted to queen of Feronia's Temple Martius in Rome so I can set all the slaves free."

She laughed. "Oh you! We will probably both live here forever, serve the master on our canes and die spinsters."

With a quick embrace they parted inside the gate and promised to meet for the evening meal. Daphne seized the moment for a quick refreshing before being summoned to the master's office. When Patharus' attention turned elsewhere, she studied his face but sensed no displeasure with her, only a preoccupation with his ledgers.

Chapter Forty-Two

...tormented with unclean spirits.
– Luke 6:18

Back in her room Kawit's teasing replayed in Daphne's mind. Why *had* Nicanor chosen to avoid her since they last met? She stood on tiptoes and peered out her window. Naked branches of poplar trees whipped, silhouetted against dark clouds that raced to usher in the first rumble of thunder.

She turned from the window. Perhaps the planned journey to Rome had spurred Nicanor to rethink about the life he would leave behind. Her thoughts ran to their last encounter. Why did she hold on to dreams of a future with him? He had never given her reason to think they....

Her chest ached as loneliness rose in vast swells and added self-pity to each crest. She sank to her knees and covered her face with her hands. Despair's roar became one with the thunder that crashed overhead. Its message of futility condemned her to a life of emptiness. For the second time that day a hunger for family flashed like the lightning outside her window. "Mother, Belte, where are you? I miss you so much."

The storm passed and the Voice interrupted the silence. *Call upon me. I am your family, and your friend.*

"Yes. Except for Kawit, no one cares."

Remember all I have promised and keep Apollo foremost in your –

Her head filled with sarcasm she could not bridle. "Can he make Nicanor care about me?"

Trust wholly in Apollo and he will supply all your desires.

Repentant, she scooted herself against the wall away from her window and hugged her knees to her chest. Apollo was her only source, her hope of a decent future. She made a mental note to spend the first moments of each day to honor him with a daily commitment and worship.

For most of the rest of the winter, Daphne stuck to her plan to give herself fully to Apollo worship and bury thoughts of a future with Nicanor. An influx of well-to-do seekers appeared each day, surely a reward for her diligence. She fussed less and less about Apollo's unconscionable advice. Sold out to his promises, she steeled her heart from the shambles greed and foolish decisions launched into the broken lives she dealt with.

She excused Apollo's harsh treatment of a man who walked away with slumped shoulders. Most of his holdings had been taken by creditors. She defended the Voice. Despite his losses, Apollo assured him he would recover if he gave him his due and became more careful about from whom he borrowed. Her conscious argued, but what will his family live on till then?

Weeks passed with no more than brief contacts with Nicanor until one evening she reported her earnings as usual and was shocked to see him in Patharus office. His eyes lit up at the sight of her, but she quickly hid her reaction. Patharus queried her at length for more details of her day. "Very good, very good, Daphne." He turned to Nicanor, Daphne earns money telling fortunes in the city for us. "Do you have any questions?"

Nicanor assured him he grasped the routine and mumbled an excuse to see Daphne to her room. She wished she had taken more time to refresh herself. At her door he took hold of her arm and turned her toward him. "Daphne, I miss you. I wish we could meet in the garden. There is so much I want to share with you. I—"

A slave rushed past and seconds later Jahtel called from down the hall. He stopped short at the sight of her and frowned. "The master has asked that you return immediately. A problem with the planting schedule has risen."

Nicanor sighed. "Always something, I must go but we will work it out, alright?" She touched the hand that held her arm and smiled in agreement.

Still, most of the time when they passed, he appeared to be distracted or buried under some pressing problem. Gossip held that Patharus had already given him responsibility over a wide variety of his businesses and some household priorities.

Weeks slipped away. She rose from the evening meal and lifted her chin and declared to Kawit, "He has forgotten and that is fine with me."

Kawit gathered their dishes. "I do not believe that."

Daphne sniffed. "Well, believe what you want." She turned and headed for her room.

"Hey, wait up! What is wrong? You are so edgy lately. I did not mean to hurt you."

She stopped and blinked away tears. "Oh, Kawit, I do not know what is wrong with me. I am so sorry, will you forgive me?"

Kawit's impish smile sprouted. "Well, I will think about it."

Daphne grabbed her friend's arm. "Come to my room for a while." They settled on her mat, and she talked about her day or anything but what was on her mind. Her head slumped to her chest as their chatter trailed. "You know it will not be long now before he leaves."

Kawit hugged her shoulders. "I know."

"Not that I care."

"Hey, it is me, remember? I know you do care."

"I have tried so hard not to. What is the matter with me? I have no reason to hold onto a hope he will, will...."

Kawit pulled her closer. "I know. The problem is the heart does not listen to reason."

The next morning, Daphne left early for the city. The warmth of the early spring sun penetrated her shawl and kept the morning cold at bay. Dutifully, she paid homage to Apollo, but despite her determination, her mind wandered.

She threw up her hands and scowled. "What does it matter, what does anything matter?"

She entered the city with a heavy heart. A prospective customer gestured to catch her eye, but she did not see him. He caught up with her in the eastern *stoa* and began to pour out his troubles. She half listened. Could he not see she carried her own heartache? Temptation to put him off withered as she reflected on Stello's unpredictable power over each of them. She quenched her reluctance and set up a place to meet.

"A high-ranking Roman is determined to possess my land." The words gushed from the lips of the slight, Grecian man. "He gave me a loan in the fall when my crops did not produce like they should, and now he demands immediate repayment." He paced in front of her. "It took all last year's profits to recoup and manage my estate."

The familiar tale snagged her heart. Exactly what her father had faced. Her voice dropped to a whisper. "What is it you desire of Apollo?"

He placed his hands on his cheeks. "I do not know… I have no more goods left to sell. Do you think the gods would have a solution, have mercy, and help me?"

"Apollo is a god of light and power. If you desire, I will call upon him for you."

She motioned for him to sit and began her routine. Thoughts of her father's burden spurred her to greater fervency. "Prostrate yourself before the great Apollo."

The man flopped with his arms out in front of him and his face on the ground.

The gravelly Voice she dreaded challenged. *As of yet you have not pursued all avenues open to you. Your wife's father is a man of great means. He has the resources to help you.*

The man shook his head and whimpered. "I, I cannot ask him. He...."

Bloated with impatience, the Voice scolded. *Would you rather lose all? Pride will destroy you and sell your family into slavery.*

Memories of soldiers about to herd their slaves from the only home they had ever known, transported her back to that horrible day in Delphi.

Pictures surfaced of how her brother staggered after a kick in his ribs, while another soldier yanked her mother to the slave monger's wagon. She could feel the terror of her little brother and the hot breath of the head soldier as he tried to convince her she would be better off as his plaything.

She wanted to cry out, to tell the man who lay at her feet of the agony a wrong decision or pride might bring.

The man pleaded. "You do not understand, my father-in-law hates me. He thinks I deceived him into betrothing his daughter in marriage to me.

Since he discovered my family does not hold the wealth he assumed was ours, he has refused to—"

The Voice broke in. *I give you the choice. Humble yourself and ask your father-in-law for help. I will move upon him to grant you favor and save your land and your family. If not, all will be lost. Now, commit your life to Apollo and give a goodly portion of your next crop to his temple.*

The man rose, visibly shaken. The pain of relinquishing his hope of an alternate source, written on his face. "Alright. I will ask him."

And what else?

"I will dedicate my life to Apollo and sacrifice generously at his temple after I sell my crops in the fall!"

The Voice faded. *So be it, so be it....* dwindled in eerie waves from her throat.

In the awkward silence that followed the man held out some coins, but she held back. "Keep them for your family and do not put off what Apollo told you to do. To be sold into slavery is a horrible thing. I…"

Stunned by her passionate admonishment, the man's expression changed. "I will go, right now, I promise." As he trotted toward the gate, she regained her composure. What happened to her vow to distance herself from people's troubles?

The day dragged with few opportunities to profit. For a while she wandered in the market and fingered some silk scarves. The likelihood of enjoying these luxuries seemed remote. The Voice promised she would prosper, but little had changed, despite a growing demand for her services. Patharus and his partners were the only one she knew who prospered from her increase.

Wearied by despair that hovered like a cagey hawk, she decided she would take a chance that the master would remember yesterday's unusually large profit, and not question today's lesser amount.

She turned into the *stoa* that led to the eastern gate. At the far end of the portico, she noticed a woman who slowly moved among the shoppers. Joy and expectation sprang in her heart. It was the young girl who Apollo had assured she carried her husband's heir. It is her, and she has the baby with her!

The sight of the young mother lifted Daphne's dour mood. She quickened her step but stopped short as she neared. Strange squalls whined from the girl. Daphne's face fell as the young woman rushed boldly into the face of all who came near. "Come, come see my baby! He is perfect! Come see my baby, look at his sweet face."

Two women more than eager to gush over a newborn stopped and peeked under the blanket the young woman held, but quickly left and did not look back.

Small children squirmed to escape their mother's grip and run and see the baby, but were hustled to the far side of the *stoa*.

The girl brazenly approached a man dressed in garments not familiar to Daphne, and howled, "come see, come see."

The man scowled and gestured at his bodyguard who took the young woman by the arm and moved her far from his master.

Daphne could not fathom what drove the new mother's behavior, to approach strangers, even a foreigner in such a manner. Hesitant, but driven, she drew nearer while the girl's attention was elsewhere. What was wrong with her, and why was everyone aghast after a look at the baby?

From behind the girl's back. Daphne whispered, "May I see your baby?"

The girl whirled. "Oh yes, do see my baby." Her watery gaze gave no indication that she remembered Daphne.

The young woman yanked back the cover and shoved her bundle into Daphne's-face. "Is he not beautiful?"

Daphne stared into the empty blanket, speechless.

Like paid mourners, the girl's voice wavered. "See how perfect he is? His father did not like that his foot was twisted, but my love has made him perfect."

Daphne backed a few steps.

The girl pressed close. "Here, would you like to hold him? Is he not beautiful? He is perfect you know."

Daphne's hands flew to her chest as the distraught mother shoved the blanket at her and continued to urge she hold the baby. At a loss, Daphne panicked, turned, and ran toward the gate. She did not stop until she could no longer hear the despondent wails.

Out of breath, she stopped in a small cove scooped from falling rocks. Sorrow ran on waves of shame down her cheeks. She sat on the lowest ledge with her head in her hands and rocked with grief. "It is my fault. It is all my fault."

She strained to remember every detail of her encounter with the girl back in the fall. The exact counsel the Voice gave, what was it?

A lone phrase drifted to her mind. *You will bear an heir….* The memory propelled her to her feet. She shook her fist at the Voice. "No, it was not my doing, it was you who promised she would bear an heir. You are the one."

My counsel was true. She bore a son.

Daphne gasped. The child was a male, but what made it seem so wrong? Had it triggered the hurtful memory of her grandmother's similar loss? The mysterious evil snicker that rumbled after the counsel arose in her mind.

Her jaw dropped. "You foresaw that the child would be deformed and that the father would command it be left to die. You knew it and regarded her misery with mirth. How could you? How could you be so cruel? Are you not a messenger of the great Apollo who is full of grace and mercy?" She collapsed in tears. "How could you, how could you?"

There was no response.

Emotionally spent but trapped in a bottomless bog with no way around the inescapable reality of her need for security, she buried her integrity and forced herself to return home.

Chapter Forty-Three

...full of deceit and all fraud.
– Acts 13:10

The weeks leading up to Nicanor's departure became a blur. Most of the household was engulfed with either his send-off banquet or preparing trunks for his extended stay. Daily, Daphne left early to avoid him. Daylight lingered noticeably now, but she did not return until near dark. On the day of the banquet, she found Nicanor waiting for her just before she reached the last rise.

"Hello. I thought it time for you to be back." Even in the twilight his smile gleamed and lit up his eyes.

Her hand shot to her lips and her heart thumped.

He cocked his head. "Are you glad to see me? It has been a good while."

She managed a weak smile and kept her tone light. "Of course. Yes, it has, but I know how busy you have been, and I have too."

His lips formed a pout. "You know I leave day after tomorrow, right?"

She avoided his eyes. "Yes, and is not tonight your farewell banquet?"

He stepped close. She could smell the musky-scented oil reserved for bathwater of the wealthy. "It is and I need to get ready." He reached out and touched her arm. "Daphne, Patharus has kept me on the run for months. I have not had a moment to myself! I want to, to see you before I go. Will you meet me in the garden tomorrow night after the evening meal?"

She thought her heart would burst. He had missed her. She fought to keep her chin from quivering. "That would ah, be nice."

A gentle smile engaged his eyes as she surrendered her resistance. "Good! I need to hurry off. They schedule my every waking moment." Already several strides down the path, he called back. "I cannot wait to be with you tomorrow night."

She pressed her knuckles to her lips and closed her eyes. He had not forgotten her. He wanted to see her before he left. Hope rekindled, boiled, and evaporated the heaviness that had simmered in her heart for weeks. She pushed aside her disappointment in the fate of the young girl, and murmured thanks to Apollo. In minutes, she reached the gate, eager to tell Kawit her good news.

She caught up with her behind one of the large tables burdened with piles of food nearly ready for the festivities. Kawit continued to wind raw fish around a mixture of ground olives and goat cheese, but insisted, "tell me again, exactly what did he say?"

"He said he wanted to see me before he leaves. I am so excited and yet so fearful. What if he tells me he is betrothed? What if he says that Patharus has found him a wife? I will die if he does, I will just die."

Kawit reached across the table and gripped her arm. "No! No, you will not die." Her eyes held Daphne's, almost threatening in their intensity. Seconds later a grin replaced the frown. "You are not going to leave me alone and friendless. Besides, he would not inform you unless his heart was not in agreement with the master's, and he wanted you to know it. Be patient, no use to borrow heartache you may never have to bear."

Daphne took a deep breath and released it. "You are right, time will tell. See you after the banquet, friend."

Chapter Forty-Four

My heart within me is broken.
– Jeremiah 23:9

Back in her room, she picked up her other tunic. Both had been issued upon arrival last summer, one replaced only because she ruined it in the foothills. She had received no more, except for the black shroud she wore as a cover in the market. She wished she could wear the lovely dress she wore to Nicanor's adoption banquet, but Jahtel had whisked it away the next morning.

She sighed. As involved as he would be with tonight's banquet, this would not be a good time to ask Jahtel for something new. She inspected her spare garment for stains. It was less tattered or faded than the one she had worn all day. She hung it back on its peg and fingered the frayed hem of the one she had on. She would wash this out tonight and wear it again tomorrow, then the better one will be fresh to wear when she met Nicanor.

On her way to refill soap at the supply room, she caught a glimpse of Nicanor as he crossed the courtyard. He wore an olive wreath on his head and a white linen Roman toga that fell from his shoulder in a lose fold that covered half his chest. A gold girdle cinched the tunic at his waist. Her eyes followed his every step until he disappeared into Patharus' quarters. The door closed on an unfamiliar, but pleasant desire that made her blush. She dismissed how handsome he looked and corralled her thoughts. Did he feel strange or unnatural in that Roman costume?

The slave's evening meal was later than usual. Most servants skipped their time together afterwards, exhausted by a full day and an even fuller evening. Kawit too, bid her an early goodnight and left.

The next day seemed a weeklong, but at last she returned and made a beeline for her room. The water in her pitcher had warmed to the day, a small compensation to sooth regrets she could only wash her face and not bathe.

She rearranged her hair, donned the fresh tunic, and wiped the dust from her only sandals. The memory of the abundant selection of shoes she had collected in Delphi, taunted her. She shrugged, "Shabby, but these will have to do."

Patharus' call came but he seemed preoccupied and quickly dismissed her. As she lined up for the evening meal she tapped her foot. Kawit caught up, "Calm down, it will be at least two hours before they finish at the master's table. Patharus requested a leisurely dinner for just him and Nicanor."

"I know, but reason cannot stop me from imagining what may lay ahead." She took little food, and they found an empty table. "How can a day pass so slowly?"

Kawit's expression sobered. "I guess it depends on what your day brings. With all the preparations for last night and the extra cleanup left for today, I do not know where the time went."

Daphne grimaced. Her task demanded much less physical effort than the work of most. "I am sorry, here I am groaning, and you look exhausted."

The gleam returned to Kawit's eyes. She pushed her face nose to nose with Daphne's and mocked a response "You are not complaining, you are just lovesick."

They finished their meal but before they parted, Kawit leaned close. "By the way, you look very nice. But try to relax or you will scare him to death."

The scolding brought a badly needed chuckle. Daphne returned to her room, sat on her mat, and rearranged her bedding for the third time.

Nicanor would not arrive for an hour, maybe more but unable to wait any longer, she left for the serene peace she found in the garden. She approached the bench, touched afresh that Nicanor had called it "ours." To wait proved as impossible as in her room. She ambled over and peered into the pond. The water was scummy and lifeless, not yet awakened to changes spring rains would soon bring.

Trees that towered over the oasis held the promise of leaves, and sprouts pushed at the soil in flowerbeds recently cleared of fall's dead foliage. She followed the path and searched for spring flowers. To her delight crocuses were up and ready to blossom. She smiled at the rare specimens she had disparaged over the previous summer. I wonder if Patharus ever comes and enjoys them. Kawit said his wife did before she was rendered disabled.

A pang of condemnation struck. Patharus had done nothing to deserve her earlier assessment that this beautiful garden should not be only for his pleasure. Clearly, he was entitled to enjoy the beauty of these special specimens and the estate he built for himself. He has been nothing but kind to me and more than upheld his promise of protection.

She continued to walk but her thoughts raced back to the bench and what Nicanor might say. A witches'-broom near the path was about to flower. She wondered why the one near the bench showed no buds. It must get less sunshine. To comment on what she saw failed to divert her thoughts, but she stuck with it. And look, that hyacinth is ready to pop. She leaned over and sniffed, but fragrance was still sealed behind purple petals that teetered on the brink of opening.

Their presence evoked a memory. Mother had promised to take her to the festival of Hyacinth before their lives were forever changed. She pushed her finger under the tip of her nose to stay the threat of tears. "It has been almost a year...." The words trailed into the stillness that surrounded her.

She resurrected her vow to keep the past buried. The sky had darkened. "She needed to get back. Nicanor may already be there concerned whether she decided not to come."

To her relief he had not arrived. She sat on the bench and tried to prepare herself for whatever might happen. Scenarios scattered her mind like startled sparrows. Her spirit soared with the chance he would ask her to wait for him, then dashed with the likelihood Patharus had much grander plans for his heir. Would he just want to affirm their friendship...let her down easy, or could there be something more?

As darkness enveloped the garden, she paced between the bench and the pond. Surely his evening meal would have ended by now. She folded her arms, leaned back into the bench, and shook off a persistent dread. Patharus probably wanted to discuss some last-minute details.

The air grew cold. Clouds blocked the moon's tiny sliver and left little light. She rubbed her upper arms against the chill, chewed her lower lip and glanced at the gate for the umpteenth time.

Moments stretched into an hour. Every excuse she conjured crumbled like stale raisin cakes.

Something rustled nearby bushes. Her heart leapt. He is here!

She jumped to her feet, expecting to hear his voice.

The sound faded. Silence closed the gap and whispered what she did not want to hear. Nicanor was not coming.

Chapter Forty-Five

Let no one deceive you with empty words.
- Ephesians 5:6

Daphne ran for her room, unaware someone watched from the shadows. She made no effort to still her footsteps as she crossed the courtyard. What did it matter if she were caught outside after dark? Life held no meaning, no hope. Pain-filled tears choked her throat.

Sobs wracked her body as she slipped through her curtain, pulled off her sandals, and threw herself on her mat. Why? Why did he say he wanted to see her and then not come? Questions and speculation muffled into her pillow for hours but found no tolerable conclusion.

She tossed, slept briefly, and tossed some more. Rejection gnawed like a trapped varmint. As Eos began his journey across the sky, she moaned into the glow. "Go back god of the dawn, I do not want another day."

The probability that Nicanor would soon leave for the coast sent her to her feet. I must leave before he does. I do not want to run into him.

She tied her sandals, grabbed her shawl, and slipped quietly down the hall. He would not humiliate her with some feeble excuse. In the dim light she bustled through the courtyard and out the gate, grateful the gatekeeper had yet to take up his post. She jogged and slowed only after she was sure she could not be seen from the estate. Servants came and left at different times, so except for Kawit she would not be missed.

The farther she traveled the angrier she became. She did not care if he was heir to Patharus' estate. What he had done was cruel. Nobody treated a friend like that." Her steps pounded the path with purpose. The sun rose and warmed her back, but the promise of a delightful spring day was lost on her.

She lifted her chin. "I am of no value to him and so shall he be to me. As far as I am concerned, he does not exist." Her stomach growled, a reminder she had skipped breakfast and eaten little the night before. She steeled herself against the discomfort and vowed to ignore any attempts to dismiss her right to be treated as an equal human being.

"Apollo is my only hope of a better life. He promised I would be free and somehow, I will find a way to make that happen." She expounded on her plans and built an impenetrable wall against the pain that stabbed at her heart with regrets over a future that was never promised.

Her distress brought thoughts of the deranged young mother, reality lost along with her baby. The cruelty imposed upon the unfortunate girl weighed heavily on her. She stopped short. The Voice. If it deceived the young mother, would it not deceive her? Was she a fool to trust it? Its promise to the girl proved to be a deception. Would her promise of freedom also be flawed?

The likelihood slowed her pace, but she soon reached the foothill that overlooked the gate. It would be well over an hour before the merchants opened their shops. She decided to wait on a grassy knoll just off the path. The bravado she declared while she walked, faded with the crisp morning air. *What am I going to do? The Voice has kept me from a horrible life but who knows if, and more likely when, it will desert or fail me?*

She threw up her hands. What did it matter? She had nothing, no future. She closed her eyes and covered her face. The lack of sleep teamed with despair and ran rampant. She had no reason to live. She would always be a slave, unloved and uncared for.

"Are you all right *Kopela?*"

She jumped, her heart pounding. Behind her stood a young man with tight curly hair. He carried a huge sack on his back. He was dressed like a slave. She poised her feet, ready to run if he moved in her direction. "Oh, I…I am waiting for the gates to open. I need to go into the city."

He sat his bag beside him and eyed her strangely. She backed a few steps, her mouth dry. He pulled out a rag, wiped his forehead and reached for his load. "The gates will be open by the time we reach them. Come along. This is not the best place for a girl to linger."

She followed him down the hill. He looked back several times but did not speak or wait for her. At the gate he joined those who waited for their goods to be inspected.

He nodded at her grateful, "Thank you." She overlooked the curiosity behind his eyes, touched that someone considered her worthy enough to be warned. Embarrassed at how she must look, she headed for the fountain, dipped the end of her shawl in the water and pressed it to her eyes. The cool liquid soothed her swollen lids, but not the pounding in her head. As soon she garnered a few coins, she would buy something to eat, that would help.

As she wandered in the *agora*, the realization hit that Patharus would likely accompany Nicanor to the coast and they would surely take the Roman road that divided the city. She chewed her lower lip. What if they decided to stop, what if they saw her.

She thought of the *palestra*. A short walk would bring her to the gymnasium where she could hide and see them approach. But when? They planned an early start and might already be on their way.

She moved to the back of the building, grateful it was empty. By late morning she began to wonder if somehow, she had missed them. By noon she was sure she must have. She left the building, but frequently checked back before she reentered the *stoa*. She needed to look for customers.

A man finally approached. Half-heartedly, she led him through the process, relieved it did not take long. He was less than generous with his recompense, but she decided to risk some of it on a small loaf of bread.

Throughout the afternoon she accommodated two more customers, still unable to figure how she could have missed Nicanor. A wagon would have been needed to carry his trunks. How did they pass without being seen?

On the way home she told herself it was not important. What mattered was that she made a decent profit.

Kawit waved and ran to meet her outside the estate. Expectancy lit her face as she plied her with questions. "I thought you would never get here. Where were you this morning? What happened last night, what did Nicanor say?"

All the pain she thought she vanquished encircled like a flock of persistent vultures. She opened her mouth but could only shake her head, her chin on her chest.

Kawit took hold of her shoulders. "What? What is it?" When Daphne did not move or answer, she steered her with an arm around her waist. "Come on." She led her around the least busy side of the courtyard, back to Daphne's room.

She sat on the bed mat with her head in her hands. Kawit snuggled close and rubbed her back.

Finally, Daphne spoke. "It is over. Nicanor did not show up last night. He—"

"He what? He did not show up? Why? Did he send word, explain?"

She shrugged. "It was not important to him. He probably forgot all about meeting me."

"I do not believe that. I know he cares for you."

"Well, you would not promise to meet someone you cared about and leave them alone in the garden at a late hour." She turned her face haggard from lack of sleep. "By the way, what time did they leave? I watched for the wagon to pass the city but never saw it." Tears she refused to release underlined the questions.

"You did not know? They left last night before dark. Patharus got a message that the ship he wanted Nicanor to board planned to leave earlier than scheduled. They needed the extra hours to get to the coast on time. I assumed it to be shortly after he met with…."

She stopped mid-sentence and tried to soften the blow. "You must have been in the garden when they pulled out."

Daphne squeezed her friend's hand. "He still could have found a minute to explain the change of plans or sent word with someone he trusted. But it does not matter now. He is out of my life, and I intend to forget him."

A servant stopped outside her room. "You are to report to the master's suite."

She groaned. "How am I going to get through that?"

Kawit soaked a cloth with cool water and helped her freshen herself. "You can do this. Hold your head up, you deserve better, anyway."

Patharus' servant ushered her in as soon as she arrived. She kept her eyes lowered, dropped her coins on the desk and backed as far as she dared.

"Well, Daphne, it seems you have had a good day."

Her head snapped up. That patronizing tone did not come from Patharus.

Chapter Forty-Six

For it is not a good report that I hear.
– 1 Samuel 2:24

Daphne's jaw dropped. Stello's smirk revealed how he relished the position of power. She nodded and returned her glance to the floor.

"Tell me, how did you come by this goodly amount?"

His syrupy tone made her shiver. She lifted her chin. He would not see her squirm "The gods blessed me with several men who sought insight into the future today."

He did not respond. Her heart began to hammer. What was on his mind? Oh, please, let him dismiss her.

"Well, Daphne, I hope to hear much more of this in days to come. You are dismissed."

Despite her hasty retreat, she hoped he had not sensed her relief.

In the days to come. That sounded like Patharus would be away a good while.

Back in her room she grew restless, rose from her mat, and paced. Where was Patharus? She hoped he had not gone all the way to Rome with Nicanor; if so, he might not return for months, and to report to Stello for that long made her uneasy.

You need not fear. I will not leave you helpless or alone.

She did not reply, grateful the Voice did not know how her trust had waned. Like neither Apollo nor his priests back in Delphi had discerned her doubts, time had proven that the Voice did not know her thoughts, only what it saw or heard.

She would guard her words. Apollo's messenger must not suspect a change, not when her favor and protection hung on her ability to receive its supernatural insights. The day her freedom came, that day she would find a way to rid herself of its presence.

She struggled to sound sincere. "Yes, you are my protection from men like Stello."

An image of the distraught young mother rekindled the battle her integrity waged with her source of survival. Her chin quivered. How long before she can escape these impossible circumstances or find a viable way around them?

She had no choice but to wait.

*****

The next day to decrease the empty hours that led to the evening meal, she lingered longer in the city. To report to Stello, the worst part of her day.

He delighted in her discomfort and dragged out the procedure. "Three drachmas. Wonderful. Now tell me about your encounters."

She swallowed the nerves that climbed her throat. As briefly as possible, she told him of a man who wanted to undermine a competitor's success, one who wanted to know if the marriage he had in mind for his son would profit the family's estate, and of two others she had serviced that day.

"Go on," he prompted.

She was at a loss. What more could she say? She could feel his eyes sweep over her. For an instant his face became that of Talsta, Apollo's murderous high priest. Panic leapt to her chest. He had eyed her the same way.

Without sound, she cried, "Apollo, please help me,"

Tell him about the dire outcome of the lust-filled man who was sent to his doom last week.

She gulped and began. "Recently, a man came to ask for Apollo's help to secure a certain woman for his bride. She had already been betrothed to his brother, but his lust was so great he could not accept it. Against all counsel, he demanded his own way."

She paused, pulled a deep breath, and continued. "Apollo granted his desire in that his brother was killed in what looked like an accident. But before he could claim her, the girl was found to be with child by his dead brother. Defiled, she became unacceptable in the man's eyes. His disappointment merged with guilt and grief for his brother. It overwhelmed him. He took his own life."

Did Stello recognize his own evil desires? She did not dare look up. Relief flowed when he quietly dismissed her.

Days turned to a week and still Patharus had not returned. Late one afternoon Kawit waved and met her and walked her back to the gate. "How was your day?"

"About the same…yours?"

"Not bad…long as I avoid Stello, I call it a good day. Did you meet anyone interesting?"

Daphne's tone was sharp. "I do not want to talk about the hateful things people do to others."

Kawit grew quiet. She put her arm around Daphne's waist, and they walked in silence.

Her eyes welled. She did not deserve such a friend. "I am sorry, *Kalon*. I cannot seem to.…"

"Hey, no need. I know how you feel about your work, but if you continue to bear everyone's pain and sorrow it will destroy you."

"I know, but sometimes despair seems to take over. Like I am not in control of my feelings." She hugged her friend. "What would I do without you?"

"Ummm…well for one thing you would miss dinner most nights. Probably waste away to nothing and I would have to spoon feed you back to health."

Daphne laughed and gave her a friendly jab. "Let us get together after dinner and do our baths and clothes…alright?"

*****

Time did not dim Daphne's pain. On walks back to the estate Nicanor filled her thoughts. How could he? Why did he not send her a message? Surely he could have found a minute to let her know he could not come.

At the hill that overlooked the gate, she squinted into the setting sun, but Kawit was not there. *Jahtel must have her too busy to meet me.*

Before she reached her room, Stello commanded she report immediately. Daphne nodded to his messenger. *Why the urgency?* She went directly to Patharus' office with dread of what new demands the overseer might make.

Stello did not look up when she placed her wages on Patharus' large desk. He swept the money into his hand. "Two drachmas. Alright you may leave."

It took a few seconds to realize she had been dismissed. She backed away and chanced a glance at him. His fingers twitched on a ledger he appeared to study. She shook her head and left as quick as she could.

"Daphne, Daphne, wait a minute."

She looked behind to see who whispered her name. "Femi. Hello. I have not seen you in weeks, where have you been?"

The girl's eyes were wide, and her chin trembled.

"Femi, what is the matter? Are you alright?

287

She put her finger to her lips. "Shhh, can we talk in your room, I am not supposed to be back here."

"Of course." She led her through the curtain. "Femi, what is it? Are you in trouble?"

The girl covered her face with her hands, then pulled them to her chin. She shuddered. "Daphne, it is Kawit. She is hurt bad, and she is asking for you."

Chapter Forty-Seven

In the day of grief and desperate sorrow.
– Isaiah 17:11

Daphne was already out the door. "What, where is she? What happened?"

Femi grabbed her arm. "Wait. You must be careful, it was Stello. Anyone who helps Kawit will be in trouble. Please do not tell anyone I told you...."

"Femi, I do not care! Where is she?"

"Down where she stays, but...."

Daphne did not wait for her to finish. She ran as fast as she could and barged through the door of the outbuilding where Kawit lived with a dozen single women. "Kawit! Kawit, where are you?

An older slave who sat near the door jerked her head at a mat in one corner.

Kawit lay in a pool of blood. Daphne's jaw fell. "Oh Kawit, oh no...." For a moment she thought she would be sick. She shook it off, dropped to her knees and lifted her friend's head and upper torso into her lap. Kawit's eyes nearly disappeared behind swollen, red bruises that extended to her jaw.

"Kawit. It is me! It is Daphne. Kawit? Kawit, can you hear me?" She rocked her in her arms. "Oh, Kawit."

She moaned. "Daphne, I...." Her half-naked body convulsed, and she vomited blood.

Panicked, Daphne called out to the woman by the door. "Please, has anyone summoned the physician? Has Halaten been called?"

The woman shrugged. "Only the overseer or Jahtel can send for him. We are not allowed."

Daphne could not believe her ears. "But she needs help! Surely they would not...."

The woman shook her head and looked away.

Daphne's anger burst like an aged wineskin. She wanted to shake the woman. With great care she laid her friend back on the mat. "I am going for help, Kawit. Please, hang on."

She ran past the woman all the way to the physician's door. "Halaten! Halaten! Kawit has been horribly hurt, please come help her."

The doctor stuck his head out and quickly shifted his eyes. "Daphne, I cannot attend a slave unless Stello or Jahtel—"

"But they are not here, and she needs you now! Please come, she is bleeding from the inside. Please help her, Halaten. I know you are a caring man. Do not let her die."

Halaten looked pained. "I cannot, but I will go and inquire of Jahtel. Perhaps he will approve a call."

She ran back to Kawit, her stomach in knots. What is wrong with them? Do they not care that Kawit may die?

She tried to hide her fear and held her friend in her arms. "Kawit, help is on the way. I am here, I will not leave you."

Kawit squinted through her blood-caked lids.

The woman by the door wandered down to look. Daphne scowled. "Please, please, could you at least get me some cold water and clean cloths?"

She peered at Kawit. "Not sure it will do her any good." At Daphne's glare, she hastened to their communal water pitcher.

Kawit opened her mouth and gasped, her breathing shallow. "Daphne, I...."

"Do not try to talk, *Kalon*. The doctor is coming."

The term brought a twitch to Kawit's lips. She groaned and grasped her stomach. "Must tell....be careful...Stello. Caught in laundry...raped... beaten to hide...." Her breath grew more ragged, and blood bubbled from her lips. She coughed and spit what she could. "eye...on you. Be care...." She choked as her eyes closed.

Where was Halaten? Her effort to keep her friend awake spiraled into desperate gasps. "Kawit, wake up!" She used the hem of her tunic to wipe the blood from her friend's mouth. "Stay with me, Kawit. Help is coming. Talk to me. Kawit."

Kawit nodded, gave a slight smile but did not open her eyes. "Too late...told you... collect...this it." Her words strangled in a coughing fit that brought up more blood.

Daphne stroked her forehead. "Shhhh, you must be still."

Kawit gasped for air. "Cannot...no time. Member, Hathor never fails...." She fought to lift her arms and make the familiar sign. Daphne put her ear close to her friend's lips. "Member...." was all she heard before Kawit's head flopped and a lifeless arm brushed Daphne's face.

Daphne's hysterics filled the room. She clutched her friend to her bosom. "I cannot live here without you, Kawit. Oh, please, please come back to me."

She was still distraught when Halaten's strong arms pried her from her friend and lifted her off the floor. A crowd of onlookers arrived along with him. He directed two of the women to take her aside. Her knees buckled as she fought to get back to Kawit. With one on each side, the women kept her on her feet.

One whispered, "Come, let us help you dear." The other added, "You will feel better tomorrow."

She gave each a vicious push, her face contorted with grief. "Get away from me!"

Halaten joined them. "Daphne, I am sorry. I...."

She lunged at him and beat his chest. "Where were you? How could you let her die? How could you?"

Halaten put his arms around her and held her. She fought to get loose and back to her friend. "Kawit, oh, my Kawit." Her strength gone, Daphne finally gave up the fight. Jahtel sailed through the door moments later, his face wreathed with disgust. He looked at the crowd, put his hands on his hips and headed straight for her. Halaten held up his hand, his frown a plea for Jahtel to back off. To everyone's surprise, the man stopped in his tracks.

The physician turned Daphne over to the two women with instructions to give her a sleeping potion. At Jahtel's nod, they led her still sobbing back to her room. One helped her out of her blood-soaked tunic while the other fetched cool water to bathe her. They gave her the doctor's potion, laid her on her mat and stayed until the remedy lulled her to sleep.

She woke often, groggy and disoriented. Each time, the horror and finality of Kawit's death crashed like a silent avalanche. Sleep did not return until fresh sobs were exhausted.

At dawn, she sat on the edge of her mat, her head in her hands. How will she stand it here without Kawit. She wailed an accusation at the Voice. "And where were you? How could you let this happen?"

Men will fail you, but I will always be here for you.

The message held no comfort. She doubled over and wept some more. "You let them kill my only friend. If Apollo is so powerful, why did he not stop Stello? Kawit never hurt anyone."

Silence filled the room.

In time, her mind ran to her father's death and the preparations she and her mother had tended to on his body. She jumped to her feet. "I need to prepare Kawit's body. No one loved her like I did."

Chapter Forty-Eight

…who suppress the truth in unrighteousness.
– Romans 1:18

Daphne looked around for her tunic. The blood-soaked garment had been removed and another hung on the peg. She reached for it and snarled. How considerate…they act as if nothing even happened.

A heaviness enveloped her soul as she washed her face and smoothed her hair. She rushed to find Jahtel and seek his permission to attend Kawit's body. Slaves milled about the courtyard, ready to eat and to secure the day's orders. Many stared as she skipped the line and went to the table where Femi refilled empty pans. "Femi, have you seen Jahtel?" Her voice broke. "I want to ask him to let me prepare Kawit's…body."

Tears sprang to Femi's eyes, her voice barely a whisper. "Oh, Daphne, there is no preparation when a slave dies. Kawit's body has already been…disposed of."

Her jaw dropped. "But what…how? Where is she? I did not get to say goodbye." Her voice rose. "Femi, where is she?"

"Is there a problem here?"

She wheeled around, aghast to find herself face to face with Stello. At the sight of him heat rose and colored her face.   All consequences of questioning an authority faded with the finality of her loss. Through gritted teeth she screamed, "You! You killed my friend. She was innocent and you killed her!"

For a second Stello stared in disbelief.

Within seconds a fist knocked her to the ground. He yanked her up by one arm and spun her around, his voice surprisingly calm. "For now, because of your grief, I will excuse your outburst." His eyes narrowed. "But do not ever let it happen again. Kawit was a disobedient slave and needed to be made an example to all who refuse to follow orders. Including you."

He tapped the lash that hung at his side. "You have ten minutes to be on your way into the city. Is that clear?"

Daphne stifled her indignation. She cleansed her bleeding lips, picked up her provisions and left for the city. Kawit's words resounded in her ears. …. *he has his eye on you, be careful.*

The dread of his brutality smothered her intentions to reveal his lie about Kawit. Failure accused and shamed her. No wonder he dismissed her so quickly yesterday. She hissed at the memory of how nervous he seemed. He knew Kawit was her friend, knew she would know he lied to cover up the rape.

….all who refuse to follow orders….

The unspoken peril behind the overseer's threat haunted her. She touched her swollen lips and shuddered. He could do the same to her as he did to Kawit, and no one would stop him.

She wished Patharus would return. What would he think of Kawit's death? Would he punish Stello if the truth came out? As terrified as everyone was of him, she doubted Patharus would ever even know what happened.

Loneliness fell like a shroud. "Oh, Kawit, I miss you already." A heart wrenching groan bellowed deep within her soul as she mourned the empty niche Kawit had filled in her heart and life.

She pictured her brave effort to make the sign of her god before she died. So where was Hathor when her loyal follower needed her? And where was Apollo when her father was killed and when the Roman stole his estate? And when we were sold into slavery and that awful captain raped mother? "Are the gods nothing but powerless myths?"

"Call on me and I will help you."

Daphne stopped and listened but heard no more from that *"gentle voice"* that first spoke to her when she awoke to the nightmare that began the family's enslavement. Who or what was it, and why would it speak to her?

The end of her day in the city could not come soon enough. Twice she had lost her concentration and failed to follow the Voice's instructions. She checked her profits. Not half of what she had earned yesterday. Would Stello reprimand her…or worse?

Like an echo from an abyss, thoughts of the man drummed up Kawit's last words, again …. *be careful, he has his eyes on you.*

She shuddered. But she had Patharus' promise of safety. Stello would not dare accost her…would he?

The call she dreaded came soon after she arrived. To her relief Stello did not mention the morning incident and seemed as anxious to dismiss her as she was to leave. For the first time since Nicanor's departure, she slipped into the garden to pass the hours until the evening meal. Spring's early blossoms and budding trees had dropped their petals, making way for summer flowers and fruit, but she hardly noticed.

Grief rose in waves of memories of Kawit she could not shake. She walked for a while, unmindful of where she stopped. The bench by the pond beckoned. Its memories of time with Nicanor rendered her as helpless to ignore thoughts of him as those of Kawit.

…let's sit here, on 'our' bench, Daphne.

His smile, his dimple, his deep blue eyes, now even the bench and the pond conspired to bring past encounters to her attention.

She sat with her face in her hands. If she could not find solace here, where could she go? Nicanor was gone and now Kawit.

Let me be your comfort. Have I not brought to pass my promises…honor, wealth, prestige?

She was too disheartened to argue. Men had begun to treat her with respect, but her prestige hinged on the name of her master. And as for wealth, ultimately it too belonged to Patharus. She sighed and thought of what her life had become since she last saw her family. That none of those things mattered if you could not share them with people you loved, would never again be taken for granted.

The Voice had neglected to mention the most crucial thing, her freedom. But she was not up to defending her failure to venerate Apollo or her failures in the city today. She left the garden and joined the others for the evening meal, aware Stello's eyes followed her around the courtyard.

"Daphne, there you are. For days I have hoped to see you."

The slave she formerly witnessed to about Apollo's superior powers stood before her. He pulled up a bench and sat across the table from her.

"You searched for me...why?"

"Yes. I wanted to thank you for what you told me about Apollo. I decided to honor and believe in your god like you said, and I was given the higher position you said would follow."

She smiled and hoped he did not sense her amazement. "I am so glad, I—"

His face glowed. "I have been put in charge of the group that is loaned out to other estates. How did you know?" He shrugged. "I guess it does not matter."

"That is great, I—"

He rose. "I wanted to thank you. I have told my friends about Apollo's power. It is greater than any gods I worshiped before."

His undeterred belief baffled her. She mumbled her thanks. Was he right? Was Apollo really the most powerful god?

She had learned about the blight that destroyed Malatus' crops, and recalled how he had scoffed and disregarded the warning given at Patharus' celebration.

She forgot about her food and leaned into her fists. Apollo did keep her from being discovered in the *adytum*, and he knew of Semiele's coming troubles. He was right about when we would leave the ship and arrive in Corinth, and as tragic as it was, he knew that poor girl would have the baby boy she wanted…and, and so many other things.

That man was right. Apollo is the most powerful god, and you are privileged to be his chosen vessel.

Daphne ignored the input, determined to sort for herself what she knew to be true. She dissected each encounter from a fresh perspective and drew her own conclusions. Having great power or knowledge of the future did not necessarily bring about good. Despite their undying loyalties, Hathor had not saved Kawit and Apollo had certainly failed her family.

Chapter Forty-Nine

…on some have compassion.
– Jude 22

Daphne was convinced Apollo's main agenda was to bring men to commit to him as their god. Setting her free might also be a distant or phony promise. Still, every morning she went through the motions, paid him homage and pledged obedience to the Voice. A ray of hope pierced her helplessness. If she tried harder, perhaps the Voice would influence Patharus to grant her freedom sooner.

Despite a resolve to keep her mind on her work, weeks of unprecedented loneliness, isolation and loss opened wide the door to despair. Many slaves avoided her, aware of the tension between her and the overseer. With no one to talk to she found herself interacting often with the Voice.

Alone in her room she asked, "Why do they shun me? I have not harmed anyone, only tried to get help for Kawit."

They are jealous of the superior treatment given you because of your gift of fortune telling. Any other slave would have been badly beaten or killed if he challenged Stello as you did.

Daphne pondered that. "But some said they admired my bravery. I know they work harder physically, but their jobs cannot be more stressful."

Others will lead you astray. I am your friend.

She blew out her lamp and lay with her hands twined beneath her head, determined not to think of Kawit or Nicanor. What was keeping Patharus? Surely, he should be back by now. "I so hope he did not go to Rome with Nicanor."

He will return in two days.

She sat up with a jerk. "He will?' Relief gushed in a sigh. Working under Stello's stare each day made her want to cover herself with a heavy wrap. Kawit's fear had become hers.

She laid down again. Should she tell Patharus about Stello's lie and his brutal treatment of Kawit? Would he believe her? She practiced different ways to broach the subject but rejected each. Why would he believe her over his long-time overseer?

More than that she longed to ask about Nicanor. If only Kawit were here, she would find all there was to know the very day Patharus returned.

Sleep evaded her for hours and the next morning she had to push herself out of bed. The summer sun grew hot as she walked to the city. She smiled at how her mother had stressed she should protect her delicate skin. With a groan she adjusted her shawl. Nothing here was the same. The memory threatened to draw her back into thoughts of her family's whereabouts. With a shake of her head, she shut the door on the hurtful loss. She threw herself into the task and praised Apollo loud enough to drown painful voices from the past.

She entered the city and had almost passed the *stoa* when she realized the distraught young mother was nowhere to be seen. Day after day the girl had appeared with a baby blanket in arm and insisted people to come see her child. Guilt dampened Daphne's relief as she looked around to be sure. "Poor thing, I wonder what had happened to her."

Her husband disposed her.

She gasped. "Disposed? You mean she is, is...."

Yes, she is no more. It is for the best. She had become a nuisance and an embarrassment to her husband.

Daphne seethed at the Voice's cold indifference. It took hours to even want to find someone who needed her counsel. As it turned out, someone found her.

"*Kopela, Kopela,*" an overweight man with a wheezy voice hollered from behind. "Are you not Patharus' sorceress?"

The caller puffed to catch up with her. "Yes, Patharus is my master. Can I seek the gods for you?"

"Yes. I need counsel...where can we go?"

"Go into the courtyard and find an empty *exedra*. I will be with you shortly."

She filled her jug at the fountain and joined the man. He stood half hidden in the shade of the opening. Perspiration poured from under his hair and down his flushed face.

She eyed him with concern. "Are you alright?"

He mopped his forehead. "Yes, but I need you to seek the gods. I think my beloved has rendezvoused with someone else." His chin quivered as he cleared his throat. "Something has changed, and I suspect my neighbor made some questionable visits while I was away on business. Can the gods tell me if it is true…and what to do if it is?"

"I am sure your answers will come. Please sit down while I seek Apollo on your behalf."

She was barely into her routine when the Voice spoke unexpectedly in the gruff tone she hated. *"Why do you seek help from Apollo when you have been heard to claim Zeus and his offspring to be a myth, and have not paid homage or sacrificed at Apollo's temple for years?"*

The man squirmed and mumbled an excuse.

Do not try to hide that it is only your own desires that you have indulged, your very flesh denies it.

Daphne could hardly believe the words that spewed from her lips. The Voice had never attacked anyone in this manner. She eyed the man and wondered if he would leave. *Prostrate yourself before the great Apollo and ask his forgiveness.*

The man did not hesitate. He fell to his knees and then on his face. She scooted to give him room and hoped his loud repentance would not draw unwanted attention. She should have chosen a more private setting.

After the man quieted and vowed to pay the proper homage to Apollo, the Voice spoke again. *"Your neighbor and your beloved are both guilty. An infirmity will come upon them both. They will be ashamed and confess their wrong and beg your forgiveness. You are to forgive and treat your love as if he had done no wrong."*

Daphne blanched. *He?*

"Do not neglect your promise to honor and pledge your loyalty to Apollo or worse things will come upon you."

The Voice faded and the man labored to push himself up off the ground. He thrust some coins into her hand and flew from the courtyard.

She swallowed her dread. "What is the infirmity that will come upon them?"

It has already started in their loins and will consume them and him too.

She gasped. "But why? Must they die even if they repent and change their ways?"

They should have remained loyal. They deserve it.

She wandered about the *agora* with a wish she could warn the man. How could the Voice be so calloused, so uncaring? By late afternoon, she counted her coins and decided to go home. It was late evening before Stello called for her report. She dashed down the hall, eager to put this behind her. She laid the coins on Patharus' desk and hoped for a quick dismissal. She lowered her eyes and waited.

Stello nodded, a slimy smile on his face as his eyes swept her form. "Well done. I have wanted to tell you that I am truly sorry I had to discipline Kawit so harshly." He rose from the desk and came toward her. "I hope we can be friends…I am really very fond of you."

She stepped back her heart racing.

He reached out and touched her arm. "You must not—"

The door behind them opened and a servant stuck in his head. Stello dropped his hand and glowered at the man.

"The master has returned…you asked to be notified immediately."

Stello waved him off. Through pursed lips, he scowled, and dismissed Daphne. She could not get out of there fast enough, worried he might take his frustrations out on her.

Chapter Fifty

Under his tongue is trouble and iniquity.
– Psalm 10:7

Back in her room, Daphne wrung her hands and paced.

Have I not told you I will protect you? He will not harm you.

"But he means to. I could see it in his face."

By dinner time, her insides had barely calmed. She sat alone, picking at her food.

Those women over there do not like you. They think you hold yourself higher than the rest of the slaves.

The women were deep in conversation. "Why do you say that? They have always been friendly."

They have seen you with the master's son. Did you notice no one sat with you to eat?

"They were all seated when I arrived, and their table was full."

Still talking, the women passed where she sat. Daphne turned as they approached. "Nice evening." No one responded.

See?

"They did not hear me, they always speak."

You will see.

She woke several times that night. Her mind jumped from Stello's evil intent, to the distraught young mother, dead at her husband's command, to the man who would follow his partner and lover in death. Did Apollo send the deadly infirmity that would kill those men? Was he behind the death of that innocent young mother who trusted him to give her the son he promised? Why was he so cruel?

Her thoughts would not settle. Back in Delphi, everyone revered Apollo. Did they know he used his power with no regard for people's pain? Her grandmother had been evasive, quick to change the subject. Did she know of his cruel streak? Did she care?

Sleep came but answers did not.

The women whom the Voice accused the night before motioned for her to join them for breakfast, but she did not see them because the Voice intervened, *Go this way and you will steer clear of Stello.* She found a table and sat by herself then left for the day.

The city swelled with people, busier than usual. At the forum, an elderly Roman expounded on the necessity for loyalty to Claudius, their emperor, and the power of the Roman army. She passed with a mere glance.

By noon only one man had sought her skills. She wandered near the baths. Perhaps someone there would have need of her. She intended to sit by the water that streamed under the building and eat her lunch, but a slave with two children in her care had claimed the spot.

Tell her something exciting is happening in the city that the children would enjoy, and she will leave.

She frowned. "That is a lie. I cannot do that."

She will never know. She will just think she arrived too late.

"No. I will find another place."

She smiled at the children as she passed. How many times had Belte taken her and Alexander into the city or to special events that preempted the festivals? Before the memory shot sprouts of regret, she focused on a place to eat and settled on a grassy knoll not far from the stream.

It was hard to leave the shaded respite but today she would report to Patharus and she wanted to earn enough to please him. She brushed off her tunic and scurried for the *agora*.

Two hours later she had gained a goodly amount. The afternoon sun was still high, so she decided to walk through the marketplace and view the fresh merchandise that arrived daily from Neapolis.

Beautiful *chitons* and *peplos'* of pure silk graced several stalls. They tugged at the memory of her wardrobe back in Delphi, but Daphne did not linger. Merchants frowned if she stayed too long, interested in paying customers not indigent slaves. The last booth sold Corinthian brass mirrors.

She stopped and held up a highly polished sample. Where was the excited young girl who stared into one just like it a year ago? The soft baby face was gone, replaced by a young woman with sharp cheekbones and sad eyes. The owner's wife stomped over, her face in a snarl. "Would you like to buy?"

Use some of the money you earned today. No one will be the wiser.

"I cannot, it is Patharus' money, not mine."

He will never know. You deserve it, go on, buy it.

The woman cocked her head.

"No. No, I am sorry, I only meant to admire your mirrors."

The shop owner snatched the mirror from her. Her expression left no doubt Daphne was not welcome.

The humiliation still smarted as she began the walk home. One day they will realize she was a person, not someone to look down upon.

Patharus looked at the coins she laid on his desk and smiled. "Well, Daphne, Stello tells me you have been very successful while I was away. Have you had any trouble in the city?

She shook her head. "It is good to have you back, Master."

"And no trouble here?"

Did he know about Kawit? Should she tell him or of her fear of Stello?

Say nothing It will only cause you trouble.

"Everything is as it was, Master."

"Good, good, you may leave."

She left, awed at how easily she lied. She had not intended to. Why did she succumb to the Voice's counsel? Patharus had given her a perfect opportunity to tell of Stello's brutality and

Kawit's death. Truth would have been a gamble, but she should have taken the risk. She owed it to her friend.

The hours before dinner were spent in the garden. Lost in thought, she stopped by the pond. Water lilies with their yellow stamens and creamy white petals had folded for the night. How different they were in the evening, as diverse as her values from those of the alien personality that sought to influence her every thought. She sighed. It is in me, operates through me, but is separate from me. It claims its agenda brings honor to Apollo. But at what cost?

She slumped on the bench. What could she do, it was her only hope of a decent future, and she could not jeopardize the Voice's promise to free her and make her equal with Nicanor.

The thought jolted her. Where did that come from? She jumped to her feet. "Stop it! Nicanor made it clear he does not care. Stop clinging to what will never be." A startled bird flew from branch to branch, its objection to the intrusion strong and shrill. Shocked at the outburst and hope she thought she buried, she retrieved her shawl from the bench. "Alright, alright, little bird I will leave."

At the gate, she vowed not to look back. Her future lay with Apollo. He sent his will through the Voice, and she must shut her eyes to his cruelty and motives. She had no choice.

Chapter Fifty-One

There is no truth or mercy…
– Hosea 4:1

Daphne's vow to shut her eyes to the Voice's evil intentions was soon tested as she walked the streets of the city.

"*Kopela, Kopela,* wait."

The man with the unfaithful lover waved at her. It had been several weeks. Was his love still with him?

He caught up, his breath in gasps. "Please, please. I did everything Apollo told me to do. I forgave my beloved and my neighbor and I have sent great sacrifices to his temple in Athens. But my beloved is very ill. You must help me. I fear he may die."

Her heart went out to him. What should she do? She listened for the Voice but heard nothing. To stall for time, she questioned him further.

The man grew quiet and stared, his face a pool of expectancy.

Her uneasiness grew as she strained to hear the inner Voice. "Would you like me to consult the gods for you again?"

"Yes, please, Apollo must help me."

Goose bumps peaked on her arms. She led the man to an empty *exedra.* Why could she not hear the Voice?

"My neighbor is very ill too. He has not come around since I confronted and forgave him. They say he will not live long."

Grieved by the panic behind his eyes, she murmured her sympathy, bid him sit before her and began to beseech Apollo.

Silence.

She tried again. "Oh Apollo, god of sun and light, full of power and victorious in battle, hear our plea." Daphne squirmed. Where was the Voice?

She eyed the man. He waited with his head bowed near the ground. She swallowed the panic that gnawed her throat. This had never happened before. Should she make up something? Would he know the difference?

Her insides rumbled as the Voice chastised her.

Apollo is not pleased that you concern yourself more with people than his wishes. Do not take your dependence on me for granted. On your own you are nothing. Tell the man Apollo says to go take care of his beloved while he can. The man will not live.

She despaired. "I cannot tell him that. You will kill his...."

Do as I say.

At her refusal, gruff words poured through her. *Apollo has deemed the man is not worthy to live, he will die. If he is truly your beloved, die with him and you will be together forever.*

The man's head shot up, his face a wreath of pain and anger. "Die with him? That is the help I have paid you for?"

His reaction terrified her. "It…it is counsel from Apollo."

He stood and screamed in her face. "You are nothing but a fake. My beloved will not die! Get out of my way."

She tried to back away but could not dodge his vicious push. Her feet tangled and she fell, curled into a ball, and covered her head with her arms. "Apollo, save me!"

His footsteps faded.

The man has left. He will not harm you. Take care you do not disobey the wishes of Apollo in the future, or you will surely find yourself stripped of his wisdom and his protection.

She crawled back under the *exedra's* cover and hugged her knees to her chest. "Yes, yes, I failed you. Please forgive me, I will do better." She rubbed the shoulder that hit the ground and peered into the courtyard, grateful no one had witnessed the ugly scene.

Weeks became months of loneliness and isolation. Without Kawit to share her sorrows or bring her out of her doldrums, Daphne found herself alone much of her free time. The Voice's negative input hung like a black fog over her head. She began to deem herself unwelcome at the evening gatherings. Rather than mingle as soon as they were excused for the night she escaped to her room.

She sought peace in the garden after an especially stressful day, heightened by an image of a funeral procession that would not fade. Summer's blooms had dried and fallen, a perfect match for her mood. She stepped around a small statue of a barely clothed nymph. "How I wish you could guide me, father."

Your father is dead, Call on me.

She ignored the Voice and reminded herself not to speak aloud of the wretchedness she felt nor challenge the evil that compounded her guilt.

The image of the funeral returned. A distraught widow with her children, men with the bier on their shoulders, paid mourners, flute girls. All confirmed the deceased was a fellow Greek.

She had swerved from the procession to avoid memories of her father's funeral, the smell of burnt flesh, the box readied for his remains. Gossip among the mourners had reached her ears. "You know the poor man lost everything, took his own life."

When news arrived at the estate earlier, she knew the dead man was the one the Voice counseled to beg a loan from his father-in-law and a sickening thud had hit her stomach.

Sorrow for the family and an endless supply of guilt blurred her eyes. She lowered herself to the bench by the pond. Did the relative refuse to help or had the man failed to humble himself and ask?

"Why? Why did it not work out? Will his family lose their home?"

The man was a fool. He tried to find a way around Apollo's commands.

She shuddered. "But his wife, his children...."

The woman returned to her father, but the children have been taken to Athens to be —

She sprang from the bench. "No! Not to be sold."

The evil laugh boiled within. *The disobedient pay dearly. He should have submitted to Apollo's counsel.*

A whirlwind of uncertainty enveloped her. Would she pay with a life of never-ending slavery though she obeyed the Voice's every whim? She ran from the garden, desperate to escape the presence within.

Mornings were noticeably cooler as she headed into the city each day. Flashes of color dappled the trees and snow circled the mountains' upper peaks. She sighed. Nicanor had been gone seven moons and she knew nothing of his progress.

She missed all the latest information Kawit shared with her. Shame followed. Kawit had been much more than a source of gossip.

She wandered the *stoa,* on the lookout for customers. Women, with servants close behind crowded the *agora* to choose the best of the late fall produce. The fragrance of melons and peaches filled the air. Bright tomatoes contrasted with shiny cucumbers, The sight of them made her mouth water for one of Belte's salads that dripped with vinegar and olive oil.

The morning passed quickly, two customers and neither with desperate needs. After a quick lunch, she walked the west *stoa*, alert to any sign of conflict.

Call out of Apollo's greatness.

Daphne gulped at the order. "Call out?"

Yes, extol him before those people sitting over there.

"But I—"

Will you refuse Apollo again?

She glanced at the group of men and women who talked quietly among themselves.

"Those people are of the Jewish sect. Their god does not allow them to seek the future, so I do not think—"

They are enemies of Apollo. Call out.

She shot another glance. Enemies? Enemies of Apollo? What did that mean?

Chapter Fifty-Two

My enemies are vigorous and they are strong.
– Psalm 38:19

Call out.

The choice was painful: harass innocent people for reasons she could not comprehend or refuse and lose her protection. A picture flashed of Kawit lying in a pool of blood. Daphne could not let that happen.

She raised her voice. "Apollo is the god of all gods."

Louder, and do not stop.

She swallowed her dread and escalated her cry. "Apollo is the god of all gods. He is the god of light and music. All power is his to do as he pleases. He is great in battle and victorious over all."

Words that once triggered denial no longer affected her, squelched by the Voice's demand she acclaim Apollo above all. She tried not to look at people gathered in the *stoa* but could not miss their shocked stares.

Heads bent close and lips moved in whispers. The group gathered their things and started to leave. Some of the men looked back and frowned at her.

Follow them.

"But they—"

Follow them and shout louder.

She choked back her tears and called out. "There is none more powerful than Apollo. He knows all things and there is none before him. All of Greece reveres him...." Perspiration beaded her forehead and prickled beneath her arms.

"Daphne, why are you persecuting me?"

She gasped. It was that same *"quiet voice"* she heard after Kawit's death, so different than the one that demanded so much of her. But who was it and what did it mean? The Voice she knew and dreaded prodded. She refocused, determined not to anger it again. Finally, her voice gave out.

She stumbled in a rut. Oh please, let me sink into the ground and disappear.

The Voice began to shout in the raspy Voice she hated. *There is none higher than Apollo and he reigns with his father, Zeus. He is god!*

It brought fear to the faces of the women she followed. Their men quickly stepped between and steered them on.

She became separated by a crowd of curious onlookers who had gathered. She crept into the courtyard and treaded for the fountain, grateful no authority followed. A cool drink soothed her raw throat. She splashed water on her face and found a quiet spot to sit and sort out what it meant. Why? Why had the Voice been so angry and why did Apollo hate these Jewish people and their God so much? And that *"other voice,"* why had her heart tugged at its gentle inquiry?

*****

The demonic spirit of divination sputtered. I do not know why you are so angry, I made sure she followed those Jews and proclaimed the greatness of Apollo. They are not likely to hang around in the agora any time soon.

The ruling prince over Greece shouted, You are so stupid. How could you have been assigned to such a crucial task when you cannot see what is in front of you?

But I thought —

Who told you to think? You are to obey orders, not decide for yourself the best way to carry out your assignment.

Well, I —

Enough! You are already on shaky ground. Our ruler has noticed your ineptness and if it were not for me, you would be sent to the bottom of the list. Do you want to be assigned to divining bulls' livers?

No, no I will —

Then be still and listen because this is your last chance. Witnesses of the Son of our ancient enemy are on their way to Philippi. When they spread their message of salvation through this Jesus, those Jews will gain new power to spread their despicable directive to the whole city. They must not find an agreeable audience and you must find a way to stop them. Do you understand?

But she is only a fortune teller, how can I---

I am beginning to see why our master is concerned. Perhaps it is time for---

No. No, you are right. I will find a way. You can depend on me.

We will see. Now be off and tend to our father's business.

*****

In the days that followed Daphne changed her course each time she caught sight of long beards or women clothed like those the Voice harassed. The way the Voice raged at them made her shiver. If only she could keep a low profile and follow Apollo's orders without....

Over there. That man leaning against the portico.

An elderly man stared, lost in thought. "He does not look like he is —"

Go ask.

Halfheartedly, she dragged herself over to the man. He did not acknowledge her. More than ready to back off should he fail to respond, she addressed him. "Sir, may I be of help. Would the counsel of the gods benefit you?"

A frown flickered and his eyes narrowed. "How...how did you know? I have debated whether to seek input from the gods."

A silent relief passed her lips. "The gods told me you have need of my service. Shall I seek counsel for you?"

He did not answer right away. Finally, he nodded. "My reputation is about to be ruined through no fault of my own. Do your gods have the wisdom I need to stop it?"

"Apollo knows things to come, let me seek him for you."

Again, the man hesitated. "Alright, but we must meet where no one will see. I cannot be seen with you."

She hid her response to the slight and pointed out a Roman temple. "Perhaps we could meet in the shaded shelter of that building. No one goes there in the late afternoon."

Time and place agreed upon, she traipsed slowly toward the temple. She sat on the grass and seethed over his comment. The man rounded the corner and peered over his shoulder. She snorted and vowed to never act like that once she was freed.

She buried her disgust and motioned for him to join her. Carefully, he lowered himself to the ground.

"Now, who or what has troubled you?"

"You do not know who I am, do you?"

Her head shot up. Should she know him? He looked vaguely familiar. "I...I am so sorry, but I am afraid I cannot—"

"Have you never heard any of my speeches from the *Bema*?"

That placed him. He was one of the elderly statesmen who frequently spoke on the platform.

She never stopped or listened. Some did, but many ignored him and others like him who appeared to love to hear themselves talk.

She squirmed. He had the power to make things difficult for her and she had probably offended him. "Of course, I remember seeing you there many times, it is that I must give my time to my profession."

The man nodded and began to enlighten her. "Philippi is the foremost city of the Roman colonies in Macedonia. We call it 'Little Rome' and have controlled it for over a century and a half, ever since Anthony and Octavia defeated Brutus and Cassius not far from here. After that Augustus decreed his conquerors be allowed to remain and establish a colony."

She ignored his patronizing tone. Why did he feel a need to tell her all this?

"The road than runs from Rome to the far-east splits Philippi, thus it is very important to Claudius, our emperor. It is his mandate that the city run smoothly with no unruly gatherings or groups prone to break laws or decrees of Caesar. And he will allow no outsiders to peddle ideologies that conflict with Rome's."

When she did not respond, he continued. "Men have come from Neapolis at the suggestion of others who want to gain my position. They have stirred up trouble among the merchants and promoted rebellion against tax on the goods they transport. Their motives are to report the trouble back to Rome and have me replaced."

He cocked his head. "Can your gods tell me how to handle these troublemakers without causing upheaval?"

She masked her irritation with the man's arrogance. "Please submit yourself to the Voice of Apollo."

She pulled out her *teraphim* and began to extol him. Forceful and loud, she followed her routine, instructing the magistrate to bow before Apollo. He looked offended but managed a slight bend of his head and chest. She continued, curious about what Apollo would say.

"Oh. great One, speak and grant your wisdom."

You alone are to blame for your situation. You have raised the taxes beyond what Rome called for and pocketed the difference. This unrest has not come from within but from the merchants that travel from Neapolis to sell their goods here. Repeal the burden of excess taxes and the problem will go away.

The man bolted upright. "Well, I have the right to charge whatever I see as fair. I will not—"

"Rome wants peace and will not tolerate fleecing the merchants. Spend more time protecting your city from intruders of other persuasions and less on lining your pockets, or the reports will continue, and Claudius will replace you."

The man stood to his feet and threw a few coins at Daphne. "I should have known better than to —"

The Voice boomed. *Bow before the powerful Apollo and give him the honor due him or you will be in great danger.*

The magistrate did a double take, his face red. "What? Did you threaten me?"

She cowered.

"Well, young woman. I will see that you are banned from plying your trade in our city." He spiraled in place and left.

Up on her knees, her hands rose to her face. "What am I going to do?"

He will not live out the day.

She gasped. "What? How?"

No answer came.

Her stomach in knots, she picked up the coins and brushed off her tunic. Could the man really ban her from work in the city? What would Patharus say, or do? Should she tell him? Did he have enough influence to dispel the threats?

The day had been long. She looked at the sun and decided to go home. Maybe the man would reconsider the consequences and honor Apollo.

Patharus called for her report soon after she arrived. With sweaty palms she entered, still weighing whether she should tell him of the confrontation.

He picked up the coins. "Tell me Daphne...."

The knock of his personal servant distracted him. "What is it?"

"An important message, Master"

Patharus nodded and dismissed her.

She did not need Kawit to hear of the servant's news. Within the hour, the unexpected death of the city's head magistrate seeped to even the lowest of slaves.

Chapter Fifty-Three

Do not deceive yourselves…
– Jeremiah 37:9

It took several days before Daphne was confident the Roman magistrate had not survived long enough to ban her from the city. She marveled anew at the Voice's foreknowledge. Forced to harass the Jews or relay callous demands to seekers sent a shiver down her back, but somehow, she would find the strength. Apollo knows the day of her freedom, she must please him, no matter what.

On her walk to the city, she passed the cemetery and thought of the distraught widow, her children taken from her and sold into slavery. A chill passed between her shoulder blades. She tightened her shawl. Would guilt over these tragedies never leave?

She entered a sunny stretch and came to the rocky cliffs where Nicanor once jumped out and frightened her. The memory of his dazzling smile and deep blue eyes taunted with a dictate she keep him in her heart. How long before he returned? Surely not before spring, not before ships could sail without the threat of storms.

She swallowed the catch in her throat. What did it matter? By now Patharus has surely picked a suitable wife for him. She must not be a fool. To gain her freedom is all she could look forward to…she must concentrate on that.

By the time she reached the city she had relegated Nicanor to a forgotten past. Again.

Eager to find a customer, she stormed past the merchants who waited to enter the city. Outside the *stoa*, a man grabbed her arm. "Whoa, *Kopela*, what is the rush?"

Her hand rose to her throat. Was this well-dressed stranger the new magistrate, come to ban her from the city? "What…."

He released her arm. "I am sorry, I did not mean to frighten you. The silk merchant told me of your skills, and I hoped to find you before you were engaged elsewhere."

Relief trickled to her toes. "Oh, well yes. What can I do for you?"

"I am need of counsel beyond that of men. Will you seek your gods for me?"

Her heart still pounded but she gathered herself. "Of course, we can meet in the—"

"It must be very private, beyond prying ears or eyes of any who have followed me."

She eyed him carefully, weighing her vow to never again be trapped in an enclosed place. She pointed at the gymnasium. "It is quite secluded over behind the *Palaestra,* will that do?"

The stranger peered over her head at the spot. "I will meet you as soon as I am sure I am alone."

"I will wait." She sauntered toward the back of the building. What all the secrecy was about.

A half hour passed before the stranger rounded the corner. He wrung his hands. "I am sorry to have made you wait. I had to be sure I was alone."

She assured him it was alright and asked him to sit down.

He lowered himself across from her. "I have come from Neapolis. I could not take a chance that a seer there might have told where I am. I have known the silk merchant for years and he assured me you could be trusted."

She reminded herself to thank the merchant. "Thank you, now for what purpose would you have me seek the counsel of Apollo?"

The man took a deep breath. "I am the owner of many ships that bring goods to Athens, Ephesus, Crete, and back to our port. I have had contracts with many merchants in these cities for years. Some competitors have accused me of a monopoly and have threatened my life if I do not release the merchants to deal with whomever they wish. They may have followed me here, I do not know how to stop them."

She pulled her idol from the pouch corded around her waist and set it between them. "I will seek Apollo for you, he has the wisdom you need. Please bow and prostrate yourself before our mighty god."

The man hesitated then kneeled before her *teraphim* and lowered his head. She was well into her routine when two men sprang from the side of the building, grabbed the stranger, and yanked him to his feet.

One pulled his arms behind him. "You are under arrest,"

She did not recognize either man. "What is this? What has he done?"

"He and his hired band have terrorized merchants in several cities. They threaten those who do business with anyone but him. Even killed a man and his family to make an example to the rest, and now we have proof. This man will pay for his crimes back in Neapolis."

She stared at the stranger in disbelief. "But you said—"

"It is a lie, *Kopela*. What I told you is the truth."

The Voice stirred within her. *The charges are trumped up. Those men in Crete killed one of their own to make it look like this man did it. They are unscrupulous ship owners who want the business at any cost.*

At the gruff Voice all three heads snapped. One authority stared, open mouthed. The other asked, "Who said that? Who are you, girl?"

I speak for the great Apollo. I know all truths and this man is innocent.

The spokesman looked at her, "How did you know Crete is where the family was killed?"

Because Apollo sees all, no matter where it happens. He is the god of justice.

Her client spoke up. "She is a Sorceress and he, I mean it, the god, is right. I am innocent and those men have threatened to kill me just as they killed that family. They intend to destroy my ships so they can have the business I have built up over the years.   Look, in my tunic is a copy of the merchants I have contracts with, each signed by the owners own hand. They agree only on prices. See for yourself. There is nothing to keep them tied to me. They do not drop me because I am fair and deliver their merchandise on time."

One of the authorities took the list, scanned it, and passed it to the other. Both kept a wary eye on her, ready to move should that strange Voice take on a presence. The second man cleared his throat. "Perhaps we need to look into this further."

The other agreed and they loosed her client's hands. "When you get back to Neapolis come see us. We will get to the bottom of this and see that justice is done."

He thanked them and assured them he would return as soon as he finished his business in Philippi. The men left for the gate to Neapolis. He smiled and shook his head. "How can I thank you?"

The Voice was forceful. *Do not neglect to pay the homage due our God at his temple and with your lips.*

"I will, I will." He handed Daphne a generous handful of coins and jogged out of sight.

She scooped up her idol, polished it with a corner of her shawl and added it to the coins in her pouch.

He will not obey my charge.

"Really? Why not?"

Because business alone matters to him. He will not take the time to pay Apollo homage or in offerings, and he will pay for it.

She asked what she did not want to hear. "Pay for it? What does that mean?"

Within the month he will neglect an opportunity to worship and support Apollo's temple in Athens. He will forfeit his life.

She hid a gasp and lifted her chin. "Then he shall pay the consequences." She hoped her stance pleased Apollo.

Chapter Fifty-Four

My soul is bowed down.
– Psalm 57:6

That afternoon Daphne sat near the fountain in the bright sunlight. No more customers had appeared, nor had she sought any. Her decision to side with the Voice left her unsettled and the fate of the stranger haunted her. Did he have a wife, children…parents who would grieve his death?

"Enough!" she scolded, pulled out her lunch, ate some and threw the rest to some sparrows. She rinsed her hands in the fountain and went to look for another customer. By late afternoon she decided she had earned what she needed.

Patharus was pleased as she reported to him that evening, attentive to what she dealt with, especially the near disaster of the stranger from Neapolis. To hide any dismay the Voice might detect, she did not speak of the sad end that awaited the man.

Back in her room, she napped and almost missed dinner. She rushed to the end of the line in time to fill her plate but found no place among the women to sit.

See, no one ever saves you a seat. They really do not like you. They are very jealous of you.

"That is not true. I am late and the tables are full."

She spotted a bench being emptied at a table filled with women and sat down. Those closest to her smiled but continued their conversation. She smiled back and began to eat. Most finished before she had hardly started and excused themselves for one reason or another.

Soon she was alone.

I told you, see none of them cared to stay and talk to you.

"They have families to attend to. I would not expect them to tarry for my sake."

She finished her meal and waited for Stello's nightly session to begin. With only the Voice to talk too, the emptiness Kawit left overwhelmed her afresh.

It seemed the overseer would go on forever. More than once his glance lingered. She shuddered and lowered hers. After he dismissed them, she headed for her room, but changed her mind and slipped into the garden. The days were getting shorter so she would not have much time. At the snap of twigs, she ducked off the path and hid behind a large bush that still held much of its leaves. One glimpse and her heart sank.

Stello jogged past, his call a loud whisper. "Daphne? Daphne, are you in here?"

She held her breath. As soon as he was out of sight she ran toward the gate, grateful it was nearly dark. She did not look back or stop until she reached her room. She leaned against the wall and groaned. "Kawit, oh Kawit you were right!

He is after me. What can I do? How can I avoid him?"

Evenings, as the grueling days passed, Daphne longed for the solace of the garden but no longer felt safe to tarry there. Time hung like the reluctant terebinth leaves that refused to drop until spring. Occasionally she would chat with Femi, but the girl had a family and Daphne did not engage her for long.

As autumn deepened, she welcomed the early darkness and retired as soon as she finished her bath. Awake hours before dawn, that proved a mistake. The long silence magnified too many things she wanted to forget.

Desperate and lonely, after months of total obedience she challenged the Voice one evening. "I have done and said everything you asked. When will I get my freedom?"

Silence.

"I know you hear me, and you promised I would be set free. Why has it not happened? I have spent many hours extolling Apollo, surely, he has heard and is pleased. Why has he not told Patharus to set me free?"

There is more to be done, work that requires my protection. It won't be long, Apollo is pleased with you.

She sighed, picked up her tub and left for the well. What was the use, he only put her off with vague promises.

Many were lined up to get their bath water. She filled her tub and turned just as another woman stepped forward and knocked most of the water from Daphne's tub.

She did that on purpose.

Daphne snapped, "Could you be more careful?"

The woman backed from Daphne's nasty frown. "I am so sorry."

Daphne grunted and refilled her tub. Those who witnessed her outburst stared in disbelief and stepped out of her way. Her cheeks flushed as she hurried back to her room. She had not intended to be rude. What came over her?

Tomorrow she would find the woman and apologize.

The Voice spoke to her silence. *That woman was pushy and should have waited.*

Daphne refused to be baited. She could not win. Why did the Voice always see the worst in people?

She lay awake rehashing the Voice's comments. No one had ever asked about her family or where she came from. Did her dissimilar background make her seem unapproachable? Was it resentment she saw in those who worked for the same master? "I need to make an effort to be more friendly."

You know no one will want to be around you after tonight. You are better off here in your room with me.

Again, she did not respond. How could she agree and stay true to her own heart? She fell asleep reminding herself of her intention to apologize. It was still dark when she awoke. Something heavy pressed her chest to her mat. Instantly, she pictured Stello. Had he secretly crept into her room to abuse her?

She tried to sit but could not move. The weight became intense. She struggled to push away whatever held her down. Her arms found nothing. More frightened than ever, she tried to scream, but her lungs held no air.

Call upon me and I will save you.

She gasped and squeaked a cry. "Yes, please… help me!"

Instantly the weight lifted but left her wheezing. "What…what was that?"

Apollo is not pleased with your questioning my wisdom. You must submit yourself entirely to my counsel and stay away from all who would lead you elsewhere.

Between sobs, she all but shouted, "But something tried to kill me! It wanted me dead!"

I am your protector. Listen to me and you will not be harmed.

She cried herself into a restless sleep. Incidents ascribed to Apollo's brutality back in Delphi haunted her. Each memory, a young girl's body tortured by Apollo's adoring muses, the sudden death of a man who maligned Apollo's status, the insanity of a woman with whom Apollo cohabited then discarded, each imparted a fear that her grandmother had ignored or tried to explain away. Dawn found her on edge, jumping at every shadow.

Somehow, Daphne made it through the day, her perspective changed: her life was on the line. No longer would she question the Voice. She needed his protection. She would do whatever he asked.

Chapter Fifty-Five

Disgust wrestled contempt for first place in Daphne's thoughts as she returned from the city. Thoughts about the day's encounter where Apollo spoke to a distraught woman, left her exasperated. She scoffed at the woman's reaction to her husband's guile. The truth had been there all along if she had paid attention.

She dismissed her mother's correction, *"Daphne, you need to apologize. Remember we all react badly sometimes."* It is not my fault Apollo exposed the history of how the man deceived his wife.

To rationalize helped, how else could she live with herself? Still, her conscience would not rest after hearing of the upheaval that followed. The authorities arrested the woman for stabbing her husband in the stomach.

He deserved it. He has neglected to honor Apollo.

An image returned of the high priest back in Delphi with blood spurting from a similar wound. The memory rushed her to the side of the path to lose what little lunch she had eaten.

Her stomach calmed and she decided to rest on the rocky overhang where she and Kawit had often met. Sorrows and laughter they shared tugged her heart.

She pulled her shawl close. The winter seemed especially cold, or was it the icy barrier she erected to protect her heart? Two months had passed since the night Apollo had nearly killed her. Months of dodging Jewish people, days of lies, deceit, and evil.

A sparrow hopped near her feet. "I have nothing to give you. I do not even know who I am anymore." Where had her will splintered and the demands of the Voice triumphed? What compelled her to comply with his every command and accept his motives as her own? From where did that irresistible pull come that stifled her ability to choose?

Or had she chosen? Regrets rose with her warm breath.

On and on, and she had done all the Voice commanded. *Tell the man it was his brother that muddied their father's good name. Inform this one that his partner is only reporting part of the profit. Tell the woman her daughter-in-law is meeting with a man who is not her husband.*

And for what? Her elusive freedom? She leaned into her hands trying to sort out what was true, caught off guard when she found herself on her feet shouting, "What does it matter if other people's lives are destroyed? Do not my hopes and dreams count? Do I not matter?"

The words echoed through the silent valley. Their ugliness assaulted her ears and sent shame down the icy slope the outburst created in her heart. She cringed and willed the words back, never to be heard. Had the Voice's influence made her act like that? Was he behind the reason his evil commands bothered her less and less? So why did today's incident upset her?

She reflected on the previous day when commanded to give the "evil eye" to a young Jewish woman. Daphne hated when the demon penetrated her eyes and terrified people. The horrified girl had dropped the shop keeper's expensive black wool and ran down the *stoa*. Daphne shuddered. How helpless she had been to refuse the task.

Its importance soon faded. What did it matter? Ignoring her conscience meant less stress.

Remaining true to what she knew to be right proved stressful, but the struggle did not lessen. She tried to dismiss an earlier incident where she had responded as heartlessly as the Voice, and it sickened her. That and a missed opportunity to show compassion to a downtrodden man. She was aghast that her thoughts had merged with those of her tormentor.

Each day she resisted its control less and less but hid her despondency when she reported to Patharus.

Past interactions with the god paraded through her mind. Her consent to marry Apollo's murderous high priest and thus save her family's estate had availed nothing, nor had the god's promised intercession. And the message through his priestess to her father held nothing but false pretenses that never materialized.

She frowned. If neither submitting to Apollo nor the prayers of his highest human authority brought change, what of the promise given her through the Voice? What if Apollo had no intention of fulfilling his promise or granting her freedom? He was a god, He could do as he pleased. What if he changed his mind? How would she bear it?

Like cloud banks back home that diminished as they passed over the Gulf, the haze that hung over her dissipated. She saw the power within for what it was. It did not care about her or her future. Apollo had no intention of granting her freedom, she was sure of it.

She sprang to her feet, clutched her shawl, and paced. This thing that lives in me is not me. Its motives and agenda are not mine, they are evil. It makes me do things I detest, and I need to be rid of it.

As the revelation swelled, so did her fear. She was powerless, trapped. If it left, she would be as vulnerable as all the other slaves, subject to Stello's whims.

The sheer hopelessness rekindled thoughts of ending her life. Hemlock grew in Patharus' garden, had she not been warned as a child to steer clear of it? Must she chew it, or could she simply swallow it? What if it only made her sick, or feeble?

She sat again. Self pity welled and tears spilled down her cheeks. A short-eared, elephant shrew studied her then dove for its burrow. She shrank at the compassion she felt for the creature and grieved at her lack of it for the people she had hurt.

A cold wind stirred and urged her to leave. She wiped her cheeks and sought to bury her distress before she arrived with little to show Patharus. Maybe he would ignore it for today or be too preoccupied to notice.

He noticed.

He studied her a few moments. "Daphne, your earnings have fallen sharply, is something wrong?"

She swallowed the lump in her throat. "I, I am so sorry, Master. I, the people, I mean many do not come to the market as much in the winter months, and—"

"That is true, but you seem weighed down, not yourself. Are you still mourning your friend, Kawit?"

Panic seized her. What should she say? Had he heard of Stello's brutality? Did he know of how she had spoken up to Stello, or of his threats? She could only nod and hope he would not force her to tell him what she knew.

Patharus waited.

A glance revealed his furrowed brow. When she offered no further explanation, he walked around his desk and stopped in front of her. She could hear his breathing and smell the musk of his scented water. He lifted her chin with his forefinger and stared into her face.

Her heart raced. She kept her eyes lowered and searched for something to say. He knew of her friendship with Kawit. Was he about to grill her on what happened to her friend?

"You have become so thin, almost gaunt. Are you sick, Daphne?

She shook her head and rummaged through the closet of her mind for some believable excuse. Nothing fell out.

He backed away. "You need to take better care of yourself. In fact, you stay home for a few days, the rest will do you good. You are dismissed."

Chapter Fifty-Six

Those who sit in darkness and in the shadow of death.
– Psalm 107:10

Daphne thanked Patharus and backed through the door. She ran to her room and lay on her mat with her hands over her face, overwhelmed by no hope of escape from Apollo's hold nor a life of endless servitude and fear. Jahtel spied relentlessly, eager to catch her in violation of some rule. Stello undressed her with his eyes, constantly on the lookout for a chance to seduce her. Her only friend was dead and gone, and now Patharus was suspicious of her ability to perform. And Nicanor…. She could not finish the thought.

She groaned and tried to envision another way out. At last sleep overtook her, filled with dreams of struggles that left her breathless.

Evenings dragged. The other women avoided her, or so it seemed. Nightly, after Stello demeaned his captive audience, she retreated to her room. Except for her ever-present loneliness, the Voice had no competition. It continually badgered, wore her down and eroded her desire to hang on to anything other than what it willed.

She spent much of her newly given time off in the garden, assured that Stello would be too busy with the day's business to seek her out. Too cold to sit, she walked. Each time she passed, the hemlock drew her attention. The brisk air she disdained on her walks to the city, now refreshed her. She pulled it deep into her lungs and like the breath she exhaled, felt her spirits rise with the sweetness of not having to confer with the Voice over desperate people.

The bench she shared with Nicanor beckoned, but she roamed in the opposite direction or deliberately studied the nearby pond. Hurtful memories would not spoil her day. She walked the length of the main path many times before her feet complained of the cold.

At dinner the second night she lined up with the others and stifled a gasp. Stripes that still oozed crisscrossed the back and legs of the man in front of her. He had been whipped! He gathered his food and drink and slowly limped toward a table. As he turned to sit down, his front exposed more bruises and a swollen black eye. When Daphne saw his face, she nearly dropped her tray. It was the man she witnessed to about Apollo's powers. It is him, I am sure of it. Whatever could have happened?

She found a seat far from where he had settled. Speculation flowed from the women she joined and one of them said, "I heard he assumed too much authority after he was given the position of overseeing a group of men the master loaned out."

Another came to his defense. "No, he is a good man and has never given anyone trouble. You know Stello, if outsiders praised the man's performance, he would find a reason to humiliate him."

Guilt squashed Daphne's appetite. She picked at her food and excused herself. Back in her room she railed at the Voice. "Why? Why does Apollo destroy anyone who tries to serve him? I know he was behind this. He granted the man that promotion after he consented to make him his god. Why must he be so cruel? I do not understand."

The man forgot who his benefactor was. Do you dare to question Apollo's judgment? Would you like to become vulnerable to Stello's whims too?

Daphne froze. What was the matter with her? Had she not decided to never question Apollo? She crossed her arms and let her head droop. "I, I am sorry. Please ask Apollo to overlook my outburst."

She lay awake late into the night, fearful of unspeakable consequences should Apollo decide to punish her. Until she found a way to be free of him, she must be more careful, keep her thoughts to herself. Tomorrow she would make sure she obeyed his slightest command.

For weeks Daphne stuck to her pledge. Early spring winds gained more warmth each day. Patharus eyed her with suspicion from time to time, but she was careful to present herself upbeat and he appeared satisfied with her earnings. She trained herself to give less and less thought to

Nicanor's return. Who knew if he would return at all, this spring or ever? If and when he did, she determined to meet him on equal ground. Despite her hatred for Apollo, she focused on survival.

Femi scolded her one morning. "Daphne you are not eating enough to feed a bird. Your tunic hangs like an empty sack. You got to eat child!"

Daphne smiled and nodded. She put a little more on her plate and took her tray to a table. Her hair brushed her food as she sat down. She grimaced. How many times had she forgotten to fasten it before leaving her room? But what did it matter?

She took care of her tray, careful to hide how little she had eaten from Femi.

The walk to the city was chilly. She wished she would have brought her shawl. To pass the time, she allowed herself a rare moment to reflect on her family. Her father and his untimely death. Anger at his poor management had passed. Her mother, beautiful and happy before tragedy upended her life. Alexander's probable fate. Had he been beaten like the man in the food line? Her heart refused to dwell on Theo. How could a three-year-old understand why his world had been destroyed? Belte…the wide grin of her servant and friend brought only sorrow. She wondered where she was…in charge of someone else's home?"

Tears of anger and resentment slipped from her eyes. The face of a surly young maid back in

Delphi flashed. She had been sent one morning to help her dress. Daphne winced. No wonder the girl acted so awful; she probably longed for her freedom too.

With regret, she shut the book on the chapters of her past. To clear her mind, she began to chant. Her efforts clanged like a sullen echo from the empty well of her broken heart. Still, she kept at it, determined to keep her vow to uphold all the Voice required.

The wind ruffled her tunic, brushing the stiff fabric against her legs. How long since she had washed it? She needed to do better, but she was so tired by the time they were excused and who really cared?

The day passed in the usual manner until she noticed a commotion near the Northern gate. A older man accompanied by two younger men approached, surrounded by many she knew to be Jews. Who were these strangers and what drew the crowd to follow them? Her heart sank. She hurried in the opposite direction. The last thing she wanted was to engage in harassing those people again.

A few days later, she decided to rest a while by the fountain. A crowd had gathered just outside the courtyard, so she wandered over, expecting to see a puppeteer or magician who hoped to elicit donations from those who watched. Always eager for a diversion, itinerant performers fascinated the merchants and their patrons.

As she approached, a woman dressed in a lovely purple robe with a complementary shawl, swiveled and smiled at her. Daphne returned the smile, her curiosity piqued. Obviously not a laborer. What would attract such a person to this gathering?

Daphne stepped further into the throng, and panic gripped her throat. The Jews the Voice had made her follow were clustered around the strangers she saw arriving earlier. Compelled, she stayed to listen.

One of the younger men gestured to his companion, "This is Paul, an apostle of Jesus Christ. He has a message that will change your life and bring you everlasting joy and peace."

The man stepped back and Paul began to speak. "The only true God sent His Son, Jesus the Christ into our world as a man to show you His great love for you. He lived a sinless life so when He died, unlike the blood of animals sacrificed for sins, His pure, sinless blood paid the price for the sins of any who would believe and submit their life to Him."

Not a few Romans stopped to listen as Paul continued to speak. One scoffed, "Hah! Claudius is our emperor. He is our god."

Another joined him. "Right! And you had better be careful, there are consequences to peddling things that contradict Roman laws."

Daphne remembered hearing how Claudius had recently deported Jews from Rome. One spoke up, "You Romans think you are so superior but we are the sons of Abraham."

But another Jew spun toward Paul and snarled. "We have awaited the coming Messiah since the beginning of time. There has been no word from the Sanhedrin. The Messiah has not come, you are a fake."

The groups fed off each other. A Jewish man called out, "Claudius is a man, not a god."

A Roman answered, "Yah, well Rome is superior to all nations and that includes your pitiful country. All you Greeks are second-class citizens."

A Grecian spoke up, "this city is part of Greece, not Rome."

Another Jew yelled, "Jehovah is the true God."

The conflict grew, each faction attacking the others and Paul. One of his men jumped up on the platform and pleaded with them to stop the harassment and allow the message to reach the many who wanted to hear.

Daphne stayed for several minutes before Paul looked around and she caught his eye. His face was aglow with compassion that spread to her and everyone there as he spoke, "Freedom from sin, guilt, shame, and all evil awaits any who desire to follow the Lord Jesus."

Her ears perked at the promise of freedom. She knew she must leave before Apollo started an assault but could not tear her eyes from the speaker. Her hand rose to her throat, she staggered backward and bumped into the well-dressed woman in purple. The lady laid her hand on Daphne's arm. "Can I help you my dear?"

Chapter Fifty-Seven

A light that shines in dark places.
– 2 Peter 1:19

Daphne jerked around. Her color drained. She muttered a quick apology and plowed through the crowd. She hoped she did not offend that woman, she seemed so kind.

At the other end of the *stoa*, she stepped into an alley and leaned against the cool exterior of the last building. The day was hot, and the seclusion and shade soothed like a forested sanctum. Perspiration oozed from under her hair, creating tiny rivulets that ran from her temple and down her cheeks. She billowed the skirt of her clammy tunic several times and touched her cheeks. Were they flushed from the heat, the awkward encounter, or the way her heart raced when she listened to the man's message?

Her panting eased and her breath settled. She rolled her head back and forth across her shoulders, closed her eyes, inhaled deeply. A narrow escape, but she had successfully dodged a possible disaster. Slowly, she released her lungs, opened her eyes, and nearly fainted.

The face of the woman who tried to help her was less than a foot from hers.

Her voice was soft. "My dear, are you alright? I was worried…is someone after you? Can I help?"

For the second time, her concern disarmed Daphne. Her lips opened but she did not respond. Why had this woman followed her and what could she possibly want? Every reason sounded lame. After an uncomfortable lull, Daphne stammered something about the heat and being late for an appointment.

The woman arched her brows. Daphne knew she did not believe her. Why did it seem she looked right through her?

After an awkward silence the woman smiled and slipped off her shawl. She put it around Daphne's shoulders. "I only live a short distance from here, I will not need this, I have several. I want you to have it." She adjusted the garment. "You should be careful my dear, the midday sun can make you very ill."

Before Daphne could protest, the woman disappeared into the crowded courtyard. She marveled that the woman appeared to have no intention to return for her expensive shawl.

A thirst for cold well water drew Daphne to search past the western edge of the *agora*, an area she had never ventured into before. Women did not normally replenish their water supplies until late afternoon so it would likely be deserted.

She entered the well's brick outer shelter and reveled in the coolness. She waited for her eyes to adjust. Blackened mildew crept up the inner walls and added a damp, musty smell to the somber atmosphere. She looked around. How could a place so vital to sustain life seem so deathlike?

A woman called out, "You...yes you. Slaves cannot draw water unless accompanied by their mistress. You need to leave." She stepped close to the entrance, her hands on her hips. Daphne lifted her chin and swayed toward the well. "My master has given me permission to fill my jug here."

"And who might that be?"

"He is Patharus, his estate is—"

"I know who he is. That does not change the law, you are not—"

"I am sorry, but I need some water. I will clarify it with him tonight."

The woman gave a huff and muttered that she would see about that. Daphne squirmed, how easily the lie had rolled off her tongue. Now she would have to tell Patharus and hope he would back her up.

A large wooden vessel hung from a bracket over the well. She braced her knees against the stones that encircled the deep hole and peered into the abyss. With practiced care, she lowered the container until she heard it hit water. When the cask nearly cleared the stones, she drained the excess back into the well. Years of respect for the value of water would not allow her to waste a drop. She filled her small jug, drank deeply, and filled it again.

After the container was secure, she found a deserted spot in the shade to rest and savor the fresh water. She put her head on her knees and hugged them to her chest. The events of the morning whirled in her head. The haunting message of freedom and the kindness of the woman in purple who followed her.

Daphne guessed her to be older than her mother but younger than her grandmother. Gray sprinkled through dark braids that encircled her head and framed an attractive face. Telltale lines surrounded her mouth and crinkled around eyes that shone with the kind of love she had not experienced since being torn from her mother.

She fingered the shawl and traced the teal and yellow flowers woven into a purple background. "It is like the lovely ones mother owned, beautifully crafted." She toyed with the idea to locate the woman to return it but had no idea how to manage that.

She returned to the *agora*, determined to concentrate on business. No one who needed help appeared so she sat by the fountain. An ugly confrontation had not happened, but unless those men left town it was only a matter of time. She dismissed the possibility and took out her flatbread and cheese. Her encounter with the shawl's generous owner would not fade. Why would such a person be concerned for her welfare?

Beresta, a slave she sometimes shared lunch with, arrived just after Daphne. She motioned and the girl joined her. Beresta was full of talk about the strangers in town and the unfamiliar god their leader spoke of. "Some have named his followers Christos, but I would not use such an unkind label."

Daphne listened and wondered what the description meant. She scoffed, the lack of morals and integrity in the gods her people worshiped could not be worse. After they each shared what they had observed, she summoned the courage to ask Beresta if she knew of the lady who had given her the shawl.

"Oh, you must mean Lydia. Was she a lot older than us with graying hair braided on top of her head?"

"Yes, and well dressed in a purple."

"For sure that was Lydia, Is she not beautiful? You know, she makes all her own clothes and dyes them with expensive dye that she imports."

"She imports? You mean her husband is in the shipping business?"

"No, I don't think she has a husband."

"Really, she must have lots of help."

Beresta tore off a bit of bread and chewed before she answered. "I think so. They say she is from Thyatira, somewhere around Ephesus. But the dye comes from Tyre, wherever that is."

"My father was in the importing business. Tyre is in Phoenicia, north of Israel, a city on the Great Sea."

"Really? Your father had a business? How did you end up, I mean—"

"It is a long story but tell me about that dye. Does it come from crushed flowers like saffron and indigo?"

"No, well I do not know exactly, but one of my master's slaves is from Tyre. He says he and his brothers were forced to dive for certain shellfish that are found in that region. Only the dye-masters were allowed to open them, take out the tiny body, and extract liquid from the vertebrae. He called them a mollusks or mollusca, something like that. A flagon of that dye is very costly, did your father ever mention it?"

Daphne shook her head. "No, I do not think so. I cannot imagine how a woman could handle a business like that on her own." She checked the position of the sun. "I need to be going, maybe I will see you tomorrow."

Beresta waved as they went their separate ways. That night Daphne paced in her room, her mind spinning. She wished she had someone to talk to, someone kind, like she supposed Lydia would be. Someone who could explain the meaning of what she heard in the market. She wondered if Beresta knew where she lived. She could return her scarf and maybe...no, the Voice would never let that happen.

Things the man called Paul said reverberated in her head. *"His name is Jesus and He has come to save you from your sin. He loves you with an everlasting love…you do not choose Him, He chooses you. He will never leave you or forsake you…."*

She curled up on her mat. Why did his words burn in her heart with such fervor, and what did he mean by sin?   And why would a god choose someone like me, and for what?

She fell asleep questioning why worshipers of such a powerful god had not built him a temple.

Chapter Fifty-Eight

But who do you say that I am.
– Matthew 16:15

The next few days Daphne kept an eye out for the man called Paul. His crowds grew larger and harder to avoid each day. She had no trouble spotting Lydia among them. When she returned home slaves buzzed about the newcomers at mealtime. While she waited to be summoned into Patharus' presence, she overheard him ask about the man.

The servant laid the requested reports on his master's desk. "They say he is a Jew but born and raised in Tarsus. That he arrived with a few others on a ship from Troas."

"Have you seen him? What is he saying?"

"Yes, on an errand into the city. You could not miss him. Everywhere he goes crowds gather. He is a small man with bandy legs and a long nose. But his face is…well, pleasant, and he is passionate about this Jesus-God he talks about."

"Passionate? About the god he peddles?"

"He believes this Jesus is the only deity who really is a god. The God of gods he calls him, and all the gods the rest of us worship are simply manmade idols of wood or stone."

Patharus grimaced. "Hump…God of gods, humm?"

"Well, according to him this Jesus is the son of the true God and He came to earth born of a young virgin."

"Sounds like all the rest of those Greek gods to me."

The servant nodded. "He says the difference is this Jesus was conceived in the girl by the Spirit of God, that he lived a sinless life before he died a martyrs death to sacrifice himself for the sins of everyone else. The man preaches that after Jesus died, God his Father raised him from the dead and He went back to heaven."

"Sounds like you got an earful. Raised him from the dead? He had better be careful. It is against the law to introduce a new religion in a Roman town. The official that replaced the late head magistrate is arrogant and power hungry, plus, he is a stickler for the law and watches for any public threat. He will not tolerate disruptions in the city."

Patharus snickered, "That is all these Greeks need…another god. Tell Daphne I am ready for her."

She ducked back from the doorway. The servant's description sounded the same as a god her mother had once described. One who sacrificed himself so his believers could be with him forever, even in death. But how could that be? People did not come back to life after they died. But Belte believed it too. Maybe she could find a way to hear about him for herself...if she could hide it from the Voice.

Preoccupied with his daily ledgers, Patharus soon dismissed her.

Morning came too quickly. Daphne had hardly slept, unable to quiet from her mind the servant's account to Patharus. She tried to grasp what he'd said, that the man spoke of Jesus as being the only true God, yet he had a Father who was God, then spoke of the Spirit of God. She found it confusing but hope swelled as she dwelt on the promise of freedom. She had heard that much for herself, but despair over its ever coming to pass rose in equal measure.

She left for the city dreading that the Voice would initiate another nasty encounter. However, the morning was slow. Daphne had hardly entered the *stoa* after lunch when she felt thrust in the opposite direction. She could hardly believe where her steps led, as if her feet had a will of their own. She grimaced. The Voice was up to something.

Step after step, it pushed her to follow the band of people who listened while they walked with the man she was desperate to avoid – the one called Paul.

"For I am not ashamed of the gospel of Christ for it is the power of salvation for everyone who believes, the Jew first and also for the Greek that all the Gentiles might hear. God willed to make known what are the riches of the glory among the

Gentiles which is Christ in you the hope of glory," she heard him say.

Some of Paul's followers smiled and others groused. According to Beresta, Gentiles were anyone who was not a Jew. Power of salvation also for the Greeks? Made known among the Gentiles? Her head swam with confusion and a hope she could not define. But had he not said it was for everyone?

She felt a nudge and dread rose in her chest. The Voice was gearing up for a confrontation and she would be at the heart of it. She kept pace as many steps as she could behind the women and children, themselves a few yards behind the men.

The group stopped often, caught up in what they heard. She lingered in the market stalls along the way until they moved, hanging on to an unlikely hope the Voice would not force her to harass them again. The heat was stifling. She pulled the drab shawl Kawit had retrieved from the clothing barrel up over her head and shoulders, thankful Lydia's lay hidden beneath her bed mat.

Paul headed for the western gate. Again, she felt pushed and found herself even closer to the women. Her mind raced while her feet dragged. To catch a glimpse of him, she rose on her toes and dodged from side to side.

Unimpressive in stature, he often turned to the people and gestured with his hands as he spoke. "There is none righteous, no not one...the wages of sin is death...no condemnation to those in Christ Jesus...having been justified by faith, we have peace with God through our Lord Jesus Christ...gift of God is eternal life in Christ Jesus our Lord...."

Reluctant to turn away but terrified of what the Voice planned, she took it all in. Did this Paul too have a voice inside that told him what to say and do? How else was he able to mesmerize those who listened to his speeches? Did he weave a spell with his words like a magician or a wizard?

Her brow furrowed. How could mere words be so spellbinding? They seemed to have a life, no, a power of their own.

She swerved in the direction of the market. She did not understand, and she was going to....

Propelled back toward the group, she tripped on the corner of a raised marble block. One knee hit the ground and she skinned her arm. "That hurt!" She rubbed her elbow. "Whatever have you planned?"

Her complaint had been louder than she meant. She examined the scrape on her knee, stood and brushed off her tunic. Had Lydia or any of the others noticed? An uneasy relief swept over her as she saw no one had turned to look and people on the street seemed occupied with their own affairs.

She did not want to harass these people. Despite the previous unpleasant encounter they shared, some had even smiled when they noticed her in the market. They were not offended or repulsed by her station in life. Why did the Voice hate them so? Why must she do this? The questions were pointless; she had no power to change anything.

Experience cautioned that the Voice would not forewarn her, that in fact it was about to manifest its evil powers through her. She shrank inwardly with a silent plea. Oh please, please do not.

The group turned toward the gate that led to the Gangites River that flowed a mile west of the city walls at the edge of the great swamp. Several times she had observed a small group of Jewish women who left through that gate and had asked Beresta about it.

"Those women go there weekly to pray," Beresta had said. "They call the day their Sabbath. Not many of their sect live in Philippi, maybe less than ten families. They do not have their own place of meeting, so they use the river. I guess the water is a part of their worship."

The girl's wealth of knowledge reminded her of Kawit. It amused Daphne that the women chose such an ordinary place to worship. It seemed pitiful to have a god so poor with no grand temple like Apollo's. His was a place where great sacrifices were offered by people in beautiful clothing and where wonderful food and entertainment were prepared in a manner fitting one's god. Strange, none of these women seemed to fret about such things. They had probably never seen a beautiful temple like the one at Delphi.

The day was nearly done, and she had seen few customers. Patharus would not be pleased, especially if he knew she spent most of her time following this band of Jews. Many native to Philippi, Greeks, and Romans alike, had joined the group, eager to hear this strange teaching. Maybe one of them would need her.

The group moved further down the outer road. The sun seared her skin and dust made her eyes run and her throat raw. She opened her water jug and swallowed most of it before she pulled her shawl over her head and across her mouth and nose. She longed to return home and bathe in cool water.

Once again, she attempted to leave, but felt herself jerked around until she faced the women who followed the men. As her pace quickened, her stomach churned. Her breath came in ragged gasps, and a low snarl drew up her nose like a rabid dog.

All followers of this man will come to a loathsome end.

Over and over villainous scourges spit from her lips, barely audible at first, then louder as she drew closer to Paul.

You are the scum of the earth. You are not wanted here. Your words are lies, a plot hatched by a false god. I curse your every movement. Only Apollo is to be revered.

She stumbled forward, unable to stifle the hateful curses that poured from her lips.

Chapter Fifty-Nine

Daphne could feel words form in her throat. Her hand rose to her lip. She clenched her tongue so hard her mouth filled with the taste of blood. Would nothing deter the voice's onslaught?

People stopped to stare. She wanted to run, to hide, but there was no escape from the presence. Her body began to sway. Her face grew long and cruelly contorted, her mouth a wide, gaping hole. A cry of protest formed in her heart but out of her throat curses shrieked in a high-pitched, nasal tone. *This man speaks lies. Do not listen to him. Only the mighty Zeus is our reigning god. He alone is the highest of gods.*

Driven by the evil within, she staggered from one side of the road to the other. People pointed and drew back. As if watching along with them, she saw her shoulders hood like a snake while her tongue darted in and out in reptile fashion. Her pupils shrank to beady pinpoints and stared with menace at any who dared return her gaze. A putrid smell rose, and she knew it emanated from her own being.

Preoccupied with her youngsters and unaware of the ruckus, a woman with two small children began to cross in front of her. Daphne was nearly upon her when another ear-piercing scream rang out. *This man will deprive you of Apollo's blessings on your crops.*

The woman panicked, yanked one child's arm, the other by her tunic, and ran. The little girl choked as her mother herded both children far out of Daphne's reach.

Those who heard her coming were quick to give her ample room. A man warned, "Watch out, she is a sorceress."

Another called, "She has the evil eye. I have seen her use it in the market."

Frightened of the peril interference might bring, no one tried to help or stop her.

The curses became more profane and could be heard over everything.

Evil will befall all who listen to this man.

The raspy, hissing she knew so well screamed. *See how he tries to deceive you. I know him of whom he speaks, and this strange god has no power.*

Bloated with anger, the voice whipped her around. She struggled to keep her balance, terrified and hardly able to draw a breath between assaults. Her throat became dry. What was riling him so, and what would he do when he reached them? The thought hung like an evil mantle, blinding all hope for a quick ending.

She whirled like a weathervane lashed by a fickle wind. It left her dizzy and nauseated. Between blasts she careened down the path. Her arms coiled and uncoiled over her head in a snake-like motion. She tried but had neither the power to stop them nor to control her steps. A foamy substance formed in her mouth and drooled down her chin.

She trembled as more taunts poured from her lips. *Apollo alone is worthy of your homage. There is no resurrection after death. Hermes alone can bring you across the river Styx and give you peace.*

Over and over the voice threatened and hissed its contempt of Paul and his followers. She was not twenty paces from the women when the voice convulsed her body. As if in a tunnel, she heard it repeat the same cry several times. *These men are the servants of the Most High God who proclaim to us the way of salvation.*

Those who traveled with Paul whipped around, infuriated at her mocking.

She closed in on the women. They gestured and pointed, alerting one another and the leader. Paul signaled to one of the men he called Silas who had arrived in Philippi with him. Silas stepped out from the group and moved toward Daphne. She could not breathe.

He raised his hand in her direction, his tone stern. "In the name of Jesus Christ of Nazareth, I command you to be still!"

She sprawled with such force she was sure he must have hit her, but he had not moved.

He remained several paces from where she lay, his eyes fixed on hers. What had thrown her to the ground with such force? Where was the voice? It had never backed down before. Why did it not speak or defend her? How like it to stir up this nasty confrontation and then disappear and leave her to face the consequences? She clutched her fists. "Where are you? Let me melt into the earth and disappear too!"

The man stood his ground. His stare paralyzed her. When he did not move, she slowly pushed herself onto her knees and then to her feet. She backed like a creature caught within reach of a swaying cobra. He watched her withdraw, his gaze riveted on her face.

Nudged by instinct, she ignored the probable consequences, spun around and ran as fast as she could. No footsteps competed with the hammering in her chest.

Sure he would follow and beat her when he caught up, she dodged people, afraid to look back. Her hand swept her shawl, and it tangled in her legs. The loose end whipped around her head and snapped her in the face. Blinded, she groped for it and nearly fell. It slipped to the ground. For a second, she debated whether to retrieve it. No, let it go.

She focused on the path until a frantic scan proved the man still watched but had not moved. "He is not coming!" She slowed but was too afraid to stop.

People she passed eyed her with suspicion though most had been too far away to know what it was all about. No longer able to see Silas, she stopped and leaned against a poplar tree to rest and catch her breath.

Filled with humiliation, angry tears washed down her face. Never had the Voice taken over to that extent. She pictured herself, helplessly in pursuit of innocent people, as curses streamed from her lips and acting like a…a what? She could not imagine.

She spat the vile taste from her mouth and wiped her chin on the hem of her tunic. Her combs had fallen, and her hair spiraled in tangles she had no way to smooth. How would she hide her disheveled appearance from Patharus? Perhaps he would be occupied elsewhere and not call for her right away.

Her left hip hurt where she hit the ground. She rubbed it, unaware of the scrape on her arm until she did so and saw that she had torn skin from her hand clear up to her elbow. "Curse him!" Whether it was the man or the Voice she blasted, she was not sure.

Still shaken, she walked and rehearsed excuses to cover her late arrival and lack of profit. She had begun to dread these daily reports. Patharus often insisted she include names and details, especially when the supernatural happened. She hated she might be forced to relive the awful loss of control when the Voice took over and attacked the person seeking his counsel. Something told her to leave out incidents concerning the band of Jews, but she was not sure why.

She scowled. How would she survive another attack like the one forced upon her today? All commitments to honor Apollo and obey the voice vanished. As if she had gotten a whiff of dung, through gritted teeth she growled, "I hate you, Voice. I just want to die."

She pressed her fingers to her tear-stained cheeks and leaned her head against them. Exhaustion drooped her shoulders. She despised everything about this life that had been forced upon her. Her life was falling apart and she had to find an escape, none but death seemed probable. She set her mind to find how best to manage hemlock.

Chapter Sixty

Spiritual hosts of wickedness in the heavenly places.
– Ephesians 6:12

The demonic spirit of divination could not get out of there fast enough. Where could he hide? The ruling principality over Greece had surely witnessed the scene and probably already reported it to the master.

Divination had tried. He had whipped his charge into a formidable frenzy and hurtled every accusation he could think of at this icon of the faith. After all, it was the apostle Paul, not some over-zealous new convert. Did not the spiritual hosts of wickedness ever consider the magnitude of his assignment?

All he ever wanted was to operate through the head pythia in the temple in Delphi, to bask in the misplaced honor given the priestess of the conjured up god humans called Apollo. Was that not his gift? Had he not been commissioned to convince people he knew the future and thereby get them to commit their allegiance to any but their Adversary. Victory would doom them to worship the god of this world, Satan himself? Was that not enough? There was nothing in his training about bringing down a great evangelist. Exactly what would the rulers of darkness have done in his place?

Divination winced at the cold wind that drew him into the presence of his superior, the ruling principality over all of Greece. He released the breath he held, relieved that the higher authority had not accompanied him.

Well here we are again, Divination. Seems you cannot avoid screwing up your assignments.

Divination cowered, no use to defend oneself against the pompous tyrant who called him out. Eons ago his superior had made sure that all spirits of a station lower than his knew he was one of the first angels to follow Lucifer out of heaven. Pride never failed to blind him to any opinion or viewpoint other than his own.

Greek's principality did not hold back, all but freezing Divination's windpipes when he spoke. I am waiting.

You have got to understand. This is no small assignment, I have....

No, I do not have to understand. Satan does not put up with failure. He hand-picked you to invade this girl, to take control and use her to influence hundreds to choose him over our adversary. Your big opportunity to do serious damage comes and what did you do? You ran!

Divination whined. But he used that name. None of us can resist that name, even you.

The principality ignored the jibe and scoffed. The Father of lies will not put up with your sniveling. You were trained to deceive and destroy, not retreat. The powerful, lying spirit you have been aided with, is teeming with deception. Use it. She is already thinking of ending her life so stay alert. Depression will hover but will not be dispatched until we are done with her. He glared at the trembling spirit. Now, what are you going to do about this?"

The ruling principality disappeared before Divination could come up with a plan. He slunk into a fold in a dark cloud to lick his wounds and think. First, he needed to convince Daphne that Apollo truly planned to grant her the freedom she craved and waylay her plans to end her life.

*****

The walk back to the western gate seemed endless. Daphne entered the city wishing she could avoid the *agora* and the *stoa* but there was no other way home. To her relief, most merchants and shoppers had left for the day. A glance at the sun told her by the time she arrived home the kitchen help would be finished with the master's evening meal. As if in response to the thought, her stomach growled. Still, food held no appeal. A bath and early to bed would be her choice…if she had one.

She barely noticed the lovely smells that drifted from the olive blossoms and the red poppies she passed. Likewise, the sound of gently bleating lambs. Instead, she saw never-ending clouds of dust that swirled about her. They billowed all the more as she quickened her pace, rising as if assigned to condemn every step she took.

Dust and rocks. They made her long for the beautiful forests of Delphi. She kicked a rock lying in the middle of the path. It tumbled and took a strange hop. She kicked it again. "Take that, Voice!"

She was sure Apollo would be laughing at her misery and making evil plans to crush all hope from her heart. Like clouds on a windless day, discouragement and hopelessness refused to disperse. It blotted the positive outlook she worked so hard to keep. How deceived she had been.

Regret and anger threatened tears. The memory of the first time she became aware of the Voice haunted her. He had seemed almost a friend, a mentor, sent to get her through a difficult time. How foolish she had been to allow it access to her innermost self.

Her steps fell harder; a fruitless attempt to stamp out her misery. Bittersweet memories returned of the doubts and exhilaration she felt while she prepared to be inducted into Apollo's temple. How wrong she had been to doubt the god's existence and power. "Oh mother, if only I could see you, talk to you. If only I had never...."

She brought herself up short. Regrets would get her nowhere. She would still have been sold into slavery and without the ability to see into the future, where would she be? She dwelt on the injustice of being considered someone's property, never free to pursue your heart's desire. To have a master whom one must constantly please was like having a pebble in your sandal without any way to adjust it, so it did not irritate or rub you raw.

She followed the path by rote. Patharus' estate had been home for almost a year now. Slaves who daily bent over crops reminded her that in so many ways she was far better off than others who shared her fate.

She took a deep breath and exhaled, her determination to make the best of things, at odds with an urge to give up and end her life. She brushed the dust from her clothes and her focus. She would never accept being owned by another nor would she assent to the Voice's evil plans. Somehow, she would find a way to make it until she received her freedom. She had to. Maybe something like today would never happen again.

Her mind closed to the likelihood that she hoped in vain.

She gazed at the fields. The slaves had yet to come in. Maybe she would be able to clean up before she had to come up with a believable excuse for her lack of profit. She slipped through the familiar entrance, unobserved by anyone other than Rybic. He barely opened his sleepy eyes to nod as she took the side path that led to her room.

She finished her bath and began to prepare for bed. The hot food Femi insisted she eat revived her and she could not wait to crawl under her blanket. She gazed with longing at her bed mat, convinced by then Patharus had overlooked their meeting. She had already donned her night *chiton* when word came, she was wanted by the master.

She redressed, smoothed her hair, and pinned it back with her only other comb. Without further delay, she made her way out of the servants' quarters and down the hall.

She waited, dreading the encounter. How many times had she come through this door? Patharus had been true to his word to protect her, but she found it harder each day to fulfill her promise. What could she tell him? She thought of Kawit, how she had taken her under her wing and guided her through the regimen of slavery.

Her warnings echoed. "No Daphne, do not ever look them in the face. Keep your eyes cast down when they speak to you. Wait Daphne, you do not walk into a room even if you have been summoned. You stand outside the door until they tell you to come in. No, you cannot question what you are told to do, in fact do not ever speak unless they ask you something."

Daphne blinked at tears the memory stirred. Kawit's counsel had saved her many a reprimand from Jahtel or the overseer.

Patharus beckoned her into the room. He did not motion for her to sit as he often did, so she stood. "So, Daphne, tell me of your day, was it profitable?"

With hardly a pause she concocted a tale of being nearly run down by a runaway team of horses outside the *agora*. He did not probe further when she professed not to know whose team it was, having been thrown to the ground when it grazed her. The lies made her squirm, but the truth would make things worse.

She gestured as she spoke and Patharus saw her injuries. "Wait, what is wrong with your hand, and your arm?" It was bright red where she had slid on the dirt. The fresh scrapes still oozed though she had carefully cleaned them in her bath.

He grimaced and muttered about untrained slaves given charge over horses. After he insisted, she see Halaten right away for some salve and attend the wound, he motioned for her to leave.

Daphne heaved a sigh. He must have attributed her lack of profit to the lie.

Chapter Sixty-One

Our hope is lost.
– Ezekiel 37:11

Sunlight filtering through the poplar trees flickered upon Daphne's face like a tiny butterfly looking for a place to land. Birds that roosted in the silver-barked trees chirped a cheerful welcome to the new day. For a moment she hovered between sleep and consciousness. She groped to sort reality from a dream that she was back in her room in Delphi. In it she reached for the little silver bell on the stand beside her bed that alerted Belte to her needs.

The clatter of sandals on the hall jolted her awake. Disappointment coddled a desire to turn over and go back to the dream. She sighed and swung her feet to the floor. A dull ache in her hip brought the horror of yesterday into focus. More pain greeted her as she stretched. She groaned and rubbed the shoulder she jammed when she fell. She peeked under the loose bandages Halaten used to cover her scraped arm and hand. Despite the salve they still oozed.

She wished she could pass her pain to the Voice. He was the one who deserved it.

Femi whispered outside Daphne's room, "Hey, are you up yet?" Without waiting she burst through the curtain. A smile leapt from Daphne's heart to her face. She treasured the bond that had formed between them after Kawit's death.

"What happened to your arm?" Femi pulled back Daphne's bandage so she could get a better look. "And your hand?" Creases rippled her brow. "You are gonna need more salve."

Her concern was all it took to break Daphne's determination to be brave. Tears welled and slipped down her cheeks. Femi put her arms around her, and Daphne gave in to the sobs she stifled all night, then sniffed back her tears. "I am sorry, Femi."

Femi hushed her and rocked her in her arms.

Daphne longed to share what happened but knew she could not. She trusted Femi but the forces that ran Patharus' estate had their own agendas, and she would not put her friend in jeopardy. Femi's childlike innocence reminded her of Belte. The same uncomplicated outlook evoked a need to be extra careful with what she said.

Femi did not pry. She hugged her again and they talked about other things. "I need to run and get the figs ready, and I will repair your tunic if I get some spare time."

Daphne splashed water on her face. Patharus would not put up with another profitless day. She finished her toilet and smoothed her hair by pulling the sides into her remaining comb and let the rest hang free. Her thoughts ran to the lovely tortoise shell and ivory combs she owned back home. She sniffed and hoped that greedy Roman woman did not have them.

She reached for her torn tunic and sighed. The humiliation of asking Jahtel for a new one would be too much. She dropped the ragged garment, kicked it into the corner, and pulled Lydia's scarf from under her bed mat. "I will show him. I will wear this to breakfast." The silky fabric shone in the morning light. She draped it over her shoulders and lovingly stroked the smooth fabric. Jahtel's vengeful sneer flashed. She grimaced. She knew she dared not and put it back.

At the dining tables she toyed with her food. She could not…could not go into the city and face what might happen again. What was she going to do?

The incessant choice loomed: Integrity or security?

She rose and dragged herself toward the door but stopped when Femi called out. "Daphne do not forget your water jug." Femi handed her that and a lunch. "See that you eat this, you hear?"

Daphne peeked into the parcel. Bread, cheese, and fresh fruit. She smiled. "You are the only good thing left in this place. How would I manage without you?"

Femi brushed off the sentiment and wished her a good day.

Daphne left and could already feel the sun on her back as it worked its way up into the cloudless sky. The heavy black shawl was too hot.

She would have to stay in the shade as much as possible. She was going to miss that old shawl she dropped.

A slight breeze feathered strands of hair that escaped her comb. "I cannot let yesterday deter me from my goal." A sousliks sat in the middle of the path but soon scampered and disappeared. "Hide, little one. I am going to escape too… somehow."

She had barely cleared the eastern gate when she noticed a small caravan of wagons on the Roman road. Her breath caught. *That is the wagon I arrived in from Athens.* She watched to see if they turned into the western gate to unload supplies from Thessalonica. They did not. Her throat went dry.

She told herself to look away from the man who sat beside the driver of the first wagon. Her eyes refused the order. They followed the wagon and ignored the lie her heart rehearsed. *It does not matter who it is…it does not matter.* The caravan passed the eastern gate and turned toward Patharus' estate.

She entered the *stoa* but struggled to keep her mind on why she was there. The Voice was strangely compliant, a far cry from its demands of yesterday. Despite thoughts that continually drifted to Nicanor, she picked up a few coins from men who sought her out. Did Nicanor even remember or care about her?

She knew she needed to abandon such hope, but could he possibly yearn to see her as much as she ached to see him? The painful memory of the lengthy wait in the garden persisted. That proved he did not care, she needed to avoid him.

In the afternoon she found herself in the southern part of the city where people had homes. Beresta had described Lydia's house, so she decided to go look for it. Maybe that will get her mind off Nicanor.

"You cannot miss it, Daphne. It is the biggest house with the nicest yard. It is two stories high, and the outside is a pale yellow."

Beresta had been right. Daphne stared at the house, careful to remain hidden behind a witches'-broom that bloomed near Lydia's stone fence. She wondered what Lydia did with all that room? Beresta never mentioned a family.

A man in work clothes came around one corner with tools in his arms. She ducked further behind the bush. He must be a gardener, or something.

He tore out some plants that had not survived the winter, immediately attentive when Lydia appeared through the back door. Daphne's heart leapt with joy. She must not let her see her.

Neither Lydia nor her gardener looked her way, so Daphne remained where she was. She peeked through the branches and wished she dared talk to the woman. But what would she say? "Why are you so nice? What is so different about you?" Nothing made sense.

When Lydia stepped back into her house, Daphne mourned the opportunity she let slip away. The gardener was preoccupied so she walked away unseen. Why was she afraid to talk to the woman? She had been nothing but kind and concerned for her welfare. Did her gentle manner remind her of her mother? Was that the pull on her heart?

The day lingered like a sundial bereft of the sun. She itched to get to the estate, to see Nicanor, if only from a distance. Still, she dreaded a chance encounter. When the shopkeepers began to pack up their merchandise, she had no choice but to return. She could not avoid him forever, so she rehearsed what she would say when the inevitable happened. She would all but ignore him. "Oh, how nice that you have been allowed a visit home. I hope your time in Rome was pleasant. Do excuse me; I must attend to my duties."

Satisfied she could control her feelings, she headed for the estate. She pulled out the cloth in which she tied her profits and counted it as she walked.

"Do you have enough?" a familiar voice asked.

Her head shot up and her mouth fell. "Nicanor..."

Chapter Sixty-Two

I will teach you the good and the right way.
– 1 Samuel 12:23

Nicanor's smile exposed the dimple that drew her the first time she saw him. "I have missed you, Daphne."

His eyes burrowed with longing into hers. She could not move or think. What was it she planned to say? Her mind whirred as she searched for something, anything. She could not help but take in his strong arms and well-defined muscles that rippled beneath his tunic. She tried to look away but the handsome face that haunted her dreams sent thrills down her spine.

She clenched her fists against her thighs to remind herself of his past neglect and to keep her from running into his arms. She swallowed hard. Stop it! That was out of the question.

He held out his hand. She pretended not to notice, pulled herself together and spoke in as cold and formal a tone as she could. "I, I am glad you have been allowed a visit home. How nice for the master…I mean your father."

Nicanor's expression fell. He eyed her strangely and stepped closer. "Daphne, I missed you. I wanted so much to say goodbye in person. Are you angry with me?"

The way he said her name nearly melted her resolve. He looked so troubled she wanted to comfort him. No, do not be fooled or forget what he had done.

"Oh, please do not concern yourself, but do excuse me. I am sure you have much to attend to as do I." She lifted her head and attempted to walk around him.

Nicanor grabbed her arm. "Wait. What is wrong? I sent word to the garden. Did you not get it?"

Her eyes sparked with the pain she had held since that night. She snapped at him. "There was no word. I waited for you that night…for hours."

His voice rose. "I did send word! When Patharus decided we had to leave early I wrote a note myself and gave it to my servant to bring to you in the garden."

She huffed. "There was no word from you." With that she pulled free and ran off. He called after her, but she did not look back.

She reached her room before she allowed herself to fall apart. She rubbed her arm that he had held, savoring his touch despite her anger, and sobbed into her pillow. "Why, why would he deny he abandoned me and pretend he sent a note?"

He plans to use you.

"Well, that is not going to happen. I will avoid him if I must stay in my room night and day."

At the call to dinner, she made sure he was not around before she joined the others. As soon as they were dismissed, she slipped back to her room. She finished her bath and lay on her mat. A picture of Nicanor's blue eyes and how his dimple showed when he smiled haunted her. The memory of yesterday's horror followed. What would he think if he knew what had happened… and worse yet if he had seen me?

She shook off the thought and let her mind drift to the look on his face when she first saw him. It lingered no matter how she tried to ignore it. The thirst in her own heart matched the hunger in his eyes, but why had he treated her so callously before he left? His every word replayed. *I desperately wanted to tell you…to tell you…*

She fell asleep wondering what he might have said had she waited. Her desire to know battled with her vow that he would never uncover her true feelings.

The next morning Femi brought the tunic she repaired, and was full of news about Nicanor's homecoming. "Did he not look handsome, Daphne? His time in Rome sure growed him up. Do you know how he spent his first evening at home?" She did not wait for a reply. "He took a walk right after his meal with the master. They did not have time to prepare a welcome home feast, that will come tonight. Anyway, some of us saw him go out to the slave cemetery where his momma's buried and visit her grave. Is that not the most touching thing ever? All who knew her loved her, especially her only son. After that he—"

Daphne could not listen to any more. "I'm sorry Femi, I slept too long, and I really need to eat and get ready for the day. Thanks so much for mending my tunic." Femi gave a cheerful nod and left. Daphne picked up the garment and looked it over. The tear was nearly hidden.

She succeeded in avoiding Nicanor at breakfast but could not escape the excitement and gossip that surrounded his return. "I heard the master has invited the fathers of several eligible young ladies to the welcome home feast tonight, sounds like he is ready to find Nicanor a wife,"

"I thought Nicanor was just home until next fall and then back to finish his studies in Rome."

"Well, that is not what I heard, I...."

Daphne could not bear it. She stood up and grabbed her tray. "Excuse me, I need to run." She could feel the eyes that followed her. Many knew she and Nicanor had been close, but none had ever mentioned the gossip that surfaced before he left for Rome.

She stopped at her room and held a cold cloth against her red-rimmed eyes. She vowed afresh to remain unaffected by all the talk about Nicanor. He had rejected her once and she would not give him another opportunity.

The morning passed quickly as Daphne went about her business in the city. The Voice remained unusually subdued as they dealt with people's needs and he had not harassed her about Apollo's demands. Only coins that jangled in her pouch testified that she had been obedient to her charge.

Her heart raced as she rehearsed a plan that had incubated like eggs ready to hatch throughout the morning. Did she dare let it surface? She assessed the coins she had earned. It was enough. Patharus would be satisfied. She stuffed the coins. She was going to take a chance.

She followed the *stoa* to the gate that led to the river. Careful not to speak her hope aloud, she mapped out her intentions. The Voice seemed to have distanced itself, if she could get there before the crowds, perhaps she could hide and hear the man for herself.

She wanted to run but unwanted attention might delay her. The area appeared deserted. Only the trampled foliage near the edge of the river testified   to the daily meetings. Melting snow from the mountains, accompanied by the early spring rains had raised the water level on the river's banks. The hot sun left her dry, so She knelt as close as she could and refilled her jug before splashing water to cool her face.

She looked for a place close enough to hear but with enough foliage to hide behind. A grove of trees with low branches seemed her only choice. She walked over, not sure she would be able to hear from there. Another look confirmed it was this or nothing. She pulled out her lunch and waited.

People began to arrive. Excited and anxious, she shivered despite the heat. Familiar faces, people she often saw in the city came in twos and threes Many shared aloud what they hoped to see and hear. She could catch a phrase or two, but most were muffled.

Her breath caught at the sight of the young man who had previously found her in tears sitting above the city, and insisted she follow him down to the gate. Her hands rose to her chest, touched at the memory of how concerned he had been that she not remain there alone.

He sat near the Jewish sect. A further glance revealed they were far outnumbered by Greeks and less prosperous Romans. At last, the man they called Paul arrived. The crowd cheered as he joined them. He greeted all and hugged many. Someone brought him a fresh jug of water. He drank it with gusto, thanked the man and shook more hands.

Fascinated, Daphne followed his every move. The man was about to begin when a group of six or eight more arrived. Her eyes shot open. Lydia was among them.

Chapter Sixty-Three

Those who seek me diligently will find me.
– Proverbs 8:7

Those who arrived with Lydia followed her lead. Paul greeted them and they joined the others on the grass. His voice rose and fell. "Friends, believe on the Lord, Jesus Christ and be baptized into His family...whomsoever believes shall be saved and become a child of God...there is neither Jew nor Greek, slave nor free, male or female, all are one in Christ Jesus."

Daphne shifted her position. Neither slave nor free? All are one? That was not true in her life.

She wished her makeshift refuge were closer. Baptized? What did that mean? She did not wonder long. When Paul finished, he stood on the banks while his helpers led Lydia, those who arrived with her, and many others down to the river's edge. Daphne rose to her knees. What were they doing? Lydia could get mud on her beautiful *peplos*.

She was the first to step into the river, kneel, and fold her arms across her chest. Daphne gasped, her jaw ajar. One of Paul's helpers put his arm around Lydia's back and a hand on her forehead before he plunged her backwards under water. "I baptize you in the name of the Father, the Son, and the Holy Spirit." Daphne could not believe her eyes...Lydia's lovely purple dress was surely ruined. Yet, the woman did not appear to notice. She came out of the water smiling, arms skyward. Over and over, she cried, "Praise your name, Jesus, praise your name. Thank you for saving me, thank you Lord, thank you my Jesus."

Daphne hung on her every word. When the name, Jesus, was spoken she felt a rumbling within, but the Voice remained silent. Jesus? Was that not the name the man spoke the day she was knocked to the ground and the Voice deserted her? And did not Paul say moments before there is no salvation in any other name by which we are saved? Daphne shook her head. She did not understand. They pushed Lydia under the water, and she came up thankful and so happy! Does this Jesus only like people who are wealthy...or free?

One after another the listeners, of whom few looked rich, lined up to submit to the ritual. Each came up from the water with the same joyful expression and cheers from the crowd. She could not tear her eyes from the strange ceremony. Amazing she had never seen such joy.

The last person was submerged, or baptized as Paul referred to the ritual, before he began to pray. "Beloved, I would that Christ may dwell in your heart through faith; that you being rooted and grounded in love may be able to comprehend with all the saints what is the width, and length, and depth and height, to know the love of Christ which passes knowledge...."

No one fidgeted or left, though the prayers and speech that went on for a good while. It was late afternoon when he finally bid them leave. Daphne too had lost track of time. After the last straggler was well on his way, she wiped the brush from her tunic and glanced at the sun. One look sent her scurrying.

She rehashed the things that stuck in her mind. "God who is rich in mercy because of His great love.... He shows the exceeding riches of His grace in His kindness toward us...by grace you are saved, not of yourself, it is a gift of God.... Her heart swelled at the hope Paul inspired, that even she could find such love and freedom one day. But how did one receive it from a man died for us on a Roman cross?"

She covered the mile back to town pondering what she heard. This Jesus was not like her god. Apollo used her and did not care about her or her desire to be free. Many of those who had submitted to the call to believe and were ducked into the water were not Jews and it did not seem to matter. Would he care about her?

So many questions. How she wished she could ask Lydia about what she witnessed. No one from Patharus' estate had been there, as few slaves had the freedom she enjoyed to come and go. Of the ones she knew in the city, none had expressed any interest in the man.

Except the Voice.

The thought brought her to a halt. Her hand flew to her lips, suddenly aware that it had not harassed her or the leader while she listened. Why? Why would it react with such violence one day and be completely quiet the next?

She had no explanation. Had it left her or no longer cared where she went? Her mind raced. What did it mean? Hope sprang at the thought of being free of its presence. In seconds it sank and left her terrified of a future without its leverage.

She stepped into the courtyard. "But I do not care, I want to hear more about this Jesus. He sounds so…."

Instantly, her insides ballooned as if they were about to burst. Her hands flew to her throat, grasping at what felt like a noose. She choked. "I, I cannot breathe." In her struggle to free herself, she fell to her knees. Nothing was there. She clawed in vain at the invisible restraint until she blacked out.

When she came to she coughed and gasped for air. Her arms flailed. No hands clutched her throat. Her heart raced. She sat up and spun around but nothing stirred. "What happened… who…?"

A large black object narrowly missed her head. She crouched to her knees. "What was that?"

Maybe you should ask that new god you are interested in.

She shuddered. She had forgotten to keep her thoughts to herself. The Voice had not left and it now knew of her forbidden desire. She rose to her feet. "I, I did not mean to…I…"

A flock of crows appeared out of nowhere and began to bombard her. She hurled herself to the ground to avoid being struck in the face. They screamed their ugly caws and came closer with each swoop. She covered her head with her arms and sobbed. A picture of the crow that disrupted her grandmother's wake sprang to mind. Had the Voice instructed the despicable creatures to harass her as it had called them to desecrate her grandmother's bier?

Do you like your new companions or would you like them to leave?

She nodded, unable to catch her breath.

You thought you were free of me, did you not? Thought you could do what you wished without regard to what I have instructed you. Now you will pay. Apollo is not pleased with you. That god you want to know about does not exist. There is only Apollo, and he holds your life and your future. You have disobeyed and now you shall always be a slave and never free.

Daphne wailed. "No! You promised he would set me free one day, you promised."

You have not been faithful to Apollo. There is no hope for you. I will no longer help you.

"No. please, no. Please give me another chance. I am sorry, I promise I will never look to another god. I will do whatever Apollo wants of me. Please, please beg him to forgive."

In the silence that followed Daphne stayed on the ground and wept. Exhausted and spent, she pulled herself to her feet and staggered to the estate. She skipped dinner but arrived before Stello sent someone to look for her. As soon as the slaves were dismissed she tromped to her room, grateful Patharus would probably be too caught up with Nicanor's welcome home feast to call for her.

The reality of Nicanor's future caused waves of sadness and despair to rush over her, submerging her in a raging surf of self pity.

She lay on her bed unmindful of the tears that trickled into her hair. The Voice was right., She had no future, nothing to live for. She needed to find a way to end her misery.

The next morning, she made sure no one saw her slip a knife from the carving table into her tunic. She left for the city as usual, but after she was sure no one watched, she doubled back and turned toward the garden. The bench where she had waited for Nicanor lay around the next bend, but she ignored it and quickened her pace.

A sob she could not stifle rose from her chest. She refused to let it rule. It did not matter…there was no hope. She had no other out.

She quickly reached the section furthest from the gate. A glance at the deadly plant she sought brought a rush of anxiety. She closed her eyes. Could she do it?

She swallowed her dread and took in the plant's myriad of feathery leaves blowing in the breeze. They swayed without malice and hid the deadly, purple-spotted stems that supported them. She stopped short of the rich, moist soil surrounding the hemlock. How could she get to it without ruining her sandals in the black mud? She rolled her eyes. Why should she care?

She stooped beneath the branches of the life-sapping plant and studied the flat-topped clusters of small white flowers. They were far too immature to produce the toxic seeds she intended to ingest. A sigh rushed from her lungs. Now what was she going to do?

Chapter Sixty-Four

Difficult is the way that leads to life.
– Matthew 7:14

Daphne remembered how her grandfather said that his countrymen used the hemlock to concoct a liquid to execute people. That in fact, the whole plant was poison. His stories of men who gasped for breath or had convulsions that ended in a coma and death terrified her. To chew or swallow pieces whole would be impossible, but she had no way to make a potion.

She glanced at the smooth hollow stems. With a fury born of hopelessness, she slashed the closest one. It swayed but did not break. She grabbed hold of it and struck the unyielding stalk again. "Why is everything so hard?"

She placed the shattered pieces in the skirt of her tunic. Through angry tears she inspected what she had gleaned and wondered what would make them work the surest and the fastest.

She backed from under the foliage and gripped the knife to chop what she gathered into pieces small enough to chew. Footsteps pounded down the path behind her. She sprang upright and clutched her chest. The bundle and knife slipped from her hands. Stello! It had to be him. He saw her turn into the garden and followed her!

Her heart pounded as she searched for a place to hide. The leaves of the hemlock were too sparse, and time prevented her from reaching another shelter before he would overtake her.

He planned to assault her. She knew it. In the seconds before he would find her, she bent down and picked up the knife. She would die defending herself even if she killed him or maimed herself in the process. She gripped her weapon and waited. She had nothing to lose.

The footsteps stopped. In the silence, jagged breathing reached her ears. Prepared for the worst, she raised the knife high.

Her assailant revealed himself, and swiftly grabbed her wrist. "Daphne! Daphne, what are you doing? Let go of that knife before you hurt yourself!"

Her chin dropped. Nicanor stood before her, dressed in his exercise toga, his face a wreath of horror. The pressure of his grip opened her hand and the knife slid to the ground. She fell to her knees and covered her face with her hands. She could have hurt him.

He knelt beside her and let her cry. After she quieted, he placed his hand under her chin. "Daphne, what is this? What are you doing here?"

His touch was gentle, comforting. What could she say? He would never understand. She blurted the first thing that came to mind. "I, I needed to gather some...herbs and I thought someone was about to attack me."

He studied her face, his brows drawn. "Who Daphne? Who would want to harm you?"

His tenderness shamed her. She tried to look away, but he held fast to her chin. "I, I am not sure, I am...I should, I must be on my way. Patharus, I mean the master, expects me to be in the city by now."

Nicanor let go and helped her up. "Then what are you doing here and why hemlock? You know it is poison, do you not?"

She nodded and backed away. "Please forgive me. I must go."

She turned and walked as fast as she could toward the gate, hoping he would not follow.

He quickly caught up and walked beside her. "I know you are still angry with me and think I left you stranded in the garden, but you watch, I will prove I sent word."

Why had he shown up? In a short time, she would have been through with all this turmoil and found peace. But he was here...now...close. She grimaced. Why would she choose death when a moment with him is all she lived for? They walked toward the gate in silence.

At the pond where their dubious meeting was to take place, he stopped her. "You need to wash your hands and where you touched your face. That plant can damage your skin." He waited while she washed her hands in the pond and rubbed her face with a dampened part of her tunic. When she stood, she staggered.

"Are you dizzy? It could be the poison. Let's sit a moment. Remember our bench?"

Her head screamed, run, but her feet would not move. Her chin dipped to her chest. She must not become vulnerable to him again. She took a deep breath, shook the cobwebs from her head and looked him in the eyes. "I am sorry Nicanor, er master, but I must be on my way, I...."

He reached for her hand and put it to his lips. "Daphne, please do not pull away from me. You are all I thought of while I was away. You care for me, I know you do."

She tried to protest but it was no use. He pulled her into his arms and kissed her tenderly. "I love you, Daphne. I have loved you from the moment I first saw you."

Over and over, he kissed her lips, her cheeks, her wet eyes. She tried to push him away, but he would not relent. The strength of his body folded her to his own. His kisses became harder, demanding she respond. For a moment she surrendered and matched his passion with all she had denied for months.

He murmured in her ear. "I do not want to know what you intended to do with that hemlock but promise me you will never touch it again. Promise?"

At the mention of the hemlock, her senses returned. What are you doing? Stop this madness! Leave before it is too late. He deceived you before, remember? Run!

Trembling, she pushed him away. "No, this is wrong. This should not be. I cannot do this. Please do not come after me. I must go." She spun away and ran for the gate.

Nicanor called for her to stop, but she did not look back.

She felt in her pocket to make sure her idol had not fallen out and sped toward the city. Work. She would concentrate on her assignment and forget this morning ever happened.

She washed the mud from her tunic and sandals in the fountain, grateful she felt no effects from the hemlock. A diligent search for a customer failed. It was just as well, her mind was far from it. Thoughts of Nicanor, the words he spoke, the feel of his arms and his lips, diminished the Voice's threat to leave her. By noon she began to worry. Patharus expected a profit. Would the Voice really desert her? She circled the *stoa* again and made sure men knew her help was available.

She sat by the fountain and refilled her jug. Anxiety billowed like a thunderhead. It brought visions of work as a field hand, or worse, coming under Stello's control. She held her head in her hands. "What am I going to do…what can I do?"

Are you ready to give up this folly of a god greater than Apollo and obey him alone?

She flushed with relief. The Voice had interceded, and Apollo must have consented to give her another chance. She jumped to her feet. "Yes, yes. I am ready. Please tell Apollo that I will never listen to another god.

Good. We have much work to do. Follow my lead.

Within the hour, two men appeared in need of counsel. Daphne finished with each and tied the coins in her cloth. She thought about the loving god the man called Paul spoke of and how his agenda differed from Apollo's. Regrets seeped like a broken cistern and spread a pool of sadness over her heart. If she wanted to gain her freedom, she must follow Apollo.

The Voice's command interrupted her thoughts. *Now, let us go to the river and intervene before any more are duped by that leader and his men.*

She hid a gasp. Surely the Voice would not force her to repeat the harassment he put upon her before. She searched frantically for a way out. "The meeting of the city council has just adjourned, there may be men who—"

Have you changed your mind or are you willing to obey whatever Apollo asks of you?

Daphne gulped. "No. I will do whatever Apollo asks."

Good. Make haste for the river.

Chapter Sixty-Five

That you may know that the Son of Man has power.
– Matthew 9:6

Daphne's insides churned as she left for the western gate. A vision of being used again to harass the man and his followers, sent chills down her spine. The closer she came the more her feet dragged. She could not go through with it.

She stopped and spun toward the *agora* but was twisted around and propelled onward through the gate. She panicked at her inability to control her body. Oh, no! Not again. Her face began to contort, leaving her mouth agape to drool that same disgusting foam down her chin. She began to sway as her arms coiled over head in a snake-like motion.

Her eyes narrowed as she closed in on the river where people were already being baptized. Heads turned as the Voice ranted.

Liars, these men are phonies! All of Greece knows Apollo is the savior of our country. His father Zeus sent him to provide all you need. Do not listen to these men.

She stumbled forward, helpless to resist the power within. The Voice grew louder as it cursed its raspy message. *Apollo has sent me to warn you to stay far from these men. They claim to be servants of the Most High God who proclaim to us the way of salvation. None is higher than Apollo. Run from them, run!*

Through her, the Voice continued to mock and threaten. People began to whisper. Some who held to their Greek heritage of many gods were noticeably alarmed. A man yelled. "You have angered the gods." His glance swept the crowd. "We do not know this man's god and Apollo will rain disaster on our crops if we disregard his supremacy. I cannot chance that, can you?"

Another shook his head in disgust. "No, no. Apollo is a myth, remember what Paul taught us? There is no other God and I for one will not be intimidated by a sorceress."

Fervent disagreements continued until Paul called for quiet and addressed them. "Beloved, remember what our Savior said, God is able to make all grace abound toward you that you having all sufficiency in all things may have an abundance for every good work. Do not cast away your confidence, believe and God will take care of your needs and your crops."

The people settled down, except for the loudest contender, "But what about her she has the evil eye and...."

Paul silenced him. "But God has delivered us from the power of darkness and conveyed us into the kingdom of the Son of His love. He has disarmed all principalities and powers like you are seeing here. But you, He made alive who were dead in trespasses and sins in which you all once walked according to the course of this world, according to the prince of the power of the air, the spirit who now works in this girl and all sons of disobedience. But by grace you have been saved through faith, it is God's gift to you. Remember, He Himself has said 'I will never leave you or forsake you.' There is no fear in the perfect love of God."

The Voice railed as Daphne drew close. A large man with a thick neck and broad shoulders shouted, "Paul is right. Lets get her!" He motioned to the two men who accompanied him. They rose as one and began to weave their way through the crowd.

Her stomach reeled. She tried to back away, but her feet felt like they were stuck in a bog. She crossed her arms over her face and braced for the onslaught.

Just before they reached her Paul called to them. "No beloved, stop! That is not our way." He nodded to Silas who quickly brushed past the three and stood between them and Daphne. Still expecting to be struck, she cowered, afraid her knees would buckle.

Paul's helper raised his arms "Brethren, there is no need for violence. Our God is more than able to dispel this demon. Please return to your seats and let us handle it."

The three groused a bit before the leader led his companions back into the crowd. Daphne's relief was short lived. She squinted at the man who rescued her. Her former encounter with him flared. He was the one who commanded the Voice to be silent and sent me flying the last time.

The Voice pushed her toward him, its message mocked louder. *These men are servants of the most High God who proclaim to us the way of salvation.*

Before the Voice could utter more the man blocked her way and looked her in the eye. He did not raise his voice but spoke with authority. "In the name of Jesus Christ, I command you to be still."

Once again, she sprawled to the ground and was unable to move. She cried to the Voice for help. There was no response. Like before, she had been left to fend for herself. Anger spewed from every pore and through gritted teeth she growled, "Why? Where are you? Was it not your idea to come here?"

Humiliated and furious, she finally pushed herself to her feet and backed away. She glanced at the crowd. For the most part their attention had returned to the leader.

To her horror, Lydia stared at her.

Beside her stood Nicanor.

She wanted to die. Her knees weakened and she fought to keep upright.

Nicanor stretched his neck to get a better look. Lydia whispered something in his ear. He shook his head and Daphne could see he was about to come after her. Adrenalin sent her scrambling. He could easily catch her. She ran as fast as she could and stopped in a densely forested area and hid behind a large boulder. She held her breath until footsteps sprinted past. A cautious peek confirmed he had not seen her. A lump formed in her throat as she watched his muscular legs carry him out of sight.

Mortified at what he had seen, she leaned into her hand. What was Nicanor doing there? Had Patharus sent him to find out more about the man called Paul? And Lydia, she saw it too. She would never want to have anything to do with her now.

She sat with her back against the rock, trying to make sense of it all. The Voice sends me to harass them and disappears when I am confronted. Why? Is it afraid of the man? She was the one who gets the brunt of it. The Voice did not run when it forced me to harass the Jews in the city…why this man? And why does the badgering stop the minute the man repeats those same words?

Slowly she repeated to herself what he said. In the name of Jesus Christ, I command you. That is what he says. Is there a connection to that name? Does the Voice lose his power to harass people when they use that name? When they command in the name of Jesus?

The sound of exuberant voices grew nearby. The meeting had ended, and the crowd would catch up if she lingered. She wondered what they would do to her. She would not blame them if they stoned her…that was what Beresta said the Jews do to troublesome people.

She left her hiding place and went back to the estate and gave her earnings to Patharus. She had managed to avoid Nicanor but knew that would not last. She treasured the picture of his face in the garden when he spoke of his love, but it soon faded, replaced by his shocked expression at the river. She clutched her waist. What must he think…what could she do?

The events of the day rolled through her mind like a runaway boulder down a mountain. The hemlock, Nicanor, his kisses, the river. Her hands shot to the sides of her head. "Stop!" She had not meant to be so loud.

"Are you alright?"

She recognized the voice of Patharus' personal servant. "Yes, yes, I am fine. I am sorry to have disturbed anyone."

"You sure? Is someone—"

She rubbed her forehead. How could she have been so careless? "No, no, I am alright, but thank you." She hoped he would leave.

"I am sorry to have to inform you that Patharus asks that you present yourself immediately."

"But I already…."

"I know, but it is his wish. Are you presentable?"

"Yes, I mean can I have a moment to freshen?"

"Yes. I will wait."

A weary sigh slid from her lips. Now what had she done? Did Nicanor report her vile behavior?

Chapter Sixty-Six

Daphne splashed some water on her face, smoothed her hair and stepped into the hall. The servant nodded kindly and led the way. Her thoughts scattered like frightened sheep as she strained to come up with a reason for the call. Being ushered in without the usual wait sent waves of dread of what might await her.

Patharus did not greet her, his tone serious. "Sit down, Daphne," She did not look up but could feel his eyes upon her. "Some information has come to my attention, and I want to hear what you know of it."He sounded upset. She nodded. What must Nicanor have told him?

"I have reason to believe the report I received upon my return after I accompanied Nicanor to catch the ship for Rome, may not have been correct. I am referring to your friend Kawit's death."

She held her breath, pulled her arms across her middle and stared at the floor.

"Look at me, Daphne. You have nothing to fear. I already know of your outburst against Stello and that he struck you, but I want the whole story, and I want it now."

She raised her head. Her lips trembled, unsure of what to reveal. Did she dare tell the truth? Would he believe her?

His voice gentled. "Start at the beginning. What did your friend confide in you about her troubles with Stello?"

She eked out an answer. "Kawit was a good girl. She did everything she could to keep from… from angering Stello." Out of habit, she lowered her eyes.

"It is alright, Daphne, do not be afraid. I have asked for the truth, and you will suffer no consequences because of it."

She knew she could trust him. Slowly, she lifted her chin and told of Kawit's fear of Stello, how she was convinced he intended to rape her. Daphne disclosed his threats in the laundry room and how he pounced on every opportunity to hover over Kawit in search of a chance to berate her. "She was terrified, knowing her rebuffs could lead to a beating or even death." Growing bolder, Daphne refocused on her pain over Kawit's torture, and the loss of her only friend. "And it did! The day she died he caught her alone in the laundry. She refused his advances, but he overpowered her, raped and beat her unmercifully to cover it up what he had done. When I heard about it, I ran to her. She was dying but she told me what happened."

Tears washed Daphne's cheeks. "Kawit coughed up blood and I knew she needed help. I ran to Halaten, but he said he could not come unless Jahtel or Stello approved it." Her voice caught. "And Stello...Stello he...he deliberately ignored my plea until it was too late. She died in my arms."

Her tears turned to sobs and bitterness coated her words. "He had no right...she had done nothing to deserve what he did...except refuse his lustful advances."

Patharus gave her time to collect herself. "And that made you angry enough to stand up to him?"

She almost shouted. "It was wrong! He would not even let me prepare her for burial or say goodbye. She was my friend! She did not deserve what he did to her!"

Patharus broke the silence that followed. "Thank you for your help. I want to get to the bottom of this and will make further inquiries into what happened. You are not to speak of this conversation to anyone. Do you understand?"

She clutched her hands. When she did not respond his brows furrowed. "Daphne? Is there more?"

"Will....I mean, will Stello know I have spoken of this?"

"No. No, I am the only one. Why? Are you afraid of him too?"

She hesitated, emboldened by the opportunity to amplify Kawit's injustice. "While you were away and I had to report to him and in those nightly meetings he, well, he looked at me and insinuated his evil intentions in the same way he taunted Kawit."

Patharus' face snarled with anger. "I promise I will see to your protection. Now be on your way."

She left the room hopeful but unable to quell a rising uneasiness.

Much of the night she tossed, her sleep ransacked with dreams that switched from the gore she witnessed in the *adytum* to running desperately down streets in Athens to escape the claws of the high priest. As in the night terrors that began in Delphi, the accusing finger of the *pythia* pointed her out. The woman's face zoomed like a blazing comet but changed to the face of Stello just before she woke in a cold sweat.

She welcomed the first rays of dawn, eager to put the night behind. Breakfast had barely been laid out when she reached the dining area. She made quick work of the wheat gruel and cream, grabbed a lunch sack, and left before a chance encounter with Nicanor occurred. Her mind whirred as she rehearsed the conversation with Patharus. Could he really keep her safe from Stello? She looked over her shoulder and shivered.

Halfway to the city the dread of what the Voice might have planned for today spread a vile taste in her mouth. She cupped her elbows against her stomach, willing the pressure to quiet her insides. Could she find a way to distract the voice and divert it from Paul and his followers?

She stopped mid step. Once again she had neglected to praise and worship Apollo like she promised. She would start again, maybe that would satisfy him.

As she walked, she cried aloud. "Oh, great and powerful, Apollo, you who are lord of the bow and of all music, I worship you. You who speak to the dawn and light bursts forth from the sun, you shine on our crops, and they grow and multiply. How great is your power and all creatures benefit from your grace. You are…."

What were those things her grandmother had instilled? She shrugged, added a few more for good measure, calling out everything that crossed her mind, but stopped short of confessing him as the god above all gods.

To her relief, the day passed peacefully with no sign of the man called Paul or his followers. Probably at the river, she noted, mindful to keep her thoughts to herself. She squeezed her money cloth and decided she needed to find another customer. No one sought her out until late afternoon. By the time the man settled on a quiet place to meet the confrontation took longer than usual. She sighed and ducked into the courtyard to refill her jug for the walk home.

The sound of a crowd alerted her to the likelihood of trouble. A quick peek out the entrance brought a shudder. Paul hustled at the front of the group and Nicanor hoofed right alongside him. Many of the people were those pushed under the water that day she went to the river, including Lydia.

They headed for the eastern gate. Daphne stepped out of sight in case Nicanor might look her way.

She had almost reached a place to hide when a man stopped her. "Sorceress, I have been looking for you. I need to seek your god for...."

What else he said did not register. Distracted, she backed away from him. "I am so sorry, but my master has commanded me to be home shortly. I will be happy to meet you first thing tomorrow and..."

"But this is urgent. Surely your master would not want you to bypass a chance to earn—"

"No, no I am so sorry." She dodged from side to side to keep an eye on the entrance near the fountain.

The man stepped closer, his frustration building. "I will double your fee, *Kopela*."

"I am sorry...please meet me here tomorrow. I will ask and I am sure Apollo will hold off your trouble until then."

The man huffed and stomped away. Daphne sighed. I hope Patharus does not hear about that lie.

The sounds of commerce fell to almost nothing before she dared look into the *stoa*. Merchants were packing up and the area had cleared of all but a few people. She gathered her courage and set out for home, grateful to have avoided another confrontation.

She pictured Nicanor's intense interaction with Paul. Why would he join the group again?

Could he…? She shrugged. No, he is probably curious.

Chapter Sixty-Seven

Power over unclean spirits.
– Matthew 10:1

Memories of when Nicanor waited along the path kept Daphne alert. She reached the final crest before the estate with no sign of him. Relief and regret mingle in a sigh.

At mealtime she entered a courtyard alive with excitement. Femi ran up to her. "Daphne, have you heard? Stello has been replaced!"

Speculation skipped from slave to slave. A woman assigned to pick fruit could hardly contain herself. "I heard a new overseer is about to be named. What a relief! That skunk will not hang around the orchard next fall with his lewd comments."

Her coworker agreed. "Yep, Stello finally got his due. Someone must have gotten brave enough uncover his vile ways or exposed his cruelty."

Random remarks affirmed what Daphne suspected to be true.

"Could be the master tired of his lofty attitude..."

"I think it was his jealousy of Nicanor..."

"Yea, me too. You know Stello expected to be the master's heir and after he made Nicanor his legal son, that is when he really started taking out his anger on us...."

"Yes, maybe the master got wind of that senseless whipping last week..."

"Well, I heard he was caught forcing himself on a young girl..."

Their reflections left Daphne speechless. She had not been alone in her dread of Stello. But why had no one spoke up? Why hadn't she? She sat at a far table with her food untouched. Patharus believed her! He listened and believed what she said. That had to have had a part in Stello's dismissal.

She did not know whether to laugh or cry. Neither could fully express her relief.

The slaves had settled, and most had finished their meal when Nicanor stepped into the outer yard. Anxious glances passed from table to table. Daphne's heart leapt at the sight of him. He was dressed like Patharus in an ornate tunic. The elegant fabric opened at the throat exposing his broad chest. She looked away.

Nicanor cleared his throat and all eyes rested on the master's son. He turned toward Stello's vacated perch, grimaced, raised his foot and shoved it off its stand. A loud cheer rose as all the slaves stood, clapped, and hooted until he raised his hands.

His eyes swept the crowd and lingered but a second on Daphne. He grinned at the people he looked upon as family. "My father, your master, has asked me to speak to you this evening. I know you have all heard that Stello will no longer be with us." More cheers rose, but he quickly hushed them. "Patharus has hired a new overseer and we hope he will arrive from Neapolis in time to meet with you tomorrow night. Jahtel will see to tomorrow's assignments."

Neapolis. Daphne's mind returned to the harbor where she arrived to begin life as a slave. Could a whole year have passed? Nicanor spoke of his assurance of Patharus' concern for their welfare and his promise to meet their needs, including no longer having to get approval to seek help from the Halaten. After Nicanor dismissed them, people surrounded and plied him with questions. She returned her tray and slipped out, grateful Kawit's death brought about some good. But, she sniffed. Had not her father promised his slaves they would be taken care of too, and where were they now?

Daylight had yet to wane, so she decided to visit the garden. The good news and the abundance of spring flowers delighted her heart. Stello would no longer be a threat. She walked the path and stopped to smell the violets or admire the poppies.

"This was your doing, was it not?"

She spun around and froze. How had Stello managed to return unseen? Her heart thumped in her throat as she stepped backwards. "I, I...."

The evil curl of his lips amplified the hate in his voice. "I know every inch of this estate and I knew you would come to the garden. You are the only one who knew what happened to Kawit and you told him, did you not?"

She backed some more. Step for step, he followed.

"You think you are better than all the others, even better than me, right? Set apart and pampered, Patharus' little profit maker."

An oleander bush stabbed her in the back. Its thick arms blocked her escape. Kawit's account of his brutality flooded her senses and terror streamed through every part of her. She was not supposed to be here, and no one would hear her call for help. "Please, I…."

"Oh yes, please." His tone mocked her plea. That is what Kawit said, "Please. Please." He grabbed her arm and pulled her close, "I am going to miss you, Daphne…perhaps you would like to give me a goodbye kiss, a little send off?"

She struggled to free herself. "Stop it! Leave me alone."

"Oh, you are a fighter. I knew you would be, but that makes it more fun."

His leer sickened her and panic swelled as he yanked at her clothes.

She screamed for him to stop, waiving consequences of being found in the forbidden garden. "Patharus will not let you get away with this."

"Ha! I have nothing to lose. He is done with me, remember?"

He forced her arm behind her back and pushed her to the ground. The weight of his body as he covered hers and wrapped her with his legs, immobilized her. She turned her face to avoid his, but he grabbed her chin and wrenched it to his. The smell of him turned her stomach, her cries muffled as his mouth encased hers.

She pounded him with her fist. He laughed, grabbed the top of her tunic, pulled it from her shoulders. She reached up and dug into his face with her nails. He howled and hit her aside the head. "You little witch."

Daphne lay stunned. She gasped, horrified at the touch of his hands. As she struggled for breath enough to call out, from out of nowhere strength she did not possess emboldened her. She worked her arm free, put her hands against his chest, and pushed. Stello flew off her as if a giant hand had hoisted him. He landed at the foot of a terebinth tree across the path from where she lay. She rose on one elbow and straightened the front of her tunic, hysterical with gratitude. She looked to each side.

No one was there.

Stello staggered to his feet. Fist raised, his head jerked in every direction. He frowned and scanned the area several times, his face contorted with confusion. His glance fell on her. She held her breath. Rage spewed from his face. She pulled herself onto her haunches, ready to run. His face twitched with indecision. She rose to her knees, her heart racing. He gave a final look in every direction, glared at her, and took off at a run.

She hugged her chest and watched him disappear. At every sound she swiveled to check for his return. When it appeared he had left for good, relief turned to sobs that resonated throughout her body. She pushed herself to her feet, not sure her legs would hold her. The ground where she had laid was undisturbed. Only the breeze stirred. "What tore him from me?"

Have I not told you of Apollo's greatness? He is able to look after his own. The man will never come near you again.

Daphne's jaw dropped. The Voice. Apollo had intervened and rescued her! She remembered the time back in Delphi when it pushed her and sent her sprawling to the ground. How could something that could not be seen exert such force? She whispered into the twilight, "Thank you… Thank you for saving me."

She brushed the dirt, and twigs from her tunic, grateful it had not ripped. Still shaken, every sound startled her. She found her way back to the garden gate, horrified at what might have happened. Her hatred of the Voice and its agenda faded in gratitude for its rescue. Somehow, she would find a way to reconcile the two…at least until she obtained her freedom.

Chapter Sixty-Eight

Men who suppress the truth in unrighteousness.
– Romans 1:18

She had not left for the city the next morning when Patharus' servant notified her that the master wanted to see her right away. She flew to his office. The latent fears that he would take advantage of her had long disappeared, but any request other than her daily report brought waves of anxiety. Did he know of Stello's assault? Had he changed his mind about the man?

Voices carried outside his door, but she could not make out what was said. She paid little attention, it would not likely concern her. She chewed her lip, waiting for the visitor to leave. The servants face revealed nothing as he led her in. She hesitated, expecting the guest to pass on his way out.

No one left.

Beside the master's desk, Jahtel stood with his fingertips touching in front of him, his face wreathed in a smirk. She hid her shock and dread behind lowered eyes. He had watched her enter, his expression of one who had achieved a well-fought triumph. She had no idea what might have displeased him, for the most part she had avoided the man for months.

Patharus motioned and she drew close to his desk. His tone was stern. "Daphne, it has come to my attention that something may be amiss. Would you tell me how you came to possess this?"

He held up Lydia's shawl.

Daphne's heart sank. How did Patharus get the shawl? It lay wrapped it in a cloth and hidden it under her bed mat. No one should have seen it. Who would have wandered into her room, lifted her mat, and disliked her enough to report it? Slaves cleaned their own rooms, and a casual glance would not have exposed it.

Jahtel watched her squirm. He folded his arms across his chest barely able to conceal his pleasure.

She searched his face. Why did the man hate her so? Patharus cleared his throat, impatience edged his voice. "Daphne?""

What could she say? Would he believe her? "Master, I, ah, ...I was in town one day and forgot to wear my shawl. As I watched for someone to help the sun became intense. While I waited, a lovely woman came up to me and told me I needed to be careful as the heat could make me sick...."

Jahtel jerked toward Patharus and gave a loud snort.

She winced but went on. "I was taken back by her concern and before I knew it, she wrapped me in her shawl. She said she lived close by, had many others, and wanted me to have it. She disappeared into the crowd before I could object, and I did not know where she lived or how to return it, so I have kept it in my room."

It took forever for Patharus to respond. Finally, he looked at Jahtel. "You seem to think this was stolen...has a merchant reported unruliness or trouble with any of our people?"

Jahtel's tone turned defensive. "Well, no, but merchants seldom are aware when someone makes off with their goods." He sneered. "Surely you do not believe a woman wealthy enough to own a shawl like this would simply give it to a slave?"

"Look at me Daphne," Patharus said. "Have you told me the whole story?"

The whole story? Her heart raced. She had withheld the part where she ran from the crowd after listening to Paul, and how the lady had followed. Should she tell him what Beresta told her about the woman? Maybe that would convince him.

"Master, I have recently learned who the lady is and where she lives. I would be glad to return it to her, or you could ask her for yourself."

Jahtel scowled, his smirk reduced to a frown. "I will see to it, Master."

Patharus laid the scarf on his desk. "No, I believe I will attend to this myself. I planned to go into the city today anyway." He looked at Daphne. "We cannot have any blemish on the reputation of our household. Leave the information you have about who the woman is and where she lives with my servant, and I will get to the bottom of this."

Daphne nodded and backed out the door. She did as Patharus asked, dashed back to her room, and splashed cold water on her face. Jahtel had searched her room. Why? Why did he want to destroy her? There had been some minor incidents early on, but…. She leaned into her hands and shook her head. Nothing added up.

On the way into the city, Daphne replayed the incident. What would Lydia tell Patharus? Would she say they were listening to Paul when Daphne panicked and ran? Would she tell him about Paul and the God he professed, how she had taken his God to be her own? And worst of all, would she tell him about her harassing the man and his followers?

The more she weighed the consequences the more she wished she had come up with a believable story and kept Lydia out of it.

Throughout the day, Daphne kept an eye out for Patharus' carriage, concerned with whether Lydia would be home when he arrived. She had not seen Paul come into the city and assumed Lydia would be with him at the river. The sun had begun its journey west when she saw Patharus' carriage. She kept out of sight until he passed the *stoa* and entered the neighborhood outside of the city.

The temptation to follow arose, to see what might happen. She rolled her eyes. Silly, they would not talk where she could hear them.

"Well, do you have time for me now?"

Behind her stood the man she had put off the day before. He looked irritated, but she was relieved a report of her lie would likely not reach Patharus. She sought Apollo for him, astonished that he had considered such a petty problem to be so urgent. To her relief, he left satisfied.

The day had been trying and long. She examined her profits and started for home. Just before she reached the eastern end of the *stoa* she paused. A man she recognized as a merchant stood with a boy about six in his arms. He talked with one of the men who arrived with Paul, but neither he nor the others were with him.

"Please sir," the merchant begged. "Please work your magic and heal my child's crippled legs."

"No, wait, you do not understand," Paul's helper replied. "My name is Luke and I am a physician, but the healings you have witnessed are not magic nor do they come through men trained in the art of healing. They are a gift of mercy from the Lord Jesus Christ whom we serve. He is the one who heals. We simply obey his instructions to lay hands on the sick and ask Him to heal."

The moment the man mentioned the name of Jesus Daphne felt her stomach wrench. She doubled over and leaned against a nearby building. There was no way around the large crowd that quickly gathered, without drawing even closer to the scene.

The merchant laid his son into Luke's outstretched arms. He held him to his chest and laid one hand on the child's legs. In a loud voice, he looked to the sky and commanded, "In the name of Jesus Christ, be healed." People pressed to see what would happen.

The boy's legs straightened, and his feet shot out. He looked at his father. Frightened but awed, he cried out. "My legs, my legs." He bent his knees and straightened them again and again. He wiggled out of Luke's arms, stood, and raised his feet up and down. "Father, look!" He ran to him and then in circles.

Along with everyone who watched, Daphne's eyes welled. People smiled and cheered the little boy whose smile matched their own. Tears streamed down the man's face as he knelt in front of Luke. "Thank you, thank you,"

"No, no! Get up. Do not thank me. Thank the Lord Jesus Christ. It is he who healed your son's legs. He loves each of you that much and wants to meet your every need and to...."

As the crowd surrounded him, they asked questions and listened to Luke tell them of the power of his God. Some requested prayer on the spot. The distractions gave Daphne an opportunity to deter the Voice's plans. She worked her way around the people, ignored the riling within, and ran as fast as she could for the Eastern gate. If she could help it, the Voice would not discredit the beautiful miracle the physician brought to pass.

She regretted her need to leave, but experience told her the Voice would not remain silent if she tarried, and it would hold her to her vow not to seek another god.

She walked and meditated on what she had witnessed. He must have a Voice in him too, one that tells him what to say and do.

The angry words of her friend back in Delphi flashed. *Go be with the evil god who tells you things.* It was true, but it stung. This man has a much kinder god, one that does good and is not out to destroy people.

Her head dipped to her chest, her heart in a battle with a reason to go on.

"You cannot avoid me forever, you know."

Daphne's breath caught. Nicanor stood in the middle of the path. The set of his jaw matched the fold of his arms.

Chapter Sixty-Nine

Nicanor had never looked more serious. Daphne released her lungs and propped her head with her fingers. The stress of last few days had depleted her. Patharus' request she tell about Kawit, Stello's attack, being accused of stealing Lydia's shawl, and a constant threat of an encounter with Paul's followers. No, not now. she could not face him now. She had no fight left. She was not ready for this....

He put his hand on her back and steered her toward a large rock that overlooked the valley. She sat down, too drained to protest.

Nicanor spoke to the point. "Daphne much has happened that I do not understand but nothing has changed my feelings for you. Can we talk about it, about us?"

Us? About Us? The words bathed like a spring shower and dissolved all reason. A tingle crept up her spine as his shoulder brushed hers. She stared at her lap fearful she would reveal the longing that swelled in every part of her being. Where would she find the strength to resist him…to even want to?

He reached and took her hand but did not look at her. "I saw you the other day at the river and I know you saw me. I do not understand what happened to you that day, but I want to, if you will give me the chance. Do you remember the first time we saw each other in Athens?"

When she said nothing, he continued. "I was horrified, you in the slave market, penned like an animal. I had heard awful tales about that place. And yet there you stood, with a beauty and innocence that belied you had ever endured such humiliation."

She did not respond but remembered being surprised and confused by his shocked expression when he and Patharus drew close to the enclosure. As he spoke, his thumb massaged the back of her hand. The warmth circled up her arm and into her heart.

He twisted toward her. "I still see you that way, Daphne. Whatever caused you to behave towards those people that day is not the real you. The real you is gentle and sweet."

Her shoulders began to shake. How could he see her that way? If he knew of the horrors she had taken part in, he would…"I cannot….You, you do not understand, you would not…."

He took her in his arms and rocked her against his chest. "Shhh." His lips brushed her forehead. "It is alright, Daphne. It is going to be alright."

Nothing within wanted to move from his embrace. She savored the tender comfort, the closeness of another human being, a rare solace since forced to leave her family.

Her sobs wound to a sniffle before he spoke again. "Before you…well before the meeting was interrupted, I heard some amazing things, Daphne. This man, Paul, is telling us about an awesome God. I heard the same things at an outdoor meeting I came upon in Rome. What they teach is different than anything I have ever heard in Philippi or anywhere in Greece."

She pulled back and stared, amazed at his passion for this new teaching.

His voice rose at the memory. "The people who embraced it were the most joy-filled people you ever saw. Few of them had two coins in their tunics, but they did not care. And if they had anything they gave it to ones more needy than themselves. Have you ever seen anything like that happen here?"

He searched her face. "Daphne, there is a power for good in this God that we Greeks know nothing of, but I am going to find it and I want it for you too, to release you from whatever makes you…."

Panic stirred at his words. "No stop," she cried and pushed herself out of reach. The Voice would not ignore talk of another god. She sprang off the rock and stopped her ears to his pleas she come back.

*****

Every form of evil.
– 1 Thessalonians 5:22

You have been called, the ruling principality over the spirit of Divination that resided in Daphne, announced. It has come to our attention that you may be losing control of your assignment. This girl is....

Divination panicked No, no. I am in complete control. Did you not see how grateful to Apollo she was after I rescued her from the overseer, and how she left the scene of that healing as quickly as she could? And just now she ran at the mention of a different god. She is totally devoted to what she is convinced is Apollo.

Divination tried not to shake as his superior rolled his eyes.

The principality over Greece huffed. You are the one who does not see. Are you blind to the effect this young man has on her? Have you seen how drawn she is to him? Perhaps you have been negligent and have not bothered to investigate why he is a threat to Satan's plans for her.

But he is only....

Only what? Only about to be swept into the kingdom of our enemy? Has it occurred to you that he will be a damaging influence on her if that happens?

Divination cowered. Why was the tyrant always picking on him? His whiney voice faltered. Well, I…

I, I, I. When will you learn there is more than your position at stake here? Have you forgotten the crux of the reason you were assigned to her? Maybe you need to revisit it.

No, no need. I am to use her to deceive men that Apollo is a powerful god who can give them what they want. As a result, they will commit and verbalize their allegiance to him and become aligned with our master. Their decision will hinder them from entering the kingdom of our enemy. Surely, he had given the right answer.

The ruling principality's voice rumbled through Divination's being. The Prince of this world has no tolerance for failure. You have not lost sight of your greater agenda, but you have been blinded to the threat you could lose her to the other side. This relationship with the young man must be destroyed, now! Do you understand?

But I don't have authority to control him.

Do not concern yourself with him, Satan has many agents. You concentrate on her.

Chapter Seventy

And He has become my salvation.
– Psalm 118:14

Nicanor let Daphne go. What brought her such panic and frightened her so? Would he ever understand her? The heat of her body still warmed his chest. He stared into the valley savoring the smell of her hair on his cheek. He rubbed the back of his neck and shook his head as a sigh climbed from deep in his lungs. Could she ever let him hold her without something scaring her out of her mind? What was it? One thing he knew, going from slave to free had to be better than from free to slave no matter your background.

He affirmed his vow to never give up until she was his, stood and started for home. At the crest he paused to watch the field hands return. Had it been less than a year since he was one of them? He rubbed his chin. Well, not wholly. For over a year Patharus had groomed him to become his heir and assigned him to things slaves did not normally take part in. He grimaced. It is a wonder some did not resent him.

Master over all those he had grown up with. For a while it had been exciting. He had conjured up changes he could make that would better the life of his people. But after a season in Rome, this new-found gain held less joy and more headaches. And, it had not filled the emptiness he often felt, a need he could not define but was sure it included Daphne.

As he jogged through the gate, the sky released the sun to slide behind the mountains and take on its twilight pallor. "Sleeping on the job again, aye Rybic?" The gatekeeper blushed and threw out excuses. Nicanor waved him off with a laugh. If he did not hurry dinner with Patharus would be ready before he was. Batano, his personal servant, had prepared his bath. Nicanor bathed and changed his clothes, hoping it would be the two of them and not another night with the master's pompous friends. But, if they are there, it might be easier to get away and attend the meeting at Lydia's.

She had urged him to come after that first day at the river. "The leader and his helpers accepted my hospitality and are staying with me," Lydia had said. "Anyone who can is invited to come to hear Paul each night." Warmth beamed from her face as she spoke. "You must come, Nicanor."

After dinner, later than he hoped, he crawled through an opening few knew about in the fence around the garden. No sense in Rybic's seeing him leave at near dark. He brushed his clothes wishing he dared take his horse, but that would get back to Patharus. No, he would walk. It would not take long.

Halfway into the city questions niggled. What am I doing? Why does that man's words have such an effect on me? I cannot listen to him enough. Am I fooling myself? What if…. Can there really be a God who cares about people rather than demand we serve him?

Despite his doubts, he hustled. Finding Lydia's house had been easy, he only needed to follow the sound of joyous singing, like at the river. He tapped on the door and was quickly ushered in. Lydia spotted him and rushed over. "Nicanor, I am so glad you could make it. Here, sit down in front with me where you will not miss a thing."

He hesitated but followed. Was there anyone who might recognize him? Slaves seldom came to town, and he had left for Rome before Patharus involved him in business in the city. He relaxed, satisfied that word would not get back to Patharus. He recognized the jailer's wife. She nodded and turned her attention back to the singing. It flowed until Paul stood up to speak.

"Friends, grace and peace to you from God our Father and the Lord Jesus Christ," Paul began. "He has commissioned me to tell you of the width, depth, length, and height of the love Christ has for you. Our God who is rich in mercy, even when we were dead in trespasses made us alive together with Christ and raised us up together and made us sit in the heavenly places in Christ Jesus. It is by His grace you are saved through faith, by believing, it is a gift from God."

Nicanor listened to the thanks and praise murmured around him. Paul had explained that day at the river how God had sent His Son, Jesus, to shed his blood and die on a Roman cross to pay for our sins, but how could so great a God love a person like himself? He shrank in his chair, convinced he would never measure up. Paul's voice rose and Nicanor's ears perked.

"If anyone is in Christ, he is a new creation, old things have passed away, behold all things become new. God has reconciled us to Himself through Christ, your old man is crucified with Him, and you are adopted into God's family, alive to the promise of new life and eternity with God."

Nicanor hung on Paul's every word, storing it in his heart like a sousliks preparing for winter.

After three hours of preaching Paul passed through the room, laid hands on people and prayed for them. Some were sick or injured. Nicanor watched in amazement at the healings that flowed, always attributed to the Lord, Jesus Christ. A man with a badly injured foot came forward and Paul laid his hands on it and commanded it be made whole in the name of Jesus. Joyful shouts of praise filled the room as the foot was restored to wholeness.

Nicanor's armpits prickled as Paul approached. "What can the Lord do for you, young man?"

He swallowed his anxiety. "I want...what you people have."

"You mean you want Jesus Christ to be your Lord?"

"Yes sir, I do, but...."

"Do you believe He was born of a virgin like I explained and that he came as both God and man?" Nicanor nodded. "Good. He gave his life for your sins son, and God, the almighty Father, raised him from the dead to be seated with Him forever in the heaven. Do you believe that?"

Again, Nicanor nodded. "Then pray and ask him to forgive your sins and come into your heart and be your Lord."

"I do not know how to pray, sir."

Paul's face shone with compassion. "Then just follow what I say, and you will soon learn." With that, he led Nicanor in a prayer asking Jesus to be his Lord. After the amen, Paul moved on, but Nicanor stood off and basked in the peace that cloaked his soul. Over and over, he whispered of the joy that filled his heart. "Jesus is my God now, Jesus is my Lord!"

Lydia hugged him goodbye as did many of the other believers in attendance. Each encouraged him to join them every night. The moon was so bright he did not need a torch to find his way home. Everything he heard and seen flooded his mind. He laughed at a nighthawk that swooped in front of him. "I cannot wait to tell Daphne. Paul said to ask the Lord for what you need, and I need her to listen to me."

His mind traveled as fast as his feet as he imagined their future together. Careful not to be seen, he reentered through the garden's gate, and headed for his suite.

Night after night, after dinner, Nicanor secretly left the estate to hear Paul. Each night had something new to offer, some new truth to ponder. He watched others receive the Lord as he had and was awed anew at seeing the jailer's wife healed of a large swelling at the base of her neck. But this night planted a special hope in his heart.

A man arrived later with his adolescent son kicking and screaming obscenities at everyone in his path. Whispers of a demonic spirit filled the room. Paul stopped the singing and motioned for the man to bring the child to him. Quiet prayers murmured after which Paul laid his hands on the squirming child. "You unclean spirit, in the name of Jesus Christ of Nazareth, I command you to leave this boy's body."

The boy fell to the floor, his arms and legs thrashing. Everyone gasped and gave them room. Seconds later the young man stiffened, let out a scream and sat up. He looked as if he wondered where he was. Joyful praise and thanks echoed from each believer as he stood and hugged his father, his face a reservoir of wonder.

Nicanor grinned. He paid no attention to the sounds of thunder as he made his way home. That kind of prayer had to be what Daphne needed. She had acted as out of control at the river as that boy. A conversation with Lydia had confirmed it. "I am sure you are right, Nicanor, I have prayed for her since the first time I saw her. God has great plans for that girl, and for you too."

Rain began to pelt with a vengeance. He paused long enough to pull his outer cover over his head. He was about to go on when lightning hit a tall terebinth tree not far ahead. The hair on his arms tingled, sending him backwards in time to avoid half of the tree that broke off and crashed onto the path in front of him. He shivered and rubbed his arms. Wow! That was close, he would have been right under it if he had not stopped minutes before. He inspected the damage, grateful he would not have to report a fire and ran for the garden where he slipped quickly inside through the broken fence.

"Is it not a bit late to be running about?"

He startled. Jahtel was the last person he wanted to run into. "Father, I…ah, did not see you there."

Jahtel sneered. "Obviously not." For a moment neither spoke. "Well, what is it? Some girl caught your attention?"

Nicanor eyed his father. Would he listen if he told him the wonderful news about the love of Jesus? He decided to try. "Father, the most amazing thing has happened to me. Come, let us sit and I will tell you about it."

Jahtel sat and listened as Nicanor spoke with great enthusiasm of his new relationship with the Lord and his new friends. He had not gone far before Jahtel jumped to his feet. "Wait, wait a minute! Are you crazy? What do you think Patharus would say to all this nonsense? He would believe he made a mistake in choosing you to be his heir!"

Nicanor shrank from his father's venomous tone but did not let that deter him. "Father, it is the..."

"No!" Jahtel shouted. "You need to forget this gibberish and make sure the master never hears of your going to those meetings. Be glad it was I who observed your coming and going and not someone else. Now get to your rooms and I will forget I ever heard of such foolishness."

With a disgusted snort, he left. Nicanor shook his head. How could he make his father understand? Would Patharus be that hardheaded too? Discouragement blindsided him, kicked him in the stomach and weighted his heart with a load of doubt and fear. The taunting stopped when he remembered to pray.

Chapter Seventy-One

…the way of truth will be blasphemed.
– 2 Peter 2:2

Daphne lay staring at the ceiling. How many times had she rehashed Nicanor's words after he waited for her along the path? *A power for good in this God…. I want it for me, and for you too.*

A power for good. The phrase would not fade. All the power she and her family attributed to Apollo had failed. The high priest's intercession, the divination given her father by the *pythia*, the temple priest's assurance of prayers to save her family's estate, all were a deception created to tie them to the temple. No evidence of power from Apollo had kept the Romans from taking everything their father owned, including his family.

If their family's god truly existed, if he had any real power, why had their prayers or sacrifices not made any differences? Why was she no closer to the promise of freedom?

Truth shone into the darkness of her soul: the promises failed because there was no power behind them.

She sat up. Yes! And the divining of her future was a lie too.

But if he did not exist then who or what resided within her and had the power to know things and do things mere men could not know or do?

Her chin fell as her thoughts replayed the times she harassed Paul and his followers. Her head shot up. Wait! What was it the man who confronted her the second time had said? *Our God is more than able to dispel this demon.*

This demon? Was a demon the force that led her to harass the group? And what had he meant by 'dispel' it? Was that what dwelt within her, a demon? And what was a demon anyway? She pulled up her blanket. She needed to find out.

She determined to sleep, but her mind wandered. What had Patharus found when he visited Lydia? He had not said a word about the shawl. Why had she not received Nicanor's note…had there really been one? She whispered into the darkness, "You seemed so sincere, Nicanor."

Remember how he clung to you? You know he has but one thing on his mind. You must avoid him, or he will prevent you from attaining your freedom.

She dismissed the threat. The Voice had no intention of setting her free…maybe it too lacked power. The enigma of the note lingered. If Nicanor told the truth who would gain by not bringing it to her?

Jahtel! Her mind raced. He disliked her and resented Nicanor's kindness toward her. She covered her face with her hands. What if the note somehow ended up in his father's possession and he destroyed it?

There was no dismissing it, it had to be the answer. No one else would dare disregard Nicanor's request or disliked her enough to interfere. She sighed, not sure she wanted to believe it. How Jahtel must hate her. She could not tell Nicanor she knew he had sent a note. He would want to know how. She would never pit him against his father. Better to let it go and rejoice in that he had not lied to her.

She lay down again. That was why Jahtel tried to discredit her before Patharus, he feared Nicanor's interest in her.

Finally, she slept. They were trapped in the ship's hold. She searched for her mother, but she was gone. She called out to her brother, "Alexander, where are you? Mother, please, come back. Take me with you, Mother." A door slammed down the hall.

Her plea faded with the dream. She sat up. "Oh, Mother." The pearl-gray dawn stole through her window. Its lonely light spread over her and her dismal possessions.

Reality revived in its wake. She groaned. "I am as trapped now as I was then." She swung her feet to the floor and leaned her elbows on her knees. Chancing a failed escape and being branded or beaten added to the horror of losing her master's protection.

Daphne's ineptus to be shielded from abuse secured the entrance of her snare, keeping her helplessly trapped in the ruse. Thoughts of her on-going dilemma rose like a child's kite. She let it unwind, persuaded the winds of her current circumstances would not change.

You need not feel trapped. I will never let you come to harm.

Daphne ignored the Voice as she realized this mystifying being did not suspect she was confident there was no god, no Apollo. As the temple's revered statue, back in Delphi failed to discern her doubts, neither could the Voice. From now on, she would not let it feed her fears or intimidate her. She would monitor her words and bide her time until she found a way of escape. With a flip of her hands, she wound her hair firmly into an attractive style and left the room.

Chapter Seventy-Two

...never able to come to the knowledge of the truth.
 – 2 Timothy 3:7

Nicanor reclined on the opposite couch while Patharus expounded on his plans. Servants picked up empty lunch dishes and refilled their cups. "Oh, and one thing before you go, drop this shawl in Daphne's room as you leave." Patharus handed Nicanor a length of lustrous purple fabric.

Nicanor looked puzzled.

"You know who she is, do you not?"

He gave an elusive nod, reminded that Patharus had no idea how well he knew Daphne, much less how he felt about her.

Patharus went on to explain Jahtel's accusation and Daphne's explanation. "I am sure he meant no harm, but I could see it shook Daphne, and the woman wanted it returned to Daphne. Interesting lady, that Lydia." He paused and drained his cup. "I have known of her and her business for years but had no idea she was so successful. She seems caught up in this new religion that preacher is peddling. Hope she does not get burned."

Nicanor hardly heard Patharus' comments. Jahtel accused Daphne of stealing? A gust of rage swooped like a frightened bird up his chest. He debated telling Patharus about his feelings for Daphne and of his trips to Lydia's but felt a check in his spirit. He took the shawl. "I will see that she gets it." He left, and nearly ran over a servant on his way to find Jahtel.

His birth father's animosity toward Daphne burned in his heart. The time she took a bath out of schedule, his animosity the night she became lost and cut her knee, his unkind handling of the longer tunic she had not been told she was not allowed to wear, and now this shawl. Why? Why did he dislike her enough to deliberately try to get her in trouble? *Maybe he suspects I care for her. Would that be enough to…? Could he have…?*

Nicanor stopped, "Yes!" He switched directions and made straight for the servants' quarters. Most were busy with their assignments but the few working inside acknowledged him.

One stopped his work and cast his glance at the floor. "Master? May I be of service?"

"I need to speak to Batano. Can you tell me where he is?"

The man cocked his head as if he expected to find the answer on the ceiling. "I believe you will find him in the laundry looking after your clothing....no, otherwise maybe…."

Nicanor had already left.

He entered the family laundry and called out, "Batano?"

Surprised, his servant was quick to stand to attention. "Master?"

"Come outside, I need to talk to you." Batano set aside the bundle he was working on and followed. "Batano, you remember when I left for Rome last fall?"

"Yes. It was —"

"Listen, this is very important. Do you remember my giving you a note to give to the girl waiting for me in the garden?"

His brows became one line. "Yes. Yes, I remember. You had to leave early, and you wanted me to —"

"Batano, did you do it? Did you take my note and give it to her?"

He shuffled his feet. "Master, I am so sorry, I did not deliver it myself. I was on my way when your father, I mean Jahtel, stopped me to do something urgent. I told him I needed to deliver the note, but he took it and said he would take care of it." He hung his head. "I am so ashamed, you gave me a task and I failed you."

Boiling inside, Nicanor waved him off. "It is all right. No one refuses Jahtel." He stormed toward his birth father's quarters, the shawl billowing behind him.

Nicanor stomped through Jahtel's door. Unlike most slaves, he had two rooms, a sitting room plus a bedroom. He shouted, "Jahtel, are you in here?"

At the sound of his son's voice, he came out of the room that housed his bed. He grimaced, "Now Nicanor, I know you are upset about the dispute we had a few nights back but I —"

Nicanor's eyes grew dark, his voice a snarl. "You know nothing, Father. But I have learned plenty! Patharus told me about your accusing Daphne of stealing this." He pushed the shawl into Jahtel's face. "How could you? You know she would not do such a thing."

Jahtel's chin jutted. "Well, I, it was an honest mistake."

Nicanor's voice rose. "A mistake huh, a mistake? The mistake is yours, father and I am calling a stop to it. I do not ever want to hear of you harassing Daphne again, for anything. Do you hear me?"

Jahtel squirmed. "Well, you know she is beneath your station now and —"

With fire in his eyes, Nicanor stepped over and grabbed Jahtel's tunic. "Tell me Father, is that why you failed to deliver my note to her the night I left for Rome?" He shouted, "Is that why?"

Jahtel tried to get away, but Nicanor yanked him closer. "What made you decide you could interfere in my affairs, Father? You could not wait to push me off into the keeping of another sire. What gives you the right to decide what is best for me now?"

Jahtel's head lurched in every direction. He tried again to free himself, but Nicanor's strong grip squelched his efforts.

Nicanor gave his elder a shove. "You disgust me." He started for the door but wheeled around, his voice steady. "Let me make myself clear,

Jahtel, if I ever hear of you bothering Daphne in any way, I will see to it that Patharus replaces you. I love Daphne and I intend to marry her."

Nicanor slammed the door and left for the garden, where he paced. What should he do now? He needed tell Patharus of his desire to marry Daphne before he heard it from someone else. What would he say? Would he too think of her as beneath Nicanor's new station?

He dropped to the bench he had shared with Daphne. His thoughts wandered to the joys of being married to her. He pictured them dining together at day's end, waking up together, walking unconcerned in the garden. He sighed, his longing nearly palatable.

Nicanor wondered if Patharus was in love with his wife when they married, or was it an arranged thing? A blue jay cocked his head as if it contemplated an answer.

The night Patharus first took him in to meet his wife, he had found her to be a lovely woman with a sweet nature, eager to engage him.

She held out her hand. "Nicanor, I am so glad to finally meet you."

He took it gently in his and kissed the back as he had been coached. She lay propped in a bed, her long blonde hair spread against layers of pillows. Her smile put him at ease. "Please sit down and tell me about yourself."

They talked for half an hour before he excused himself, having been warned she tired easily, and he must not stay long. He entered his quarters shaking his head. My legal mother and he hardly knew her. How sad that she was too ill to enjoy life with Patharus. He must love her, for the only time I ever saw his shoulders droop was when he left her suite.

The jay's squawk brought his thoughts back to Daphne. What was it Paul said last night? To trust the Lord with all your heart and not try to figure things out for yourself. To honor God in everything and he would tell you what to do.

Nicanor did not remember it word for word, but spoke the promise aloud in prayer. He leaned back into the bench and reveled in the assurance that swept his heart like the gentle sway of the branch vacated by the noisy bird.

Chapter Seventy-Three

Choose for yourselves this day whom you will serve.
- Joshua 24:15

Nicanor had run out of excuses, he was stuck. Patharus expected him to stay and interact with his dinner guests.

A neighbor approached. "There you are, young man, I have been wanting to talk with you."

Nicanor hid a grimace. Here we go again.

The man stepped close, almost as if he intended to block any escape. He covered him with flattery, expounded on how he knew Nicanor would be a great asset to Patharus. Finally, he arrived at his poorly veiled intentions.

"You know, I would really love for you to come and see my estate. My olive trees are in full bloom and the view from my bluff is amazing. It would be a great chance to meet my family. I have two sons, and a beautiful daughter who has just become eligible for marriage."

When Nicanor did not respond, the man went on about how important it was to have compatible people in one's family.

Nicanor forced a smile. "I would enjoy seeing your land sometime, please excuse me." He ducked around the wine *krater* in time to avoid another determined-looking father of eligible daughters. Three in one night! He must tell

Patharus of his plans to marry Daphne and end this torture. He is already suspicious of my indifference. Much later, the last guest left and Nicanor decided to go to Lydia's anyway.

He rushed to the city, gave the door a tap and entered Lydia's home. The singing had evolved to deep worship. He slipped into an empty spot and stood with the rest, raising his heart and his hands to his Lord. After an inspiring message on the value and need for continual prayer, Paul directed them to gather in groups of three or four to pray for each other. Nicanor stiffened. How could he pray for others? He had so much to learn.

Paul encouraged them. "Remember prayer is simply talking to your Heavenly Father. There is no formula, just ask."

Nicanor welcomed the reassurance and joined another man who motioned for the jailor's wife to join them. The man asked Nicanor how they could pray for him. He squirmed, unaccustomed to being open about his private affairs. The kindness written on their faces gave him courage. "I, I need God's help to share this good news with my adoptive father and to tell him I want to marry a girl who…who is a slave."

The man smiled. "Paul says we are all slaves to our Lord Jesus Christ."

The woman nodded. "I guess we are all pretty new at this but let us try."

The man prayed first. "Lord, we beseech You on Nicanor's behalf. We ask that his father would be open and receptive to the good news and Nicanor's wishes. You are the one who opens hearts to truth, Lord Jesus. Please reveal God the Father to him and transfer him from the kingdom of darkness into Your kingdom of light."

When he finished, the woman asked Nicanor if the slave girl knew the Lord. He shook his head, and she prayed that the love of his life would also become a follower of Jesus.

They prayed for the other man's need of a healthy crop, each becoming more comfortable with the process of asking. After that, Nicanor boldly prayed for the woman, that something would open her husband's heart to receive the good news and become a believer. At the finish, they hugged like old friends.

Someone had brought refreshments, offering them to any who lingered. Everyone seemed excited about the time of prayer, sharing confidence God heard and would act on their behalf.

Paul's conversation with his close companions caught Nicanor's attention. "It is annoying, and it sorely grieves me." He helped himself to a cup of wine. "I admit I am troubled by it, but I am waiting on the Holy Spirit. He will give discernment when the time is right."

Silas, Paul's companion spoke up. "You know the peril an upheaval could bring on us and all these new believers. And more importantly, it could shut down our opportunity to spread the Gospel here."

Paul agreed. "That is the dilemma. There are still many here who have not heard or yet believed. That demon's agenda is to destroy or damage our message, but God's plan is greater than that of any unclean spirit."

The men who traveled with him committed to saturate it in prayer. Nicanor basked in Paul's confidence that whatever the concern, God would prevail. He bid his new friends' good night and left.

Arriving home, he slipped down the hall to his suite aware of the late hour. The meeting had gone long but his heart swelled with the joy of sharing his beliefs with others who believed. He stopped. Someone lay in front of his door. He squinted into the dim light and nudged him with the toe of his sandal. "Batano, what are you doing here?"

His servant jumped to his feet. "Pardon me, Master, I did not mean to doze." He straightened his tunic, his eyes pleading for understanding. "The master asked me to send you to him no matter how late you returned…said he would be in his study."

He sent his sleepy servant on his way and took a deep breath. What could he tell Patharus but the truth? "Lord, please be with me, open his heart as the man prayed."

A light shone beneath Patharus' door, erasing Nicanor's hope that his father had given up and retired. He knocked. "Come in, Nicanor. I will be with you in a moment."

He sat on the edge of the couch as Patharus finished some paperwork. He did not look upset, but Nicanor silently prayed, Oh, Father God, give me the right words.

Patharus left his desk and sat opposite his son. "So, Nicanor, what is it that keeps you out at such late hours?"

Silence hovered before Nicanor lifted his head and looked at the man he called father. Patharus had held nothing from him since the adoption, completely open about everything. He owed him the same.

"Father, I have wanted to share with you an exciting thing that has come into my life, but it is all so new to me that I decided to wait until I could explain it more fully."

Patharus nodded. "Go on."

Nicanor explained how while he stayed in Rome he had heard a group of people proclaiming a new God. "It was so uplifting, I found myself frequenting their meetings as often as my studies freed me to attend."

Patharus did not appear disturbed by that, so Nicanor continued. "To my delight, a very learned man who preaches this same God arrived in Philippi last week. He taught down by the river

Gangites some days ago on the day the Jewish people call their Sabbath, and—"

"Wait a minute, Nicanor. You mean this is a Jewish god?"

Nicanor hesitated. "Well....yes, but actually He is the God of heaven, the God of us all." Patharus' face darkened but Nicanor plowed on. "This man, Paul, has been teaching at Lydia's home every evening. You remember, she is the lady who gave Daphne the shawl. Have you heard of his teaching, Father?"

Patharus gave a slight nod. "I have heard from several sources. But a Jewish god Nicanor? Not even Greek?"

"I know it seems strange but—"

"Very strange, and remember you are a Roman now, and Rome does not recognize these foreign gods." He rose from his seat and folded his arms across his chest.

Nicanor stood and faced his father, the decision his: cower and deny his need of the Savior, or confess Jesus was his Lord and would always be first in his life. His insides shook but peace descended as he spoke. "Father, I have taken this Jesus as my true and only God. He is the Son of the Lord God Almighty, the God who created the world and everything in it. His agenda is nothing but love and help for all our needs. I will do nothing against your will, Father, but I cannot deny he is everything to me. I only wish that you would come—"

"No. No, I am not interested in a Jewish god."
Patharus' face bristled with disappointment as he
studied his son. "I will not try to dissuade you,
but I ask you to be careful and to weigh what you
hear with an open mind and the intelligence you
were born with."

He put his hand on Nicanor's shoulder and
reminded him of Roman customs and laws. He
kept his voice low. "This teacher of yours is
treading on shaky ground and the new head
magistrate is a man who loves to flaunt his power.
Mercy is not a concept he holds to, and I would
not want to see you caught up in the trouble this
is likely to bring."

His eyes locked on Nicanor's. "Let us get some
sleep and we will talk more of this if need be."

Nicanor left for his room wondering about the
prayer that his father's heart be opened.

"The end is not yet, trust me."

Nicanor smiled into the darkness and
whispered, "Thank you, Lord."

Chapter Seventy-Four

For you have delivered my soul from death.
– Psalm 56:13

Daphne left for the city early to avoid running into Nicanor. Lydia's shawl hung past her waist. She stroked the corners, amused to have found it on top of her mat with a note she assumed was from Patharus. "This is yours now, enjoy it."

Her thoughts ran ahead. Pretend to praise Apollo…watch what I say…be alert, avoid Paul and his followers….

Listing her goals helped her focus. She repeated the praises taught her by her grandmother and added a few of her own. Flattery, she discovered, appeased the power within, so she kept it up.

As the sun peaked, she looked for Beresta near the fountain but did not see her. All morning clients had searched her out, so Daphne finally granted herself a leisurely break. She lifted her face to the warm spring sunshine and checked her profits. *I have earned plenty, I am going home and spend time in the garden.*

She worked her way down the crowded *stoa*, surprised at how busy it was. The reason brought her hand to her throat. Large crowds blocked the corner she normally crossed to the eastern gate. In its center stood the man called Paul.

Like the shadow of a windswept cloud, panic shrouded all reason. The man had not conducted a meeting in town before. Why now and why here? Where had all these people come from?

Anxious for a closer look at the town's newest distraction, the throng quickly increased and pushed her forward. She searched the area. Surely she could find another way out of here.

She decided to go back and wait by the fountain but could not fight the crowd. Without warning, the Voice joined the thrust and propelled her toward the speaker.

She cried out, "No!" Those nearest turned and stared, their curiosity quickly displaced by their desire to see what it was all about. I cannot do this, her heart screamed though her lips never moved. Already, the transformation she so dreaded had begun to manifest.

Her shoulders hooded, giving way to the serpentine motions she was helpless to control. She hissed, *He is a liar who wants to deceive you.* Soon, her cries turned to raspy threats. *Do not listen to this man, he says our mighty Zeus is as nothing.*

Her chest heaved and fueled the fire that burned in her lungs. She gasped at the pressure, unable to expel the disgusting foam that drooled from her lips.

A pitiful wail rose in her throat and whined its singsong mockery through her gaping mouth. *These men are servants of the most High God who proclaims to us the way of salvation.*

Threats followed, shrieked in high pitched taunts. The uproar drew the attention of all who heard. A woman screamed. "She has the evil eye."

Those within hearing scrambled to get out of Daphne's way. Soon there was no one between her and the man she strove to avoid. Amplias and Sergius stood to one side along with a group of Romans. At the sight of her, Sergius' jaw went slack. He stared, his pretense of uprightness warped by curiosity. Believers, along with Nicanor and Lydia, formed a semi-circle behind Paul. Daphne's knees quivered at the sight of them. Oh no, Daphne despaired, please no!

The Voice would not let up and forced her ever closer to Paul. Curses spewed from her mouth, rendering some of her words unintelligible. Her thoughts flew back to the *adytum*, where the *pythia* babbled under what people believed was the influence of fumes from the decaying python. The poor woman had no choice and neither would she.

As the Voice drove her toward Paul and his companions, it roared, *These men are servants of the Most High who….*

Paul gestured in her direction. "Bring her to me." As one, the crowd gasped, sure he would succumb to close contact with the power of her evil eye.

Daphne's heart sank. The man had to be furious, what would he do to her? Weary of the battle, her shoulders slumped. She stumbled, unable to maintain the fight. Let the power within have its way. If this man's God is more powerful, as he claims, let his God do with her as he pleases, she no longer cared.

A quiet enveloped her from within, but the Voice continued to lash from her throat. She scratched the face of one man who propelled her forward and bit the hand of the another. It took two more of Paul's strongest followers to finally escort her to him.

Despite her writhing body and villainous tirades, her evil eye and blustering rants did not intimidate their leader. His eyes held only love as they locked on her. Over the ruckus he addressed her. He did not shout but pointed directly at her and spoke with authority. "I command you in the name of Jesus Christ to come out of her."

Daphne could not grasp what was happening. At the name of Jesus Christ, the Voice demanded she resist.

He will leave you a slave with no power or way of escape. I am your only hope. I am your only friend. You will be subject to Sergius' lust and more. Ignore him, do not listen....

She shut her eyes and will to its pleas. Its threats found no anchor. They floated far from the harbor upon which her mind had already embarked. Still gagging on the residue that drooled from her lips, she growled, "I want to be free of you!"

Instantly, her insides felt like they exploded and flew in every direction. Something kicked her in the stomach. She convulsed and doubled over. It threw her to the ground where she writhed and hissed like a snake. From deep in the bowels of her being, a blood-curdling scream crept up her lungs and rang from her lips. A strong suction drew from her stomach. The pressure spewed something vile out her mouth and through her nose. At last, her body quieted. She tried to get up but fell whimpering at Paul's feet.

He took her hand and helped her up. She staggered and nearly fell. Her gaze traveled to his face. It held nothing but joy and acceptance. He motioned for Lydia to come help her. "You will be fine now. The demon is gone for good."

Chapter Seventy-Five

Whose mind the god of this world has blinded.
– 2 Corinthians 4:4

Lydia took Daphne by the arm and led her from the center of the gathering. Her legs shook so badly she welcomed Lydia's invitation to lean on her.

Paul spoke to the crowd. "The demon that possessed this girl is gone. The Lord has delivered her and never again will she tell fortunes or mock the Lord Jesus Christ."

Those in the crowd who had seen and heard Daphne scorn the God the men spoke of, shook their heads in wonder. Confusion reigned in many who had dealt with her as a sorceress, inspired by Apollo, the god they had long revered and feared.

But the believers cheered. One shouted, "There is none like our God."

"He has more power than all the evil in this world," another added.

Their cheers lit up the rest of the faithful followers and for a short time they danced and shouted praises to the King of Kings.

Loud enough for all to hear, Paul cried, "This is the power of our King, the Lord Jesus Christ whom we serve. He cares for each of you and desires only that you…"

"Stop that man! He is breaking the laws of this Roman colony. To call this God a king is contrary to the decrees of Caesar and employs a title only our emperor is worthy of."

Totally spent, Daphne turned from Lydia's shoulder in time to see who spoke. Enraged at the loss of his profits, Sergius stepped into the opening around Paul. He shouted again, bent on stirring up the crowd. "It is against the law to disturb the peace of our city. All who take part in this civic rebellion will be held responsible when the magistrates arrive."

His words incited the mob that surrounded Paul. Angry words and accusation flew from the different camps.

A believer shouted, "Jesus is the author of true peace."

"Claudius, Claudius, Claudius," rang from a group of Romans.

Sergius motioned for Amplias, and with the help of those dedicated to the strict letter of Roman law, seized Paul and Silas and dragged them into the marketplace. Many of the town's people and most of the believers fled to avoid a clash with Roman soldiers.

Daphne caught Sergius eyeing her before he left. Was he anticipating the loss of Patharus' protection over her or his loss of the profit she earned? Both induced pictures of what might come to be, and she panicked. Before Lydia could turn back from those she had been trying to calm, Daphne slipped away.

*****

Spiritual hosts of wickedness.
– Ephesians 6:12

The demonic ruler who posed as Greek's Apollo, stood with folded arms. "Well, Divination, fine mess you made of that.

But, but I…

No buts about it. Perhaps you do belong in the bowels of some temple…an obscure place where you cannot screw up important assignments.

The spirit of divination shivered. How he hated having been evicted from a warm, comfortable human…. again. He knew he was in trouble. He had not meant to ignore his superior's previous warnings or let things get out of hand. How was he to know she would find the courage to defy him? I hope she gets what is coming to her.

You have an appointment with the powers in high places in an hour. Make sure you are on time and do not bring any of your lame excuses or it will go even worse for you.

Divination whined. No….Principality, you know I tried. I cannot face the one whose power has influenced all of Greece. I cannot stand before the one they call Zeus. You know what a difficult assignment my girl was and how I had no choice when they used that name. Please, intervene for me…they would listen to you.

Hah! And what would I say? I am sorry but this fallen angel you put under me was an incompetent fool. He believed he could bombard her with his cohorts…let me see, despair and a lying spirit, were they not? And this spirit schooled in divination did not have enough insight to attack her mind. He allowed her to vacillate from total dependence on him, and to make a decision that ultimately led to his displacement.

No, and you can bet your next assignment will be assisting a lying spirit to deceive some back country people who still believe in the ancient gods…you know the ones who still sacrifice to mother earth.

Well, if despair had done his job and lying had worked harder to dispel her disgusting sense of honesty, I….

Principality stepped close and roared in his face. Despair became ineffective and your charge disregarded the lies because you failed to lead them in the battle. You did know you were in a battle for the souls of men, did you not?

Well, I, of course I….

Your neglect weakened those we aided you with and sanctioned both to be cast out along with you.

Divination twitched. He searched for a valid argument, but nothing came to mind. What could he do? He had to avoid that appointment. You know, Principality, it is not necessarily over. She has not committed to our great enemy yet. Perhaps I can find a way back in before she accepts the truth or learns how to protect herself from us. I have no doubt she is still fearful of the future she faces without my help.

His superior's head tilted. True. I do not relish having your failure on my record. Maybe I can postpone your appointment. His lips twisted, his tone a threat. For a very short time.

Divination breathed a sigh of relief. I will get right on it. I know where she is, and I am sure I can pile enough fear on her to reopen the door.

Not so fast, underling. I happen to know there is a herd of swine not far from here and if you screw this up again, there is a good chance one will be your next dwelling place. I will give you until morning to make it happen. He pulled his finger across his throat.

Chapter Seventy-Six

...share with me in the suffering of the gospel.
– 2 Timothy 1:8

Nicanor followed, aghast at what was happening. He watched Sergius and Amplias goad the crowd to force Paul and Silas up onto the *Bema*, the elevated part of the forum where all would be assured to see the proceedings. Within minutes, the magistrates arrived, eager to judge as well as enforce the law.

The head magistrate strutted past Paul and Silas, followed by two others. He sneered and made no effort to hide his delight in this anticipated confrontation. The crowd quieted. He puffed himself up to full stature and addressed Sergius. "So, what is this all about, friend? Why are these men here?"

"These Jews have exceedingly troubled our city's peace, your honor. They teach customs which are not lawful for us being Romans to receive or observe. They have riled crowds with speeches that have impacted our weaker and more gullible citizens."

The head magistrate nodded. "Go on."

"Well, they have promoted a foreign king and dishonored Claudius, our Emperor." Sergius followed that with every negative aspect of Paul's address to the crowds. He did not mention that it had blown away his hope of future profit.

The head authority folded his arms and flicked a brief wink at Sergius. Momentarily, he conferred with the other two magistrates, glared at the prisoners and stepped toward the crowd. "I decree that these men are a public danger to our political life and the wellbeing of our city." He twisted toward the soldiers who held Paul and Silas. "They are under arrest. Tear their clothes from them."

In expectation of what would follow, the crowd roared their approval. The magistrate lifted his chin. "Give them the beating they deserve and cast them into prison. "He brushed his hands on his vest. "Perhaps that will teach them authority of Roman law is not to be trifled with."

Several soldiers shot into action. They tied Paul and Silas to posts at the back of the Bema and picked up their rods. Nicanor cringed with every stripe they laid on the back of God's servants. What could he do? What would Patharus say if he got involved? His promise not to do anything against the will of his earthly father weighed on his conscience.

Blood spattered and the crowd cheered, egging the soldiers on. Nicanor could not believe his eyes. He had seen slaves beaten for running away, but these men were innocent. He looked around for Paul's supporters. Unnoticed in his Roman attire, he alone had remained, helpless to defend Paul and his colleague.

As the jailer prodded them off the Bema, Paul spoke boldly to Silas. "Have courage, my friend. We have had the privilege of taking part in the suffering of Christ."

A glorious smile spread Silas' lips before the jailer hurried them up out of the *stoa*, across the Via Egnatia to the city's upper area. Nicanor followed as the soldiers dragged his mentors up steps that led into the upper city and those into the prison. The jailer pushed them through the small, rocky opening of the cramped dungeon that had once been a Roman cistern.

He shuddered. Would they be taken to the innermost section? Patharus once described it as the area where dangerous prisoners were chained to the wall. Moments before the jailer emerged, Nicanor heard a loud clank that sealed off any hope of escape.

His eyes teared at the cruelty endured by those he had come to cherish. What would become of them? Concern for Daphne suddenly replaced his fears. He wheeled around and headed back to the *agora*. When he saw a woman in purple, he shouted, "Lydia, Lydia, where is Daphne?"

"She is gone. I swerved to comfort some believers who were paralyzed with fear at the arrest, and after I prayed—"

"Where would she go? Lydia, we must find her. She will surely be afraid and confused by all that happened."

She laid her hand on his arm. "Yes, but remember she is free of that controlling spirit now. She will be able to think clearly, and she will know what to do."

He tried to hide his impatience. "I know, but please help me find her. Could you go back and look in the city? I will take the path to our estate and see if she decided to go home."

She assured him she would search the city. "But if we do not find her by dark, I will need to be home. The believers will want to gather to pray for Paul and Silas."

Nicanor took off at a run, each step a blend of fear and anger. "Where are you, Daphne? Why would you run off like this?" His heart raced but softened as he remembered how confused she looked after the deliverance. *Please let me find her, I loved her and want to protect her.*

Last night's meeting at Lydia's slipped into his thoughts. How full of the joy of the Lord Paul had been, and now he lay beaten and imprisoned. He envisioned Silas with his hands raised, praising the Lord louder than anyone. Paul confession of his annoyance with someone replayed and brought Nicanor's feet slid to a stop.

"That had to have been Daphne! She was the one Paul spoke of." He began to walk, the realization condemning. He should have known, he could have warned her. *But no, it is better this way. She is free of that thing that bound and frightened her so.*

He needed to find her, to hold her close and comfort her. Halfway to the estate he hesitated. She could not have made it farther than this. As he ran, he called out her name, assuring her of his care and desire to help.

*****

It was nearly dark before Lydia gave up the search. She had scoured every side of the deserted *stoa*, checked between all the buildings and behind the *Palestra*. Where else could she look? Weary and worried about her mentors in that dismal prison, she headed home. How would they survive in that filthy place with cuts on their backs?

She prayed as she walked, her heart heavy.

A soft call reached her from behind some bushes. "Lydia. Lydia, will you help me?"

She stopped. That had to be Daphne. She stretched her neck and whispered, "Daphne, is that you?"

She waved from behind a large aloe bush. "Yes, over here."

Lydia rushed to her side. "Oh Daphne, we have been so worried. Why did you run off?

"Please, I will explain, but I cannot be found. Could you help me find a safe place to hide?'

"No, I want you to come home with me. We are almost there. Hurry, I will not let anyone hurt you."

Daphne nodded and followed to the big yellow house she had only seen from the outside.

*****

The prayers and songs ceased, and quiet returned to Lydia's house. Daphne peeked from behind a curtain that led to the upstairs. "Are they gone?"

"Yes, you can come out now. Let me fix you a nice cup of tea. These herbs will help you relax so you can sleep."

Daphne followed her into the kitchen where Lydia hastened to brew the tea. She set a cup in front of her and one across the table for herself. Daphne inhaled the steam and savored the scent of oranges and herbs she could not identify.

"How do you feel? Have your insides quieted?"

She closed her eyes. "Oh Lydia, I, yes, I am much better, but I feel so strange, like I am empty...but it is a good feeling." She put her hands on the sides of her face, opened her eyes, and shook her head. "But I do not know what happened there in the city. I do not understand it."

"Of course, you would not. The power of the true God is something you have probably never experienced. But He has cared about you since before you were born. He loves you, Daphne."

"Before I was born? But Lydia, I am not a Jew. I do not even know one or what they believe. Well,

I guess I do know some, but only by sight." Her voice dropped. "My mother tried to explain the Jewish faith to me, a long time ago."

"It does not matter, dear. I am not a Jew by birth either. I came from a city far from here where no one had ever heard of Jewish people or their God. But when I moved here some kind Jewish ladies introduced me to their God. My heart warmed and I knew I wanted him for my God too. So, when Paul came with the message of our God's Son, the Lord Jesus Christ, and his sacrifice for me…well I knew I wanted him to be my Lord too."

"But will not his Father be mad that you have left him for his Son? I remember how Zeus was not always pleased with his son, Apollo."

Lydia smiled. "There is so much I want to tell you, Daphne, so much to learn. But no, God the Father of the Jewish people is delighted when one of us decides to make His Son our Lord. I do not want to confuse you, but you see the Father and the Son are one. Actually, there are three. God's Holy Spirit is also our God and the three of them are all different but also all one and all God."

Daphne's brows scrunched. "Three gods who are one?"

Lydia nodded. "In time you will come to understand. But you do not have to know or grasp it all to become one of God's children. For now, the most important thing is for you to decide if you want the God who drove that evil spirit from within you to forgive your sins and ask His Son, Jesus, to be your Lord."

"But why? Why would He bother with me? I have never done anything to deserve that kind of love, in fact I—"

"Oh, child, it is because before the world was made, He knew you and chose you to become His own. At the right time He gives you the grace to see and understand that He loves you exactly as you are right now.

Daphne's eyes filled. She knew in her heart that Lydia spoke the truth, but could not grasp how that could be.

Chapter Seventy-Seven

Those who receive abundance of grace.
– Romans 5:17

Nicanor did not stop until he reached the Eastern gate. His breath came in pants as he leaned on his knees and studied the city. Except for a few torches set to burn through the night, only a full moon shadowed the marketplace. He could not quit searching. She was out there somewhere, alone, and probably frightened.

A breeze brought a whiff of a late-blooming fruit tree. He drew in the scent and remembered Daphne laughing with her friend Kawit, each with a blossom pinned in their hair. The memory pushed him on.

Alert for any guards, he walked into the city and searched the *stoa,* behind the *palestra,* the library, and the baths. To his relief, despite the uprising no security had been posted. He walked over to the *Bema.* The only sounds were echoes he could not relinquish, rods tearing into flesh. He shuddered.

His thoughts returned to Daphne. He should check with Lydia, maybe she had found her.

An inner compulsion led him to check out the prison area. He hopped up the steps to the upper city and nearly ran into two men coming down.

One grabbed the other's arm. "Hurry, the third change of the guard is about to happen, and we do not want them looking into why we are here."

Nicanor assumed they were Paul's supporters, but what if they were thieves looking for an isolated place to rob someone or worse? He decided to follow his instinct and fell in behind them. When the men turned he recognized them and they stopped well out of sight from the prison.

One of them spoke up. "I am Luke, and this is Timothy. His glance fell on Nicanor's Roman toga. "Are you part of the Roman—"

Nicanor saw his alarm. "No....no, I am a follower of the Lord Jesus Christ and I...."

"Welcome, brother," Timothy said. "We need all the followers we can find to help with our prayer vigil."

Nicanor held out his hand. "My name is Nicanor. I have not been a follower of Christ for very long and have much to learn about prayer."

"Then you saw what happened this afternoon?"

He nodded. "Harsh punishment for so slight a crime, and that filthy prison is no place for open wounds. It is full of rats and varmint droppings."

Luke scoffed. "That head magistrate is in dire need of our Savior. What an ego."

Timothy touched his shoulder. "Have faith my good friend. God will redeem our loved ones from that prison. He is faithful and his loving kindness never fails." He looked at Nicanor. "But we need some serious prayer."

They bowed their heads and both men fervently prayed that God would intervene and bring good from the affliction their friends suffered. Nicanor looked up at the clear moonlight and added his amen.

Luke followed his gaze and suggested they go back. "The changing of the guard should be well settled by now. Want to join us?"

Nicanor nodded. Should he tell them about Daphne? Perhaps they had seen her.

"Could I share something before we go?" They listened as he told them about Daphne and who she was to him.

Timothy's voice was full of wonder. "You mean the girl with the demon that started all this?"

"Yes, but aside from that, that thing, she is a wonderful girl. But she does not have any knowledge of God or of what happened to her, so she ran away. You did not happen to see her, did you?"

Luke shook his head. "No, and we were at Lydia's, and she did not say anything about her."

Nicanor's shoulders drooped. Lydia's was his last hope.

"You will not likely find her in the dark. Let us pray and turn her over to the Lord. Then come with us and we will see what is going on at the jail."

Timothy's confidence in God's protection swelled the peace the Lord placed in Nicanor's heart. He headed back up the steps with them and nearly stepped on a gopher snake that slithered across their path. It disappeared and left him to wonder why it would come out at night. Like most Greeks, his mother had considered snakes sacred, symbolic of underground gods. He shook his head. Few of our people know the difference between myths and the true God.

Chapter Seventy-Eight

He gave them power over unclean spirits to cast them out.
– Matthew 10:1

Lydia smiled. "Think back Daphne, do you remember a time in your life, maybe an incident where you felt something tug at your heart, a strange wooing wrapped in love? A kind of knowing you might not have understood, but recognized there was someone or something greater you had yet to discover? God fashions those moments to awaken us to His presence."

Daphne's thoughts flew to her beloved mountains in Delphi. "I think I know what you mean. Once in the foothills of Mount Parnassus I had an overwhelming sense that some being had put them there. I remember being awestruck."

Her eyes glistened as her mind traveled back to a moment when God seemed to reached out to her. She patted her chest. "It was a certainty in here that something much greater than the god my family worshiped was in control and had placed in perfect order all that was before me. I wish I had remembered that when..." Daphne broke off, her eyes glistened as her mind traveled back to that moment.

Lydia broke the silence. "And you will probably remember many more incidents in time.

It is one way the Lord lets you know He exists and wants you for His own."

Daphne's lips twitched. "Do you really think so?" At Lydia's nod she asked, "How can that happen?"

"You simply tell him you believe in God the Father who sent His Son, Jesus Christ to die for your sins, and that He rose from the dead by the power of the Holy Spirit. Then you ask him to forgive you of all your wrong doings and for making a god of anything else in your life. You invite Him to come into your heart and be your Lord. He is the God of all gods."

Daphne grew quiet. The God of all gods....no wonder she could never attribute that to Apollo... or that power within her.

Lydia freshened their tea. "Child, you have been through so much. It must have been awful for you."

She squirmed at the ugly memories Lydia's sympathy ignited. "But I have done so many evil, things too despicable for your God to forgive." Her voice wavered. "I helped that demon hurt people...I even spoke counsel that caused deaths. You cannot imagine what..."

Lydia reached across the table and took her hand. "No Daphne, no. It is not like that. Everybody has sinned...everybody. Paul taught us that one sin is as bad as any other. All Jesus wants you to do is admit it and ask his forgiveness. He is here right now, waiting and wanting you to ask Him to be your Lord. It is a gift. No one deserves it, no one. It is His gift to us."

Daphne chewed her lip. "My grandmother always told me I had a gift, that my spirit was tender, open to truth, that I should cherish it."

"Did your grandmother worship Apollo?"

"Yes, my whole family was deeply involved with Apollo's temple."

"Perhaps that is why this is so hard for you to understand. There are other demonic spirits, one called a 'familiar spirit' that can prey on a family for generations, blind them to truth, oppress and keep them from understanding or receiving the love of God. Because you came from such a strong tradition, I believe the Lord is showing me you need to be delivered of it before you will be able to understand."

Daphne jerked to her feet. "No! No Lydia, I could not go through that again."

She walked around the table and put her hands on Daphne's shoulders. "No, it will not be like that, dear. There are many demonic spirits that simply oppress people. They disrupt our lives and try to keep us from God's will and His best for us. I will just pray and command the unclean spirit to leave in Jesus' name and it will have to go. It will not be like that stronghold that gripped you before."

Daphne searched her face. "You are sure?"

"Yes, I am sure. Do you want to be rid of it, Daphne?"

She nodded and Lydia prayed. "Father, please lead me as I come against this evil spirit that deceived and held Daphne's family in bondage for so many generations. I thank you that you told us to ask and that you are faithful to do what is in your will."

With that Lydia opened her eyes and spoke firmly. "You familiar spirit that has harassed Daphne and her family all these years, I command you to leave her now. You are found out and she has announced her desire to be free of you. Leave now, familiar spirit, in the name of Jesus Christ."

At the name of Jesus, a heaviness rose in Daphne's chest. She coughed several times, took a deep breath, and looked at Lydia. "I do not understand what happened, but something rose up and when I coughed, I felt it leave."

Lydia hugged her. "I am so glad. You have had quite a day, are you tired?"

"Yes, but I want Jesus for my Lord too." Her face clouded. "But wait, the *pythia* in the *adytum* cursed me and said I would always be bound by evil. Will that keep me from…"

Lydia frowned and Daphne realized her mentor had no idea what she was talking about.

"I am sorry, Lydia. A *pythia* is a woman who gives divination for the god, Apollo, in the bowels of his temple. She works in the *adytum* where it is forbidden to go, but I snuck into it to see if Apollo was real, and she saw me and…."

Lydia held up her hands, "No, no. It does not matter. She had no power to curse you, and anyway God promises that an undeserved curse will not stick. Do not worry. Apollo is a myth as is all the lore connected to him. What dwelt within you was a demonic spirit sent from hell by the evil one who posed as a messenger of Apollo. At some point in your life, you must have committed yourself to one other than the true God, and that opened the door for you to be indwelt by that demon."

"Oh, Lydia, I did, I did! When I joined Apollo's temple, I had to declare Apollo was my god. Does that mean I cannot—"

No, no. You can still become a child of God. But you must denounce that vow and ask God to forgive you."

She sighed. "Then I can ask Jesus to be my Lord?"

Lydia's eyes shone. "Oh, my yes. You surely can."

"Will you help me?"

She took Daphne's hands. "I will say the words and you pray it back to the Lord, alright?"

Daphne followed Lydia's prayer, from denouncing her vow to Apollo to the amen. She looked up and grinned. "It happened, did it not? I mean I do not really feel different, but somehow, I know that I am. Oh Lydia, thank you! Thank you." She threw her arms around her and held her tight.

Lydia laughed and hugged her back. "Praise the Lord. The angels are rejoicing with us."

Daphne threw up her arms and whirled around, "I feel so free, so happy. All the guilt that hung over me is gone…it is really gone!"

"I know, I know. God is so good! It is late but there is one more thing I must explain. It is about the Holy Spirit."

Daphne eased onto her chair, chin on her fists, eyes fixed on Lydia.

"You see Jesus came to earth as a human being and yet God to save sinners. After he died on the cross, He rose again, and He returned to his Father in heaven. The way He can always be with us as He promised is because He sent His Holy Spirit back to live in each of us." She waited to see if Daphne followed her explanation. Satisfied, she continued.

"Each of us is born with a spirit, but it does not come alive until we ask Jesus to come into our heart. That is when He sends the Spirit of God to connect with our newly born spirit. The Holy Spirit within us whispers to our spirit, who speaks to our soul, the part of us that is our mind, emotions, will and personality. Thus, we can commune with him and know and understand what God wants us to do. Does that make sense to you?"

"Well, it is a lot to understand, but if you will help me, I know I will learn fast."

"I believe you will too. And one more thing, when a person is delivered of such demonic strongholds as you harbored for so long, it can leave a void within you. So, it is important for you to ask the Lord to fill you, to baptize you in His Holy Spirit and fill that gap with Himself. We do not want anything to make room for those spirits to return and invade you again."

Daphne froze at the thought of the Voice returning.

Chapter Seventy-Nine

He who is in you is greater than he who is in the world.
– 1 John 4:4

Lydia recognized the panic that threatened to choke the young woman she had brought into her home. "Do not be afraid, Daphne. Paul teaches that the Spirit of God that is now within you is greater than those evil things that prowl the earth looking for someone to oppress. Think back, was there any time when you were able to hear Paul that the Voice within did not object?"

Daphne cocked her head. Her face brightened. "Yes, yes there was. I once slipped down by the river and hid behind some bushes so I could see and hear Paul. It was the day when his helpers pushed you and all those others under the water." She frowned. "Why did they do that? Must I be pushed underwater? I hated seeing your beautiful dress ruined."

Lydia laughed. "I will explain about that later. I did not know you were there, but why do you think you were not harassed that day?"

Daphne shrugged.

"It is because we have power over those evil spirits if we belong to Jesus. Days before that happened, I prayed and fasted for you. And on that day, I had already asked God for a hedge of protection around you. I bound all the evil spirits that hindered you from hearing this wonderful news one day soon. That rendered the demon ineffective for a season.

Like sunshine after a storm, light spread across Daphne's face. Her voice cracked. "You did that for me?"

Lydia smiled. "But now you have Christ for yourself. Just pray and ask God to fill those voids with his precious Holy Spirit…it is something you must do for yourself."

Daphne closed her eyes as she had seen Lydia do when she prayed. "Lord Jesus, I am not sure how to say it, but please fill me with your Holy Spirit and fill the void left in me when the evil spirit of python or divination and any others departed. And please fill the empty place that remained when that familiar spirit that plagued my family left. Thank you for sending Lydia to help me. Amen."

She opened her eyes, surprised to see tears on Lydia's cheeks. Dread gripped her heart. "Oh no, did I say it wrong?"

Lydia reached over and hugged her close. "No, not at all. I am sure God is very pleased with you."

The breath Daphne held gushed from her lungs.

"But tell me, how did you know that Voice you heard all that time was a spirit of python or of divination?"

Daphne's lips parted but nothing came forth. She shook her head. "I do not know how I knew. It seemed that something inside was leading me to pray that way." She grimaced. "Or maybe it was all the lore my grandmother crammed into my head about Apollo slaying the dragon or python. The temple built for him was famous for the divination that people believed came from the *pythia* in the *adytum* where the slain monster supposedly lay…and is not divination a form of fortune telling?"

Deep in thought, her eyes glazed. Lydia waited. "What are you thinking, Daphne?"

"That it was then when I first heard the Voice. I was knocked unconscious and when I came to it started talking inside of me." Tears ran down her face. "That is when it happened. That is when the demon first came into me, I am sure of it."

Lydia put her arm around her. "I believe you are right. And that it was the Holy Spirit speaking to your spirit to help you to understand. Just as the evil spirit spoke to you then, now if you listen, you will hear the voice of God's Spirit speak to you to help you.

"You are way ahead of a lot of believers, Daphne. You have learned the truth and that has enabled you to receive Christ and be freed of all demonic oppression. But come, let us get some sleep. You will have a lot of explaining to do when you go back to your master tomorrow."

Daphne's jaw dropped. "Lydia...I cannot go back there. I can no longer tell fortunes, it was the Voice that told me what to say, so I have no value now. I will be put out with the field slaves, vulnerable to the whims of the overseer or anyone who wants to make sport of me. And I will lose my protection from people like Sergius, he is one of the two other men who own me. I cannot face that, Lydia. He tried to rape me once and now I will have no defense." She gripped the table. "Please do not send me back."

"I am so sorry, I did not know. But I am afraid you will have no choice if you are to obey the Lord. Jesus taught that we are to remain in the state in which we are saved. If a slave you are to obey your master and not seek freedom unless it is granted. You are to accept your lot and serve the Lord where you are.

Daphne's tears turned to sobs. "Lydia, that is too hard. I cannot, I cannot."

She put her arms around her and rocked her against her chest. "There, there, little one. We will pray and God will make a way. You must trust him. Come let us get you to bed."

Daphne followed to an upstairs room, and after a warm bath, Lydia tucked her into a clean, soft bed. She took Daphne's hands and asked the Lord to help her face what she needed to face and to make a way of escape from the fears that overwhelmed her. Daphne clung as if she might never let go. Lydia brushed back her wayward locks and lifted her chin. "Get some sleep now and we will talk some more in the morning, alright?"

As she blew out the lamp, Daphne snuffed her tears and tried to smile. In the dark she whispered, "God, I want to trust you, but I am so afraid. Please do not make me go back there." She listened long into the night, sure the Holy Spirit would tell her what she desperately wanted to hear. But when no answer came, she concluded he was not listening or maybe he changed his mind about her. She would not blame Him, after all she had done.

Hours of empty silence quelled all hope from her heart. She sat up and listened. Nothing stirred. She folded the lovely nightdress Lydia had lent her and laid it on the bed. Her tunic hung on a chair. She frowned at the life it represented but picked it up and redressed. As she tiptoed out into the night, she whispered, "Goodbye, dear Lydia. I am so sorry but I cannot risk what going back would mean."

Chapter Eighty

By pride comes nothing but strife.
– Proverbs 13:10

Dinner had been served and still Nicanor had not returned from the city. Patharus paced. Beyond irritation, his anger festered like the sun on a hazy day. "It is a lack of respect, that is what it is. No, it is that new god and those people he has attached himself to…he never acted like this before."

He called for his servant. Always within hearing, the man hurried in. "Yes Master?"

"Send for Daphne. She had not yet returned when first summoned, she must have had a big day."

The servant left and returned after some length. He waited to be addressed. Patharus barked, "Well, send her in." Instantly he regretted his tone. Nicanor's inconsideration was not the servant's fault. He waved at servant. "Sorry, send her in."

The servant bowed. "Master, Daphne is not in her room, and no one has seen her since breakfast."

Patharus rose from his desk. "What? Where is she?"

"No one seems to know sir. Shall I summon Jahtel?"

He stared as if he the man asked for the moon. "No…no. It is not yet dark. I will wait a bit and let her explain the late hour. You are dismissed."

The servant left and Patharus questioned his decision to wait. First Nicanor and now Daphne. What happened to his orderly household?

He had hardly sat down when the servant interrupted. Patharus sighed but kept his tone civil. "Yes?"

"Master, Sergius is here to see you. He says it is urgent."

Patharus nodded and Sergius barged through the door. "Well, what do you think of what happened today? And what are we going to do about it?"

"Hold on, what are you talking about?"

Sergius gloated. He seldom had the upper hand over his partner and sometimes rival. "You do not know?"

"I am not in the mood for games, Sergius. Are you going to tell me what you are talking about or not?"

"Is Daphne here?"

Patharus hesitated. "No, she is evidently having a big day and has not yet returned. I expect her shortly."

"Well do not count on it. Our little money maker has probably run for the hills."

Patharus stood to his feet, leaned over his desk, and glared. "Either tell me what is going on Sergius or get out of here."

"All right, simmer down." He recounted the scene and described the crowds right up until Daphne was brought before that man Paul. "And when the man called out, her body contorted and she screamed and hissed insults at him, then fell and lay helpless at his feet."

Patharus's jaw went slack. How could what the man yelled knock her to the ground? And why did Sergius believe she no longer had the skill to earn money? "How do you know she lost her ability to tell fortunes?"

"Well, I have not seen her since, but I heard that man Paul and those people who follow that new god were all excited about it and sure she would never again harbor that power."

Power. Patharus sneered. There had not been any evidence of any "god power" the day he begged them to save his son or heal his wife. He snorted. "I do not hold to all this "god stuff," but something gave her special abilities. Where did she go after that?"

"I do not know. Amplias and I convinced the crowd the leader had disturbed the peace. Before we knew it, the whole mob got behind us. They helped us drag him and one of his partners to the Bema where the magistrates held a fast trial. They had them beaten and thrown into jail."

Neither spoke for a moment. "Say, Nicanor was there, what has he said about it?"

Patharus lowered his eyes. "He is not home yet, either."

"We should send out a search for Daphne. She is still our property and maybe we can get her back to her former state."

"You are right. You and Amplias sit tight. I will send my men to find her and find the truth."

With that he practically ushered the man out of his house. Patharus crumpled onto the nearest couch and held his head in his hands. "Now what? What am I going to do, about Daphne… about Nicanor?"

He waited until late evening, hoping one or both would show up. Finally, he called his servant. "Have my horse saddled. I am going to town, but no one is to know…understand?

*****

Believe on the Lord, Jesus Christ, and you will be saved, you and your household.
Acts 16:31

Nicanor followed Timothy and Luke back toward the prison, each careful not to be heard or wake the guards." They crossed the Roman Road and moved stealthily up the rocky steps that led to the jail's opening.

Timothy put out his arm and stopped the others. "Listen, do you hear that? It is Paul and Silas, and they are singing!"

Luke smiled. "That is Paul all right, no jail cell will keep him from singing hymns and praying at midnight."

A smile swept Timothy's face. "Guess that cancels our need to be quiet, you know how loud Silas is."

"But how will we...." Nicanor stopped mid-sentence and looked at the others. "Did you feel that?" All three fell on their hands and knees before any could answer. Nicanor shouted, "It is an earthquake. We get a lot of them here. Just stay where you are, there is nothing above us to fall and crush us."

The ground heaved like waves of wheat, tossing them on their sides and backs. Nicanor continued to assure them they were safe. "This is a big one, but hang on, they never last more than a few minutes."

He glanced back at the *agora*, shocked to witness the collapse of some buildings. Both the library and the *Palestra's* upper stories rocked dangerously. He gasped as parts of each fell, thanking God it was late and nobody was likely around. His thoughts ran to Daphne. "Oh Lord Jesus, wherever she is, please protect her, do not let her be hurt."

As the tremor settled, Luke pointed at the jail. "Nicanor, it looks to be an old cave. Do you think...."

"It was carved out of solid rock years ago. It should be able to stand the shock. Let us go see."

They arrived right after the jailer who had been awakened by the earth's shaking. The prison doors were wide open and the jailer assumed the prisoner's had escaped. Knowing Roman law and that he would be held responsible, he drew his sword. Better a quick death than to be hung.

Paul called out in a loud voice. "Stop! Do yourself no harm…we are all here."

The jailer dropped his sword and called to his assistant. "Quick, get me a torch, and hurry. Surely it is their God who has shaken the earth!"

He grabbed the light and ran into the prison. Nicanor and the others tried to follow, but the assistant stopped them from going further. They peered around the man, anxious for the safety of their friends. They could not see anything but heard a shaky voice cry out. "Sirs, what must I do to be saved?"

Immediately, Paul spoke from the cavern. "Believe on the Lord Jesus Christ and you will be saved, you and your household."

The jailer emerged from the prison with Paul and Silas right behind. He called to his assistant, "Take care of things here. Make the doors as secure as possible. I will return shortly."

With that, he led them all to his house. Luke and Timothy joyfully embraced their friends, clamoring to hear all that had happened inside the prison. Nicanor followed, smiling broadly as the jailer summoned all in his household to hear

Paul speak of the God who had become his Savior.

The jailer's wife grinned at Nicanor, "Who would have thought an earthquake would be the answer to our prayer?"

The jailer's family and even his servants listened as Paul explained God's love, his forgiveness and desire they become His children. At his invitation all responded and received Jesus, followed by a baptism in the trough where the jailer's herds were watered.

Afterward the jailer took soft cloths and personally washed the backs of Paul and Silas, charging his wife to spread a healing balm over the bloody welts. She found each a clean tunic and his servants quickly prepared a feast for the prisoners and the household.

Everyone except the jailer sat down to eat. He insisted on serving Paul and Silas himself, darting back and forth with choice dishes. Everyone rejoiced openly at the amazing goodness of their new God.

Dawn had yet to arrive when Paul's friends watched him and Silas return to the prison. Nicanor whispered to Luke, "Why is Paul so confident they will be released?"

Timothy shrugged. "He has something up his sleeve, Luke?"

"I have a hunch but let us wait and see. The magistrates will probably call for them the first thing in the morning."

Nicanor hated to leave. "I will try to be back for that, but I need to find Daphne. She may be in trouble. I keep feeling she needs my help."

Luke touched his arm. "Then go, my friend. We will continue to pray for her and you too.

Nicanor thanked them and headed back toward home.

Chapter Eighty-One

…you have overcome the wicked one.
– 1 John 1:13

Daphne cleared the fence around Lydia's yard and ran as fast as she could. She stopped to catch her breath near a stone wall and almost stepped on a snake half-hidden in the grass. She kept her scream to a yelp as both she and the reptile scattered. Further on a large whip snake coiled on the path, its scales glistening in the moonlight. She gasped. "Why are they…."

Her question hung midair, swept from her lips by the heaving ground. She tripped and fell, rolled and tried to get her bearings. "Earthquake! She had never been alone in earthquake, what should she do?"

In a flash she remembered why those snakes were out at night. According to her father they were underground gods that feel the quake building and come out of the ground or rocks, so they will not be crushed. She shivered and checked around, remembering the one she had encountered on a trip to the temple. Her father may have been right about snakes, but he was wrong about the gods. There is no other God but Jesus.

She rolled to a stop and reached for a sharp brick that poked her back, only to discover it was her *teraphim*. Its face smirked in the moonlight daring her to ignore it. She could almost hear the Voice taunt and threaten a horrible life without its power. An icy blast reaffirmed her desperate need for security. Maybe she ought to....

The Spirt of God's love rose within her, and with a strength not of her own, she cried aloud, forgetting the need to keep from being heard, "No! You will never be a part of my life again. Never, never!" She pushed herself to her knees and threw it as hard as she could into an adjacent field where a group of swine milled. "That is where you belong among the pigs. You are worthless and have no power and I will never give heed to that miserable demon again."

A strong aftershock followed. It scattered the animals. Daphne sighed and treasured the assurance of peace and freedom that engulfed her.

The ground still trembled from time to time but with less vigor. She startled when a house to one side of the road collapsed before her eyes. She cried out and ran to see if anyone needed help, but her feet would not stay beneath her. She half crawled, stirred by the sight of a man that staggered with a toddler in his arms. He handed off a small child to an older one. Daphne put her arm around the frantic young girl and asked if she could help.

The man looked past her and cried, "My wife... my wife."

Daphne followed his ghastly stare to a woman's arm that protruded from the rubble.

Another aftershock sent them all to the ground. As soon as he could manage his footing the man grabbed both children and ran toward a neighbor's.

She passed another house that lay in ruins. A faint cry turned to a whimper and then silence. She pointed out the area to people who came from everywhere and began to dig frantically with their hands or whatever they could find. Mangled piles of masonry and twisted metal lay everywhere.

She held a crying toddler while his mother tried with no avail to free her husband. The woman finally gave up and clutched her only survivor. Without strength enough to move heavy bricks or be of much help, Daphne left and went into the deserted market.

*****

A man's pride will bring him low.
– Proverbs 29:23

When his horse's legs buckled, Patharus had already reached the crest where the path looked down on the city. The animal righted itself briefly, but reared and threw Patharus to the ground. He stood, ready to curse the beast, but found his own legs jerked from under him. He sat up. "Earthquake! No wonder the horse panicked."

The critter's legs buckled several times before it gained its footing and bolted toward home.

Patharus would have thought it funny if he were not so angry at being without his horse. He whistled for the animal, but it was gone.

He started for the city while the ground still heaved, stretching his arms to keep his balance. He hardly recognized the eastern gate. Stones that were not on the ground had large cracks that threatened to give way at any moment. He passed the *palestra* shocked to see most of its upper story collapsed.

The library too had large cracks on the front portion. He had almost reached the main door when an aftershock shook the ground. Before he could back away, a portion of the upper story slid to the ground and pinned his right leg.

Sweat poured from his head as pain seared up his leg and into his hip. He cried out, "Help, help, is anyone around? Please, I need help."

While he could hear cries and shouts, no one appeared to have heard him. Like a bad dream, the tremor seemed to last forever. Fear clutched his chest as another part of the building teetered above him. He called out even louder. "Help, help. Can anyone hear me?"

Why did he not bring someone with him? He knew the answer. Pride kept him from wanting anyone to know things were not perfect at his estate. He scoffed. Patharus, the pillar of perfection. Ha! And look what it had gotten him.

He tried to remain calm but could not keep his eyes from returning to the threat. Nicanor was not ready to run his estate and all the other holdings. He had not even had time to tell him about some of them. He could not die here like this!

Every few minutes he called out, but no one came. Probably afraid to be in or around these old buildings…smarter than him.

Exhausted, he rested his head on the ground and closed his eyes. His leg had gone numb, dulling the pain except for the sting of a few deep gashes. Nothing to do but wait and hope someone found him before that thing fell and crushed him.

*****

…because fear involves torment.
– 1 John 4:18

Daphne stumbled aimlessly through the city, not sure what to do. She tripped over the ruins of a market stall along the cluttered *stoa* but caught herself. She wandered into the courtyard grateful the moon's light covered the open area. The bricks around the fountain had been pushed to one side and water gushed over the walkway.

She sat on her familiar bench pleased to find it undamaged and wondered if the aftershocks were over. In the silence, Lydia's unwelcome explanation about going back to Patharus' rushed back. She tried to remember the things she learned, especially about God's great love and mercy. Maybe He is not mad at me. He must know I would not survive that kind of….

A sneering image of Sergius interrupted her thoughts and sent a shudder right through to her toes. "I cannot Lord…I just cannot. I want to be one of your followers, but I cannot go back."

"Trust Me, Daphne. Turn it over to Me and choose to obey. I will never leave you or forsake you. Trust me."

She recognized the voice she heard so long ago, when the slave monger carried her and her family away. So different than that of the demon. The gentle voice of Belte's God had urged her to call on Him. How she wished she had, and that Belte could know He was now her God too.

Dust from the rubble filled her lungs. She coughed and squeezed her forearms into her waist. Dread and fear of a future apart from her new God swooshed, danced on the polluted air, and refused to leave. What was she going to do? She had nowhere to go, nowhere to hide. Maybe she could appeal to Patharus. He had always been understanding and kind. Maybe she could work with Femi in the kitchen, but what if he sold me off to Amplias, or worse, to Sergius?

She leaned her head on her hands. She needed to be far from here by daylight. Maybe she could find her way back to Neapolis and earn enough money to take a ship to Athens.

The idea stuck. She hopped to her feet. That is what she would do and hope that God would not be mad at her. She would do whatever else He asked.

She grieved over the damage in the *stoa* as she left. A dismal picture of the broken lives and hopes of people she had known there. None were real friends, but the stalls of the silk merchant, the lady who sold wonderful bread, even the crabby lady with her mirrors and things ladies loved, they and many others had lost everything in the quake. Would she lose the peace and joy she had found? The thought urged her on.

She passed the *palestra,* mourning the loss of its beautiful façade. She worked her way around the damage wishing the ground were clear so she could run. The next two buildings appeared to be intact, but moonlight revealed a great deal of damage to the library. She groaned, Oh no, not the library. It meant so much to the people.

She had stepped past most of the rubble when she heard someone moan. She stopped and listened. A man's voice called out. "Is somebody there? Please, help me if you are there. Please do not leave, please help me."

Chapter Eighty-Two

And you shall do what is right and good in the sight of the Lord.
– Deuteronomy 6:18

Daphne bit her lip. You cannot stop, someone else will surely come along and help him. Her conscience refused to listen. She disregarded her better judgement and edged her way toward the sound.

The man cried out again. "Please do not leave. I need help."

She picked her way toward what was left of the building. At least she would do what she could and send help back with the next person she saw. A body lay close to the ruins. She gasped. A large piece of the building covered one leg. His dilemma made her heart sink. There was no way she could move the piece that trapped him. She ran over to him. "I am sorry that I will not be able to move that off of you, but maybe I can...."

The man turned his face toward her. Both jaws dropped. Unbelief, relief, and pain shot from his eyes. "Daphne, what are you doing here?"

She swallowed her shock. "I, I can explain, Master. I...." What could she tell him? She was no longer of any use to him, and she was running away? "Run!" her insides screamed. She looked around and backed a few steps.

"Daphne, I am trapped and that piece of the building above me is teetering a little more with each aftershock." As if to underscore his words a slight tremor sent another shudder. Both stared at the swaying facade. Patharus barked, "Run Daphne, run, it could crush you,"

Her feet itched to obey, but her heart refused to comply. Her voice cracked with fear. "No, we must find a way to get you out of there." When had she made that decision? She knew only that she could not leave him to die.

She ran and found a plank that looked strong enough to make a wedge. She dragged it over and placed it on top of a nearby block that had fallen, and wedged the other end as deeply as she could under the piece that held Patharus. She pushed down as hard as she could on the end of the plank. It did not move. Frantic, she searched for another way but found none.

She pulled up her tunic, hiked herself up onto the plank, and crawled near the end. The slab moved some as she bounced, then fell back in place and sent her sprawling. She rose to the sound of marble cracking.

"It is no use, Daphne. Get out of here before the rest of this thing falls."

"No! I can do it...somehow. I just need more leverage." She found a sturdy piece of metal and dug deeper under the board. With all her might she wedged it beneath the stone.

Patharus groaned. She patted his arm and swallowed her dread he might not make it. "Hang on, Master. This should work."

"I will be alright, but please leave. I do not want to see you hurt."

Tears flooded her cheeks as she climbed up on the board for another try. It jerked and resettled with enough force to knock her feet from under her and send her flying again. She sobbed. What could she do? She did not know what else to do. "Lord, please send someone to help me."

"Daphne. Get out of here! Now! And that is an order!"

She ignored him, and was about to try again, when she heard someone call out.

"I heard voices. What is going on? Does somebody need help?"

Relief flooded her heart as she recognized Nicanor's voice. She called out, "Nicanor…over here."

"Daphne? What? Where are you?"

"In front of the library. Hurry, the Master is trapped under some rubble."

He rushed over. "Father? What are you doing here? Your leg, is it bad?"

Patharus made a brave effort to hide his pain. "I will be alright, but you need to get her out of here, that wall could fall any minute."

Daphne gestured at the rock and board she used to try and move the rubble. "My weight was not enough, but with your help I know we can get him out." She pointed at the wall. "We have to hurry, that loose portion sways more with every aftershock."

Nicanor's glance brought a gulp. He grabbed a piece of loose metal and they both dug further under the mass that trapped Patharus and shoved the board deeper beneath.

He pulled her to her feet. "That should be good. Let us pull hard on the board and see if it will move." They tried, and it rocked but would not give way.

Pebbles fell from beneath the facade. Patharus groaned and Daphne shuddered. Nicanor winced and tried to push the board deeper under the mass, but it would not budge. "Alright, let us climb up and use both our weights."

He crawled up onto the board with Daphne right behind, but it still did not give way. They slid back down. "I will see if I can slide the board any further under the rubble."

Their eyes met for a brief second before he hustled to the task. "Alright, you climb all the way to the end and, when I say now, try to bounce on the board and I will see if I can wedge it under further.

On her hands and knees, she rocked the board at his every call. With each effort the board dug deeper beneath the mass of rubble. Nicanor climbed up with her. "Alright, when I say now, let us both bounce and see if it will roll. He shouted, "Now!"

The board creaked and both fell as it pushed the wreckage far enough to clear Patharus' leg. Daphne clambered to her feet. "We did it! We did it!"

Nicanor was already at Patharus' side. He lay very still. "Father?" There was no response.

Daphne's hand flew to her throat. "Is he, is he…."

He placed his hand on Patharus' neck to feel for a pulse. "He is alive. He must have passed out when that weight lifted off him."

In unison, their eyes shot to the dangling structure, relieved it had not moved further. "We must get him away from that danger."

She heaved a sigh of relief. "I will help you move him…as far as we dare without hurting him more."

Nicanor checked his father's leg. "It is hardly bleeding but it must have crushed the bone." He took his shoulders and with her help they dragged Patharus from danger.

She knelt beside Patharus and brushed some debris from his face. "What now? How are you going to get him home, to Halaten?"

Nicanor grimaced and shook his head. "I cannot leave him, I…."

Daphne leapt to her feet. "I will go. I know that road so well I can easily find my way in the dark and the moon is…."

"No. It is too dangerous."

"Nicanor, you cannot go. He may wake and need you to…to, well you must stay with him. I will be fine." She started to leave. "I will send the wagon and have Halaten come with them."

He seized her wrist. "Daphne, I do not know where you have been since…since yesterday but promise me you will not leave or run off again. Promise?"

"You do not under…."

He frowned. "No. No more of that. I know all I need to know. Promise?"

She nodded. He pulled her into his arms and held her like he would never let go. Exhausted, she melted against his chest, but forced herself to back away and leave for the estate.

She ran until her sides ached, then walked until she caught her breath. Between spurts her mind raced. Nothing had really changed. She still had to face Patharus and tell him she no longer had the ability to tell fortunes. What would he do with her? She plotted again how she might get to Neapolis. But what about Nicanor? What about her promise? And what about the vow she made to make Jesus Lord of her life and God's mandate she obey?

When she reached the estate, Patharus' household quickly readied the wagon. Halaten quizzed her about the injury as he packed his satchel. Shaking his head, he ordered a huge pile of blankets, a board to use as a splint and jugs of water be thrown into the wagon's bed and they

were on their way in minutes. She paced after
they left, knowing she should try to sleep but just
as sure it would not come.

Chapter Eighty-Three

For He shall pluck my feet out of the net.
– Psalm 25:15

Patharus groaned. "Where am I? Where is...."

"Hush, father. I am here."

He sucked a deep breath. "Nicanor...I am so relieved. Where is Daphne...is she alright?" He raised up on one shoulder, but Nicanor gently pressed him down.

"She has gone to get the wagon and Halaten. They should not be long. Is your pain bad, Father?"

"My leg...oh, I think it is broken."

Nicanor suppressed a smile. "I think it might be, but try to rest, help should be along soon.

Patharus struggled for breath to speak. "Nicanor do you know what Daphne did for me?"

He leaned in close. "Do not try to talk, Father. Just rest."

"No. One never knows how these things might go...and you need to hear me."

He did not argue, thinking it better his father not become agitated.

"She found me trapped under that fallen mess and tried to release me...by herself! That little wisp of a girl! Sergius came by earlier this evening and told me what happened in town. I am sure she feared what might happen because of it, but she stayed to help me anyway."

He tried again to lift himself, but pain forced him back down. He grimaced. "She put herself in danger for me. Damaged parts of the library swayed above me, but she would not leave, just kept trying to release me until you came along. Son...."

Touched to hear Patharus called him 'Son,' Nicanor pleaded, "Please, Father, you must be quiet, you could...."

His eyes locked on Nicanor's. "No, like I said, if this thing takes a nasty turn and I do not make it...." He held up his hand to halt Nicanor's instant protest. "If something happens, I want you to buy out Sergius and Amplias' interests in Daphne. Pay them whatever they ask but make it legal. Then, I want you to grant Daphne her freedom. Give her enough money to go back to her home in Delphi or wherever she wants to go." He closed his eyes. "Is that clear?"

"Very clear, Father. But you see there's a problem."

He forced open his eyes. "A problem?"

"Father, I have not found the right time to tell you, but I guess this is it. I love Daphne. I have loved her since the first time I saw her, but she continually put me off because of that awful thing inside that controlled her life. She hated it, Father. She hated the evil things it did to people through the counsel it gave. Even if she were able to get rid of it, she could not bring herself to deny it because she knew what her life would be without the ability to bring you and the others a daily profit."

Patharus' eyes welled at the passion in Nicanor's voice.

"It was evil, Father…evil. And it was tearing her apart. I even found her about to ingest hemlock in the garden one day. She would not admit it, but later I understood how desperate she was and without hope."

"I had no idea. She never complained, only about Stello killing that good friend of hers.

"I want her for my wife, Father. She may not be from one of Rome's better families, but no other woman will ever interest me."

Patharus closed his eyes and gave a weak nod. "I…I know about that, Son. You would do well to take her for your wife. That girl has more proven character than ten of the Roman girls' pushy fathers have paraded before me in hopes of access to my estate." He tried to chuckle, but a groan displaced it.

The wagon arrived and on the ride home, Patharus lost consciousness. Halaten had tied a splint to the damaged leg, and pain had returned with a vengeance. Even the laudanum barely dulled it. Nicanor sat on one side keeping him covered as Patharus' body trembled with shock. He tried to warm his father's upper torso with his own, quietly begging God for mercy. Daphne met them at the gate. She jogged alongside the slowing wagon. "I thought you would never get here. How is he?"

She stood back as the wagon came to a stop and Patharus' servants carried him into his quarters. The gentle handling by all who helped spoke volumes of their regard for the man who owned them. Nicanor filled Daphne in on what the doctor did and of the agony of watching his father suffer. His voice cracked as he spoke. "He could lose part of his leg if infection sets in. I do not think I knew how much he means to me until… until this."

Daphne clutched her fists to her sides to keep her arms from reaching out to comfort him, to hold him and take away his pain. She turned to leave. "You must go to him, he…."

"No, Halaten is seeing to his injury. We need to talk." His tone left no room for discussion. "Come, let us sit here where they can find me if…." He broke off as dread trailed his fears for his father.

He led her to a bench not far from the rooms Patharus occupied alongside his wife's. "Daphne, so much has happened. I know you have felt you cannot trust me but there is something I want you to know, to prove I never lied to you."

Her heart raced. He had made plain his desire for her back at the accident. How could she resist when a longing to hold him flooded her heart like a raging river? "I, I…."

He pressed his fingers to her lips. "No, do not say anything, just listen. I know about Lydia's shawl. How my father…" The muscles in his jaw clenched. He began again. "I mean how Jahtel tried to cause trouble for you after he searched your room and found it."

She jerked to face him. "I…." The cock of Nicanor's head said "wait."

"It set me thinking. Why did he have it in for you? Except that he seemed to know how much I care for you."

She turned her eyes from his and swallowed the lump that rose in her throat like a thunderhead.

He placed his hand on her cheek and turned her face back to his. "It was not a great leap from there to figure out who kept the note I sent that night from reaching you. Jahtel commandeered Batano to run an errand for him and promised to deliver the note in his place." Bitterness edged his voice. "Of course, he never did, and I feel so bad about it."

With little success, Daphne tried to stifle her tears. "It is alright, Nicanor. I knew Jahtel destroyed the note."

He spun on the seat. "You knew? How?"

"It just came to me one night, same as you. Nothing else made sense. I knew how much Jahtel hated me, and after he found the shawl and took it to Patharus, I knew he had somehow gotten his hands on the note and saw to it that it never reached me."

Nicanor frowned. "Why did you not tell me? You knew how much I wanted you to believe me."

"Jahtel was your birth father. I could not come to you and accuse him without proof...."

He reached for her hand and caressed it with his fingers. "No. No, of course not. And to this day he would never understand your choosing to protect him or me over yourself."

Neither spoke for a long minute until Nicanor broke the silence. "Daphne, while we waited for the wagon before Patharus passed out, he told me of how you tried to help him. How you put yourself in danger of being crushed along with him."

He held her eyes with his. "He was so moved by your unselfish courage that he insisted I know his plan in case he...well, the pain was bad by then. But he wanted to make sure his will would be carried out, instructed me to buy out Amplias' and Sergius' portion no matter what they demanded and to set you free. He..."

She shot to her feet. "Free? I will really be free? Nicanor, are you sure? Tell me again, exactly what did he say? You have no idea what this means to me."

He chuckled and relished her excitement. "Sit down, sit down a minute." His smile was electric." I think I am getting the idea. You will soon be free, no longer a slave." She sat down and he repeated the whole scenario, patiently answering her interruptions. When she quieted, he took her hand again. "But Daphne, there is more."

Chapter Eighty-Four

*...believing you rejoice with joy inexpressible and
full of glory.*
– 1 Peter 1:8

"Nicanor," a voice called from the doorway. "Your father is asking for you."

"Coming." Midway to the door, he spun around, his face stern. "Do not leave Daphne... promise?"

She promised and he sped off.

There is more.... She wondered what he meant by that. Would stipulations be added to being set free? She scoffed at her doubts. Do not be so suspicious, he would not have been so happy for her if limitations were placed on her freedom.

Eager for any hint of how Patharus was doing, she paced outside his door. Funny, she did not know how much he meant to her, either...until now. Free! The word chased a path of delight through every thought that assailed her. Free. She was free of that demon and no longer a slave. Oh, God...or should she say Lord Jesus? She would have to ask Lydia about that.

She decided on Lord Jesus. "You worked it all out, Lord, just like Lydia said you would. Even when I struggled to trust you, you cared enough to make a way for me."

"No, my child, though you wanted to run off, you made the way when you decided to stay and help your master. It was then you chose to trust me."

Daphne fell to her knees. Tears mingled with the praise and gratitude she heaped on the Lord.

A feeling of well-being surrounded her. Gone was anxiousness about not measuring up, shelving even the guilt and regrets that lurked, eager to accuse. Reminders of the shameful deeds she had taken part in lost their grasp. In their place, the blessing of God's presence rolled over her. Like a warm breeze, it left only the fragrance of his love and an awareness of his acceptance.

She struggled to understand it all. Change so real, so tangible, she thought to examine her body to see if she looked different too. Peace wrapped her in a cocoon of love. Its fibers held her close, draining all desire to be free of this encompassing comfort.

She did not know how long she sat rocking herself like a mother with a hurting child, easing all cares far from her. She knew she was different. Hope bloomed within, nothing would keep her from her newfound faith. Assurance of its permanent joy crept from deep in her being and rose in her chest until she could not contain her joy.

It burst across her face. She stood and stretched her arms toward the sky. "Yes, yes, yes! Thank you, Father of my Lord Jesus. Thank you that you sent your Son to this cruel place to die for me.

Thank you, Jesus that you loved me that much. You knew all the evil I took part in, and yet you forgave me. And I believe it. Is it not amazing that I know it?"

She whirled around, her arms lifted in praise to her newly adopted God. "Thank you, thank you, thank you!" As if a dam had burst deep in her being and the water carried every truth she had learned in a torrent of joy, her praises continued up and out in gratitude to the Lord.

Finally, she fell to her knees near the bench and began to simply talk to the Lord. "Father" suddenly shy and halting, "do I call you Papa, Father of my Jesus? I do not understand why you would love me or want me to be your child, but Lydia said you do and inside I know it is true. I do not know how to talk to you. I do not know what I can do for such a great God."

"She says you want nothing but my heart and my life. I do not know how to give you such a thing, Father. Please show me and teach me. I have no earthly things, but I am strong and can work hard."

Her mind ran in a hundred directions. How did you serve a God who wanted only to love and give to you? Apollo and the gods she knew about ruled with unpredictable terror and demanded service and sacrifices. "I will learn, Father of my Jesus. I will find what you want from me, and I will obey your plan."

The wind rippled her shawl as she stood. She caught her reflection in a small pool in Patharus' courtyard. The face that stared back was of a long-lost stranger. The pinched lips were soft and smiling now. Her dull, sunken eyes were wide and shining. The frown burrowed between her brows had disappeared and her face glowed with peace.

She laughed and declared into the wind. "It is me, I am new on the outside too!"

"Daphne? Are you alright?"

She twirled and came face to face with Nicanor. "Your father...Patharus, how is he? Is he...."

"No, he is alive. He regained consciousness and the laudanum helped. His leg is set but Halaten says it could be days before we will know if...well if an infection sets in. His knee and his foot appear to be intact, but the large bone that leads to his foot is broken in several places. Daphne, he wants to see you. Halaten told him he should rest, but my father insisted. The healer asks that you to stay only a moment."

She brushed at a rush of nerves that tingled her arms. She tiptoed into the room where Patharus lay on a large bed. She knew wealthy people did not sleep on mats, but the enormity of it and all the lush furnishings amazed her. At the physician's nod, she made her way to her master's side.

Halaten whispered, "She is here, Patharus." The Master opened his eyes, found Daphne's, and reached for her hand. "Daphne…"

Surprised by his gesture, she took the hand he offered and knelt beside him. Tears coursed down her cheeks. "Master, I am so glad you are going to be alright."

"Well, that remains to be seen, but I wanted to thank you myself…while I can." He brushed off her denials. "Nicanor informed me of the horror you have lived, and I am so sorry. I had no idea what having a, a well whatever it was that tormented you and made your life so miserable."

She squeezed his hand. "It is alright. We will talk later, you need to rest."

He increased his grip. "No, you need to hear me. Considering what happened in town today, you were very unselfish to put yourself in danger to try to help me. You must have been worried about your future, and yet you chose to help me. I am awed by your courage and your integrity, Daphne."

For a moment he was quiet, then spoke again. "Nicanor told me he explained my intentions to set you free. As soon as it can be arranged it will be permanent. No one will own you or be your master. I shall ever be grateful to you."

Then he closed his eyes, and panic bounded like a frightened rabbit up Daphne's chest. She searched the physician's face. "He, has he…."

"No, he is alright, the powders have dulled his pain. He has fallen asleep," Halaten assured her.

"Oh, thank you Lord." The healer shot her a quizzical glance, but she ignored it. "Nicanor is right outside. I will send him in."

"No, tell him his father is asleep, and at this point rest is the best thing for him."

She nodded and went to find Nicanor. "He is asleep, Halaten said that was best for now."

Nicanor exhaled in relief. "What did he say about you?"

Her smile lit up his own. "That I will soon be free. That no one ever again will be my master." Except you, Lord.

Chapter Eighty-Five

...in the valley of decision.
 – Joel 3:14

Daphne and Nicanor went to sit on their bench in the garden. Finding Patharus trapped and injured and her relief when God sent help, replayed in her mind. "I am so glad you were in town, Nicanor." She frowned. "But why were you there at such a late hour?"

"Searching for you!" His words blared as if she should have known he would be. "After what you had been through, I knew you would be afraid and confused. I knew someone needed to find you. Where were you all that time?"

She told him about going to Lydia's and how she had kindly taken care of her.

"Then you were there when the earthquake hit?" Concern knitted a wedge between his brows. "Was Lydia's home damaged? Did you have to leave...was she alright?"

"No, I mean yes, I had barely left when it hit, but I looked back and her house had not fallen." She told him about the damage she saw in the area, of the injured people and how helpless she felt to assist them. To avoid telling him why she left, she elaborated on the damage "Where were you when it hit?"

He recounted being just outside the city, how he had run into two of the men who traveled with

Paul and how they had gone to the prison to check on him and Silas. He mentioned the gopher snake and they laughed when she told him about her near encounters. "But what happened at the prison is amazing."

Her ears perked. "What…what happened?"

He divulged how the earthquake broke the prisoners' chains and sprang the doors wide open. With joy, he recited how the jailer was saved and how they watched his whole family be baptized before he cleaned the prisoners' wounds himself and fed all involved. "Then Paul and his helper insisted they go back to jail. They wanted to be there when the magistrates came to release them in the morning."

She jumped to her feet. "Nicanor, if your father is all right, I need to go and be there when the magistrates come to check on them this morning. I want to be present. I want to thank the man who gave me back my life." She pointed to the east. "Look, the sky is already beginning to lighten. I need to hurry."

He reached up and pulled her back down on the bench they had moved to. "Wait, wait a minute. I told you there was more, remember?"

An overwhelming urgency crept up her heart, a mandate she must arrive in town before she lost her chance to thank Paul. The need swelled and threatened to burst the seams of her patience. What would Nicanor have to tell her that could not wait?

Her heart softened as he took her hands in his. "Daphne, I have loved you since I first saw you. From that time on, I knew you would be the only girl I would ever want in my life. I want to marry you, Daphne, I want you to be my wife."

Time stood still. She could no longer remember why she felt an urgent need to leave. Nothing felt real but this moment. Disbelief poured from her eyes. "Marry me? You want to marry me…me?"

His grin stretched to his ears. "Yes, you! Tell me you will marry me, Daphne. You love me, do you not?"

She could not escape his demand for her answer. "Love you? I have loved you since I first stumbled and fell into your arms. But you cannot marry me, Nicanor. You are the son of one of Philippi's leading citizens and none of your father's peers would ever accept a former slave as your wife."

He laughed and pulled her hands to his chest. "It does not matter, Daphne. I told my father of my desire, and he was fine with the idea. He said I would do well to marry someone of your character."

She gasped. "He said that? Oh, Nicanor, have you thought this through?"

Her hesitation brought a frown. "What is it? What is bothering you? I know you love me, nothing else matters."

"I do love you, I always will, but…being married to you would mean a lifestyle I am not sure I could manage. My life is going to be so different now. Please, let us hurry into the city and give it some thought."

He pulled her into his arms and kissed her, a promise of desire that raged to be set free, then murmured into her hair, "Alright. I know being free changes things for you, but do not let it change our love. I will never give up, I could not live without you by my side."

The passion of his embrace nearly extinguished her reluctance. Lord, what should I do? How can I tell him I belong to you now and must use this freedom to follow your path for my life? I will not let you down again, Lord, I promise.

She closed her eyes and vowed to trust God with her future.

Nicanor made sure Patharus still slept, and no immediate danger threatened. He had two of his horses saddled and helped her up onto the smaller one. "You do know how to ride, do you not?"

She cocked her head and laughed, aware of how little he knew of her past life. We have so much to share, Lord. Will it ever happen?

The thought stayed with her as she followed behind him into the city. She was free. That meant she could go back to Athens and try to find her family. She would have to find a way to make some honest money so she could buy their freedom from whoever owned them. And what about those she knew back in Delphi? They were as much a slave as she had been, but to a much more evil master, one that would go to any ends to keep them from knowing her Lord. When had her goal of being free to live her life changed to living to see others set free?

Chapter Eighty-Six

O full of all deceit and all fraud…
– Acts 13:10

The head magistrate eyed his fellow judges with disgust. "Our position grants us the authority of judges as well as peacekeepers. We were within our rights."

"But I am telling you that earthquake was Jupiter's vengeance, punishment for acting too quickly and beating those men without a proper trial. The whole city will hold us responsible for all the damage it caused."

The third magistrate echoed his support. "He is right. It was a reaction to our wrongdoing. That trial was a fluke."

A grimace underlined their superior's contempt. "You two would fear the glimmer of a lightning bug." He leaned his elbow into his hand and ran his fingers over his chin. "Alright, alright, let us put this behind us. Send a soldier to tell the jailer those men are exonerated and to let them go."

The three huddled in their office, going over plans to avoid paying for the damaged businesses, should there be a surge of blame. It seemed the messenger had hardly left when he returned, panting. Irritated at the disturbance, the head Magistrate barked, "Well, what is it?"

The soldier hesitated. "Sir, the jailer, I mean…."

"Spit it out man, we do not have all day."

"Yes sir. It is…it is that it turns out the prisoners are Roman citizens. Paul, the leader, knows of the law of Valerius, that a Roman can never be beaten or thrown into prison without a trial and legal sentencing."

All three jaws dropped. "They are Romans?" The question came in unison.

The soldier nodded.

The voice of one judge wavered with fear. "We have betrayed Roman law."

The other added, "It guarantees their legal rights, a fair trial. We are in big trouble. What are we going to do?"

Indignant at being caught in an error, the leader held up his hands. "Wait a minute. Let us not lose our heads." He turned to the soldier. "Did not the jailer tell them they were free to go?"

The man shuffled his feet. "Yes sir, he did, but they refuse to leave. The one they call Paul insists that you come and usher them out yourselves."

He waved the soldier off. Relief filled the man's face as he hustled to be spared his superior's ire.

One judge rose. "We must go. If they report this the consequences could be enormous. To start, we would lose our positions."

His superior held up his hand. "I know, I know, let me think." He paced for several minutes, rubbing his chin and his forehead in turn. The thought of apologizing turned his face purple.

Finally, he stopped. "We cannot take a chance. It is early. Let us hope word has not gotten out and we can do this quietly without anyone knowing."

Chapter Eighty-Seven

For you will be His witness to all men of what you have seen and heard.
– Acts 22:15

Daphne could not believe the size of the crowd that gathered around the prison. Nicanor tied their horses near the eastern gate, and they continued on foot.

"Make way for the magistrates" a soldier on horseback called. Behind him the three men walked swiftly to the prison's entrance. Each kept his head bent and avoided eye contact. Pulling Daphne along, Nicanor pushed their way to the front of the crowd.

A man shouted, "These men deserve to be freed. They are innocent and look at what you have brought upon us! Free them!"

The crowd picked up the chant. "Free them, free them," soon rang from the mouths of even those who had propelled the prisoners toward the Bema the night before.

The head magistrate glared at the crowd before he turned his attention to the jailer. Daphne could not hear what was said but saw the jailer nod. As he entered the prison, a big smile stretched his lips. Moments later, he returned with Paul and Silas one step behind.

Daphne nudged Nicanor. "They look like they spent the night in a fine inn and not a prison."

He nodded, unable to suppress a grin. "Remind me later to tell you what his friend Timothy said last night."

They both turned back in time to see the head magistrate walk over to Paul. "I am here...." He cleared his throat and began again. "We have come...."

Paul interrupted. "Speak up man. I am sure these good folks would like to hear what you have to say."

The magistrate's face turned ashen, then bright red. His whole being appeared to shrink. "Yes, ah well, a mistake has been made...."

Paul's eyebrows rose high into his forehead. "A mistake? And who is it that made this mistake? Who would order a beating and prison before a proper trial and sentencing for Roman citizens?"

The crowd roared while the magistrate squirmed. Many were Greek merchants who merely tolerated the presence of the Roman law. "Free them, free them," broke out again.

Quiet finally returned and Paul addressed the man. "Well, did you have something to say?"

The magistrate looked like he might faint. He tried again, flailing when Paul insisted he speak up. "It has come to my attention that I, we, mistakenly proceeded in a fashion contrary to Roman law." His voice dropped. "I extend an apology and am sorry for the mix up."

Paul smirked. "What was that last sentence? I do not believe everyone heard you."

The man's patience snapped. Through gritted teeth, he nearly yelled. "I said I am sorry and I apologize! You are both free to go."

"Well thank you," Paul said. "We will accept your apology."

Cheers rose from the crowd, drowning out the magistrates' request that they depart from the city. The jailer waved them off, straining to hide his joy from his superiors. Those who had become believers rushed to congratulate Paul and Silas. Word quickly spread that they would be at Lydia's for a brief good-bye, and all were welcome to join them.

Daphne moaned to Nicanor, "I did not get to thank him."

"Come on, let us go to Lydia's. Maybe you will get a chance there."

Lydia's house was nearly bursting at the seams, so everyone gathered outside instead. Paul stood on the top step of her porch where he could be seen. He recited all the details of the night before, glorifying God for his faithfulness to them and to the jailer's family. The short good-bye became three hours of teaching the love of God and what true freedom meant. "And so, you will discover as we have, that whom the Son sets free, is truly free indeed."

Daphne smiled. Free indeed! Yes, she was free inside and out. Thank you, Lord.

"Now, the grace of the Lord Jesus Christ and the love of God and the communion of the Holy

Spirit be with you all until we meet again." With that, Paul stepped down and motioned his team it was time to leave.

Daphne could not lose her chance. "Nicanor, I must reach him." She wound her way through the crowd of those who desired to give Paul a personal send off. Many gave him small gifts she assumed was money, but he did not linger. Within reach, she pleaded at his back. "Please, only a moment, sir."

Paul twisted around. Suddenly, shyness swallowed all she wanted to say. His eyes glowed with love. "What is it, daughter?"

"I, I am the girl that caused you all that trouble yesterday, and I…."

"Yes, I know the one that had the demon. Have you been set free?"

She swallowed her fears. "Yes Sir, and I wanted to thank you." Tears surged and cascaded over her cheeks. "You have given me back my life and I am so grateful. Thank you."

"No, not me child. Thank the Lord who delivered you. Take your newly found freedom and use it for him. That is the true outcome of gratitude."

He turned and left with the others. Daphne watched until they were all out of sight.

"He is quite a man, is he not?"

She swerved and fell into Nicanor's arms. "Yes, I wish he could have stayed. There is so much I wanted to ask him."

He held her close, assuring her of his love. Suddenly she pushed herself from his embrace. "Nicanor, I need to tell you something. I...."

"Wait. Let's go back to the city and sit by the broken fountain, no one will be there today."

She nodded and walked beside him. How could she tell him, Lord? Paul just confirmed what you want me to do, to take my new freedom and use it to help set others free.

They sat quietly beside the fountain until Daphne gathered courage to say what was on her heart. "Nicanor, something has changed in my life, besides being set free from slavery. While I was at Lydia's, she explained what happened to me yesterday. She said it was the Lord Jesus Christ working by His Spirit through Paul that set me free of that demon that controlled my life."

"Nicanor, my heart leapt at what she shared with me, and I, well, I made Jesus my Lord too".

"Daphne, that is wonderful!" He pulled her into his arms, locked his eyes on hers and chuckled. "And I have been waiting for a chance to tell you that I too made Jesus my Lord one evening at Lydia's house. Paul spoke there every night and I left after dinner and attended every meeting I could."

Daphne's heart soared at the news. "Oh Nicanor, I am so glad." She backed out of his arms, blinking tears that threatened to spill. "But you see, that is why I cannot marry you. I know God wants me to go back to Athens to track down my family and find a way to free them. And after that, I need to use my freedom to go back to Delphi and see to all those who are enslaved to the myth of Apollo. They need to hear the good news and be set free too. It is not just about me and my freedom now. I am free of slavery but now I am a slave of the Lord Jesus, and it is he who is my master. I have been set free to go and share this wonderful news so others can find Jesus and have the same new life I have found."

Nicanor stared at his feet. He had not interrupted, nor did he try to dissuade her. He turned his face to her, and in a sorrowful voice whispered. "Let us go home." He led her to where they left the horses. The slump of his shoulders as she rode behind broke her heart. Why God? I love him so. How could she bear to leave him?

"Trust me."

Neither spoke on the way home. At the estate, he saw her to her room and bid her get some sleep, assuring her Patharus or he would see to her freedom as soon as they could pay off Sergius and Amplias.

"Nicanor? I want you to know…．

He kept his focus on the ground. "No, Daphne, hush. I cannot fight the Lord. I will see you tomorrow. Please do not mention your decision to leave to my father until he is…well, until he is better."

He walked down the hall and turned into the family's quarters. She went to her room, fell onto her mat, and sobbed into her pillow. "Oh Lord, I love him so much. This is so hard."

"Trust me, Daphne."

She sniffed back her tears. "Yes, Lord, I will trust you."

Hours later, she finally slept, only to be awakened by someone calling her name. She sat up. "Is that you, Nicanor?"

"Yes, I need to see you right now."

She jumped up and pulled a cover around her, swept the curtain aside and squinted at him. The corridor's dim lamps exposed the glow on his face. His voice reflected an equal light. He backed her into her room. "Daphne, I know this is not proper, but I could not wait for morning. I have been talking to the Lord and he asked me, *"Why would you not go with her?"*

"Nicanor…really? You would leave all this and come with me?"

"Why not? We do not have to be gone forever, do we? We could wait until my father is back on his feet, or his one foot." He hesitated, looking embarrassed at how that sounded. "What I mean is, he could have the joy of seeing us marry and send us off with his blessings! Will you? Will you marry me, Daphne, and let me go with you?"

She threw herself into his arms. "Oh Nicanor, yes! Yes, yes, yes!"

He picked her up and swung her around. "Thank you, Lord," he called into the heavens. She smiled. "Lord, you have truly set us free, and even made a way for us to find your path together."

•••••

In *Free Indeed*, the final book of *The Snare of the Fouler* series, Daphne has chosen to give up a pampered life in Philippi with her beloved Nicanor. The apostle Paul's admonishment she use her newly found freedom for the Lord, has captured her heart. Her spirit plummets over the plight of those back in Delphi, ignorant of the true God and grounded by the evil one in the myth of Apollo. Please join me in book three as her journey home brings her face to face with powerful, demonic opposition. Can deep gratitude for her Savior's saving grace spur her on to continue the battle for the souls of her people?

Characters in
Whom The Son Sets Free

Daphne — thirteen years old

Tribia — Daphne's father

Hebee — Daphne's mother

Alexander — Daphne's brother, eighteen months
   her junior

Theo — Daphne's three-year-old brother

Belte — long time servant, friend to Daphne

Yahyah — Daphne's paternal grandmother, family
   matriarch

Zeus — believed to be Greece's highest god

Apollo — son of Zeus, god of Delphi, Greece

The Voice — a demon of devination who posses as
   a messenger of Apollo

Principality — the territorial demon over Greece

Cyrene — Daphne's closest friend

Talsta — high priest of Apollo's temple in Delphi

Bentalla — fellow slave in Athens

Patharus — leading owner of Daphne

Sergius — one of Daphne's new owners

Amplias — one of Daphne's new owners

Nicanor — slave/heir to Pathrus' estate

Kawit—fellow slave, Daphne's good friend

Stello—overseer of Patharus' estate

Jatel—manager of Patarus' household

Rybic—gatekeeper

Femi—fellow slave

Halaten—estate physician

Beresta—friend Daphne sees in market

Lydia—woman who hosts Paul and team

Botano—Nicanor's personal servant

Paul - Apostle to the Gentiles

Silas - companion of Paul in Ministry

Luke - author of the Gospel

Timothy - Paul's spiritual son

Carol Lacey

I hope you enjoyed both my books in *The Snare of the Fouler* series, and follow Daphne's journey to the end in Book 3 *Free Indeed*, to debut in Fall 2023.

I have been writing for thirty years and was published in many Christian magazines, like *The Christian Reader*, *Evangel*, *Woman Alive*, a United Kingdom magazine, *Impact Magazine*, a Singapore production, my local paper, and others.

My blog, is called *Nuggets from God's Word*, where I focus on things God teaches me, life lessons from His Word, or whispers in corrections. You can find it and other resources by visiting my website at www.CarolLacey.com.

It is my hope that my books will shine God's light on the reality of the kingdom of darkness and our ability in Christ Jesus to overcome the evil one through the power of the Holy Spirit in us.

God bless your journey,
Carol Lacey